This Book Belongs To:

The Clockwork Pen

By Jennifer Haskin

Book One of the *Sublunary Devices* Series

The Clockwork Pen Copyright © 2024 by Frontpage
SUBLUNARY DEVICES SERIES

All rights reserved. Printed in the United States of America. No part of this book may be used or reproduced in any manner whatsoever without written permission except in the case of brief quotations embodied in critical articles or reviews.

This book is a work of fiction. Names, characters, businesses, organizations, places, events, and incidents either are the product of the author's imagination or are used fictitiously. Any resemblance to actual persons, living or dead, events, or locales is entirely coincidental.

For information contact: jenn@frontpageediting.com

Cover art by Seventh Star Art
Map by Haskin Originals
Chapter designs: Ekaterina Ilinskaya
(iStock ID 1224825385)

ISBN (paperback) 9798326598950
ISBN (hardcover) 9798332703409

First Edition: [August 2024]
10 9 8 7 6 5 4 3 2 1

This book is for...

All those who daydream in class,

Those who need a fantasy world because the real one hurts too much,

Those who journey far and beyond,

Those who need to be lost,

And those who need to be found.

Enjoy Sepherra; it's only the beginning of the journey.

~Penn

Table of Contents

Prologue..9
Chapter One...17
Chapter Two..34
Chapter Three..60
Chapter Four..83
Chapter Five...105
Chapter Six...113
Chapter Seven..128
Chapter Eight...149
Chapter Nine..179
Chapter Ten...207
Chapter Eleven...213
Chapter Twelve..234
Chapter Thirteen..259
Chapter Fourteen...281
Chapter Fifteen..299
Chapter Sixteen...305
Chapter Seventeen...325
Chapter Eighteen...349
Chapter Nineteen...364
Chapter Twenty...381
Chapter Twenty-One...392
Chapter Twenty-Two...417

Chapter Twenty-Three	442
Chapter Twenty-Four	453
Epilogue	467
Dear Reader	471
Acknowledgments	472
About the Author	473
Other Titles by Jennifer Haskin	475

Sepherra

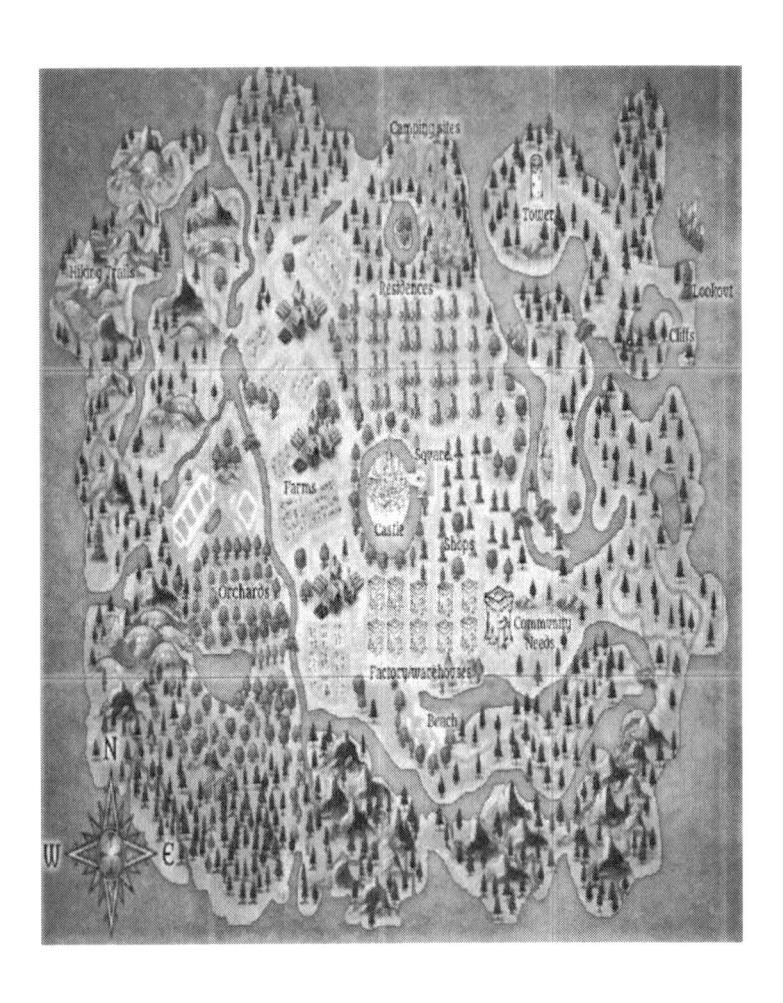

Prologue
Eighteen Years Ago

The clamor of the winners was significantly quieter this late at night. These were the black-market games. Nobody gambled here if they could help it. These games were for the down-on-your-luck thieves, your addicts in withdrawal, your broken, diseased, and most desperate of the fallen.

Eugene clutched the last bills in his sweaty fist. He stood near a blazing trashcan for heat, the mist condensing on his coat lapel, and tried to stay in the dancing light. He didn't trust the people he could see, let alone whoever was lurking in the shadows. It was the last game of the night, and Eugene had lost almost every bill he'd come with. He wiped a shaking hand across his forehead, smearing the beaded sweat with his grimy palm. He looked down at his dirt-smeared hand.

Though he was pale-skinned and red-haired, his beautiful wife's complexion was the color of deep copper. She would hate that he stood here, with the degenerate filth of the community, but she was in a hospital bed, her condition worsening. Her fate would be sealed if he couldn't produce the funds for an experimental procedure. He turned his hand over to check the time. The nurse was going to be furious that he was out so late. His heavily pregnant wife was surely asleep, though. He tapped his foot impatiently. *Come on, hurry up.*

The man next to Eugene blew a whiskey-laced burp in his face. "Last game. You in?"

"Yeah." Eugene tried not to show his revulsion and handed the last of his money to the bookkeeper. "All in." He frowned.

The small group huddled around a wooden pallet converted into a worn blackjack table that they used for dice games. The dealer called, and everyone threw in their last hopes for a win. *Last chance. Saturday night.*

The dealer opened his mouth to start the game, but a filthy drunk man across from Eugene called out, "Wait!"

"Throw it in." The dealer stared hard at him.

The man's face shined with the reflection of perspiration. It gathered in the wrinkles around his eyes and ran down to his chin. He wiped it with his sleeve, then ran his fingers through his grease-clumped hair. He mumbled to himself and shoved a hand in his ripped and dirty jeans pocket. He pulled out a fancy, metallic fountain pen with a glass reservoir. Thin bands of brass spiraled up the cylinder, and both ends, with the cap on, were crisscrossed with spiral webbing. He laid it on top of the pile of bills.

"We don't take free bets," the dealer said. "It's got no value."

The Clockwork Pen

"No!" The drunk man shoved his hand out and swayed slightly. "Iss not just any pen. Iss a *magic* pen. Very v-valuable."

The men—gathered around the mound of bets on the "table"—laughed raucously; some pointed, and the man nearest to him slapped him on the back. "Sure it is," he said. Most of them eyed him with sympathy. They were all two games away from abject misery, and everyone there understood. The rest glared at him.

One of the men laughed and sneered, "If it's magic, and *so* valuable, why are you throwin' it in?"

The man looked down and mumbled, "It ruined my life," but he was drowned out by the jeering.

Eugene thought about what he could do with a magic pen. *I could make a whole new world for her. Maybe she would get well. And our little girl could grow up and have a place to live away from the bill collectors and sickness. Someplace that feels like home. A place where I am in control and she will be respected and safe, and we can live there together, the three of us, away from this world of pain.*

The drunk man teetered and pleaded with the dealer, "C'mon. Iss last call. I got nothin' left."

"Maybe you should go back to the shelter, Stan." The dealer sighed and shook his head slightly.

"C'mon, man. I can't..."

"All right. It looks expensive. I'll give you $25 credit for it." The dealer looked around. "The pot's good, gentlemen."

The men nodded and leaned forward, ready to do business.

The acrid smell of burnt oil and nervous sweat assaulted Eugene's nose with the wind, and he watched the other players shifting from foot to foot. One man blew on dirty hands with black-crusted fingernails for warmth. At least half of them looked—and smelled—as if they lived in the tent colony that had taken residence under a bridge near the train tracks. They played for a few rounds, but the game wasn't long.

Eugene began to sweat and moved closer to the board as the dealer began the last roll. He'd be forced to sell their house if he didn't win something big in this game. His family would be destitute *and* homeless. All he needed was a four and a six. Common numbers. He could still win. The dealer's hand shot out like a striking snake, and the dice flew. They tumbled against each other, rolling across the board. Eugene's breath was a plume of white mist before him. The first die came up with a six, and Eugene clenched his jaw. If the next one said four, he would win the whole kitty.

Just as the die landed on four, it slid off the edge of the board and rolled onto the gravelly concrete to stop on two.

"I win!" crowed a greasy fat man with a cough.

Eugene thrust his hand out. "Wait! It rolled a four! You all saw it. Right?" He looked around at the haggard faces expressing uninterest and exhaustion.

The Clockwork Pen

"No way," the fat man yelled. "It plays where it lands. Right, Joe?"

"But—" Eugene was ready to fight for the amount. He took a deep breath and clenched his fists, ready to argue with the man.

"He's right," the dealer said decisively, but not without a small measure of sympathy. "He wins." He pointed to the fat man.

Eugene's stomach roiled, and his head spun. He'd lost it all—every dollar he'd come with. His ears rang. The fat man quickly scooped his belongings into a nondescript tote, but Eugene grabbed his sleeve. "Listen. I'll make you a deal. Whatever I can do. I need that money. I should have won it. You saw it land on four. I know you did." He gulped. His pride stripped bare, he nearly whispered, "Please. It's not for me."

The man coughed and appraised Eugene. He dug into his bag and tossed the pen toward him. Eugene caught it instinctively. "I don't need no *magic* pen." The man chuckled with a sneer. "There. You won somethin'. Be happy, it's *magic*," he taunted.

Eugene worked hard to keep his face neutral and pressed his lips together in a thin line. He knew the man wasn't going to relinquish his winnings. Defeated, he pocketed the pen and turned to walk dejectedly from the empty shell of a roofless warehouse. After a few steps from the ring of light, the drunk man stumbled up next to him. "Um, you won somethin' of mine." The man looked strung out, with long, brown hair hanging in strings over his eyes.

"Yeah?" Eugene gave him a side glance and sped up. "Sorry, mate. You lost it. And it's all I got."

"No. I mean, I don't want it anymore. I just brought you this." He held out a small jar of black liquid with a cobalt blue stopper full of tiny air bubbles.

"What's that?"

"Ink." He held the bottle out, and Eugene took it.

Eugene fished his keys out of his pocket, and as they left the dark warehouse for the streetlight-lined lot, Eugene made a beeline toward his tan, four-door sedan, holding the pen tightly inside his pocket. He needed to hurry home. Magic, if it was real, could heal his wife. "If it's magic, what can it do?"

The man whispered, "It creates. Anything you want. It can make any world you can imagine."

He stopped. Maybe he could make the treatment his wife needed without having to pay for it. He clicked the key fob, and his lights flashed with a quick beep. *Magic. Humph.* Eugene realized the foolishness of his thoughts and laughed, then began walking again. *The man is crazy.* If the pen was truly magic, surely the guy would've made himself some money a long time ago. *Should I just give it back?* Not if there was a minuscule possibility that it could help him … he needed a miracle. "Thanks, fella, but I've got to go."

If there was any chance in hell that pen worked, he needed to try it. He'd tried everything else. He couldn't even afford hospice care with what he had. How was he going to tell her that his PTO had run out, along with their funds?

The man chewed his lip with brown-encrusted teeth. "It's more of a pain than it's worth, really. I was holdin' it for somebody else, but it's better at the bottom of the ocean."

They stared hard at each other for a moment. The man nodded and walked off. Eugene opened his car door and paused, then turned back. "Hey, what do I do?"

The man turned back. "Put the ink in that pen; the bottle never runs out. Whoever holds it just needs to think of what they want and draw it or write it out. If I were you, I'd look up 'man-made dimensions.' You could make a whole new country and be president ... or a king. You could be King Whatever-your-name-is."

Eugene snorted. "I'd never use my real name if I was king. Can it make medicine?"

"I never tried. But it can make anything you want if you're holdin' it."

"That it?"

"No. Some powerful people knows about it, too. But don't worry, I won't say nothin'—I jus' wouldn't stay in town too long if I was you."

Eugene didn't believe in the man's discretion, but he hoped that magic was indeed real. His fear of loan shark thugs didn't match his fear of losing her, not even close. The light of his life, the woman of his dreams, she was the only one who would give him their perfect little girl. He'd believed in magic as a child, maybe he'd been looking in the wrong places for his miracle.

> *"Rumored to have celestial origins—according to antiquities dealer, Mr. Haversmith—the Clockwork Pen [see illustration below], said to create life, was disclosed as one part of a larger secretarial set, and reportedly stolen from the National Antiquities Museum in London in the early 1900s. The fountain pen is used exclusively with its pair, a bottle of infinite black ink."*

Chapter One
Under the Stairs

Could this get any worse?

Wyll gaped at his parents across the living room, slumping back into the worn armchair. This "family meeting" was really an ambush. He'd come in from the garage, covered in grease, proud to tell them that he'd managed to put the alternator in the car when his mother told him there'd be a quick meeting. He had cleaned up and sat with a smile; then, his father dropped the bomb. His father had never been a man of many words, but suddenly, he was full of them, and none made any sense. His mother stood next to the sofa, listening and pulling tissues out of the box like there was a prize at the bottom. She twisted them into spirals.

"Wyll, Sweetheart, what your father is trying to say, is that we have decided it will be better for everyone if we get a divorce." Wyll's mother was squeezing the tissue, looking down at his father, seated on the sofa.

The floor seemed to slide out from under him as the finality of the words hit. *Better for who?*

Why hadn't he realized there was a problem? Sure, he'd spent the last year holed up in the garage—rebuilding the car Dad said he could have if he got it running—but when had everything gone so wrong? The idea of change made his clothes feel like they were shrinking around him. He tried to reach for a lifeline, but security was a floating balloon with a string that seemed to dance perpetually on his fingertips. It seemed like no one else had any problem grabbing the strings while he was bolted to the ground. With his emotions untethered, he felt too vulnerable. *Better to get mad than be hurt.* He let himself stew in his anger. How could they do this to him? He couldn't think of one response that wouldn't have him yelling, so he just sat there, flexing the muscles in his jaw as he ground his teeth together.

"Wyll." His father looked sideways at his mother. Overnight, the lines in his father's face had deepened, contrasting wildly with the photos from his younger days—looking just like Wyll—chiseled jaw, blonde hair spilling over his brow, tall and lanky with a killer smile. The signs of his mortality angered Wyll, throwing fuel on the fire. He didn't want to think of his parents getting old—like breaking up—it was just one more thing doomed to change his life. "We want this to be easy for you, Son. So, we want you to think about whom you'd like to live with."

Right now, Wyll didn't want to live with either of them. He wanted his family—*his life*—intact. He wanted things NOT to change. His temper flared. *How could they even ask me this?*

"Honey, don't get all hung up on it. You know how you get when you overthink things. We are trying to make this simple. Talk to us." His mother sat on the faded, navy-patterned sofa, tearing the tissue into confetti-sized pieces. "I knew this wasn't a good idea. Maybe we *should* call that counselor to mediate…"

The fibers fell to her leg, drifting to the floor as if filmed in slow-motion, her face covered in a mask of worry. For once, her blue dress didn't match her shoes. She was always put together, not a hair out of place, and seeing her this way made Wyll uncomfortable. He didn't want to feel sorry for her right now. His father perched next to her on the edge of the cushion and looked like he wanted to bolt at any second. So did Wyll. A sudden need to escape the situation overtook him. He couldn't deal with this right now.

He stood, and his parents rose as well. Done with the conversation, he headed toward the hall.

His father boomed in his *I'm serious* voice, "Where do you think you're going? We haven't finished—"

Wyll interrupted him. "To my room."

"But we need to talk…" His mother warbled through fresh tears, hiccupping.

If he stayed in the house, he was going to have to listen to her crying through the wall. "Actually, I need to go out." He spun and headed for the front door, passing them.

"You can't just walk away from this, Son." His father laid an arm across Wyll's broad shoulders, but he shrugged out of the hug.

"What about *me?*" Wyll knew he was shouting, but once he lit his fuse, he *wanted* to explode. It was better than melting into a puddle of anxiety. He'd single-handedly rebuild a fleet of cars before he'd willingly deal with emotional pain. Anger was safe; it covered him in defensive barbs. "Didn't anyone care what *I* would think?"

"Of course we do. That's why we're talking to you about it." His mother pulled a fresh tissue from the box.

"You're only talking to me because—it doesn't matter." He dropped his shoulders in defeat and sighed. "You can't do this. How long have you been hiding things from me? Were you even thinking of how this would hurt me? I'm just a kid."

Looking at each other, his parents both barked a dry laugh.

His mother shook her head slowly as she spoke. "I love you, honey. You are my only child, and I'm not trying to hurt your feelings, but you are leaving home next year. It's time to grow up. You've got to get over that eighth-grade bully and move on; he doesn't own the rest of your life. You are still so hurt inside that you've treated everyone so ... so ... distantly. Now, don't try to deny it. For the past few years, you've been so moody and mopey.

Are you even concerned that *we* are hurting or just how it affects you?" She released a broken sob, but his father didn't hold and comfort her as he'd always done. It was the last straw.

"I'm leaving," Wyll said, daring them to argue. He pointed at them both. "I need to think. Away from all this."

"If you're leaving, don't forget to walk the dog. She hasn't been out all day." His mom sniffed as she clapped for TeaCup, their beagle pup.

"*Are you kidding?* You want me to do chores *now?* Is this whole day some kind of punishment? You guys make me want to—to—" Giving up on the idea, Wyll growled out loud, grabbed the leash by the door, and clipped it to the ring on TeaCup's collar. "C'mon, Tea, let's go." Then under his breath, he said, "This sucks."

"It's just a walk." His father crossed his arms.

Wyll stomped out of the house, slamming the screen door.

Trudging to the sidewalk, he heard his father shout out the door, "You'd better come back with a better attitude." His mother's lonely crying faded away.

Wyll struggled not to drown in despair. He didn't want to feel this way. It wasn't that he didn't care. The problem was that he cared too much. And now was not the time to deal with it. *Better to ignore the whole thing.* He shook it off. To him, there would never be a good time to think about his shredding soul. He shoved the emotions into a little black box in his mind as he walked. Wyll's tennis shoes gripped the concrete, and he pulled his phone from the pocket of his cargo shorts, scrolling to punch the right number.

"Hello?" A rasping voice came from the speaker, accompanied by a sniff.

"Hey, Derec."

"What's up, man?"

"Wanna go somewhere?" Wyll stopped to let the dog pee in his neighbor's yard, watching them scowl through the window. He smiled and waved.

"It's too hot. And your car isn't working. Where would we go anyway?"

Wyll racked his brain for a place where he wouldn't have to see anyone he knew. He wasn't in a state to be around people—Derec didn't count. They'd known each other their whole lives, always lived a block and a half apart. They hadn't hung out at school for years, but after school and summers, they were always together. Wyll considered Derec more as a constant than a friend—a brother, but not in a bromance way—and he really needed something stable right now. He thought of his home and felt his lungs constrict—he took a deep breath.

"You okay?" Derec's voice crackled over the line.

"Not really. I need to get out of the house. Wanna walk to the Quik Mart? I got fifteen bucks. It'll get us lunch."

Derec sighed. "I guess. I'll meet you."

They always met at the fire hydrant on Bennet Street. It was halfway. Wyll arrived first and sat on the

The Clockwork Pen

yellow-painted hydrant. He looped the leash around the top knob and sat back against it, absently chipping off crispy flakes of yellow paint with his fingernail to expose the gray metal underneath.

He wiped the sweat from his forehead and upper lip with the bottom of his t-shirt, exposing a taut stomach. A red car zoomed past him with the windows down, the radio blaring. Two girls he knew from school, really stuck-up types, turned their heads and gawked.

"Take it off!" the driver yelled out.

The girls cackled as they sped down the street.

Wyll chuckled. He was getting used to it, and it felt good. Ever since he'd made varsity on the football team, he'd reached a new social status, and ever since last year's growth spurt, he'd had to start blocking the over-giggly girls from his phone.

Where is Derec? The charcoal color of his shirt soaked up his sweat, as well as the sun's rays. Summer was just getting started, not that he had any plans. Apparently, now he had to figure out which one of his parents' hearts he was going to break. It had always been the three of them. What was he supposed to do now? He reminded himself that he only had one more year till he was out on his own anyway and pushed the whole problem out of his mind.

"You don't look too good." Derec came up the sidewalk to Wyll. "You sure you wanna walk?"

Wyll pushed his fingers through his hair. "Yeah. Let's go."

They were at the edge of the oldest portion of the neighborhood and past the old, abandoned residence that the neighborhood kids called "the mansion" when Wyll got an idea and stopped. The large house—with a weed-riddled front yard—had been vacant of inhabitants for as long as he could remember. Supposedly, they left suddenly and never returned, but their cars still sat parked in the garage. The elementary kids of the neighborhood all thought it was haunted.

"Hey." Wyll elbowed Derec. "Let's go check out the mansion. I feel like an adventure. Remember when we were kids, and we'd make up all that crap about pirates and cowboys? Let's go on a treasure hunt. I heard all the stuff is still in there."

"You sure you're okay? You haven't wanted to go on a treasure hunt since middle school."

"Yeah. I'm fine." Wyll chuckled as he wiped the sweat from the back of his neck onto his shirt. "Come on. For old-time's sake. I mean, we've only got one more year left, right?"

"Is something going on with you, man?"

"Nah, not really—just feeling nostalgic. Come on."

"Um…" Derec's brow bunched in doubt, but Wyll knew he was a follower. Derec would do whatever dumb thing he suggested—if he pushed hard enough. Luckily, he knew all Derec's buttons.

"I don't think that's a good—"

Wyll held his palms up; the leather leash looped around his wrist. "It's abandoned. What could go wrong?"

"A guy in my Chem class says they do drug deals in there. The mafia—"

"The mafia of Olathe, Kansas? Are you kidding me? There's no such thing." Wyll stared hard at his companion and narrowed one eye. "Are you up for it?" It was a clear provocation. *Are you man enough?* Derec didn't like being directly challenged. It was a pet peeve that Wyll often used to his own advantage.

"Fine." Derec's right hand shook at his side like he was waving off a bug. When he lifted his chin and pulled his shoulders back, Wyll knew he was in.

They crossed the stone path to the front door. Wyll reached for the door handle.

"It's not going to be open," Derec said.

Wyll tried it anyway, to no effect. "Come on," he called, striding to the edge of the porch and jumping off. TeaCup leaped next to him, and they headed toward the side of the house. TeaCup yipped, and Wyll stopped to look back. Derec's hands were cupped around his eyes as he peered into a curtained window.

"Psst." He waved toward himself, and Derec jogged to catch up. The house was massive. They traced along the bushes lining the front to the side yard, where a smooth driveway led around the building to the back.

"Aha," Wyll said, spying a door. The curtains in the door's window framed a bright kitchen decorated in Italian stone tile and black marble. He turned the knob and found the door unlocked. Wyll quickly tied TeaCup to the outside water faucet. The sun beat down, cooking the pavement, so he turned the faucet on and let it trickle, then pulled the trash cans over to give her some shade.

They only had to take one step inside the house to realize it was an oven—the torrid air nearly stifling. It blasted them with a sauna-like gust.

A walnut table and three chairs stood before the windows on the other side of the kitchen. Their tennis shoes squeaked on the tile. "Let's start down here." Wyll passed his fellow adventurer and stepped into the hallway. The heat baked his sinuses as he listened to the silence. Rounded archways led to rooms with beautiful hardwood floors, dull with age and covered by thick and dusty rugs in earth tones. Spider webs hung from the corners like filmy, cotton candy hammocks. The furniture was an academy of apparitions, hovering over the floor under dust-covered white sheets. He peeked under one to see a shiny black piano and pressed a key. *Ding.* The tone rang throughout the house.

"Shit," Derec jumped and spun toward him. "Be quiet. What if we're not alone?"

"So what if we aren't? Anybody in this house is trespassing. They'd be in as much trouble as us."

"What if—"

"Stop being a weeny and look for some treasure."

"A weeny? Really? It's like you've regressed to the seventh grade today."

"What do you want me to call you? The Big D?" Wyll chuckled while he picked up a towel draped over a shelf in the dining room.

"How 'bout you just shut up?" Derec flipped him off, turned, and walked away.

Wyll knew he wasn't really mad. Blowing it off, he focused on the pictures. There were several frames filled with a grinning couple and their little girl. Was this their house? He plopped in a chair at the head of the oversized table, letting his long legs sprawl. He dropped his elbow to the table, tapping it with his fingertips. This sheet looked like a tablecloth. He peeked under the corner to see a rich mahogany wood. He brushed his hand over the silky-smooth texture, running his finger along the grain. His nails were filthy.

He turned over his other hand and stared at the picture he held. There was something oddly comforting about it. The clothes were vintage. The woman's skin was a coppery shade of brown, and the man was a ginger, but the photo had also aged with an orange tint. Nestled between them, a cherubic little girl with big, shining eyes sported a huge, laughing smile. She was eerily beautiful, her features promising an evolution of stunning beauty as she matured. *Yeah, she'll be hot someday.*

"Wanna go upstairs?" Derec entered the room.

Wyll replaced the photo and said, "Sure. Come on. We'll check it out."

They took their time leisurely searching ghostly bedrooms. Wyll thought it odd that someone would leave a house behind with so many personal items—like picture albums and toothbrushes. The little girl's room was painted a sunny yellow, with white furniture. On her dresser stood a tiny glass horse. He considered taking it, but it was too fragile to put in his pocket. *And face it,* he told himself, *it would last about two minutes before I forget and hit it against something.* He placed the delicate glass sculpture back where he'd found it.

They were descending the back staircase, returning to the main floor, when they heard male voices in the kitchen.

"Sshh." Wyll stuck his arm out, blocking Derec mid-step.

"Who is it?" Derec whispered.

Wyll rolled his eyes, shaking his head. "How should I know, stupid?"

The conversation rose in pitch and volume as if they were in an intense argument. Derec's eyes widened like twin moons. Wyll put a finger to his lips and pointed to the wall. They inched down the stairs, sliding along the wall, and heard the voices clearer as they neared the kitchen.

Crap. That's our way out. And even if we find another exit, I'll have to pass the kitchen windows to get the damn dog. They'd have to wait until the men left the room. Wyll wasn't too worried since they were all in the wrong, but he was pissed at the complication and didn't want to spook anyone or cause a confrontation. He lifted weights every football season and knew he could hold his own, but he was smart enough to know when to stay out of a fight.

"Where is it? It's got to be here somewhere. You have three seconds to produce it or name its location," the deep male voice echoed through the house.

"Yeah," a second, nasally voice pitched in.

"I—I was told it was here. I don't know exactly where! I've never seen it myself, but I— No. No, wait. I—I can find it. I know I can! No, please!" The third voice shook and then was cut off.

THWWAAAP.

Wyll didn't recognize the sound, but he knew it wasn't good.

Feet scuffled. "If it's here, we'll find it ourselves." The first man's ominous statement set Wyll's nerves on edge.

He felt the vibration of a heavy thud through the floor. Something had fallen—or someone.

"Don't get blood on the tile this time," the man said. "Ah, what do I care? You're cleanin' up anyway."

"Sure, boss."

Wyll peered at Derec. The poor guy looked like he was ready to blow his lunch. *Lunch.* His tightly clenched stomach reminded him they hadn't made it to the Quik Mart. *Crap.*

They reached a shadowy hallway full of doors. When footsteps sounded in the dining room, panic gripped his heart. Wyll pointed to the door nearest them, and they inched it open, sliding through.

Wyll would have fallen down the staircase if Derec hadn't caught him by the arm. Wooden stairs descended to a concrete basement. He could see the glow of sunlight at the bottom, so Wyll thought there might be a way out. They tiptoed down the steps slowly to keep them from creaking.

At the bottom, cases of wine were stacked against the far wall of an empty concrete room with piles of what looked to be burlap in the corner. Most likely left from some squatter, the burlap was formed like a nest. The light they'd seen came from two small windows set high in the wall. *We aren't getting out that way.* He could barely see the grassy yard outside. They were in the back of the house. If they could squeeze through the narrow window opening, at least Derec could—

"Can we stack the crates and fit through?" Derec whispered.

Wyll looked around the shadowy expanse of the basement for anything else to use. He lifted one of the crates, testing its weight. They were made of thick wooden slats—each one full of wine bottles. That was a ton of wine. *I'll have to remember that.* He replaced the burdensome crate. *Too heavy to carry.*

Scraping the crates across the floor, even if they could move them, would make too much noise. He paced to the other corner, where reams of burlap lay in heaps, and looked for a closet with tools. With something metal, he could pry the crates open, pull out the bottles, and carry the empty boxes to the window—or possibly find a storage area where they could hide if needed.

His eyes flicked along the wall. *There.* He elbowed Derec and pointed. Under the stairs hid a small door with an old-fashioned-looking key sticking out of the lock. He turned the knob and found it locked, so he turned the key until it clicked, then pulled the door open. The fit was tight, and he pulled hard. The small door protested loudly from its hinges, but once he could see through the frame, he opened it further, letting out a strident creak.

"Shhh," Derec whispered furiously. "What are you doing?"

Wyll stood paralyzed in front of the opening. "Look." He pointed through the door.

Derec joined him, and they gazed—unbelieving—into another empty basement room. There were five or six stairs in the other room across from them, leading to a closed door at the top. Mold-covered windows gave the room a green tint.

"I thought it was a closet," Derec said as if looking for logic. "It's under the stairs. That's not possible—and there's no house next door. Where does it go? We must be turned around, and it's part of the house we didn't realize."

"No, dude. That is the backyard." Wyll pointed to the concrete wall.

"So where could it possibly go? It's unbelievable ... not possible." Derec looked allergic to the paradigm shift and shook his head, backing up a few steps. One way to really freak Derec out was to watch late-night episodes of *Extraordinary Unexplainable Tales*. He existed on logic, and Wyll could tell he was gearing up for a full-blown anxiety attack.

"Only one way to find out," Wyll said as he shrugged, ducked through the door jamb, and stepped into the other room. "Come on. Let's explore. There's got to be an explanation."

Derec was looking up to where the house was and measuring the distance of the yard against the foreign basement. "It can't—. It's just not possible," he repeated.

Wyll faced Derec—standing on the other side of the doorway—and shivered, rubbing his biceps. "It's really cold in here. They must have the air on high or something. Are you coming or not?"

Derec stepped backward and shook his head, his wispy black hair following his movement. "I can't. It's too weird. I—"

"You don't want to be stuck in there, do you? I mean, what could this be?" Wyll gestured to the room around him.

Derec crossed his arms and planted his feet. "Better here than the Twilight Zone. There's no way I'm going in there."

Wyll gave up and walked back toward the doorframe.

Suddenly, the door they'd come through at the top of the stairs creaked open, and they heard a heavy footstep thunk onto the first stair. "I thought I heard something down here."

"Like what?" the other voice asked.

"I don't know. A noise. But there's not supposed to be anyone else here."

"Go check it out. I'm going upstairs." The voice in the hall faded. Then, the squeaky steps resumed as the mobster slowly shifted his weight to the next step.

Wyll and Derec froze. Derec's face lit up, and he held his hand up for Wyll to stop.

Wyll motioned with both hands for him to come through the door. Fine black hair fanned through the air as a calculating statue of Derec shook his head. The heavy steps got louder, and Derec snapped into action; his brows perked up, then he waved to Wyll with a smile and quickly closed the door with Wyll on the other side.

Chapter Two
Horror Movie Victim

What is he doing? Wyll tensed and worked his jaw in the green light of the new basement. He realized as he found himself in a strange place that Derec was stuck in the other basement with a thug. He considered pounding on the door, but that would definitely get Derec in trouble—or send the hitman after himself. If the man saw Wyll, he would appear to be a threat. Just seventeen, he was already six feet tall, with wide shoulders and an attitude. Wyll wasn't particularly worried about his friend, though.

Derec was a Boy Scout. *For real.* His parents—modern immigrants from China—were divided on immersing Derec into the full American experience. Derec and his dad—an engineer—spoke English, but his mom didn't care to learn more than what she had to for the grocery store and church. She was old-school religious. His dad always wanted to grow up in America, though, so he enrolled Derec in every traditional American-child activity—even made him play baseball with his allergies.

Derec was the sole reason that Wyll got through middle school, mostly by sharing his homework after school. He was a smart guy. Of all the people Wyll knew, he could probably handle himself. He was probably hiding.

Oh well. Wyll shrugged. Nothing he could do about it. He wouldn't worry too much about it yet—he'd come for an adventure, and he found one. *Each man for himself, right?*

Really, Wyll knew he sometimes lacked a socially acceptable level of empathy. He didn't deal well with conflict and emotions. His mother called it absent morality, but Wyll disagreed that it was anything malicious; he just didn't worry about how his self-preservation methods affected other people. *"Take care of thyself." –Me 24:7* Wyll chuckled. A counselor once told him that he did it to eliminate the risk of rejection. He supposed it could be true. Deep down—in a place he refused to recognize—he cared deeply about what others thought and felt, *but why put yourself in that position?*

Sometimes gripped with the tight, feverish sweating of his insecurity, he worked so hard to remain strong and steady—and unaffected—he convinced himself that he didn't care at all. *Who am I kidding?* He would always be this way—passive and fearful deep inside and cocky on the outside. Still, he warred with himself about leaving Derec behind.

The thug must be gone by now. He put his head up to the door but didn't hear anything. He turned the knob, but it was locked from the other side. Derec must have the key. He pressed his ear harder to the rough panel of wood but still heard nothing. He tapped lightly and waited. *Nothing.*

Aside from all the sensible arguments flashing through his thoughts, he didn't really want to go back. He wanted to have an adventure to take his mind off his home life. If he went back, he'd have to face the loss of his family unit. No, it was better to explore the mystery before him. Taking in his surroundings made his blood bubble with excitement. He smiled, inhaling the stale air, smelling the touch of mold.

Derec is always right—this must lead to another part of the house, and we got turned around. Well, he wasn't going to stand there all day. He kinda had to pee. Giving in to his need, he crossed the green-lit room and tiptoed up the stairs. Derec would figure a way out. Wyll needed to take care of himself and figure out his own way. TeaCup was probably becoming a "hot dog" by now; he'd better get moving. He chuckled at the groaner and was glad he'd left the water on.

The door at the top of the stairs opened smoothly, and Wyll found himself in a small house that was obviously not the modern mansion he'd just been in. He emerged into a short hallway. "Anybody here?" he called. He didn't want to freak anyone out.

The Clockwork Pen

The front room was small and brightly lit. A brass telescope rested next to the large window, striking, in front of rich, wine-colored curtains. The fabric—open in the center—framed a huge piece of glass, paned in oak, and etched with scrolling designs. Sunlight poured in, and the space was cozy, but it didn't put him at ease. He shivered, envying the outside heat—his fingers were freezing. There was no answer, so he continued.

It was exquisite—everything gleaming and intricately decorated, with a thin layer of dust. The air smelled stale, and he wondered if the house had been vacant for long. It was furnished, like the mansion, but everything was different. The walls were a rich golden hue that reflected off the polished walnut floors. In an alcove, a table for four stood on a rug under a hanging bulb encased by an amber-colored glass shade. On a nearby hutch, a black top hat slouched to the side, a pair of goggles perched on the brim. Not for swimming, they were made with brass spikes and dark lenses.

Wyll crossed to a wrought-iron cabinet with glass shelves, peering at unfamiliar gadgets lined up next to each other, one a coil of wire with decorative ends, another a copper canister that might have been a teapot, and several beakers that his science teacher would kill for—delicate and held in a metal stand covered with wire filigree. *Where am I? What is all this?* He began to feel like he might not be in Kansas. But that wasn't possible. He pushed out any feelings of panic.

Derec's face flashed in front of him. He was so afraid of the illogical because he enjoyed the tales of aliens and alternate dimensions and magic, believing in theory—they were just too terrifying for reality. Wyll only believed in what he could see. The problem was that he could see this and had to agree it didn't make sense. Was he in a secret place? The door was hidden under a set of basement stairs. Surely, there was some kind of secret involved. *But magic?* He decided to hold his suspension of disbelief a little longer. There must be an explanation here.

He found a short hallway leading to a small bedroom. The wrought iron bed was made up with a purple velvet duvet and covered by a canopy of sheer cream-colored fabric. He ran his hand through the soft fronds of a large vase of feathers, letting them slide through his fingers. It sat on a dresser with metal gears for knobs, a large peacock feather rising from the middle of the bunch.

This was the coolest house he'd ever been in. *But who lives here, and where are they?* He sniffed the musty air. *How long have they been gone?* He hadn't noticed any little houses in the mansion's backyard. And the place wasn't like any carriage house he'd ever seen. Then, through the window, he heard people outside. He relaxed somewhat, knowing he wasn't alone in this foreign place. How could he be in a magic land if there were other people here? He should head out and ask someone. He

The Clockwork Pen

used the bathroom but had to figure out where to flush the stupid thing because there were several parts to the toilet.

When Wyll walked out the front door, he was assaulted with the knowledge that he was far from home. Instead of the humid heat of summer, the air wrapped him in a chill that immediately gave him goosebumps, but it didn't feel too bad since he generally liked the cold. *Could I have entered a portal to another part of the planet where it's cold?* He stepped off the porch and noticed the ornately built houses were close together. People rode strange bikes in the street, and others strolled down the sidewalk. *Maybe a time-traveling portal?* He saw mountains in the distance and remembered how the Rockies looked from the edge of Denver.

He certainly wasn't home—there were no mountains in Olathe, Kansas. Not even close. Wyll's skin crawled. He couldn't decide if he was fascinated or terrified. He debated running back to the basement door but squared his shoulders. He was here now; he had no desire to go home, and it was a mystery ripe for his exploration. For some reason, he needed the answer to this riddle so much more than heading back toward what waited for him.

The sky was deep blue, but the airship flying overhead stole his attention. It was a huge contraption that looked like the Goodyear blimp in gold lamé, covered in cables and carrying what looked like a huge wooden bullet with a flat bottom. The people passed him going down the street as he stood on a little walkway leading to an iron pipe gate. He had to find out where he was. Every instinct he had, said this was a secret—a land apart—like Middle-Earth. Only not. Deciding to explore further, he glanced at the house for distinguishing features to remember where he'd come from. It said *2224 Olathe*. He cocked his head in wonder. Was that a joke? *Where is this place?*

The people on the sidewalk looked at him strangely as he stood shivering in his cargo shorts and t-shirt, and he stared at them in their striped skirts, ruffled shirts, and leather boots. They were all dressed for the weather—not like it was a freak occurrence in the middle of summer—wearing long coats and hats like the Kentucky Derby. One couple strolled by him and then whispered to themselves. The man's handlebar mustache tickled her ear and caused the feathers on her hat to flutter. They looked back at him and laughed. It kinda ticked him off. He definitely felt out of place.

Before he could pull the anxiety on like a coat, the couple passed, and Wyll saw twin cylinders on the man's back, strapped over his shoulders and around his waist. *A jet pack?* Did it work? He would have thought he'd walked into a steampunk-type of Renaissance Faire, but the houses across the street all carried on the theme and looked like they'd come from a Victorian catalog with tall, vaulted roofs and decorative trim. His inner pilot light flared to life. He pushed aside his apprehension—he

The Clockwork Pen

wanted to see everything and noticed every magical detail.

He listened to the people speaking and realized he couldn't understand them. *Another language? How could this be happening? Am I in Europe?* He decided to ask someone for information. Standing up straight and taking a fortifying lungful, Wyll opened the gate and stepped onto the sidewalk. The street was cobblestone, and he saw several bikes, motorized with shiny gold-trimmed glass canisters, but no cars. He walked up to a gentleman with a cane and a high collar.

"Hi." He stuck out his hand. When the man looked confused, he said, "I'm Wyll. Does anyone around here speak English?"

The man's eyes widened, and he looked around. He stared meaningfully at Wyll and shook his head. Wyll reached out toward him as he turned to walk away, and the man glared at him, saying something low and quiet before stalking off. Wyll's brow wrinkled, and he leaned back against the fence, wondering what the man had meant.

A minute later, a woman walked up to him, pushing a baby carriage with one hand, the other holding a delicate umbrella over her head. The hem of her dress was higher in the front, showing off some nice stems in pointed white boots. Her cropped jacket boasted twin dragons that blew fire up to her ruffled collar. So cool.

She smiled at him. *Not bad.* He returned the smile and asked her, "Do *you* know anyone who speaks English?"

She blushed and tilted her head but kept looking at him.

"English?" He pointed to his own mouth, then to her mouth, and raised his eyebrows.

"Sepherran." She looked around and touched his shoulder. She continued, saying more things he didn't understand. When she realized he wasn't comprehending, she glanced both ways down the sidewalk. She shook her head at him sadly and started to pass him.

Wyll touched her sleeve, and she turned back.

"I really need to talk to someone who speaks *English.*" *There should be someone, right? The doorway leads here from an English-speaking country, after all. Someone* knew it was there.

She put a finger to her lips and shook her head.

"You want me to be quiet?" He didn't understand.

She sighed heavily and motioned for him to follow her. He didn't have anything to lose, and he wanted to explore the place, so he followed her as she made a U-turn and walked down the sidewalk the way she'd come. They passed men in velvet vests with leather trim and buckles. As they walked, Wyll pushed his finger against the wooden points of the white-painted fencing that came to his hip. It ran the length of the block, every house nestled in a perfectly square little patch of yard. Wyll and the

The Clockwork Pen

woman squished up against the fence for a pair of ladies to pass with half masks in black crystal and velvet, ribboned to elaborate hairdos.

They passed homes with a plethora of uniquely styled windows, archways, and decorative woodwork. The woman stopped before a house built mostly of brick, with a shiny dome on top, small peaks surrounding it, and huge round windows. The biggest window in front housed an enormous clock in iron and glass, with silver scrolls. She opened the gate and motioned him inside the yard.

It was only about ten feet up the walkway to the door. He turned to see her still standing on the sidewalk. She motioned for him to continue, so he knocked on the heavy door's oval etched glass and looked back again. She smiled and nodded her encouragement.

A man pulled the door open, filling the frame. Even Wyll could give the man credit for being more than handsome—his glossy black hair was swept back and fashioned at his neck. Two gold hoops hung from his ears, and a belt full of bullets hung diagonally from his lean hips. He wore fitted, black pin-striped pants and black boots better than any runway model, and his high-collared shirt was open a few buttons. He swirled a glass of amber liquid and looked at Wyll with raised eyebrows. He waved at the woman on the sidewalk and smiled. She returned the gesture.

The man said something Wyll didn't understand in a jovial tone.

"Dude. I can't understand you. I don't know why she brought me here, but I really need to talk to someone who can speak *English*." Wyll stressed the last word loudly.

The man's eyes widened, and he looked up and down the block as the woman had.

"Do *you* speak English?" Wyll was hoping the word meant something to them. But the man put a finger to his lips and a hand on Wyll's shoulder, pulling him inside.

The man waved again at the woman on the sidewalk and shut the door. He muttered in his strange language, going to the side table and tossing his drink down his throat before pouring another glass.

The man motioned for Wyll to sit in one of the grape-hued satin chairs, then left the room. Wyll chose the seat next to a grandfather clock. With nothing to do but stare at all the wonders around him, he drank up the differences between this world and his own boring home with the floral wallpaper and lumpy navy sofa. The levers and pulleys of the clock were visible through the glass casing, with tall tin gears on the wooden base in designs of rabbits chasing each other round and round.

The front room resembled the house he'd emerged from, with more furniture. Between the satin chairs sat a matching sofa in velvet, but this house also had a bright copper birdcage, floor lamps, and an elaborate-looking stereo in dark wood with shiny brass details. The rafters were exposed beams of mahogany contrasting with the pale lilac color of the walls and high ceiling. Two round doorways led to other rooms, and a spiral staircase in the corner went upstairs. Wyll really liked the maps on the walls in elegantly gilded frames. His heartbeat transcended the rhythm of the ticking clock. He was excited and a bit nervous. He'd feel better once he could speak with someone to make sense of all this.

The man returned, setting his glass down on the sideboard. He picked up another glass and half-filled it, handing it to Wyll. Then he rifled through some papers in the sideboard drawer. Wyll sniffed the drink. Alcoholic for sure. *Strong.* Not wanting to appear unrefined, he leaned back and propped one ankle on the opposite knee. He swirled the drink around the glass and poured it down his throat. The fire began in his airway and grew into a blazing inferno in his stomach. Fumes shot through his sinuses, bringing tears to his eyes and stealing his breath.

When he could inhale again, he attempted to talk to the man, who only gazed at him sadly and shook his head. The man pulled a pocket watch out of his vest and then stood in front of him. The man put both hands out toward him like he was saying, *"Stay there."* Wyll nodded.

The man walked over to the door and pointed to himself, then to the door. He pointed to Wyll and then to the floor. *Yep. Stay here.* Wyll nodded again. The man would go, and he would wait. *Fine.* The room was spinning a little bit anyway. The man buttoned his collar and put on a leather coat that reached his ankles, a pair of oval glasses, and a slouchy top hat. He looked like that older actor in an 80s vampire movie he'd seen. Wyll was comfortable in the chair and leaned his head back as the man jingled his keys, locking the door when he left.

When Wyll again heard the rattle of keys in the lock, he opened his eyes to a dark house. He must have crashed from his adrenaline high. Couldn't have been the drink—he could put down a six-pack in the first thirty minutes of a kegger. The man walked into the house and immediately flicked on the power. The lamps brightened to a warm glow, and the man turned to see Wyll sitting there, squinting as his pupils adjusted. He smiled and sighed with what looked to be relief—it stoked Wyll's curiosity. What was such a secret? Why would he care if Wyll was still there?

The man closed the curtains in the front window and motioned for Wyll to follow him. Wyll stretched his legs as he rose, shaking out the kinks. He put his hands on his hips and popped his back. The man cringed just like his parents did, which made Wyll chuckle. Smiling kindly, the man led him through the house to the kitchen, tiled in slate gray. He reached into a shiny wooden cabinet door and took out a key he tucked into his pocket.

He gestured for Wyll past a pantry decorated with iron squids to a table that looked like a giant steering wheel from a pirate's ship. It was encompassed by a round booth in shiny sea-blue vinyl. Wyll felt cool as hell sitting down at it until he whacked his forehead on the octopus-shaped chandelier hanging low over the table. He rubbed his temple in the dim light of the round bulbs dangling from each tentacle. The man pulled out two big cookies and handed them to him.

Wyll bit into one with curiosity. It had a thin layer of something savory. The flaky cookie tasted like a beef potpie. It was really filling and surprisingly delicious. He hadn't realized he was hungry and gratefully shoved both meat cookies in his mouth. He accepted a glass of water decorated with tiny black metal flowers vining around it and turned it to follow the vines, finding the glass sparkled with iridescence. He realized he was frowning in concentration and relaxed his forehead. The mystery man stood at the back door, holding out a long coat, smiling at him with the same curiosity he felt.

He set the glass down and scooted off the bench, accepting the coat. It stretched across his muscled shoulders, and the long sleeves nearly reached his wrists. When he was covered, they went out the back door into a crispy, cool evening. Wyll followed the man down the back path, passing a small garden space and a shed made with exposed beams and steel pipe accents. Their shoes crunched on the pebbled alley dividing this street's backyards and those from one street over. The houses were as elaborate from behind as they were from the front, the yards really more garden-sized, a few sprouting dead grass, and many tilled and spotted with dead plants. A few blocks of silence didn't bother Wyll; he was absorbing.

They emerged from the neighborhood, looking both ways before stepping onto a *perpendicular* sidewalk. *Yay for geometry.* The man's cane tapped the cement as they walked. The pace was brisk, and Wyll puffed out wispy white clouds, watching them dissipate as he walked through them.

The man practically ran as they entered a large open square of concrete scattered with sculptures of geometrical shapes. To his right, the moon's reflection glowed on a wicked-looking castle elevated over a lake-like moat, complete with pointy turrets. Wyll wanted to stop and look or get closer, but the man pulled his sleeve and then put a finger to his lips when Wyll opened his mouth, ready to protest. They moved on.

Is this guy a speed walker? Wyll's breath was deep and forceful. They traveled along a commercial street, and he peered in shop windows displaying shadowed wares—all closing for the night. Pulled along by his arm, Wyll gave up fighting the guy and followed him.

"Fine," he whispered.

The buildings grew larger and further apart. They were the only people out this far from the neighborhoods he'd started in. No lights shined in any windows; no shadowy figures moved in his periphery. The cane's click echoed off the glass and metal exteriors. *Click, click,*

click. Wyll's pulse was loud in his ears, the exact source of his anxiety unknown, but *something* was going down. The poor guy leading him was sweating and looking over his shoulders for some anonymous threat, and it set Wyll's nerves on edge.

Wyll's thigh muscles were warming, and he pushed them harder when the man pointed to a boxy structure ahead and took off at a jog. Through the glass, he could see giant machinery—huge drums and gears the size of his body. Rusty metal staircases ran rings inside the structure, leading up to towering levels of glass-encased offices and more machinery. They huddled together in front of the glass door, and his guide pulled the key from his pocket. When they entered, the ceiling was so high it didn't feel like they were inside at all, except for the absence of the frigid breeze.

The man turned the deadbolt behind them. Lamps dotted the walls, but everything was dark, stationary, and covered in dust like it hadn't been used in years. He followed the stranger behind the machinery and along a back wall of concrete to a seamless door that was practically invisible. He entered the hallway and descended concrete steps, sliding his palm along a pipe railing, focused on the hanging lightbulb shining at the bottom.

Tripping on the last step, he barreled into the back of the man, who stumbled forward. They were in a dark hallway full of spiders, and he ran into a string of spiderwebs hanging from the ceiling. Wyll shivered despite himself. *I hate spiders. Where the hell are we going?* Should he even be following a stranger down a dark hall? He wanted to smack himself. It was like every dumb horror movie he'd ever seen. The whole time, you're yelling at the screen, "Don't go in there!" And they always do, and you think, *How stupid are they?* He stopped. About as stupid as he was, apparently.

"Hey, guy? I ah, I think I'm going to go back." He pointed over his shoulder just as the man opened a door, and light spilled into the hallway. The man removed his glasses and smiled genuinely, gesturing for Wyll to enter. He approached cautiously, puffing out his chest as he passed in case the guy had any ideas. The room was large, with rudimentary furniture. It was nothing decorative—a big studio apartment, really—with a bed, a small kitchen with a table, a couple of chairs, and a sofa. *Was he supposed to stay here? Were they going to lock him up?* Wyll began to lose a measure of his cool.

No one knew he was there. If they locked him away, there would be nothing he could do. He glanced around, looking for chains. *Shit.* He'd seen something like this in a movie. His ears filled with the rush of blood from his instantly panicked heartbeat. He turned to leave and saw the man blocking the door.

"No." Wyll shook his head as if there was any doubt about what he was saying. "I'm not staying here. I don't belong here. Dude, *I'm sorry*. I'm just gonna go back to where I came from—pound on the stupid door."

The man stood sentinel, watching him curiously, both hands on the ball of his cane. Wyll pointed to himself and then pointed to the door. "I need to leave."

The man shook his head, frowning, and stood firm.

Wyll was gearing up to ram his shoulder right through the guy when a side door opened. He could see a short person, lit from behind by the bathroom light, their face in shadow. But with an hourglass figure like that, he guessed it was a girl. He slowed his panicky nerves and watched her.

She stepped under the light of a hanging bulb, and he took in her brown suede jacket with bell pulls on the shoulders. A deep brown top hat decorated with gold leaves blowing across one side, perched on a nest of dark red curls. An open-geared clock sat on the brim in front of an ice-blue swatch of fabric that matched her eyes. Tiny rectangle glasses sat on her nose, and frothy white fabric ruffled from her cuffs and at her neck. He took in her slim legs, clad in form-fitting black pants with boots to her knee.

"You done looking me over?" She put a hand on her hip.

He realized his mouth was open. *Again.* He was usually on the other side of this reaction. He casually straightened his posture, flexing his lean upper body.

"Well?" she asked, her brows raised and both hands gripped her hips.

"You speak English." It was like his brain had succumbed to dementia. What was wrong with him? He talked to girls all the time. *But none this intimidating.* She was petite, but she filled the room with her presence.

He liked it.

"Yes, detective obvious. And so do you. So … what are you doing here?"

It wasn't the welcome he'd expected—and he had questions. He frowned. "Where am I? And why doesn't anyone but *you* speak English?"

After a few moments of staring him down, she sighed. "Okay, fine. It's another dimension. Now, you tell me how you got here and who you are, and I might answer more questions."

Another dimension? He didn't feel like that answered anything. But there were more pressing issues. "Are you planning to keep me here?"

"For the time being, yes. So, start talking." She walked to the sofa and motioned for the men to sit. She said something to the man in their language, and he nodded.

"What language is that?" Wyll asked.

"Sepherran. Start talking." She perched one ankle over her opposite knee and sat back.

That was what the woman on the sidewalk had said. *Sepherran.* He'd almost flunked geography, but he was quite sure that wasn't one of the languages he'd ever been aware of. She sat waiting for him to speak. The man picked up something like a magazine and leafed through the pages.

"Maybe start with your name?" She raised her brows.

"I'm Wyll Brey. I was checking out this abandoned mansion when we found a door—"

Her eyes lit up. "Tell me about the house."

"Ah, everything is covered with sheets? There's not much to tell. But in the *basement*, there's this door ... and I came through it to find myself here. Then everybody freaked out when I tried to talk to them—"

"That's because English is illegal here. You said *'we'* found the door." She was leaning toward him now.

He waited for her to say more, but she didn't.

"If it's illegal, then why do *you* speak it when no one else does?" he asked. "And he stayed there."

"I'm bilingual. I moved here when I was nearly five. The king outlawed English years before I came, so he'd know any time someone found him from the real world."

"This isn't ... the real world?" He was trying to wrap his head around the new information.

"No. The king created it. We're in some parallel man-made dimension, *whatever*. He makes anything he wants. He made this entire world and all the people. Everything." She shook her head. "It's too much power

Jennifer Haskin

for one man to have. I've been trying to get out of here for years. *Finally,* you're here. Did you bring the key with you? Where is it?" Her eyes lit from within, and she held out her hand.

Wyll was struggling to believe it all. "He made the *people?* But how—I don't understand."

"That's okay. You don't need to. Just give me the key, and I'll get us back home." She closed her extended fist and opened it again.

"I don't want to go home. Right now, my home sucks. I want to stay here and explore. If I'm lucky, they'll miss me. Maybe then they won't—. Well, I can't, anyway. I don't have it."

"What do you mean you don't have it?" Her eyes narrowed to slits.

"When I came through, I was with this other guy, right? He stayed there and shut the door. Some bad guy was coming."

"What bad guy?"

"How the heck should I know? Just somebody else in the house. We heard these thugs hurting somebody, and we ran." He shrugged and pulled a hand through his hair. "I wasn't going to stick around to find out."

"But what happened to the other guy and the key?" She sounded panicked.

"I'm sure he's fine. Nobody's going to hurt a skinny Asian kid with glasses and allergies. He can pass for a thirteen-year-old; he probably said he got lost. And Derec is obviously not a threat."

The girl turned to the man reading the magazine and spoke Sepherran. His eyes grew large, and he answered her.

"Do you know where you came out?" she asked.

"Yeah. I remember. I don't know which street, but I know the house," Wyll said. "Why's it such a big deal? Can't you go out another way? Or find another key?"

"No," she said, as though she'd sucked on a lemon. "There's only one door to this world, but until you, I never knew where it was—though I suspected one of the houses. I suppose I should be grateful for that. But there are only two keys. One is in the real world, with your *friend*, I guess. And the other one is around the king's neck."

"Oh. Sorry... So, we're both stuck here?"

She took off her glasses and rubbed the bridge of her nose. She looked familiar to him for some reason, but he didn't see how that would be possible. "I've been stuck here for over twelve years, waiting for the day I can go back to the real world. I really thought this was it..."

"I hope Derec remembered to grab my dog." Wyll still didn't want to go home—he was too upset—but eventually, he would need to figure out a way. And he didn't want to tell Mom he'd killed her dog.

The other two spoke back and forth for a few minutes.

She turned to Wyll. "Are there many people in the house? If we banged on the door, would your friend be there?"

"I doubt it. I don't know what happened; maybe he hid. But I'm sure he's gone home by now."

"But if you heard bad people, why did you leave him?"

"What could I do? He's the one who shut the door. I had to take care of myself—that's who I'm responsible for." Wyll felt like he was being chastised, and it ruffled his feathers. She looked at him like a bug in a geology lab. "Hey, I knocked lightly, just in case the bad guy was there. I tried to help him. Was I supposed to stay there forever in case thugs caught him?"

She didn't answer.

He couldn't remember ever feeling so inferior to another person, let alone a girl. It made him nervous, but he didn't know why—and that made him angry. "You know what I mean, right? If you don't take care of yourself, no one else will." It wasn't like he didn't care about Derec, but once he'd shut the door, Wyll had no choice but to carry on.

She looked disappointed, and he couldn't understand why it bothered him so much. "You are *so* wrong; I don't think it would make a difference what I said."

The Clockwork Pen

When she spoke to the man again, Wyll had enough. "Hey. I'm right here. If you're going to talk about me, I want to know what you're saying."

"Oh, I forgot. I brought you this." She fished out a small contraption the size of the tip of his pinkie from her pocket. "My father made me this when we moved here, so I'd understand before I could speak Sepherran. Put it in your ear."

She handed him the device, and he placed it in his right ear. It settled in nicely. He waited to hear them speak.

"If he doesn't have access to the key, we are back to square one. But now with a new problem. Who knows what the king will do to him if he finds him? He will never believe the Resistance had nothing to do with this." Indigo closed the magazine and furrowed his brow.

It sounded to Wyll like they had already planned their exodus. He didn't really care about the details. He was content to check out this crazy new world while they figured out the way to send him home. He was in no hurry to see Kansas—or his parents. *And when they worry, maybe they'll think about what they're doing to my life. Maybe they'll see how wrong they are, and things will stay the same—safe and permanent.*

But he knew they probably wouldn't worry. They'd naturally assume he was at Derec's. He and Derec had spent summers together since they were in the third grade at one house or another. They were supposed to be seniors this year—if he ever came back. If Wyll searched his feelings, he'd realize he would hate to forgo football season, with its bonfires and tipsy cheerleaders, and all the senior-year hoopla. But he was happily in denial for the moment. There might be a power-hungry king here, but power-hungry lawmakers already infected the real world. How could this be any worse? It was a magical land, for crying out loud—the stuff of stories.

"Well, Indigo. We will just have to go back to the plan we made originally," she said, and they nodded together somberly.

"What's the plan?" Wyll asked.

"I'm not sure we should include him in our plans," she said as she watched the man rise and held up two fingers horizontally.

The man, Indigo, walked to a counter and opened a fancy glass decanter. Holding the ball stopper, he poured three glasses. "We might as well. He needs to get home eventually. His family will be worried. Surely the king wouldn't really hurt him?"

"He isn't the same anymore, Indi. You know he's lashing out at anyone he can get a hold of who even *smells* of Resistance. He's just now starting to realize that he's losing control of the people, and it's obvious that he rejects the idea entirely. He won't believe this kid wasn't smart enough to bring the key with him, and it's no secret how I feel." She took the glass that Indigo offered her.

Wyll took the last glass from Indigo and nursed it this time.

"Until we know more, we'd better keep him hidden." Indigo drained his glass and wiped his lip with his thumb.

Hidden? Hidden from what? If the king was law around here, these guys would be the outlaws, right? Were they the good guys or the bad guys? What had he gotten himself into?

Chapter Three

TWISTED KITTENS

"Yeah," the girl agreed with Indigo. "I think you're right. We should keep him in here. No one will find him."

"Hey—" Wyll leaned forward, so they both had to look directly at him.

"I can send Malynda to check on him tomorrow," Indigo offered, leaning to the left.

"That would be great, thanks." The girl rose from the sofa, brushed her hands down her jacket, and then took her glass to the sink. *She doesn't* seem *to be an evil hag in disguise...*

Indigo rose as well. "If that's all you need, I'll get going."

"Yes, everything's fine. Go before you're missed." The girl turned to Wyll, sitting in his chair, as Indigo left and closed the door behind himself. "You'll have everything you need here. You're safe, comfortable... I'll be back tomorrow night."

The Clockwork Pen

"Excuse me? You can't just leave me in here, like some dungeon. How do I know you'll come back?" Wyll's anxiety flared into anger. "I'm not your prisoner."

"I'm not locking you in here or anything. You are free to go home,"—she motioned toward the door with both arms—"but how are you going to do that?" She looked at him pointedly. "Until we have a plan, you must stay out of sight. It's the only way I can protect you."

"From what?"

"Not what. *Who.* The king would—well, honestly, I don't know what he'd do. But he's on the hunt for anyone who seems to resist him right now. He thinks killing the rebellion is the answer to keeping his control. And you being here threatens his hold on this entire world. Understand? He *won't* be happy to meet you."

Wyll imagined an incensed tyrant with a torture chamber of gears, cogs, pipes, and wire. "I'm not part of any Resistance. I haven't even been here long enough to be a threat. So, this Resistance—I'm guessing you guys head it up. Are there many who resist him?"

She sighed and sat back down. "You need to understand that these people may be adults, but they have only been alive for about eighteen years. That's when he created the world. Granted, the adults matured very quickly, but how many eighteen-year-olds want to do what their parents tell them? Especially if your 'parent' is a sovereign who holds your life in his hands. He can write away your existence instantly or take your home, wife, and children. Or he could make a torture device designed specifically for use on you until you do what he wants. All they want is independence."

"Why would he do that?" Wyll's mind flashed to a torture scene from a gruesome movie he watched recently, and he shivered involuntarily.

Her eyes stared at the wall next to him, but her gaze was somewhere far away. "He's not a bad guy. I mean, he wasn't. In fact, he used to be a really great man. He came across a magic pen when he was in the real world—he doesn't tell people how—and discovered that it creates whatever he wants. The power of the pen changed him. The more he uses it, the more his mind slips away. He's slowly going crazy, but he won't stop using it. He doesn't believe his precious pen is causing the problem, and he won't leave the world he's created. It's his legacy."

She let her shoulders drop. "If we could get that pen, the Resistance could take over and make a new government, and I could make new keys for the door or make a whole new door that would let me out into the real world. Most of the people here don't believe there is another world, but a few in the Resistance have suspected it for a while. Your existence will only solidify their desire to know if the human world really exists—where they wouldn't be persecuted."

"Human world? Aren't you human?" *What else would you be? Aliens? Zombies?*

She blew a curl from her face. "I'm human, yes. Apparently, the pen only makes *clockwork* life. Their souls are human; they have a mind, body, and spirit like anyone else. They're real people, except actual humans have a support system of bones and organs, and these people have a framework of gears, pulleys, and flesh. But they are as human inside as you or me." She pinched her forearm when she mentioned herself.

"Do they have doctors?"

"Of course. Though some ailments call for a mechanic."

"That's why everything— Wait, how do they have children?"

"The king gives them a baby. In the beginning, he made entire families. Then, he designed an orphanage with children so that couples could choose one to adopt. If they want a specific baby, they petition the king. He rules everything." She appeared to wilt from exhaustion, dropping her head with a little shake.

"It sounds like he's just trying to make everyone happy. But if he's crazy... Those people don't often make sense. I don't get why you feel so stuck here, but honestly, I don't think the real world is ready for clockwork people."

"Probably not, but they deserve to have choices— and a government that won't kill them for it. This hasn't been a bad life for them, but things are changing. The king wipes out any instances of perceived rebellion as soon as he sees them, and the people are growing more than wary. They need a government where they have a voice."

"Sounds like my parents." He chuckled, but she stared at him.

"You have no idea, do you? You don't even care. These people belong to him. They have no choice but to obey him or be punished—or wiped out completely. But they're people; they should have rights. We should be free." She stood as she spoke so passionately, Wyll was taken aback. She was beautiful this way, in her strength. "Nevermind. You'll find out soon enough."

"Hey, I'm not stupid. I get it. I just think you're not looking at it from all angles, that's all. If you don't think it's right here, you *should* leave. But you need to save yourself. I will help you, but I don't know what to do. I can't just step in and be your hero here. Sorry." It frustrated him that his words weren't coming out like he meant them. "I'll go with you when you leave and everything, but I'm probably not good for much else here." He shrugged. "Nobody needs my opinion to do anything." *A bit melodramatic, Wyll?* He could hear his mother's voice. *Why don't you do more?* He couldn't afford to care for these people. If he broke the dam of his repressed emotions, he might have to deal with everything—and he wasn't ready.

She stared at him like he'd sprouted wings, then she shivered and blinked. "I, uh. I have nothing to say to that. You certainly aren't what I thought you'd be."

The Clockwork Pen

"What?" he asked.

"My first human. Other than my own father, of course. You're the first human I've met since…" She cleared her throat and squared her shoulders, making the fringe bounce on her sleeves. "Since my mother died. I imagined you'd be more like her, I guess—a kind and caring person with humanity. I'm sorry I was wrong. I guess people are the same everywhere."

He didn't want her to think he wasn't kind. He did care that her mother had died but knew from her rigid posture that she didn't want his pity, and he respected her for it. She wasn't like the girls back home. She wasn't like the girls anywhere. He wondered what she would do when she eventually made it back to the real world—when *they* made it back. Maybe if they got out before school started… He imagined taking her to the bonfire after the Homecoming game this fall and smiled genuinely at her. He would enjoy teaching her about things she'd missed.

She looked angry at first, then exhaled as she shook her head and grinned at him with a kind of ease that was … cute. She looked like the tiny leader of a great army. Her attitude was sassy, but he could tell she had a sense of humor.

"So, you'll be back tomorrow?" he asked, measuring their chemistry. It might be unsteady, but it had a heartbeat. Her body in that leather called to his, and electricity buzzed between them. Did she really not know any other human guys? Wyll wasn't good at relationships, but her charisma attracted him like a moth to a bug zapper.

"Yes. Tomorrow evening I can get away, but not for long. I need to talk to Indigo and figure out our plan. You need to get home, where you belong. And if the only way to get you there just happens to complete my goal, I can't really turn down the opportunity, can I?" She slipped her glasses onto the end of her nose and looked at him over the lenses, flashing a conspiratorial smile.

"Guess not. But you don't need to hurry." He yawned through the second adrenaline crash and glass of whatever. "I want to see everything."

She stood and tipped her hat. "We'll figure it out. Just lay low. Someone will check on you tomorrow morning."

He gave her a "thumbs up" and let his arm drop to the sofa.

She flicked a lever on the end of her cane, and the bottom quarter of it glowed inside an iron-framed lamp with a long curling wire burning brightly. He would never have guessed it was there. Like her hair, the cane was dark red wood, and the lighted portion was covered in red glass. It was a beautiful piece of hardware and only piqued Wyll's excitement to see the rest of this world.

Raising the cane to light her way, she tucked the other end under her arm. She slipped into the cavernous hallway and pulled the door closed. He hoped she'd be okay, but then again, he thought, if she was right, she was safer here than he was. She was a strong girl; she'd probably be fine. He rose slowly and saw a small lamp glowing by the bed, so he turned off the shaded overhead bulb, dropped onto the mattress, and then rolled over to mash his face in the pillow. He inhaled the scent of lavender on the pillowcase and relaxed into sleep, wondering if the scent was hers.

Wyll rolled over, feeling rested and perkier than he'd been since he was a kid. There was an entire world out there—like a Christmas gift—wrapped in glittering tape and folded bows, waiting expectantly for him to rip it open and drink it in. And he wouldn't mind seeing *her* again. Wyll smiled at the memory of her feisty temper. He didn't necessarily align himself with her crusade yet, but he admired her drive to lead people, fighting for their freedom. Wasn't that ultimately what he wanted for himself?

He had no idea what time of day it was. In fact, the room looked identical to the way it had appeared when he went to sleep. Shadows crept along the walls, and the only light he could see was from the lamp beside the bed. It was in the form of a small animal. He hadn't noticed last night—it was a wire-rimmed crow covered in a translucent silver-blue material. Like the fabric on the girl's hat had been … and her eyes. Why hadn't he asked her name? Why hadn't she told him? He shrugged it off. It hadn't come up. He'd given his; she hadn't.

He allowed his mind to run along a bunny trail as he rose and rifled through the drawers next to the sink, looking for anything he could use to make coffee. He marveled at the drawers of gadgets and found what looked like loose-leaf tea, but when he boiled it, the brew strangely smelled and tasted enough like coffee to satisfy his brain. He sat at the table, full of energy and maybe a tiny caffeine high. He tingled but felt a bit grumpy, like when he slept too long on Sundays because his mom was at church and didn't bother him.

"Crap. What am I supposed to do here all day? For all I know, it's two in the afternoon, and that other lady didn't show up because they've all been caught." He knew it wasn't true, but he needed to work himself up for what he knew he really wanted to do, which was go outside and see what wonders this city held. He'd forgotten to ask about the flying ship. *What else was out there?*

"I owe it to myself and the girl from last night to check out the safety of the situation." He flipped the light on in the bathroom and saw men's clothes hanging on three hooks over a padded bench that extended a footstool when he sat on it. He removed his cargo shorts and t-shirt. The brown trousers were thick, but they molded to his legs like baseball pants, and the boots were a half-size tight but doable. He buttoned his collar but had no idea how to tie the silk thing. He knew it belonged around his neck, but that was about it. He shrugged into a patterned vest that matched the silk and reached into the heavy pocket, his fingers brushing a watch on a chain. He connected the dangling chain to a buttonhole on his vest and threaded the leather straps through the buckles across his chest. He was more of a baseball hat kind of guy and knew for certain that he could not pull off the look as Indigo had, but he ran a hand through his hair and pulled on the hat. He donned the long coat. In his mind, it was still summer, and the coat's warmth made him sweat.

No one will know. No one will care. He was dressed in their awesome clothes and would fit right in. He coached himself out of the room and into the black hallway. He felt for the railing and slid his hand along the iron pipe as he strode down the corridor. The light at the foot of the stairs was off. On second thought, for all he knew, he might have slept for three hours, and it was two o'clock in the morning. Alarm bells rang in his head, and he stopped, but Wyll saw a faint line of light several feet in front of him. It came from the bottom of the steel door. He tripped up the first concrete step, banging his shin.

"Damn." He felt around the rivets for a smooth handle and yanked it down.

He emerged into the room of immense machinery. *What was this made for? What did it produce?* He wondered if the king had created things to create things.

Jennifer Haskin

It was about the only way he thought most of this was possible. He couldn't wrap his head around it. He didn't believe in magic. He'd been told faith was believing in something that makes no sense to your brain, but you can't stop yourself from believing anyway. His mom always said his faith was in his *truth*.

Wyll guessed this was his new truth. Not sure how he felt about it, he watched the dust motes flying through rays of sunlight like bumper cars in the atmosphere. He smiled. It was daytime—surely there were amazing things to see. Excitement pulsed through his blood; he crossed the room and flipped open the lock on the glass door. He inched it ajar and peeked out, looking both ways down the street. Though he saw no one, Wyll could hear the voices of many people. *Clockwork people. Hmmm.* It appeared he was in a bunker hardly conspicuous but not too far from the action. He walked a few blocks in the direction they'd come from the night before, toward the neighborhood where he'd arrived.

First, he smelled the nuts, the warm, sweet scent of butter and sugar browning in a copper tub, being tossed about with a pipe-handled wooden paddle. Wyll inhaled. Then he watched as the street ahead—clogged like an artery on Thanksgiving Day, ready to burst—moved with a heavy beat. A steady whirring of gears, clicking spikes, and the whoosh-and-bang of pistons filled his ears. He was knocked into the street and nearly run down by a pair of neighing horses with wheels for legs. No, one wheel on

The Clockwork Pen

each side, the poor horses' legs were joined together in iron castings. When the horses leaned left and right, the wheels moved to pull the carriage that followed.

He could barely see the inhabitants of the vehicle past their frills of fabric or past the heads of women in hats; some tall, some wide, some miniature. The men joined in the style parade with their displays of imaginatively designed facial hair with tiny, curled mustaches and bushy beards. Eye patches seemed a trend—unless the king had taken to giving many of them a bad eye, but that didn't seem logical. *He isn't logical, though, from what the girl said.*

He passed tiny shops of sweets, teas, medicines, shops of automata, and clockwork repair. Taking his time, he took in everything. Glass balls hung from wires in many windows with tiny fish and little green plants inside. He felt like he could almost stand in the narrow street and reach out to touch the stores on either side. The blank spaces were full of children playing with the shop carts lining the alleys between buildings.

He bumped into a man who said something, and Wyll mumbled an apology, knowing the man couldn't understand him. He knew better than to say the word *English*, but the man looked at him with a squint. Wyll slowly nodded at the man, keeping eye contact. He thought he looked cool doing it. The man shook his head and walked on. He caught the eye of several ladies and walked with a swagger, then thought it was probably better to blend in. He watched a man with a pipe, resting on a bench near him. As he came closer, the area opened into the square he'd seen last night.

Toy carts delighted all ages there, with little steam-powered bunnies that hopped in circles, their legs reaching out behind them and their little front paws outstretched. A small girl clapped as the toymaker lifted a fairy in his hand. When he tossed it up in the air, the fairy spun in circles as it fell and landed in the girl's small white glove, like a flower on a lily pad. She looked up to her mother with joy and questions. Wyll half-grinned, but the mother saw him, frowned, and turned away. *Hag.*

He sat on a bench and watched an animated toy cart. A baby doll with a turnkey stayed in a crawling position, but its elbows and knees moved adjacently, making it crawl when it was wound. The man on the bench next to him was eating something that looked like a dough pocket but smelled like a sausage, egg, and cheese biscuit—his favorite fast-food breakfast. His stomach growled loudly, and Wyll covered his middle with his arms. He hadn't eaten since yesterday's cookies, and he was a big guy. The man offered him a pastry, and he gladly accepted.

He hadn't counted on the man talking to him.

"Beautiful day." The guy looked like someone he wouldn't have been friends with at home—he was the library-type.

The Clockwork Pen

Wyll shifted on the bench, smiled at him while chewing, and pointed to his mouth. When he finished his bite, he took another … and another. When he finished, the man sat waiting, his head tilted and his eyebrows somewhere near his hairline.

"Good *Bierocks*, yes? The king's own recipe. My cook makes me more than I can eat for lunch." The man patted a spider-shaped basket with a blood-red cloth inside, curved legs forming the basket, and lifted the spider's body to take out a large cookie. He broke it into two pieces and handed half to Wyll. "You are feeling better, yes?"

Wyll had been trying to hear both what the man said through his borrowed hearing device and the words he used in order to say something. He caught the word for "yes" and repeated it with a nod. He might have said it wrong from the man's eyebrow lift.

The airship flew above them, and its shadow fell over the bench, making Wyll shiver, but his mind wasn't on the cold. Wyll exhaled as he looked up and soaked in the gold-lined port holes, billows of steam spewing from twin engines, their shining silver bodies lining the boat's top deck. He couldn't see any people—they must be inside. He thought he could see shadowy passengers through the glass panels on the bottom.

"Have you ever been on the Zamboni?" the man asked, pointing up.

Wyll stifled his immediate burst of laughter. Mostly. *That's not a Zamboni*. What did they call an actual Zamboni? He shook his head.

"I hear it's the fanciest place in the world. It even has moving pictures. I can only imagine … flying high and seeing forever. I'm saving up."

Wyll nodded and fished his watch from his pocket, the chain pulling his vest, and tapped the clock face a few times. He rose and yawned, stretching his arms, but as he turned to leave, the man stood before him and stuck out his hand. He was as tall as Wyll, with narrow shoulders that held his clothes like a hanger.

"I'm Luc Tailor."

He smiled and took the offered hand, squeezing lightly. "Wyll Brey."

"Ah. You do speak. I was afraid you might be broken." Luc laughed lightly and stepped closer. "I haven't seen you around. Are you, ah, new?"

Wyll tried to pull his hand away, but Luc held tight. "Not unless you let me buy you a drink."

Wyll understood but couldn't afford to say anything. He didn't want to be rude or have the guy think he was a homophobe, but he was supposed to be laying low, not out for drinks.

He gently pried his hand out of Luc's grip, smiling as if bashfully declining, and muttered an apology. An older couple nearby cooed as they looked on, and Wyll got a hot, heavy feeling. Luc wasn't going to let him get away that easily.

"At least tell me where you live so I can talk to you again." Luc looked like he was losing his favorite toy, and Wyll could do nothing but stand there. This wasn't an uncommon occurrence for Wyll, though he never did the right thing, no matter the situation.

He looked at the couple, who motioned for him to go on. He even opened his mouth like he might say something, anything, but he spun and pushed through the masses of people like a line of tackle. He could hear Luc calling behind him. *Geez*. Were they lonely here? How big was this city? He started noticing things like every couple appeared to be in some kind of mixed relationship. Rarely were they the same race or opposite genders. Why would the king make races at all just to mix them up like that? Or did the people all choose that way? Had he made families out of people who had nothing in common? There were old people. *Why would he make people already old?* They'd been alive eighteen years but would die before everyone else. They did die, right?

He wasn't sure if it was crazy or cruel.

As he barreled past one woman, Wyll grabbed her by the arm to keep her from falling into the street, but when he stepped back, he knocked over a display of boxes holding mewling clockwork kittens. They pounced from the overturned crates with large skulls and long bending necks. Their spiky legs reminded him of crab legs, but they were furry. Wyll cringed at the monstrosities, picking their way between ankles and under feet. He bent down and grabbed one in each hand, holding them out to the shop cart keeper, but the man was shouting and calling, trying to round up the merchandise. Wyll kicked a crate upright and dropped the kittens in it. He followed two more of them down the sidewalk.

    He swept them up and was walking back to the cart when he saw the keeper pointing at him and talking to what Wyll could only describe as a cousin of the Terminator. Maybe it was a steampunk Iron Man because it had a glowing disc in the middle of its gilded chest. He didn't know if there was a man inside that suit or if that was all there was, but he didn't want to find out. He dropped the kittens and pivoted, diving into a sea of citizens.

    Wyll glanced back. Two lines of rivets followed the metal man's thigh, his metal-booted feet clomping hard on the cement, his face a smooth metal mask with glowing blue goggles. His chest—girded with strips of brown leather alternating with strips of copper—was a mass of wires and clockwork gears behind glass. Brass fists clenched, the pistons at the soldier's elbow worked as he pumped his arms, and tubes flopped when he impacted with the cement, propelling him forward with increasing speed.

    Wyll was fast, and he might have gotten away. He might have remembered where the correct building was and even let himself back in, but an eight-foot-tall brute of a man with a barrel chest, suspenders, and a strong-man mustache grabbed him by the collar and spun him around to face the metal man.

"Here you go," his captor said, offering Wyll to the metal man.

"Thank you, citizen." A man's voice emitted from the horizontal line representing a mouth on his mask. Wyll was more than curious if a man was inside the alloy-jointed limbs. *A clockwork man*, he corrected himself.

He yanked out of the large man's grip and growled at him, but the man laughed at him and walked off; *laughed* at him. Wyll could literally feel steam rise from his head; he'd never been so pissed.

The metal guard held his arm out and grabbed Wyll's shoulder, saying, "For disrupting the street traffic and losing the shop's inventory, you will be fined. What do you plead?"

Was he holding court in the street? Wyll couldn't plead anything, or else they would know his secret. He kept his mouth shut.

The guard shook him. "What do you plead?"

Wyll made the motion of zipping his lips and tossing the key, which made the guard groan.

"I will take you in if you don't cooperate. Speak, or you will be uniquely tortured until you do so."

"Tortured?" *What the hell?* Oh, that changed the situation entirely. He would say whatever the metal thing wanted him to say. No one was going to inflict pain and anguish upon him. He wasn't *totally* stupid. "Look, I accidentally spilled those boxes, but I was helping him gather the kittens. You don't need to take me in." He laughed. "I'm just clumsy. No harm, no foul, right?"

He watched the metal guard as they stood in silence. The guard's gears whirred, and Wyll watched a dial spin on his shoulder next to a skull-shaped shoulder pad that made him look like a TV wrestler.

Wyll was inching backward, preparing to bolt, when the guard vibrated, emitting a series of alarm-like beeps, and said, "English is prohibited. Where did you learn this language?"

"My mother?" He squinted one eye and shrugged his shoulders.

"Incorrect." The guard switched his grip from Wyll's collar to his wrists. He slapped on a set of leather strips buckled in a row of grommets, then took a dull brass clip and hooked the two cuffs together with matching D-rings.

Wyll flexed his arms and tested the pull on his bonds. He was sweating. The crispy bite of the breeze chilled him now while the sun faintly warmed his face. He was lost for ideas on what to do. There wasn't much he *could* do. He couldn't have stayed inside that room and just waited for someone when there was an unexplored world before him. He didn't regret going out, but he vastly regretted getting caught.

The Clockwork Pen

In his peripheral vision, he noticed a tall woman watching them and wringing her gloved hands. She carried a basket on her elbow and a messenger bag on her shoulder. She looked invested in his situation, and he wondered if that was Malynda, the woman who was supposed to check on him. He smiled at her, hoping she was a friend, not a foe.

She wrinkled her brow in frustration but gave him a small smile. She was beautiful. Olive-skinned and dressed in high fashion—she sported a wine-colored hat with pink roses piled on the right side of the wide brim, an elegant scrolling design shaved into her closely cropped black beard. It gave her a startling effect. He could imagine her with Indigo—a power couple.

As the guard hauled Wyll toward the square, Malynda grimaced and spun on her heel, marching the other way. He hoped she was going to get help, but he had a feeling the Resistance wouldn't be troubling with him if he wasn't going to follow directions. How could they expect him *not* to be curious? Still, he knew he screwed up.

"Where are you taking me?" he asked while struggling to keep the pace the guard set.

"The Reformatory."

Doesn't sound so bad. At least it wasn't prison, probably a reform school of sorts, girls in short plaid skirts and knee highs. The castle came into view when they exited the square on the far side. It was palatial—

obviously—shining a dazzling white in the morning sun. Turrets sported round-topped glass windows lined up pane to pane. Buttresses held up tall white towers with pointed roofs and decorative designs, peaking in spikes all around the top. It was built entirely of white stone and brick, with silver-plated roofing tiles.

The construction didn't sit inside a moat but over one. Tall, wide stone pillars rose from the still, inky water to an enormous platform that suspended the castle over flocks of ducks floating in lazy circles. Well, they were kind of like ducks—repulsive ducks. Wyll shivered.

The guard walked him up the left side of a twin set of marble stairways curving away from each other and back again, to meet at a landing over the water, and turned into one wide set of stairs leading to the first platform. The wrought iron railings, painted white to match the marble, held decorative spikes every five feet or so above the forest animal designs that lined the steps.

"Come on." The guard yanked Wyll's cuffs, pulling him up the stairs.

Wyll saw fish in the moat as he looked over the railing, well, some big fins in dark water. He shivered. "Do you always have to walk up all these stairs?" he asked as they climbed.

"Stop complaining. You will have plenty of time for that." The guard gave a short burst of laughter, obviously thinking himself funny. Wyll was surprised the

The Clockwork Pen

guard knew what he was saying, but he guessed they must be programmed to know the language to recognize it.

"Great. How long are you going to keep me here?" He panted. *Do all clockwork people have this kind of stamina?*

The guard stopped and looked down at him. "Unsure. This is unprecedented."

"Did I just make you famous? Wow. You must be so proud."

They stood staring at each other. Wyll imagined he could hear the gears in the guard's mind turning. Then he grabbed the back of Wyll's collar and propelled him up the last few stairs.

The tiered castle's entrance was impressive; a red carpet led to two doors towering twenty feet tall. They were gold-leaved, and the working gears were enclosed between the glass layers. Golden fairies, dragonflies, crows, and a large buzzard on each door flew in synchronized patterns on the door panels. They didn't go that way. The lower level was nothing to sniff at, either. At a similar set of smaller doors, the guard punched numbers in a pad, then turned a buzzard that flew into a tree, moving a swing back to hit a bunny, who ran into a bush, sending a flock of birds into flight. A series of clicks followed as the door opened itself inward. Wyll realized there was no handle. He would have never figured out how to get in—or how to get out, for that matter. As they walked into the darkness, he realized he was genuinely trapped. What if the Resistance didn't come? What if they came and failed? What if he *couldn't* go home?

Chapter Four
NOBODY'S HERO

"This way." The wanna-be tin soldier dragging Wyll growled a very animal-like sound of frustration as he pulled Wyll toward a plain wooden door, the same way he had to jerk TeaCup's leash when she saw another dog. He thought they were walking into a closet; the space was so dark. But the guard stepped down and then again, leading Wyll behind him into the abyss. Wyll was only momentarily disappointed at not getting to enter the main doors and view the opulent interior, wondering how extravagantly the king would have created his own home; the thought evaporated as soon as he was submerged in inky shadow.

At the bottom of five thousand stairs, spiraling into the pitch-black—gripping a steel arm covered in hissing tubes like snakes—Wyll found himself in hell. It was a dark, cavernous space divided into arched cells and thick iron bars. He could barely make out the shapes. The air was cold and damp, and he realized—with mounting dread—that they were *under* the moat. He swallowed. His mouth was so dry the lump in his throat felt lodged. He breathed through his nose, which was a mistake. The prevalent odor was urine. *It could be worse,* his mother's mantra invaded his thoughts. Wyll snorted. *Yeah right.*

While he stumbled on the uneven ground, trying to keep up with his captor, he tried to peer into the arched cells as he passed, but beyond the bars, it was black and cold as space. When they passed the occasional dimly lit hanging bulb, he squinted again to see the outlines of shadowy spines, curved in dejection, but nothing clear. Suddenly, a man jumped up and grabbed the bars, scaring the hell out of Wyll and making him fall backward.

"Run!" the prisoner shouted. "Run now! Before they lock you up! Hurry! It's your last chance!"

Wyll saw the wisdom in that advice and took advantage of the fall, ripping himself away from the soldier and leaving him with a handful of frilly white collar. Wyll broke into a flat-out sprint. Soon, he was only twenty feet from the stairs.

"Geffen!" the soldier yelled.

Wyll didn't listen, didn't look back, or see anyone ahead, and there was no chance of him slowing down. *Twenty feet from the stairs.* He could see the red light at the bottom getting brighter. He was sweating, breathing with force, and he pushed his muscles harder than he ever had before. Wyll was ten feet away from the open doorway to the stairs of freedom. He was flying pell-mell toward the light. He reached his hands out toward the doorway reflexively. He was almost there.

The Clockwork Pen

Suddenly, an arm shot out in front of him. A thick, rock-hard pipe of an arm appeared, swinging forward just before impacting with his clavicle and proceeding to crush his throat. His feet flew forward, and Wyll hung by his neck for just a moment before he dropped hard, straight to his back on the stone floor, knocking the wind from his lungs. He rocked back and forth, coughing, choking, and gasping for air. Rough pebbles ground into his shoulder and hip.

He was still coughing when the first guy hauled him up by his arm. The new soldier smiled at him, and Wyll tried to clear his throat.

"You're a dick." His voice was raspy but clear.

The soldier narrowed his eyes but obviously didn't know enough English to figure it out. Wyll chuckled. He could immediately imagine the things he would say to this guy. The amusement only lasted for a few seconds. In the darkness, his mother's face flashed in front of him. He could see her so clearly. She was usually smiling, but he watched her face turn to worry, then she scrunched her brows and frowned at him. *Why aren't you home yet?* she seemed to ask.

He hadn't meant for this to happen. Things were starting to feel too real, and he released a great measure of his cocky attitude. He didn't know what they had planned for him, but he was fairly certain he was done with this place. Not even that girl was worth this garbage. The Resistance would send someone to help him, right?

Did he have any value to them at all? This wasn't really his fault. All he'd done was knock over some kittens. Real cops wouldn't even give you a ticket for that, and he was down here in the cold emptiness of … whatever this place was called.

The floor slanted down as they continued forward, always veering toward the left. Wyll imagined he was inside a giant snail shell winding toward the middle. Would there eventually be a space the perfect size for him to sit? He felt hot as the corridor seemed to close around him. When they had gone deep into the bowels of blackness, they stopped, and the soldier pushed Wyll to a cramped opening in the bars. He gripped the bars on either side of the doorway and hunched to make it through. But he couldn't see anything in front of him, and his forehead bounced off the metal bar at the top with a ringing clunk.

"Ow."

The guard barked a laugh and pushed him through the opening. Colors bloomed in his vision like fireworks in July. The gears in the lock ground as it turned. No back wall was visible, though he hoped to God there was one. As much as he didn't like small spaces, the thought of an open black tunnel going to who-knows-where really creeped him out.

With nothing better to do, he explored the cold, hard surface of the wall next to him. It was uneven rock, like the floors and ceiling. He wondered if the entire place was carved out of a huge layer of stone. *Of course not,* he

The Clockwork Pen

chided himself. *No one carved this. It was created to be here. Hello, stupid.* Why didn't he just stay in that crappy little room? It was a whole lot better than where he was now. Not even the Resistance could help him down here. It would be too much trouble to find him. And why would they? Indigo was obviously the head guy, but Wyll didn't know if the man would risk the safety of others just to liberate a punk kid.

He hoped so.

Seconds later, he bashed his shin against a metal bed frame and fell forward onto the thin mattress, hitting his head on the cell's back wall. Flopping over onto the mattress, he sat with his knees out and leaned back against the rock. He laced his hands over his stomach and concentrated on his breath for a few minutes. He'd left his cell phone in his cargo shorts when he realized he didn't have service in this dimension but longed for it. At least he could have played solitaire until the battery died.

He listened to other prisoners calling and talking to each other, some crying and some moaning or singing. Sometimes, it was hard to tell the difference. He might have dozed a bit. Who knew? Who cared? Bored brainless, Wyll started trying to imagine his favorite movies. Something about being in complete darkness made pictures appear in front of him easily. He entertained himself until he fell asleep directing the next Fast and Furious.

The next day—he assumed it was the next day from the guard change, but he could have been wrong—the screaming began. He was just thinking that the sentence was not so scary as terribly boring, and the constant darkness only irritated him when he heard the first man start shrieking. He was terrified. The man gurgled like he was in a state far beyond fear—like Derec did in haunted houses. But Wyll could relate. Even he'd had a few of those times, like when you enter a room thinking about something else, and someone jumps out at you, and you're so scared, you can't scream, you can't move, you stand there and kind of jog in place for a second with your mouth open, making a guttural noise in your throat. That was the noise. Wyll panicked and echoed an exhalation of intense fear.

And on and on it went. Each man sounded as tortured as the one before him. After a while, a smaller figure came by and gave him a small loaf of bread, an apple, and a cup of water. He thought it might have been a woman in a robe by her size, but he couldn't tell, and she wouldn't answer him. Probably some poor kitchen girl, too scared to speak to the prisoners.

"Thanks," he told her as she was leaving, and she stopped, but only for a second.

The pain was coming. The wailing was getting closer. He paced the cell, finding a toilet—or what passed for one. Which was good timing as his stomach turned

The Clockwork Pen

upside down. He wiped his mouth and laid back on his bed.

"You there!" a voice boomed, and sudden light blinded him.

"What?" He didn't even lift his head. *Why should he make it easy for them?*

"Get up. Now."

Wyll reluctantly pulled himself to his feet and could see behind the light the outlines of a machine that moved around. It seemed to breathe audibly as if alive, but it looked like a microwave on top of a washing machine covered in tubes and gears. Of course, there was more to it: square-shaped blinking eyes and a row of teeth in a slot that looked like you'd feed it floppy disks and tons of working pieces with steam vents hissing. But it didn't have the shape of anything you'd want to be alive. The worst part was its legs. They looked like sickly human legs on either side of the machine, maybe lumpy stork legs with bare feet. It stood with its legs shaking, kind of bending its knees in what looked like anticipation. Maybe it couldn't hold its own weight?

"What is it?" He pointed to the monstrosity.

The soldier laughed. "Oh, Teri? One of the king's best creations." He patted the machine like it was a good dog, and it rubbed up against him. "This baby can read your deepest fears and create them for you; put you right in the middle of it. Your brain can't tell the difference from reality. To you, it will be the worst experience of your life."

"Why would you do that?" Wyll said as a tingle of fear pricked the back of his neck, and his shoulders seized with terror. *Your worst fears?* That's why all those men sounded so haunted. It was tailor-made insanity.

The man smiled at him and shrugged. "It's fun."

"I'll tell you whatever you want to know. You don't even have to use that … whatever. You know? Just ask me." For now, he abandoned all shame. The acoustics of the rock ensured he heard the other inmates as if they'd been next to him. At this point, it was one for Wyll and all for Wyll. That's why he couldn't be trusted in the Resistance. He was suddenly glad he didn't know that girl's name so he couldn't get her in trouble.

"Oh, I know you'll tell me everything. But I ain't asking till later. Don't worry. We do this a lot. You're nothin' special. Now, jest relax. It takes him a minute to warm up."

Wyll waited, his body trembling. Suddenly, the black cave lit up like there was an industrial spotlight on—or it seemed that bright to him. He squinted in the brilliant light, his eyes unfocused. Then he could hear the clatter of trays on Formica tables, the hum of so many conversations at once. He knew the smell instantly and blinked his eyes to see his high school lunchroom. Then, every head seemed to turn in his direction, and they were all laughing and pointing at him. His face burned at their mocking, and when he crossed his arms, he realized he was completely naked with nowhere to hide. He was embarrassed and tried to run, holding his junk, but his running feet kept slipping around in that spot, and everyone watching him roared with laughter.

In the back of his mind, though, he thought, *I didn't think that would be my biggest fear. I thought it might be spiders or the...*

Instantly, the room became a jungle, and he was finally moving. His feet sped down the dirt path until the earth gave way, and he fell into a pit, dropping into a pile of leaves ... with legs? No, mounds and mounds of crawling spiders. He wiggled his bare feet, feeling the mass shift, and dropped to the bottom of the pit, spiders to his knees. He lifted his feet, swiping them off, quickly flinging them from his fingers. Then he sank to the real bottom, with spiders up to his chest. He danced in place, trying to get away from them, feeling their legs pull his body hair as he shook violently, sinking further. He could feel his weight squishing their soft bodies under him with every step. He was pouring sweat now and sweeping them off his raised arms. He screamed as one did its best to crawl up his nose. They were crawling inside his ears. As much as he wanted them out, he couldn't force himself to touch them to pull them out or shove them farther in.

"Get off, get off..." he cried out, choking on his tears, then closing his mouth as they covered his face and pushed past his lips to fill his mouth. Wyll could feel their little legs gripping his eyelashes. But through the horror, that thought in the back of his mind wanted to finish itself with another fear he had. A worse fear. He didn't want to experience it, so he tried to keep from thinking it, but that never worked. He would do *almost* anything to get out of that pit…

Suddenly suspended in black coldness, Wyll rocked with the force of a powerful current, knowing without a doubt that he was in the deepest parts of the frigid ocean. A filmy light blue glowed so far above him that he knew he floated below a fathomless depth but nowhere near the chasmic bottom. He could breathe if he put effort into it, but that thought didn't calm him. Not at all. In fact, he began to hyperventilate. He could hear the call of sea life in choirs of squeaks, clicks, and ghostly whale songs, the woosh of saltwater rushing past his eardrums.

Creatures could surround him—but he saw nothing. The not knowing … the blackness all around… He pulled his legs up near his body, pushing water around him with his hands, trying to stay upright. He didn't know if he wanted to put his feet down to kick up—or not. He felt something swim beside him and lightly touch his ankle, bumping his hip. He screamed, but no sound came out. He kicked out, but the water slowed his movements. He was shaking violently, surrounded by an ocean of dark space farther than he knew he could imagine in all directions, filled with living things, spikes, fins, tentacles, teeth.

Screw this, screw this.

He heard the screams of whales lumbering above, blocking out the small measure of light, and then he saw something enormous with a bioluminescent fin coming his way. It moved side to side like a snake approaching its prey. He tried to back up, but there was nothing to push against. Slowed down by the water, he couldn't swim fast enough. This thing had to be the size of his mom's minivan and moving just as fast. He knew most things this far down had wicked teeth. Even if it only nicked him, the scent of his blood would travel miles to the olfactory sense of every shark in the vicinity. He'd be eaten before he had enough light to see what tore him apart.

Fear clawed up his throat, along with bile. His body was stiff and shaking so badly that he felt like he was having a seizure. He curled into the fetal position, gritting his teeth, and seized with terror. *Get me out of here*, his mind screamed, and then he started forming a thought...

Immediately, Wyll stood in his living room. Shimmers of heat vapor danced in his vision before a backdrop of spreading orange light. The crackling flames were already licking the ceiling like a thirsty kitten, the drapes an undulating inferno, as well as the couch. The roar was loud, and the air was dry and hot. It seared his lungs, and they seemed to shrivel, the room a vacuum, sucking from his mouth and his blistered sinuses. He'd been there for seconds, and he could feel his flesh crisping, his eyes instantly dry. The hair on his body melted into little black, smoking beads like pinheads. Still naked, he dropped to his knees, trying to find his way out, and could barely see through the smoke. There was a little more air on the floor, but the drapes had fallen, and there was too much fire by the door to get out.

There. The back window. He might make it if he held his breath, jumped up, and ran, crashing through the glass. He saw his mom fainted on the kitchen floor to his right, but he heard his father—stuck—calling for help from the office to Wyll's left. He could feel the meat under his skin cooking. Little white bubbles raised up all over his arms. A few swelled up quickly and popped, giving a little sizzle as the hot air met the water inside. He had to close his eyes while he thought.

I'll never make it out if I don't move soon. I might be able to help one of them, but only one—and that's pushing it. He caught his reflection in the cracked sliding glass door his father bolted shut, and his bald skin was cracking into fissures branching like tributaries. Crawling, he turned to see the stairs and the flaming railing. A piece of the ceiling fell behind him, charred and smoking. He stayed there gathering his courage, trying to decide. He wanted to help. More than anything. Who lived? Who did he love more? He couldn't make that kind of decision. He could see the bright and boiling afternoon sun out the living room windows. He *might* be able to make it if he let them both die, but could he live with himself if he did? Flames erupted along his arms, the skin burning like tissue paper, and he screamed in pain.

As he screamed over and over, something in the back of his mind whispered, *this isn't real*, but he couldn't hear it. The flames were caressing him as he fell and lay curled in impotence.

And then it stopped. Still in a ball, he was back in his cell and lay crouched on the ground, his stomach still seizing. He was afraid of what was coming. Wyll bathed in white light from the machine. He could see the inside of his cell—and all the bugs that ran away—as someone also shined a hand-held light on the wall. He didn't know who to thank but was grateful it had stopped. Not sure if he could have handled it much longer, his next fear was unthinkable.

Even now, his mind was thinking of new tortures he feared. Phobias that made him want to vomit, like having his fingernails and toenails pulled out with pliers, and those fish in the Amazon that swim up streams of urine until they're in your body. He had immediate sympathy for those prisoners who'd been there the longest. He put a hand up to shield his eyes.

"Who's there?" he asked.

"Well, I know who I am," the voice drawled with an almost southern accent. Wyll imagined the Cheshire cat. "The question is, who are you?"

He'd had enough torture, and he spoke toward the blinding light. "I'm Wyll. Brey. Listen, I don't know shit. I found the door by accident. I'll say whatever you want—I just want to go home."

"No doubt. Surely just a mix-up. I rule here. King Rozam. Did you give her the key?"

"Who?" He could barely see the man through his bars. "What key?" Wyll's mind had blanked.

"*Did you give her the key to leave?!*" he roared.

"No, I didn't bring it. My friend shoved me through the door and locked it."

"Do you expect me to believe you are that stupid?" The king stepped forward, and his silhouette appeared to shake as if he was losing patience—his shadowed visage hidden behind the bars.

Wyll just stared back and shrugged in apology. *What do you want me to say?*

"Maybe you are… And I'm sure my daughter convinced you to take her with you, is that it? She's planning to use you for her little Resistance? She's not one of them, but she's in a rebellious phase, just an innocent, daydreaming child."

"Your daughter? I don't know any princesses—or children. I've never even been to the castle before. I only met two people since I got here." He vaguely wondered if that girl was a princess, but he didn't see it. She was bossy enough. Logically, it could be true, but the girl he'd met

The Clockwork Pen

was definitely not a child—built well in all the right places.

"Hmmm. If you haven't, you will soon. Sira wants to explore that vicious world of yours. She's got all sorts of people thinking they want to make their own decisions. She has a bleeding heart and knows of a Resistance, and I want to know where they are. I have an idea, and you are going to work for me. Right?"

He didn't like where this was heading, but there was exactly one word right now keeping him away from that freaking torture machine restarting. He nodded.

"Good. You will let her break you out of here, and I will give them a reason to get together."

"How? You going to follow me or something? How will I get home?"

"I won't need to follow you." Keys jangled, the lock's gears scraped, and Wyll's cell door opened.

A soldier—they all looked identical to him with their helmets on—escorted the king to Wyll. The sovereign wasn't what he'd thought the king would be. His tall hat had a gleaming bat in gold that reflected the light, and his frizzy red hair tumbled to his shoulders. His ginger mustache and soul patch were long and bushy, and his sideburns had a scrolling design. He wasn't wearing military garb like foreign leaders on TV. Rozam sported a matching vest and coat with a high-pressed collar and red silk tie. He removed his monocle and looked at Wyll.

"Give me your hand." The king held his palm up.

Wyll laid his hand in the king's and chewed his lip. The king pulled a pen out of his breast pocket.

"Is that it?" Wyll asked.

"Yes ... this is the pen." The king looked at him and smiled. "You've heard of it." Then, he drew an angular shape on Wyll's wrist, but as they watched, the ink disappeared.

"What happened?" Wyll looked at his wrist up close and heard a faint ticking sound.

"I put a chip under your skin that will tell me your location. Just stay with her."

"Wha—What if they suspect?" Wyll wasn't good at keeping secrets. Ever. He poked the edges of the tiny rectangle with his fingertip. It didn't hurt. It was the foreign living body in his arm that bothered him.

"Make sure they don't. I made this entire world for *her*. I must squash this rebellion so Sira can lead a happy life here, forever. She encourages them but will get sucked in if she's not careful. She's just testing her limits. One day, *she* will wield the pen and be the queen."

"When I do this, you'll send me back? Nobody gets hurt, right? Your princess can stay in her castle, and I can go home?" *Who wouldn't want to live in this cool world if you lived in the castle and had whatever you wanted? She'd appreciate it eventually.*

The king smiled and clapped his hands. "Absolutely."

The Clockwork Pen

"Okay, I guess I'll help you. Does that mean I can be done now?" Wyll pointed a shaky finger at the terror machine that shifted a step closer to its master. He shivered involuntarily.

The king laughed. "Oh, I guess. You're lucky I came down here when I did. I shall have to pay better attention to the time." He turned and began walking out but continued speaking. "Enjoy my city, Wyll Brey. Do *not* enjoy my daughter. Are we clear?"

Wyll nodded, and the king turned back with an eyebrow raised.

"Oh. Yes. Okay, I got it. Leave your daughter alone. Then you'll send me home?" Wyll's hands curled into fists. He inhaled deeply to stop himself from saying more and risking the king renegotiating on the terror thing. Thank God they were taking the machine away. It faced him until the soldier turned it around and pushed it down the tunnel.

"Actually, I have a gift for you... Soldier?" The king cackled and nodded to the nearest soldier, who approached Wyll and pulled his arms behind his back. Wyll felt an automatic urge to struggle and wiggled his shoulders. The soldier tightened his grip as the king stepped a foot in front of him. The king grasped Wyll's chin and raised it. With his other hand, he pulled out the magic pen. Wyll tried to struggle, but he was held tight. The pen burned the skin of his neck like acid. He screamed, and the pain traveled through his skin to his throat. It felt like he could breathe fire. He blew it out in great gusts, but no flame emerged, just air. He struggled for breath.

"What have you done to me?" Wyll shouted as the king turned away, but he got no answer.

The crazy king took the light with him. It faded down the hall, and Wyll flopped onto the bed, once again plunged into eternal night. Tears leaped to his eyes. He was thankful for the darkness and wiped them away. At least he could see the cell in his mind now, and he replayed the conversation over and over. Would this princess come for him herself or send the adults like Indigo and his followers?

He absently rubbed his neck and allowed himself to wonder if *the girl* would be there. He wondered if she was the princess. She didn't dress—or seem—very princessy, but what did he know? They would have told him. She let him know so many other secrets. Besides, isn't that one of the first things a girl would want to tell you? *Hi, I'm a rich princess, la di da.* He could imagine the child princess in flouncy frills, like those he saw in the street, and a floppy hat. Maybe that was her in the carriage—no wonder he'd been caught.

But his mind followed his desires, and a memory of the girl's petite features heated his belly. Had he imagined it, or was there chemistry there? Her face turned in his mind, the light bouncing off her high cheekbones, her smile lighting her eyes. She was pretty, but more than that … she was determined, brave, and passionate about her beliefs. She was acting to make change where it was needed. He admired those qualities. It's probably why he was so sad.

What he was doing would deceive the Resistance. He didn't want to betray her. When he sold out the princess, would the girl be forced down here in his place? Remorse tightened around his chest like a steel band. He wouldn't be able to leave her here. What he wanted was to leave *with* her. What was he doing? The threat of tears again squeezed his throat, and he clutched his sore neck, the skin still tender to the touch. He could feel a raised design but had no idea what it looked like or meant.

He knew that if the Resistance came, he would go with them to get out of there, and he had no choice but to betray them. No one had ever asked him to be a hero before—he had no practice. It never made sense to put someone else's life before his own. Especially people he didn't know. What if he helped them, but no one helped him? Could he risk it? Was it worth it to be exposed before people he knew? What if they learned about the true Wyll—middle school's token punching bag? *I can't do that again. It's too dangerous.*

No, it's not, he heard Derec in his mind.

Shut up, he answered.

You play with girls' feelings, and you know it. It doesn't matter the reason. And all your friends are jerks.

He imagined Derec's arms crossed over the chest of his ironed button-down shirt tucked into belted khakis.

He's right. A guy like Wyll hid too much to land a girl like that—better to stay unattached and protected. He tried to think of other things, but he would catch himself thinking about her loose curls of deep red hanging over her shoulder or the way her forehead wrinkled when she stared at him. He tried to think of sports cars and Guitar Hero—watching the little colored dots sliding away from him in the dark. But then he saw the shadow of her jaw. The light reflected in her icy blue eyes.

He wished he could take her home. His mom would love her—probably want to take her shopping and do female stuff with her. He didn't know; he never brought girls home. Then he thought of his mother. She was going to be worried after a while when he didn't call. His mom thought he was worthy of anything—that's what she always used to say, anyway. Maybe they'd actually be glad he was gone? The thought had too much possibility for him to consider.

He wondered how often that machine came around. Would he always have that much notice, or would he be the first next time? He fell asleep, wondering what other hideous clockwork life this king had made.

A slew of pebbles hit his body, but he couldn't make sense of what was happening.

"Pssst. Hey. Hey, wake up."

The Clockwork Pen

Wyll heard a voice and the scrape of the lock turning. He sat up. "Who's there?"

"It's your fairy godmother, stupid. You didn't think we'd discuss our plan with you and then leave you here, did you? Even though we should, because technically, we already had you safe, and you are the idiot who got yourself caught, right?" The tip of a red cane came to life, and he saw her smile.

"Is that a rhetorical question?" He grinned at her as he squeezed through the cell door. When he stood in the tunnel, he noticed Indigo behind her. "Hey. Thanks, guys."

"Of course," Indigo said.

"Wait. You understand him?" She turned to Indigo.

"Yeah, I did. What did they do to you?" Indigo tried to look Wyll in the eye, but he kept his head down.

"I don't want to— We should hurry." Wyll grabbed them both by the shoulder and pushed them forward.

Each time they walked under a light, Wyll tried not to check out the girl's leather pants and the way they swung with her steps. It was pretty much all he *could* see. They walked in silence, sliding along the tunnel's far wall across from the cells, darting along the periphery of the barely glowing bulbs. A few times, Wyll bumped into the girl or stepped on her foot, and he felt terrible, which he tried to remember when he felt a push from behind or had his Achille's heel assaulted by Indigo.

"Nearly there," Wyll whispered as they passed under the red light at the bottom of the stairs. Where were the soldiers? The Resistance surely knew the guards' schedules. *And*, he thought, weighed down with guilt, *the king wanted us to escape.* He began his ascent, pushing harder with every step. "I'm so glad to get out of here."

"Save your breath," Indigo said softly behind him.

The girl chuckled, and Wyll smiled into the dark. His thighs were heating up. Each step was another ounce of energy spent as they climbed. He had remembered the room at the top of the stairs being much brighter, but when they emerged from the heavy iron patterned doors, he realized it was nighttime. *Of course.* Had it only been one day?

As soon as they hit the bitter night air, they ran. Wyll imagined he heard the clomping of boots right behind him. Or was that blood thumping through his ears? Erring on the side of caution, he pushed them forward and ran full tilt.

Chapter Five
HIDE AND SEEK

Sira was going out again. Keylin pulled back from the doorframe, hiding behind the ornate wooden door between Sira's sitting room and bedroom. She'd come to ask Sira about a song she couldn't put a name to but ducked back when she realized Sira was inside her massive closet dressed all in black and swinging on a short, hooded cloak. It was cold outside—and nighttime. *Where is she going?* Keylin squinted her face up in determination. This time, she was going to follow her.

They'd always had each other and were still close, but Sira was keeping secrets, and Keylin didn't like it. She wasn't sure if she felt more hurt at being on the outside or jealous that her best friend had somewhere to go. She vacillated between going to fetch her coat and worrying that she would miss Sira if she did. When a head of dark red curls darted stealthily out of the room, her course was decided. Keylin waited behind the door while Sira left her suite, then ran behind her to the hall. She held back, then followed her to the stairs and waited until Sira had gone down a few flights in the atrium's open staircase. To be expeditious, she decided to slide along the inside railing and careened down one flight, hearing a rip in her skirt and nearly falling on her face. She covered her mouth as a shriek escaped. Abandoning the idea, she skipped down the steps as quickly as possible.

When she reached the first floor, Keylin stopped. She assumed that Sira had gone the back way through the kitchen as usual, but everyone knew that no matter how one left the castle, they must eventually use the main staircase outside to leave the castle grounds. She turned and crossed the great hall to the empty entryway and the main castle doors. She hefted one side open and peeked an eye out. Sira hadn't had enough time to reach the stairs yet. She was probably talking to one of the guards. They all liked Sira; some flirted, but she didn't encourage them. Still, they let her do whatever she wanted.

Their castle wasn't typical of the old kingdoms from the "other world" and didn't have the same kind of soldiers as the castles in the history book Sira let her read. She'd taken it from her father. It said those regal palaces were fortified and had guards on ramparts, drawbridges, and porticos. They didn't let people in or out. But here, people seemed to come and go from the castle at all hours, though traffic trickled at night. The king liked things formal at the castle, but Keylin had always considered it home.

Keylin knew the story well. Even though her mother took care of little Sira, she had petitioned the king

The Clockwork Pen

for a child. At that time, the king hadn't made his wife yet, and he spent the evenings with Sira, so Keylin's mother wanted a child of her own. The king thought it was a clever idea for Sira to have a playmate, so he made Keylin a year younger than Sira. Clockwork people could be created at any age, but apparently, once the magic gave them life, they aged like all living things.

Though the king clarified that *Sira* was the crown heir, she never made Keylin feel like anything other than a sister. Keylin's mother had rooms adjoined to Sira's sitting room, and Keylin shared her mother's quarters. They had a quaint sitting room, a bedroom her mother used, a feminine little bathroom, and a small office where Keylin slept. Sira's office operated as their school room. When classes were over for the day, Sira worked on the management duties her father assigned her, and Keylin began her tiring job serving in the castle. She held a strange position as *honored staff*. It was easy to forget and pretend she belonged there when she was young, but now that they'd mostly aged out of their classes, she was constantly reminded since she was "staff" all day.

She saw Sira's shadowed form emerge from the left, hugging the railing over the moat that curved under the main staircase. *Does she think she's fooling anybody?* She was lucky no one doubted her or cared where she went. Of course, Sepherra wasn't a very big place. As an island, there was only so far she could go. She wouldn't be lost or harmed. No one would cross the king that way.

Especially not lately. Keylin shivered. Sira said the power was too much for him, and when he'd come unglued the other day, shouting about people challenging him, they'd all given him some space.

When Sira got to the plaza at the bottom of the staircase, Keylin squeezed through the doors and tiptoed down the stairs, ducking under the railing whenever Sira looked behind her. She was heading North, toward the neighborhoods. *What is she doing?* Keylin hated being left out. It soured her mouth, thinking Sira didn't tell her everything as Keylin did. Maybe she was just taking a walk? *Dressed in black leather?* Keylin shook her head. Was she hiding something that was illegal—or just fun? The secrecy was tearing holes in her organs. She struggled to breathe. Her heeled shoes weren't made for speed walking, and her pink and white skirt suit, with a ruffle at the bottom, was not meant for outdoor warmth.

The neighborhoods were dark and shadowy, and she'd let Sira have too far a lead. Keylin blew on her hands and peered down a street with four porch lights on, but no one was in sight. She jogged gingerly to the next street. There was movement to her right, but it was just an animal, eating trash. She huffed out her frustration in a cloud of mist. She'd come all this way, freezing, with sore feet, just to lose her. Maybe if she waited, Sira would come back. *Maybe not.* Was it a house party? Were they playing games? Drinking? She so badly wanted to go to a party. By the time Sira returned, all the fun would be over anyway. She gave up and trudged back to the castle with a disappointed sigh.

Might as well go to bed. What a waste of her time off. She'd get to the bottom of this, though.

Where are they going? Alva—Sira's governess and Keylin's mother—held the basket of sheets against her hip as she watched her daughter spying on Sira from down the hall and following her. From her cloak, she assumed Sira was going for a walk. She did that more and more lately. Alva sighed. She had never stopped her charge from escaping, knowing that the pressure of being a princess and dealing with the king could be incredibly stressful for her at times. She knew Sira liked to walk alone, but she never worried for her safety. However, the king had been randomly judging people, assigning ulterior motives to their actions, and becoming irrational in his outrage. Lately, Alva kept Keylin shielded from his line of sight whenever possible.

So why was Keylin following Sira? Did she know something Alva did not? Did she suspect something nefarious? Or was it a game they were playing? With those two, she could never tell. Something niggled in her brain, though.

"Be careful what you tell Keylin about the other world," Alva told Sira several years ago. *"She should be happy here. Not wishing she was somewhere else."*

"Like me? Is that a terrible thing?" Sira looked up at her innocently.

"No, no. I know why you want to go there. But I don't want you to get your hopes up, either. Every place has its unique problems. There is always a bit of bad mixed with the good. Be wary."

"What's that?" she asked.

"It's like being cautious. Think of both sides of an argument. Think of more than one possible outcome in different situations. Trust people but expect they're on their best behavior—don't expect them to disappoint you, but don't be surprised if they do." Alva stroked the girl's hair. *"You are a smart girl and a good friend, and Keylin loves you. One day, you may leave here, but she will not. She will miss you terribly, but her place is here—with me."*

"I would never hurt her. She's the only sister I have. I'll protect her."

Alva wondered if Sira was mixed up in something she shouldn't be. She wouldn't risk taking Keylin along if there was danger, but she wouldn't be sneaking away if it was anything else. She twisted her mouth to the side in thought. *Maybe I should see what this is about.*

Alva deposited her laundry basket just inside the door to her sitting room and plucked her coat from the hook. Striding down the hall, she was buttoning the clasp at her throat when the king's wife barreled out of their suite and nearly knocked Alva into the wall.

"Oh! Sorry, your majesty." Alva bowed her head, surprised to see the woman outside their suite at this time of the evening.

"Very well. Very well. The king wants something to eat. Go get it, please." She spun to return to the suite.

"Um…" The woman would never understand that Alva wasn't her personal servant. When she'd mentioned that fact once recently, the king's wife had sneered, *"Well then, what are you here for? The girl doesn't need a governess anymore. Does she?"*

The look in her eyes said the same thing tonight. She turned back to face Alva and squinted her eyes. "Wait. Why is your coat on?"

"I was just going out," Alva stammered, inching a few steps down the hall.

"Going where?"

"Just going to meet—ah, for a walk, I mean."

"Who meets this time of night? Or walks, for that matter? What are you really doing?" The woman raised an eyebrow and cocked her hip.

"Really, your majesty. I was just going for a walk," Alva said quickly, unclasping her coat before the woman pressed further. "I'll go get something from the kitchen right away."

The king's wife frowned. "Yes. And hurry. I will keep him occupied." Then she grinned slyly at Alva as if she'd be envious.

Alva's stomach turned, but she schooled her face. "Yes, ma'am. I'll be right back."

The king's wife nodded and walked back into his suite, mumbling about how people shouldn't be going out at night anyway, up to no good. Alva was okay with being suspected of strange activity if the girls were safe. She threw her coat back on the hook and grabbed her laundry basket to carry it to the kitchen and exchange it for a sandwich.

Chapter Six
THE NEWEST RECRUIT

They were safely in the underground room, and Wyll sat around the small kitchen table with his rescuers. The girl stared at Wyll's neck until he covered it.

"Sorry." She shook her head briefly. "I'm making you uncomfortable. The tattoo must be why we can understand you in Sepherran. It looks cool, though."

"What's it look like?" He lowered his hand slowly and tilted his head back, lengthening the column of his throat.

"It's like liquid silver scrolling; some words I don't recognize."

"Do you have a mirror?" He felt the raised edges with his fingertips.

She brought him a heavy, long-handled mirror. Wyll gasped at his reflection. The tattoo wrapped his neck in elegant coils, just under his Adam's apple. She didn't know the symbols because they were Latin, but that's all he knew. It said, *"Et loquimur intellexerunt."*

He put the mirror down in disgust and covered the words again self-consciously. He was dying for a signal and a charging cord. It looked like it said something about intelligence. Two seconds on the internet, and he'd know. Maybe it was a hex. Maybe it said, *Hi. My name is stupid. I've got a tattoo on my throat.* He knew they couldn't read it either, but he was self-conscious, knowing there were words on his neck that he didn't understand. How did anybody know *anything* before Google? They grew silent.

Looking around, it occurred to Wyll that this was probably the girl's apartment. He wondered if she'd let him sleep here again. Indigo walked over to the kitchen, comprised of a small countertop. An upside-down teardrop-shaped glass container held up with delicate metal legs had a spigot in the bottom. He placed each glass under the faucet and pulled the lever, filling the glasses with blue liquid.

Wyll sniffed it. *Fruity. Non-alcoholic.* It tasted like blue Kool-Aid. *Could be.* Maybe they were really hiding in a large Kool-Aid factory, except it was a flavor they didn't like… *A sandwich would go great with this.*

"…Wyll?"

"Huh?" He looked up from his glass, and they were watching him.

"Maybe that's the answer to your question," the girl said to Indigo.

"What?" He was confused.

Indigo chuckled. "I asked if you were suffering mentally from your stay under the castle. Some people do not come out quite … right."

The Clockwork Pen

"I won't say I could have handled any more of it, but yeah, I'm okay. Thanks for asking."

"Good. Sira felt terrible about you being in there." Indigo looked at the girl, and she nodded.

"The king said she'd probably come to break me out. But I didn't know if she was coming—or sending you two instead." Wyll smiled. "What are you staring at?"

"Of *course* he talked to you about it. What else did the king say?" The girl's eyes narrowed. "He'll have a plan now. Crap."

"Oh. Ah, he wants his beloved child to stay here. Something about him making this world for her. But I am totally with you guys." Wyll didn't really know yet whose side he was on. If he did what the king wanted, he would get sent home, but these people would suffer. *Damn.*

He only had a *chance* of going home if he stayed with these people, but they also hadn't put him in the Reformatory and tortured him. It occurred to him that the king might not keep his deal, either. She was right. It was too much power for that man to have. He had to choose the Resistance and help take down the king. He wanted to help her. He really did. As long as no torture was included…

"Did he say how he plans to get her to stay?" She held her hand up toward Indigo, who looked like he would burst.

"No. But he says she encourages you guys with a bleeding heart. He just doesn't want her to get very involved with you. I think he wants me to convince her or something." Wyll kicked himself for lying. He wanted to say he was supposed to turn her over, but if he played things right, he could discover just what kind of chance he had here. Then, if they were just a bunch of dreamers, he could finish his deal with the king to see if he'd keep his end of the bargain. He'd go back, make a copy of the key, and return for her. If the thing with Rozam didn't work out, he could still help the Resistance take the crazy royal down. He just wouldn't tell anyone the plan. He was a guilty double agent, and it cramped his stomach.

The girl jumped up out of her chair, growling. She paced quickly on her side of the table with her arms crossed. "Who does he think he is? Planning against us. What kind of—I mean, does he really think I'd be so shallow? Really. I don't get it, Indi. Of all the stupid ideas. Who does he think I am? Helen of Troy? Send in a Trojan human boy to change my mind?" Her voice rose in volume and pitch.

Wyll was about to ask Indigo, *"What's wrong with her?"* when it hit him.

Indigo gave a short laugh, held his hand toward the girl, and said, "Wyll, meet Sira, the, ahem, next to inherit Sepherra."

"*You* are the princess?"

"I am not going to punch you right now because you don't know how I feel about that word yet." Sira leaned down and spoke in Wyll's face. "I am *no* princess.

My father is *not* a king. He's a regular man from Kansas with a magic pen—who is slowly going crazy from its power—and I must stop him."

She flopped into the chair as if she'd just lost a long race.

"But you could have whatever you want..." Wyll tried to wrap his head around the idea.

"What I really want? If you could be happy here, you wouldn't understand." She looked at her hands on the table. "What I want is the life he took from me."

"The boy doesn't understand because he comes from a place where he is already free." Indigo put his hand on Sira's.

"It's not like I don't get it." Wyll tried not to sound as irked as he felt.

"What I want is to know the real world—*my world*—where I was happy ... where I had friends and a mom. A whole planet of humans—a place where my father doesn't have every last word. When you discovered our world, didn't you want to know all about it?" Sira spread her hands, palms up, and her bracelet cuff jingled against the buckle on the back of her leather fingerless gloves.

He was still amazed. Of course he wanted to know more. "Sure."

"That's because this is something you don't already have. I want what's out there, what I don't have.

To go back to where I came from—where I belong—to be happy again." Sira's wet eyes shone in the lamplight.

"A place where all the people are free…" Indigo stared at the wall, imagining his picture of freedom.

Wyll's heart clenched. "You'll get there." Wyll couldn't imagine anything standing in her way, and it was suddenly important that he help her do it. The waffling in his brain stopped. She was the plan for now.

Indigo made sure Wyll was settled and left to go home.

"Tell Malynda I'm sorry," Wyll said. "And thanks again."

The man tipped his round-topped hat and bit the end of an elaborate ivory pipe. "I will. Goodnight."

"I'm sorry I called you the 'P' word." They sat on the sofa with their boots lined up next to each other on the coffee table. They watched a little clockwork beetle scuttle across the surface, its tiny gears spinning, needle-like legs making barely audible clicks.

Sira laughed softly. "I suppose it's not the worst word in the dictionary."

"Did you go to school here? I can't imagine your parents at career day." He smiled.

She tilted her head. "Career day? Everyone here has schooling of some kind. The people had to learn their jobs and the basics of Sepherran and math. It was all 'learn at your own pace.' The smartest people don't need their classes after a few years, but many of them go to new classes just to get ahead."

"What about you?" He imagined her studying with him, lying on his bed, leaning on her elbow, and chewing her pen.

"My governess taught me, along with her daughter—we're the same age. We finished the required schooling last year. Now, we choose things that interest us. I'm supposed to prepare to *rule*, and she works in the castle. She's my best friend, I guess—more like a sister. I try to protect her from what I can."

"That would have been nice. To grow up with somebody else. I was always so bored—just Mom, Dad, and me, and they aren't the most stimulating people." Wyll still wasn't sure this world was as bad as Sira thought, but then its creator's face flashed through his mind. The room seemed to darken quickly. His chest constricted, and he unbuckled the leather straps across his chest, concentrating on his breath for a few seconds.

"My mom was great. I barely remember her, but I always see her at the park where we played. She wore a faded yellow sweater, and her black hair was long and curly. She always sat under the big tree because she didn't want to freckle. I loved her freckles. The funny thing is, I don't know if that park was in your world or here." She stared at nothing, seeing a picture in her mind.

Wyll suddenly remembered the striking couple in the photo at the mansion of the white man and his African American wife and their striking little girl. It was Sira.

That's why she looked familiar. Suddenly, all the mixed couples made sense. The king must have made every couple mismatched so that no one was out of the ordinary. He liked the idea. *And she did grow up hot*. He appreciated their closeness and the warmth of her body radiated into his side.

"So, did your father ever re-marry?"

"He created a sweet, docile wife who wouldn't think of contradicting him. I really don't think she can. It's not in her DNA," Sira sneered. "She doesn't say much to me, trivial things mostly, but she watches me. You get used to it, but it's harder to sneak away. Fortunately, she is fully devoted to my father all evening. *Blech*." She performed an exaggerated shiver.

Wyll didn't know if he should be disgusted or admire the man. Really, what would any man do, given the opportunity to create a whole new world? Then he thought of the Reformatory. Not everyone would do that, would they?

"How can your father torture and kill his own creations, though? I don't get it. Can't he see they're actually people?"

She swept a lock of hair away from her cheek and tucked it back into the elaborate hairstyle of curls looped high on the back of her head. "He sees himself as their god. He doesn't see them as living beings that deserve independence and figures that if he can create them, he can do whatever he wants with them. Absolute power is dangerous. If he dismantles—kills—them all, he thinks he can find the flaw and will simply create more and better versions. But his creations are not as sturdy as they used to be. They break. Or they are made with malfunctions. I think it's connected to his mind; they're both coming apart. The more he uses the pen, the worse it gets."

"But they are real people with personalities, jobs, and feelings. He's surrounded by them. He can't know one person if he's able to do that." *No, not every man would do this.* Unless it was the pen's fault. They had to get it away from him before he made something stupid that could kill them all.

"I know," she whispered. "It's why I have to stop him. The people could run their own government. I could go home. I could take care of him—get him some help."

They sat silently for a minute, the clock on the wall echoing, *tock, tock, tock*.

"So, I guess this isn't your apartment?" Wyll smiled.

Her eyes squinted with her grin. "No. And yes. I live in the castle. But this is my home away from home, I guess. The Resistance uses it sometimes to meet. We try not to gather too many people at once to be safe."

He wouldn't have thought of that. "Who makes the plans?"

She leaned back against the curve of the sofa—one elbow perched on the dark wood of the arm and her other arm draped over the back. She propped her ankle on her knee, and her boot bounced up and down, making the metal chains jingle. "There are five of us: Indigo; his wife Malynda; Nally, the best baker in Sepherra; Kipper, a miniature clockwork mechanic; and me. Every one of us has a team that meets in groups of five at most, and they have teams of their own and so on."

He turned toward her, one knee on the sofa and his elbow resting on his other knee. "What have you done so far?"

"Nothing effective. Mostly, we rescue our own people from the cells. It would be ideal to apprehend the pen, but he keeps it hidden. He started to increase the number of people he arrested over the last year. We know we must do something soon, but most are too reluctant to go to war against their creator. If he knows they are coming, he only needs the time it takes to write them out of existence."

The clock's steady rhythm was soothing.

"Man." Wyll hung his head and shook it slowly. "I hadn't thought of that."

"Yeah. It's where we get stumped. No one agrees with any of the ideas that have been presented yet. Not enough to risk their life for it. Maybe your arrival will be the catalyst we need."

The clock's low *dong, dong, dong* startled them both, and they sat up straight.

She laughed. "I'd better get back so you can sleep."

The idea of being alone in the dark room made him think of the cave-like cell. "Yeah. Sure." His voice warbled.

"Will you be okay?" Her brow wrinkled.

There was no way he was going to look like a wuss in front of the only girl he'd ever wanted to have more than a five-minute conversation with—let alone one who rescued him from the most traumatic experience of his life.

He kept his voice steady. "Oh yeah. Sure. I'm good. Go ahead... Ah, when will someone be here tomorrow?"

She smiled. "I'll try to come over in the morning." She looked around the room. "I'll bring you breakfast."

His mouth watered at the thought. "Great." He watched her leave and admired the confidence of her walk.

"Goodnight," she called as she pulled the door behind her.

"Goodnight," he said, seeing her cane light up before it disappeared.

Wyll felt the shadows creeping in from the corners of the room. He left all the lights glowing and hurried to the bed. He moved the side table, then pushed the bed against the wall and curled up with his back against it. It wasn't worth his energy to bother with the covers; there was no way he was going to be able to sleep. His mind was still going a hundred miles an hour.

The next thing he knew, Sira was tapping him on the shoulder.

"Wake up," she said softly, her fingertips like a butterfly on his shoulder.

"Huh?" He lifted his head and looked around. He didn't even remember falling asleep. "What time is it?"

"Not sure. I left at six, but I took the long way not to be seen with that." She pointed to a wire contraption with four thin legs holding it upright and one big, fat wheel between them. The top was a basket constructed from strips of wood and leather woven together, and from behind it rose a handle not unlike those on a stroller, except for the wires and pistons on the sides. Wyll inspected everything. He was fascinated.

"Why did you bring it then?" he asked.

She crossed the room to retrieve it, pulled a lever on the handle, and the legs shot up into the piston-looking cylinders. He smiled as she rolled the basket to the bed and pushed the lever down, the legs shooting from each corner. When the basket righted itself, Sira flicked another button, and the basket itself came apart at the seams, flattening out into a table for two. In the center sat two huge berry muffins in brown paper, a glass container

The Clockwork Pen

of bacon, and a flask of orange juice. She divided up the food, poured the juice, and pulled a chair over.

Wyll shoved the first half of the muffin in his mouth without even tasting it. The orange juice didn't last long, either. He crunched the crispy bacon and looked up to see her watching him.

"What?" He wiped his mouth in case.

"Nothing. I just... I thought meeting a human would be so different. But you eat, sleep, and feel just like everyone else. I guess I thought you'd be more *real* than the people here."

He nodded while he chewed. She slid her bacon over to him, and he ate it gratefully. He didn't know where she was going with the whole "human" thing, but he was preoccupied and didn't give it much thought. If she wanted him to know, she'd tell him.

He was dusting crumbs off his leg, and she was picking at her muffin when a small man came running into the room, looking around frantically. When he saw Sira, he approached the bed and bowed his head.

He touched his cap, weighted to his head by goggles with at least five different magnifications. Wyll guessed this was the mini mechanic.

"What's wrong, Kipper?" Sira stood from the bed to take his shaking hands in her own.

"In the square. Did'n ya see it? The Resistance members want ta know what ta do." His shirt was filthy;

the sleeves rolled up to his elbows, and a pair of leather suspenders held up his brown trousers.

"What's in the square?" Her voice shook on the last word.

"A woman. She's been—well, ya need to come see for yourself. She's nay in good shape."

Sira narrowed her eyes and stared straight ahead. "He's playing a game. Making his first move. But he's already going too far… How will we rescue her from the direct sight of the castle, let alone in the light of day?"

"Tha's what ever'one wants ta know."

She dropped Kipper's hands. "Let's go tell her that we will get her out as soon as we can. Wyll, can you fill this with water?" She dropped something in a flask and handed it to him.

He took it to the sink and filled it, screwing the cap on. "I'm going, too."

Wyll shoved the canteen in his pocket. Sira pulled the basket over to the wall and faced Wyll. She buckled the straps over his chest and adjusted the collar on his shirt.

"Are you sure?"

He nodded. "I'm part of it now."

"Welcome to the Resistance," she said. "I know what you said—"

"It's okay. I'm ready." He smiled and nodded toward the hall. "Let's go."

The Clockwork Pen

Kipper held the door open, and they jogged outside and down the main street of shops, slowing to walk through the throng of citizens on the sidewalks.

When they reached the square, people stood in a semi-circle facing the woman, gaping and whispering animatedly. A huge iron sculpture of a rectangle encased a woman in her nightdress like she was standing in a doorframe. She wilted inside the structure—hanging by her wrists—held by chains connected to the top corners, her feet wide and chained to the bottom corners. Her gown was torn in many places, exposing skin blotched in variations of violet and red.

As they propelled themselves to the front of the crowd, Wyll could see that the woman was unresponsive, her knees bent inward, her chin tucked to her chest. Sira pushed her way through the mass surrounding the drama full of fascination. He followed as close as he could. Next to the slight woman hung a sign saying:

This is what happens when you are the Resistance.

"Give me the flask," Sira said, holding her hand out toward Wyll.

He gave it to her, and they stepped close to the woman. A curtain of silky black hair shrouded her face. Sira gently scooped the strands aside, took one look at the bruised and swollen face, and screamed loud enough to wake the dead.

Chapter Seven
FARKING PTSD

"Ya know her?" Kipper asked with his arms out to steady Sira.

"Alva's been my governess since I was three years old. She isn't even one of us. Why would he do this? He knows she'd never—" She held her clenched fists next to her chest and looked at Wyll and Kipper pleadingly. "We must do something. Alva? Alva?"

Sira gently stroked Alva's shoulder. The woman roused and blinked at them. Wyll remembered what it felt like to see the outside after being in the immense darkness of the Reformatory. Like a mole out of its den, her eyes were slits. The day was overcast but still bright enough to hurt Alva's eyes.

"Sira?" Alva began to cry. "Sira, I didn't do anything. I didn't—"

"Shhh. I'm here. I'm here, and I'm so sorry. I've done this to you."

"This is *your* fault?" A girl emerged from the front of the crowd. She could have been Derec's sister—a much prettier version. She wore a skirt that ended higher in the front and showed off her white boots, laced to the knee. Her hair was fixed in a pile of shiny, black curls, with a tiny top hat perched to the right, sporting a large feather the same burgundy color as her dress. Wyll thought she would have been immensely popular back home in a cheerleader uniform. But the way she was glaring at Sira had him grinding his teeth.

"No," he said in a lowered voice, covering his throat with one hand and holding the other toward her. "It's the king's fault."

A few people in the front row gasped.

Sira pulled his sleeve and whispered in his ear. "Not here. They'll think you're with the Resistance. Want to go back to the cells?" To the girl, she said, "I'm so sorry, Keylin. I had no idea. He's trying to punish me."

"By nearly killing my mother?" Keylin shrieked.

Ah—the girl she grew up with.

Sira pulled her to the side, and Wyll followed. Kipper held up the flask for Alva and wiped her nose with his handkerchief.

"This is what he does. You know that." Sira held both Keylin's hands. "He's not the same as he used to be. I just didn't know he'd hurt people I love to get back at me."

"The sign next to her says something about a Resistance." Keylin looked at them both and then squinted her eyes at Wyll. "Who are you?"

"There's a lot you don't know. You remember I told you there's another world that I came from?" Sira asked.

Keylin nodded, but her one raised brow said she was doubtful.

"He's from my world." Sira nodded in Wyll's direction and smiled.

He flashed his dimples at them. It was his best smile. Sticking out his hand, he said, "I'm Wyll. I'm sorry about your mother."

She took his hand hesitantly but turned to Sira. "What about this Resistance? Mom knew nothing about resistance, and she wouldn't risk it anyway."

Sira looked around. "I can tell you more later. How is she?"

"Miserable. And I don't know how long she will be there." Keylin's eyes filled.

Wyll had a flash of emotion. He owed them his assistance. Hell, he was putting them all in danger just being around, but no plan was coming to him. Maybe it would help to be the offense. "We'll get her out of there." Wyll surprised them with his offer to help. "Right, Sira?"

Sira sighed. "The Resistance will take care of her. They won't let her stay there."

He finally realized how deep this secret must be.

"I want to help, too." Keylin crossed her arms. "And if you know anything, you'd better spill it now."

The Clockwork Pen

"Key, I can't. The more you know, the closer you are to that." Sira tilted her head toward the torture device in the square.

"I don't care." Her tiny chin pointed up in defiance. "If she's punished for them, I want to know more. You know you've already told me more than you should."

Sira paused in thought, crossing her arms. "Fine. Wyll, can you tell Kipper we need to call an emergency meeting to figure out a plan?" Sira patted Keylin's shoulder and continued to Wyll, "Have him take you back to the apartment. I'll be back as soon as I can."

As Wyll walked with Kipper toward the hideout, he tried to absorb everything they passed. He wanted to buy one of the globes of little mechanized fish, or a turnkey turtle with jewel colors inlaid across his shell and wheels for feet, or one of the tiny insects the size of a half-dollar. They had the tiniest gears along their bodies, long wire antennae, and delicate wings adorned them, with spiky little legs. Many lit up, and most had beautiful colored glass in their design. He was enamored, but he had no currency here.

Kipper saw him staring at the table of insects. He passed a few coins to the merchant and said, "Pick one."

"Thanks, man." Wyll smiled at him. He chose a little bug with an iridescent round body, like a tiny marble, and shimmering wings. Its teeny antennae curled, and it crawled on his hand. It was the coolest thing he'd ever owned. He tucked its box in his pocket.

They were passing a little shop with a big front window paned in lead, which looked like a lion's head from across the street, but up close was a random mosaic of colors. Wyll entered behind Kipper, and the bell above the door jingled.

"How can I help you?" The shopkeeper sat on a stool behind a case of knick-knacks, toys, and gadgets. Wyll couldn't place a purpose for many of them. His leather apron creaked as he stood up and faced them.

Though no one else was in the store, Kipper said in a low, quiet voice, "This be Resistance bus'ness."

The shopkeeper nodded gravely.

"And I'm needin' some parts." Kipper wrote down a list of items that Wyll couldn't read.

Wyll's little bug carefully picked its way over his palm while the men spoke in hushed tones. The little shop was cozy. Not much bigger than his bedroom at home, it was paneled in dark wood, with glass cases of merchandise displayed on blue velvet-covered shelves.

"Let yar people know aboot tonight," Kipper told the merchant.

When they had all they needed, Kipper led them back to the apartment.

"I'm sorry ta keep ya shut up in this room," Kipper said. "But I might be able ta help with somethin' else..."

The Clockwork Pen

He set up all his tools on the table and shook out the pieces he'd purchased from the store.

Wyll held the back of the chair across the table and glanced at Kipper with his brows raised.

"Yeah. It's okay. Sit doon." Kipper pulled his goggles down and flipped on a light at the corner that Wyll hadn't even seen. He was astounded by the tech here. It seemed so chunky and exposed, almost crude sometimes, but the things they could make it do were amazing. He wondered where the line drew between skill and magic.

After a long while, unaware of how many hours had passed, Wyll's eyes started crossing as he watched Kipper soldering with tweezers and wire. His stomach growled, so he checked out the cupboard—it was olive green metal with shiny wooden doors and iron latches. He could see through the decorative mesh that covered the cutout in the doors that not much was in it.

He opened them anyway to find unfamiliar packages with strange writing on them. He didn't know what anything was. Choosing something that looked like a candy bar, he opened it to find a long, square-shaped granola bar. It wasn't bad.

Soon, Kipper looked up and stretched his neck, rolling his shoulders. "Here it is." He held up a strip of leather that sported a manly collection of gears and tooling that looked almost tribal. He'd used the wire to burn designs into the leather.

"What's it for?"

"Ta wear." Kipper held the strap up against his own neck. It dawned on Wyll—it would cover his tattoo.

"Thanks so much." He felt a rush of gratitude and took it from Kipper, pulling it across his throat and turning the closure in the back. He rolled his head on his shoulders to get used to the feeling of the band. He felt less exposed already.

Wyll didn't see or hear the door open, but he knew the moment Sira arrived. He looked up at her somber face and gave a little smile. Sira smiled, then laughed lightly and shook her head.

"How's it going?" he asked.

She perked up a bit. "Everyone's coming here as soon as the sun sets."

"Everyone? I thought you said—"

"No, no. The main team. The rule makers and those on the action panel." She looked around, and Wyll watched Kipper leave the room. Her hands rested lightly on the chair across from him. "This is new. He's never been so blatant about it. It's like he's calling us out. Today was about me."

"No, it's about *them*. He doesn't really think you're one of them. He is probably warning you that something bad could happen, so you should stay away."

"That just makes me want to fight harder." She growled, tensing all her muscles at the same time. She pulled the chair around and plopped down, defeated.

"Maybe you could, though. Stay away? I mean, the guys and I could go and rescue her, and you could get stuff ready for us to bring her back—"

She cut him off. "Excuse me? If you thought you knew me enough to suggest that, you were wrong. There is no way I'm staying here. Actually, I'm going to help Kipper with the chairs for tonight."

She stormed out the door.

It took Wyll a second to understand what had happened. He'd only suggested that she stay back. He couldn't tell her that the king would know where she was while she was with him ... but he kind of wanted to. Oh well, let her walk it off. She'd be fine. He'd keep an eye on her, too. The king would have to go through him. But he really hoped it didn't come to that.

He straightened the covers on the bed, tossed his clothes under it, and helped set up the chairs into a big circle. He bent over the back of a chair, folding the seat down, and wondered where his bug had gone.

"I'm sorry for snapping at you like that." Sira unfolded the last chair across the room and smiled sadly. "I'm a little stressed."

"S'okay." He grinned at her.

"I like your new band." She pointed to her own neck and smiled. "It's neat."

"Thanks. Kipper made it."

They stood staring at each other. She bit her lip and glanced away. It turned him on like a forest fire. She turned to him, and their stare crackled with energy. Her eyes wandered, and Wyll could feel her molten gaze through his skin. His breathing quickened. Her cheeks tinted, and he looked at her hungrily.

Kipper cleared his throat. "Ahem. Sira?"

"Yes." She blinked, looking like the kitten who ate the canary. He shuddered. *The kittens around here are creepy.*

"They're comin' now. Sun's down. I'll clean up my tools an' get ma bride."

"Sure. Go ahead," she said.

"See you, Wyll," he called.

"Hey, thanks!" Wyll cupped his hands around his mouth as Kipper jogged out, buckles jingling.

The room soon filled with people decked out in all sorts of gadgets. Wyll felt like he was at the best steampunk con ever—and it was all clockwork. *Staggering.* He nodded at the few he knew. The others eyed him warily from the side, wondering who he was and what he was doing there. He let them wonder. Sometimes, he knew he was a jerk, but what else was he supposed to do? This wasn't *his* meeting.

"Welcome, everyone." Indigo stood before his chair as everyone took their seats in a circle around him. "You've all seen the woman in the square. She is Sira's governess—" People gasped and whispered. He spoke a little louder, "Her name is Alva Yardager. And this is her daughter, Keylin."

Keylin stood up next to him, twisting something in her tiny hands. It looked like a piece of lacey cloth, maybe a fancy hankie.

"She has come to us requesting our help in freeing her mother. I feel it is our duty to do so, as she is being punished on our behalf. The floor is open." Indigo and Keylin sat back down.

A few people popped out of their chairs with varying opinions. Another woman stood in shiny purple satin from her high buttoned collar to her lace boots. "Is she one of us or not? We risk our own identity by helping. And prisoners have never been so public before. What if we're seen?"

There was murmuring, and Indigo said, "She was not one of us previously, but her daughter assures us that they will join us if we assist in her rescue."

Louder murmuring commenced, and Keylin stood firmly, wringing the handkerchief into a spiral. "Please help her. You must. She's only hurt because of your revolution. She never did anything wrong ... and she's all I have."

Everyone was quiet, watching Keylin take her seat. She readjusted her miniature hat.

The bits of conversation he caught weren't positive. They were actually considering leaving that poor woman out there, cold and beaten, just because she wasn't already part of the plan? Indignation infected him, and his temperature rose with his temper. He could feel the beat of patriotism in his core—the feeling that one's life was a worthy price for curing injustice.

Sira stood. "We all know the facts. There are two options: rescue her or let her die. Her life is on us. Yes, the king has called us out. We don't know if he'll be watching, but assume he is. Everyone wear their face masks and bring your weapons because I vote, we do it tonight."

People spoke loudly to one another in a jumble of words.

Indigo watched them all as he sat back and casually checked his pocket watch. He turned his head to listen to various arguments thrown around like flaming-hot potatoes. Then he stood up and put his hands out. The group quieted. "You've all been heard. It's a blind vote. Everyone, turn your chairs around, please."

Wyll was confused, but he mirrored the people around him and turned his chair around to face out. He looked over his shoulder and saw Indigo still in the middle of the circle. His voice was smooth, and his top hat tilted. "Please, hold your hand high. Now, if you vote to perform the rescue, open your hand. If you vote to stay, close your hand in a fist. Eyes forward."

Wyll sat with his hand held high like when he was a kid, and the teacher asked for an answer he knew. It took all his concentration not to look around, and out of his peripheral vision, he saw his neighbors looking straight ahead with their arms raised, though he couldn't see their hands. It was a fantastic way to vote—no cheating. They waited for Indigo to tally the responses.

"Okay, team, turn back around. Looks like we're moving out. Any other questions or business?" Indigo sat and crossed his legs so eloquently that it didn't seem unmanly at all. Chair legs squeaked as they were scooted around the floor to face inside the circle again.

Sira turned her chair around. "I have business. Before we break, I propose spreading the news and having an all-inclusive meeting. Indigo has found a building near here where we can fit everyone. We need to move on our plans to take over the king as soon as possible. We'll meet in a few days. Everyone's ideas are requested in this brainstorming session. Now that he's pushed us, it's time to fight back."

"Why now? It's only one woman—unconnected to us. He's reaching." The man speaking twirled the edge of his mustache.

"It's my governess today and your daughter tomorrow. He won't stop. We know this. And now we have a complication—or rather, an opportunity. We are also being called for aid to help Wyll get back home." Sira motioned for Wyll to rise. He stood with confidence, dressed in high-society fashion and kick-ass boots. He smiled at the panel, but the people didn't appear enthusiastic about this at all.

She smiled and pointed at him. "This is Wyll. Remember how I told you that I come from another world? Wyll is from my world. He managed to get here, but now he needs assistance returning to his family. We can help him if we have the pen, and it's been our mission to retrieve it; then, we can do anything. We will finally be the ones with power." She stopped to catch her breath. "It defeats the king and helps another human who needs us. We must do it. We've worked on this, talked about it, and made plans. Now, we must speed up our timeline."

Many people wanted to know why. Why was it so important to help a human? What made a human boy any more important than a clockwork one? They were going to vote no. He could smell it in the air like a sulfurous odor. Unhappy conversations rolled like ocean waves.

He didn't know what possessed him. Maybe part of it was his desire to impress Sira or the adrenaline rush shaking through his system. Gearing up to go into battle, he stood with his newfound voice. "Look, you people don't even know how utterly oppressed you are. Everyone should be free to say what they like in any language they choose, like where I come from. You shouldn't have to live in fear. Your creator should appreciate you, and he probably did, but he's losing his mind. How many of you have been to the Reformatory? It's the result of a madman with too much power. And what happens if he loses the rest of his mind and decides to wipe out the city to raise pretty-colored horses or decides you are all too rebellious and writes a virus that will subdue all your mutinous emotions? If that doesn't scare you, it should. Sira's right; it's too much for one person. You owe it to yourselves to unseat your king."

"Who chooses to meet in a few days?" Indigo clapped his ringed fingers together.

Most of the hands went up—enough to make a noticeable difference. Sira's smile lit up the room. Her skin glowed, and she looked angelic. Well, if angels could be badass chicks. His blood boiled with want and determination.

"Tell your group leaders tomorrow," both Indigo and Sira said.

He was proud of her and riding the high of madness that comes before risking your life for a cause bigger than yourself. He was ready for the first time, and they weren't moving fast enough.

"For the Resistance!" Wyll roared in anger. Sira's eyes widened as he stood, brimming with testosterone, ready to rescue Alva. He surprised himself, too. It was a night for winning, and the desire for it pumped through him like a thumping heartbeat. It felt good to voice an opinion and take a risk that benefited someone else. "Let's go!" He was caught up in it as the group cheered and raised fists. They simultaneously took action, chairs scooting as they rose and scattered to prepare.

Then he realized the king would track them. His shoulders dropped, and his stomach shrank into a black pit. He could feel venomous snakes roiling inside him and biting him everywhere. He had to warn her.

The members fixed their masks and ran out in groups. Some masks half and some full, gears and feathers and wire mesh adorned them. Many wore a type of chemical filtering mask with skull creations and metal galore. They pulled out weapons that impressed him. Strapped under coats or inside boots, they were some of the coolest pieces of hardware he'd ever seen.

The man next to Wyll pulled back a lever on his homemade bronze shotgun of sorts, with designs engraved all along the barrel, and a series of lights flashed green. There were cylinders on the sides that Wyll couldn't think of a reason for, and the sight was a smaller piece of pipe mounted on the top. A thin chain hung from stock to barrel. The man gave a hoot and took off for the door.

One of the women in pants—with a gun belt slung across her hips and a mask over the left side of her face—smiled at him and handed him a gun. Her short hair surrounded her head like a halo, held back with goggles, and her ebony face contrasted with her bright smile. "You'll need one of these. I'll be close," she said, patting the gun and leaving.

The gun was smaller than most others, more like a pistol, but the leather handgrip sported elegant tooling. He turned it over, looking at the cylinders and tubing that linked them. What would it do? He tapped the dial above the trigger, but it remained fully leaned to the left. He flipped the gun over, avoiding anything that looked fragile, and saw three buttons. He was about to push the first one when Sira grabbed his arm.

"Come on!" She smiled and pulled him into the dark hallway. His calloused hand enveloped her tiny palm. He had a battle partner.

They ran a few feet down the inky hallway, and he immediately tensed up in the blackness. He couldn't see, and then he wished he couldn't. Since his stint in the Reformatory, he now saw his own fears in the dark, as clear as if they were real. He dropped her hand and stopped, backing away from the visions. The gun shook in his grip, and he pressed his shoulder to the wall, gripping the iron pipe railing.

"...Wyll? Wyll?" Sira's voice warbled in his mind, but then her cane flashed on, and Wyll could breathe. He focused on the coil of glowing red. "Are you okay?" Her concern was obvious in the shadowed wrinkles on her forehead.

"Yeah. I just. The dark. Sorry." He cleared his throat. "Can you, ah, leave that on? Just down the hall?

"Sure." She closed her hand around his arm, just above his elbow, grounding him to reality. As his mind fought to unravel, he centered his breathing and focused on the safety of her grip. He wondered how long the dark would bother him like this. He'd be so pissed if the king gave him farking PTSD. He sat next to a guy in school who did a report on PTSD as related to freshman year girls, but he only remembered the title: *Potential To Suck D*. That kid failed. Not just the essay and not just that class.

With his mind distracted, they resumed their jog down the hallway, Sira's light shining on the backs of people who'd passed them. He could hear more clomping steps behind them. At least he wasn't alone. Finally, they were in the glass building with rusty rivets decorating huge cylinders like polka-dot trim. Rust ran down the sides in blood-like drips.

They ran around the edge of the mechanical structure.

"Be alert," Sira said, holding the outside door open for him.

"Shouldn't you be up front or something?" He realized he was still holding his gun in two hands and let one swing.

She smiled. "Indigo is up there. They don't need me. But you do. You sure you're okay? You can stay back—"

"No. I really want to help. He shouldn't have that pen … and I wouldn't mind going home."

She took off in a jog, and he kept pace with her. He breathed deeply as they sprinted past a cross street.

He continued, "I mean, this place is great and all, but I'm just starting senior year, and—well, I want to help get us there."

"I'm glad," she said just loud enough for him to hear.

They were almost to the square when Sira said, "Oh crap, I've got the chain cutter."

Pushing his muscles to the limit, Wyll ran with her to the metal structure in the square. A few people huddled around Alva; others stood facing out and pointed their weapons in large arcs around them. Figures were scattered around the square, holding position, eyes ready. They dodged a few gunmen to reach the small group with Alva, and Sira announced she had the cutters, so they made way for her.

Wyll hung back and said to Indigo, "I don't feel right about this. I think the king will try something."

Indigo patted his shoulder. "I'd be surprised if he didn't. It's okay, Wyll. Everyone here knows the risk."

A collective sigh around the prisoner meant that at least one limb was free.

"It's not fast enough," Sira whisper-shouted to Indigo. "What else can we do? Kipper's saw would draw too much attention."

"How much faster would it be?" Malynda asked, sliding up to Indigo and standing shoulder-to-shoulder with him.

"Probably twice as fast, but much louder." Sira winced. "Captain?"

"Captain?" Wyll asked.

"Nickname," Indigo said, chuckling. "Go ahead, Sira. Either they know we're here, or they don't. But whatever happens, Alva retreats with us."

Sira nodded and spoke to Kipper, who picked up a long electric hacksaw resembling a giant vegetable peeler. It lit up with a line of ice-blue light and screeched when held against the thick metal. There's no way they weren't attracting attention. Wyll saw a window light up across the square and winced.

The harder Kipper pushed, the faster it cut and the louder it screamed. It raised the hair on the back of Wyll's neck. He held his weight on one leg and then the other. Thinking about the chip in his hand, he stepped away from Sira, inching backward casually across the square. *What are the soldiers waiting for?* Wyll was practically running in place by the time the first shot fired.

Everyone started yelling at once. Some were general screams of fright, and some were instructions to people. Things like, "Get down, people!" or "Everybody, move!" or "Protect Sira!" That one got his attention. Resistance members ran in every direction, and he wasn't exactly sure where to fire. He spun around, pointing his pistol forward with both hands, looking for Sira. She was on her knees, helping hold the cuff away from Alva's ankle so Kipper wouldn't cut into it with the saw. Wyll was halfway to her when he saw a soldier walking purposefully toward him. He held up his gun, his hands trembling, and pulled the trigger. He prepared for the

The Clockwork Pen

kickback, but nothing happened. The soldier continued steadily forward as Wyll pulled the trigger repeatedly.

"Damn it!" He looked around wildly. "Somebody help me with this gun!"

The woman who'd handed it to him ran up and pushed the center button on the side of it, then she smiled and ran off. The gun buzzed in his hands. It pulsed with power, and little lights all along the cylinders showed yellow, white, and blue. The soldier stood several feet away, aiming at his heart when Wyll shot. A blast of light and heat burst from his gun and hit the metal soldier in the hip, causing him to lean to the side. The robot-looking soldier gripped his hip and lifted his arm again. Wyll shot and hit him in the opposite shoulder, the energy glancing off. "Damn it!" *You've got to hit them where it counts.*

The soldier went down to his knee but lifted his gun and pointed it at Wyll, so he aimed his final shot and ended the soldier's clockwork existence. It wasn't much of a consolation, though, knowing how real the people were.

"Sira!" Kipper's voice carried to Wyll, though he couldn't see them.

He ran around citizens and shot wildly at soldiers as he shouldered through people near Alva. Bullets and quick laser beams of colored light buzzed randomly through the air like a mortar malfunction. Alva slumped against a man in a dirty shirt and suspenders holding her up. He wore an apron of sorts—a tradesman. A soldier pointed his weapon at the person uncuffing Alva's ankle chain. *Sira.*

It happened in slow motion. Sira looked up, and the soldier stepped back as he recognized her. She held up her hands, and he raised his weapon again to fire. Wyll charged forward, aiming to kill the guard, but the guard saw him and swung the weapon in his direction. There were three shots so close together that their ears all rang from the three-second boom. The guard's bullet hit Wyll in the collarbone. Wyll's bullet went wide, and Sira's gun smoked as she held it aimed at the guard's forehead.

"Wyll! –yll –yll!" Her voice echoed in his ears as he flew backward, light shooting across his vision, his head bouncing off the stone of the cobbled square.

Chapter Eight
Good Goals ... For Later

Vicious pain throbbed through Wyll's body. It was all he knew. Not even his name registered as he lay prone, enduring agony that made colors bloom before his eyes. He blinked, but all he saw was a swirling mix of colors and shadow.

"Wyll," Sira said quietly next to him. "Are you awake?"

"Shhh," he whispered. "Not so loud."

"Head hurt?" She placed an ice-cold pack on his forehead, and the pain eased momentarily.

He sighed in relief. "He shot me, didn't he?"

"Yeah ... but you fell backward into someone else's shot and got grazed across your forehead."

His headache made sense. The energy beams that surrounded the artillery burned. He felt his forehead, but bandages wrapped across it. He peeked at his shoulder. Same.

Squinting, he pushed himself to a sitting position. They were back in the apartment, sitting on the bed, and she faced him, just visible in the glow of the bedside lamp.

He remembered the rescue and looked around, but they were alone.

"Did we get her?" he asked with a black hole in his stomach, imagining that poor limp woman in the Reformatory again.

Sira's hand rested on top of his. "Yes. She's fine. Keylin said they had family that would take them in."

"Take them in?"

"They've always lived near me in their own apartment in the castle. But Keylin doesn't want Alva going back there, and I don't blame her. I don't know what they'll do for credit now, though. I'm sure I'll figure something out. The Resistance takes care of their own," she whispered passionately.

He relaxed. "You did great. I mean, out there. In the square." He remembered her straight spine as she knelt before Alva, how regal she looked, bowing to cut the chains.

They stared at each other. As he searched her eyes, they suddenly shined with unshed tears, so he said nothing, just in case. Girls were often difficult to understand, but he learned that part at least. He just waited. He knew she was attached to her nanny, and she felt responsible for what happened to her.

Sira ducked her head and blinked the tears away, then smiled and looked up at him. "You were really brave... Don't get mad, but I really didn't expect you to step in like that."

"I'm not mad. It was worth the fight." He shrugged one shoulder with fake aloofness. "I mean, why not join a cause? Right?" He smiled softly at her, and she returned it with a shy smile of her own.

Would she run from him if he let down his walls? He didn't want to treat her like the others, but it was too easy to be a jerk and hide—*risk nothing*, his protective mantra. Though he'd never analyzed it this closely, he might have been kidding himself if he believed he wasn't still protecting his own interests. She would hate him if she discovered his part in her father's plan—*when* she discovered it. What would he risk to keep Sira with him? He didn't know yet, but her gravity pulled him in like a planet holds its moons.

They both jumped at the sudden knocking on the door and chuckled together. Sira went to the door and flipped on the overhead bulb. She let in a man in a black bowler hat and goggles with a white-splotched vest, carrying a tray of food and the most mouth-watering scented pastries.

"Come on in. You can set those on the table." Sira swung her arm, motioning toward the "kitchen."

He looked up at Wyll and smiled. "I hope you don't mind grilled sandwiches."

"I love panini." Wyll sat forward, but the motion pulled his shoulder, and he sucked air in through his teeth.

The man's brow bunched in confusion as he placed the tray on the table.

Sira came over to Wyll and pushed him back into the pillows. "You stay here."

"Pa-ni-ni?" the man asked.

"Yeah. That's what they're called. Well, where we come from." Wyll pointed to Sira and himself.

"Hmmm. I like that. It's easier to say." The man walked over to shake his hand. "I'm Nally."

"Oh my gears, I totally forgot to introduce you. Nally, this is Wyll. He's the one I told you about, from the human world." Sira stood next to them. "Wyll, this is our favorite baker, Nally."

"Favorite? I thought I was your only rebel baker?" Nally looked hurt but winked at Wyll.

She was flustered then. "I mean—"

Nally boomed with laughter so loud, Wyll was glad they were underground. It bounced around in his aching head but was endearing. The man could play a mall Santa with a "ho ho ho" like that. He'd make bank.

Wyll's stomach growled when he thought of the panini, and Sira went to make him a plate. Nally pulled two chairs over next to the bed for himself and Sira, and all three balanced tin plates on their laps. When they were finishing, Wyll took a drink and was suddenly exhausted. His eyelids grew thick and heavy.

He could hear Sira cleaning up, heard her bidding Nally goodnight. Then he heard the ring of metal unbuckling as she stacked her gun belt, shoulder holster, hat, vest, and chains on the coffee table in front of the

The Clockwork Pen

sofa. When the bathroom door closed, the room echoed the patter of water hitting the shower floor, the whoosh of it flowing through the pipes. He let his eyes close and felt himself start to snore.

He thought she'd gone for the night when he heard a noise in the room with him. She'd turned off the main light, but he could see her laying blankets on the stiff-backed sofa.

"What are you doing?" he murmured.

She stood up, her arms full of a patched quilt. "That soldier in the square. He recognized me. If I go home now, I could be in big trouble. The king might lock me up where I can't do anyone any good. Then you'd have to meet about rescuing me."

"Would the king hurt you?" Wyll was suddenly awake at the thought of Sira needing him.

"I don't know what he'll do to me. I need the arrest order to get to him so he can cancel it before I'm found. And at least give him some time to settle down."

Wyll remembered the crazy king's face and how completely rational he appeared to be, especially when it came to knowing he was protecting his daughter. This whole thing stemmed from a father's love for his child. He'd tried to make a better life for her than he could provide in the real world. He made her a princess. Like, what little girl wouldn't want that? Then he looked at Sira. *She wouldn't.*

"He might be crazy, but he does love you. I know that. In his mind, you aren't part of the Resistance. You never will be." Wyll's mouth felt like it was full of cotton. He reached over to the bedside table for his glass of water. It made him feel instantly better, and he was surprised. He took another large gulp.

"Be careful with that. Doc Azona put something in there for your pain." Sira came over to the bed. "How are you feeling?"

"I'm fine. Better now. You don't have to sleep on the couch, you know. I do know how to keep my hands to myself." He smiled at her with his eyes half closed, then laughed as she returned a nervous smile that resembled a grimace. He held his hands up. "Really. I'm too tired to try anything."

His eyes drooped as she looked back at the sofa and then Wyll, practically wringing her hands. He figured she'd be more comfortable if she didn't see him, so he rolled over and faced the wall. A minute later, he was weightless, slowly slipping into unconsciousness, when he felt the mattress dip behind him. He smiled into the dark corner when he felt her tiny hand rest against his back.

He slept fitfully. The pain returned, and he trembled, pouring sweat. He was in a boat, rocking, rocking, and it was on fire. He was a flaming inferno but couldn't make it to the side to throw himself overboard. When he bolted for the rail, his feet didn't move. They were melting into the deck like it was quicksand. His legs were so heavy it was fatiguing. He tried calling out, but his voice only made unintelligible noise. The louder he tried to force the sound from his throat, the closer he came to the white-hot pain. Wyll woke, tensing, as Sira gently shook his shoulder.

"Drink your water," she mumbled.

He woke up enough to chug a third of the glass. In his blissful state of relief, he rolled back over to his side and faced her in the dark. She watched him. He smiled in the dark; she mirrored him. Wyll put his arm around her, and she snuggled closer to him. She looked up at him, the shadows lining her face in geographical blocks. He knew that look but doubted she was conscious of it. His body wanted to respond, but his strength was quickly draining away. He leaned forward, kissed her forehead, and tried to think of something else.

"Thanks," he said, drifting. "For everything."

"Thank you ... for waking me up and encouraging me to stop talking and begin fighting."

"And don't forget, being your first human." He flashed his dimples at her with his eyelids half closed.

"It's nice to have a friend from the real world." Her voice was as soft as her hair looked, curled around her upper arm. Her tank top and trousers exuded her warmth mere inches from him. "Who could have guessed it was you?"

"Anybody, I guess. Not me. I had no idea." He struggled to gaze at her intensely, his eyes slightly narrowed in consideration. "But I'm not sorry."

"Really?"

"Absolutely." He poked her shoulder.

She chuckled, and the sound rang in his ears like he was hearing her down a long tunnel. He laid his head on the pillow, resting his jaw along her brow. He inhaled the scent of her spicy cinnamon soap and relaxed into sleep.

When he woke, Wyll was stiff with pain. His shoulder throbbed, and his forehead felt like someone hit him with a hot poker. He groaned, curling inward, and pressed his body toward the mattress, realizing that he was hugging something and rolling it under him. His eyes shot open as he realized he was nearly smothering Sira to death.

"Wake up," she said, her lips pressed to his neck.

He quite enjoyed the feeling of her mouth against his skin and realized he needed to roll away quickly. He sat up and reached for the glass of water. His dominant shoulder screamed in pain as he reached with it instinctively. He let it drop and picked up the glass with his left hand. Whatever medicine they used was much better than anything he'd had in Kansas. Not that he had anything good to compare it with—or that he'd ever been shot before.

"Are you okay?" Sira's hand skimmed the length of his back.

"I'm, ah, I'm fine. I'm just going to—" Wyll jumped up and hopped out of bed. "I'm gonna take a shower."

He hurried to the bathroom and leaned against the closed door. He took the longest shower ever, scrubbing layers of grime from his skin. When he was drying off, he felt more like he was polishing. There was a knock on the door.

"Just a second. I'm almost done." He rubbed his hair into spikes.

"I know." A voice came through the door. "Nally brought you some clean clothes."

"Oh. Thanks." He opened the door wide enough to take the pile of clothing and shut it.

He was surprised at how well Nally's clothes fit him. The boots were a bit snug, but he filled out the pinstriped trousers with his muscled thighs, and the shirt fit his broad shoulders, though he didn't care for the extra material at the cuffs and chest. He put on his leather collar; it was already more pliable than it had been to start with. Even the hat fit. It was a short top hat like he'd seen Indigo wear, and he wondered if it made him look nearly as cool.

The feathers were blue and purple. He tucked the monocle and watch into the pockets on his vest.

Wyll emerged a new man, proud of himself for being such a metrosexual. A pair of younger teenagers had joined Sira and Nally, and they sat around the table, discussing something new in the square.

"What's there now?" Wyll asked, grabbing a folding chair by the wall and dragging it to the table.

Sira waited for him to sit down. "The king started questioning people. He's bringing them in and forcing them to admit they're part of the Resistance or identify someone else as a member."

"I would have admitted to anything to stop that torture," Wyll said, working to keep his mind from going back there.

"Exactly," Nally said. "They're all confessing."

"So, he's putting them in the square? Like Alva?" Wyll imagined the iron sculptures littering the square, full of bruised and broken people chained and left to die.

"Most," a guy in a pageboy cap and circle glasses said. "Some are worse."

"Worse? What do you mean?"

Sira watched him. "Some of them are forced into uncomfortable positions that will cause loss of limbs, even if we get them out. We'll have to push our meeting ahead—tonight—to identify everyone on our side and brainstorm some plausible ideas. Then we'll all swarm the square and rescue the people. That's all we can do."

The Clockwork Pen

With everyone in agreement, they readied to spread the news. The network of teen followers would let their team leaders know the plan, and it would flow from there. Nally would tell the other council members, and Sira needed to get a message to her team leaders.

The others filed out the door, each to their own tasks. Wyll got up and pushed in his chair.

"Where do you think you're going?" Sira planted her fists on her hips.

"I'm going with you."

"Oh no, you're not. Your wounded self will stay here and heal. How am I supposed to hide you and keep you safe if you're traipsing through the city?" she asked.

"Aren't you on the run just as much as I am?" He paced four steps one way, four steps back. "You can't go *traipsing* through the city at all. Besides, the two of us can see more and assist each other better."

She groaned. "You're not going to sneak out if I leave you alone, are you?"

"I can't promise anything." He crossed his arms and smiled.

She gave a shout of frustration. "Fine. Grab your coat."

He followed her outside and chuckled because she was still stomping. The sky was dark, the clouds pregnant with rain. A few fat drops fell here and there, and another strange, long-bodied, feline-like creature crossed the street and ducked into a hole in another factory.

"What is that thing?" Wyll pointed. "It's not like the kittens I saw in the market."

"That's a goran. They come out at night and eat the garbage, then go sleep somewhere all day. Some people have them as pets. They dispose of trash and are lovable like cats or dogs but with hyper-active personalities."

"I haven't seen many dogs around." He looked down the narrow cobblestone street both ways.

"He doesn't make them. They crap on everything. And the king hasn't made a creature that eats dog poop yet." She laughed.

"You always call him 'the king.' Do you call him that at home?"

She barked a short laugh. "No, I call him *Dad* at home. But I don't associate with the things he does, especially in public. I don't like reminding the Resistance how close I am to the problem. What if they decided to put me up for ransom? That's another reason for the smaller meetings."

"Oh."

Light misting looked like fog rolling down vacant streets in this neglected section of town. They went a new way. As they approached a busy street, Sira pulled the sheer fabric from her hat down to cover her eyes and nose and handed Wyll a black leather mask like a doctor might use, with a brass hexagon of wire meshing over his mouth. The rivets and nose strip were all made of matching metal,

The Clockwork Pen

and he fastened it on. It wasn't difficult to breathe through at all. In fact, the air tasted *cleaner* somehow. He couldn't explain it.

Wyll's heart galloped out of his chest. The closer they came to people, the closer he was to being exposed. Or caught. And the thought of going back in the dark made him cold. He shivered.

"You okay?" Sira peered up at him. All he could see was the outline of her dark lashes in the shadow.

"Yeah." He smiled with his eyes. "What's the plan for us? I mean, what's our part of the plan, not that there's an us. I mean ... shutting up."

He watched her mouth curl into a delicious smile. He needed to tell her about the chip in his arm. But he liked this smile so much he couldn't bear to change it. She would be devastated at his ruse. Maybe he didn't have to tell her at all. Maybe they could fight their way out. If not, he'd tell her later.

"Our part is to give the news to my team leader—she'll gather her messengers—and head back to the dead zone. The warehouse we're going to tonight is just down the street from the apartment, so if you're up for it, I'm going to clean and set up chairs. But if you need to rest, you can drink your water and take a nap. I'll have help."

He nodded, but his head was already beginning to throb, and it felt like his hatband was tightening. His shirt collar was shrinking, too. They ducked into the mass of sidewalk travelers, and he followed her with his head bowed. Soldiers dotted the streets randomly, watching people. He didn't know what they were looking for, but it could be anything. He reached out and pulled the hood up on Sira's stunning hair.

They passed shop after shop, with alleyways so narrow the buildings' gutters nearly touched each other. Her slender fingers brushed the back of his hand as their arms swung naturally, and he felt a spark of temptation to grasp her hand. Buildings were peaked and edged in dark wood, and rounded display windows adorned the fronts of the shops with paned or etched glass, giving the whole street a uniform look.

They stopped at a horseshoe-shaped wooden door. Sira opened it, and a blast of warm air shot out. Wyll backed up. The thought of being in a little store of wood didn't bother him, but he couldn't handle the aroma. It rivaled the Yankee Candle Company store. Not that it was an unpleasant smell, but with his headache, the rich scents were so overpowering he couldn't see straight.

"You go ahead. I'll keep an eye out." Wyll let go of the door.

"Are you sure?" Her eyebrows raised.

He nodded and waited for the door to close before he inhaled. Taking a few steps to the side, he leaned back against the building, favoring his shoulder. He liked to people-watch. There were hardly any good places to do that anymore without someone thinking you were a creeper. His parents told him they used to go to the Great

The Clockwork Pen

Mall to watch people, but it was torn down ages ago. He liked going to Oak Park Mall sometimes; it was the only good mall around anymore. He liked Zona Rosa, too—it was an outside mall up North. But this street topped even the Plaza.

He saw so many unique and distinctive styles attributed to the same general outfits, and women wore everything from the fanciest, laciest frills to rugged pants and vests. It was like he'd gone back in time, yet it resembled a distant future involving unimaginable tech. The sky rumbled, and a few umbrellas popped open.

A soldier came to stand two doors down, and Wyll turned slightly in the other direction. He realized he was shaking his knee and turned it into a slow heel tap to look inconspicuous. Luckily, no one noticed him. His mask was not out of the ordinary. He inhaled and wondered again what made the air so fresh. Maybe the mask had some type of magnetic filter? The soldier watched all the people who passed, his glowing blue gaze landing on Wyll. So, he kept his cool and tipped his hat like Sira did. The soldier nodded and turned back to the crowd.

What was taking her so long? The door finally opened, and she stepped out. There was something different about her, but the soldier called, "Hey you! Wait. Stop."

Wyll looked around Sira to see the soldier coming their way, and his heart leaped to his throat. Wyll grabbed her arm and propelled her in front of him. He pushed off to sprint when he heard the voice say, "Gotcha."

He glanced back to see the soldier pull an unsuspecting man by the back of his hood. Wyll didn't stick around to watch. He turned back to Sira and drove her ahead.

"What took you so long?" He knew his biting comment was the result of his pounding head, aching shoulder, and the heart attack he nearly had, almost getting caught.

She ignored his attitude and smiled at him. "She had clean clothes for me. And I can't attend this meeting or lead anybody like I was."

That's what the difference was. Her eyes were lined, and she looked like she was blushing. She was the prettiest girl who'd ever cared about him. Wait, *did* she care about him? His stomach warmed at the thought. He watched her long coat sway as they walked down the alleys to the place she'd called the dead zone.

"You should rest. We have a long night ahead of us." They stood at the corner of the warehouse building, the machinery looked so grand through the glass. It must have been a sight to see when it was working. She waited for his answer.

He should tell her about the chip. *Now.* But there wasn't anything he could do, was there? Everyone had already been invited to the meeting. *Besides, what would she think of his deception?* He knew her enough to know she'd be angry, but would it hurt her? He couldn't do that. Not now. He couldn't bear to have her look at him any other way than she did at that moment. If it was up to him, she'd *never* know. He'd only accepted the king's assignment out of cowardice and the fear of more torture. He didn't want her to know any of it.

He might have found a cause to get behind, but he still needed to protect himself and his reputation—and he hated it. He was kidding everyone but himself; he was worthless. Suddenly, he felt the crash of his adrenaline rush.

"I'm going to stay here. You go ahead." He waved as she walked backward a few steps.

She waved long, slender fingers and ducked her head as she smiled. "I'll bring back dinner before we go. Have a good nap."

He watched her coat swish from side to side as she walked away, then let himself into the building. He was so focused on his self-loathing he forgot to fear the dark hallway and ran his hand along the wall, counting the beams to the door. *Twelve.* The lamp was still on, so he walked toward the yellow glow and sat on the bed. For being a big, strong football player, he was a coward. He threw his boots on the rug, but the concrete floor muted the satisfying thud. It was anticlimactic. He hung his coat and hat on the bedpost and laid his vest on the bed. The foamy fabric on his chest was making him crazy, so he removed his shirt, easing it off his shoulder.

The water beckoned to him from the bedside table, and he downed the last of the glass. *She'd better have more of that.* Falling back on the pillow, Wyll relaxed his muscles. The medication washed over him, and his limbs grew heavy. He could see how addicting it could be to feel this good. It was like a step above pain-free. It was ... bliss.

He'd always preferred to sleep in the dark before, but now he liked to know the light was on when he closed his eyes. He could open his eyes when the visions came, and they'd disappear. Somewhere between awake and asleep, Wyll dreamed of home. His father flipped through the morning paper on his laptop while his mother put eggs on his plate. *Must be Sunday, then. He joined them and sat in his place.*

His mother looked upset. She kept setting her phone down and sighing.

"What's wrong, Mom? I'm right here." Wyll tried to touch her hand but passed right through it. "What's happening?"

He felt the darkness pulling him backward. He tried even harder to grip the table, or clutch his mother, to keep from falling into the pit behind him.

"Mom!"

She turned her head and looked steadily at him, despite his panic, and said, "Men of honor will always—"

"Wyll." He heard his name called from far away, but he needed to know what his mother was trying to tell him.

"Always what, Mom?" he called. "Men of honor will always what?"

"Wyll, wake up." Sira's voice accompanied her hand on his good shoulder.

He could sense she was there, but he was angry. What was Mom trying to tell him? Men of honor lose? Or win? Or maybe they always bring a weapon or always think twice? She could have been saying anything.

The dream's hopeless anger translated into subconscious anxiety when he was fully roused. Sira sat on the bed, leaning over him, a wrinkle of concern on her forehead. He realized he was half naked and sat up. He was pretty proud of his build, but this early in the summer, he was ghostly pale, especially compared to Sira's bronzed skin.

"I need a tan," he said, attempting to lighten his own mood.

"I don't think you would stand out here. Though in the summer, we do swim sometimes." She stood up. "Are you hungry? I brought food."

He smelled spices and hot bread wafting from the dining table. "Sure. Let me put on my shirt, and I'll join you."

"Okay," she said over her shoulder, walking to the door. She hung her coat from a curved pipe on the wall. There were four of them, so he guessed they were meant to be hooks.

He knew she'd changed clothes, but he didn't realize what that meant until she removed the coat, and his mouth fell open. Her hair was done up in a flurry of curls with feathers tucked into the back, and a couple ringlets hung down to her neck. He hadn't noticed with her hood up. The woman gave her a skirt with tiers of ruffles that fell to her knee but longer in the back, showing off her boots, laced up over her ankles. She faced him, and he noticed the swell of her chest as her bronze-colored corset hugged every inch of her. A miniature jacket with spiky teal feathers rested on her shoulders, with lacey sleeves that covered her hands and fluttered when she talked. Its hem was unique and made a half circle from the clasp at her throat to her armpits, effectively framing a pair of perfect breasts.

He cleared his throat, then realized by her raised brows that she'd said something.

"You like it?" she repeated, motioning to herself.

"Yeah. It's really ... pretty." He wanted to face-palm. Was that all he could think to say?

The Clockwork Pen

It didn't seem to matter as she smiled and ducked her head. She was so cute when she was nervous. Maybe there was a possibility he could tell her about the chip without making it his fault?

She motioned for him to sit, and they faced one another. She took off fingerless leather gloves and picked up a leg, like chicken, but it was huge.

"Is this a chicken leg?"

"Yep." She bit in and chewed while she smiled.

He shrugged. They must have huge chickens around here somewhere. It kind of gave him the creeps. What if only their legs were big? He stifled a grimace because she was watching him. The chicken was delicious, juicy, and tender.

He realized he was stalling again. "I want to tell you something."

She wiped her mouth with a cloth napkin and tilted her head. "Okay?"

"I think the king might try to ambush us tonight." There. He'd said it. *Done*.

She laughed. "I doubt it. He doesn't know we're meeting, and he doesn't know where. It's no place we've met before."

His stomach fell. *Of course*. He'd have to try harder. "Sira. I mean it. We should be prepared. Have people watching with guns."

She narrowed her eyes. "Why are you telling me this now?"

"I just want you to be careful. It's dangerous, and you can't trust anyone." *That was the truth.*

She relaxed and raised a fork of baked potato in front of her. "Don't worry so much, Wyll. Don't let the Reformatory change you."

"I'm not paranoid. I'm being *cautious*. Oh geez, I sound like my mother." He rolled his eyes in mock despair, fanning his face with effeminate flair.

She snorted, which made her laugh harder. He laughed with her. A tear rolled down her cheek, and she wiped her eyes.

He didn't want her to stop, so he thought of the first joke he could remember. "Hey, why can't you hear a pterodactyl pee?"

She looked so confused. "I have no idea."

"You can't hear it because they have a *silent P*."

She burst into laughter. "Tell me another one."

"Um, what did the grape say when he was pinched?"

She sputtered. "What?"

"He didn't say anything. He just *wined*." Wyll pretended to drink with a wine glass.

"You crack me up. I only know one joke."

"What is it?" he asked.

"What's the difference between ignorance and apathy?" She sat up straight and mimed a teacher holding a book and pointing.

"What is it?"

She leaned back in the chair and relaxed, throwing her hands up. "I don't know, and I don't care."

"That's funny," he said with a chuckle.

After a few seconds of silence, she said, "So ... you know my life goal: stop at nothing to get home," she said. "But what's your goal? When you're back there—in real life?"

Wyll thought of his parents' situation and the desire to escape reality that led him here. But for some reason, running away didn't seem like the goal of a healthy, sane person anymore. "I guess it would be to start over. I thought I wanted to go somewhere else, but I miss home. I don't want to lose my family; I just want to start a new life. One where I'm not—" He stopped, realizing he was talking aloud and unable to show her how truly lost he was. But her presence made him want to be responsible, be a man. It bolstered his confidence.

"Where you aren't what?" She cocked her head to the side, and her earring dangled.

He studied it, trying to rescue himself from the unbearable truth. He didn't want to be insecure any longer, fearing everyone's intention to harm him. He struggled to find an answer that wouldn't expose himself. "I just don't want to be the jerk I always am." He felt a rush of blood heat his cheeks. It was still too real for his taste. What if she thought he was weak and stupid?

"I get it. Don't worry. I don't think you're a *total* jerk." She grinned, then lowered her voice. "I tend to hold people away from me, too. It's a coping mechanism. I don't like to lose people, and I sometimes remain cold until I'm sure of their motives before jumping in."

"You seem pretty nice to me." He smiled and took a bite.

She peered over his shoulder in thought for a moment. "Yeah. I don't know why I trusted you so easily. Maybe, maybe, I know you don't want to hurt me." A pretty blush tinged her face as well.

It felt like they were two awkward preteens having a nervous conversation, and he didn't want to add any more, so he just nodded. He worried that she might actually trust him when he was set up to betray her. What was he going to do? It would ruin everything. He'd wait and see if he could get out of this. He smiled as he racked his brain for an alternate solution.

They finished eating, and the clock sounded.

"It's time to go. We can clean this up later." Sira wiped her mouth and hands on her napkin.

Wyll pulled on his vest and grabbed his coat off the bed. Its olive-green wool was scratchy, but the leather patches on the shoulders, pockets, and trim were soft and smooth. He swung it over his shoulders and felt the beginning of an ache deep in his shoulder. He touched it and groaned.

"You drank all your water." She seemed to notice a lot of details, just like he did.

"Yeah."

The Clockwork Pen

She went to the pantry and took a flask and a bottle from the cabinet. She filled the flask with water, added a few drops of the liquid from the bottle, and then shook it. Wyll took a sip. The flask fit perfectly into the pocket inside his coat.

"Hang on," she said, reaching toward him. Wyll stopped, and she grasped his open vest with both hands. For a moment, they stood still as she clutched the material, looking through him. He tipped up her face, her wet eyes full of desperate hope that he was ... what? What was she thinking? He swam in the liquid pools of her eyes—in his imagination, learning everything about her. She stared at him like she was drowning, and he might be the breath she needed. He felt the same way. He leaned toward her, and she snapped to attention.

"Oh! Sorry." She gave her head a small shake and buttoned his vest. She lightly tapped his chest and blushed. "There you are."

"You ready?"

"Yeah. Sorry about that. With all that's going on, I'm not myself. Let's go," she said.

He flipped off the main bulb, and she switched on her cane. Pointing it forward, it lit the area around them. Sira had the handle end tucked under her arm, and she looked so cool doing it. He appreciated her and how big her personality shone. Somehow, it wasn't as dark with her around. If the king were to win, it would be Sira stuck up in her palace forever. He couldn't imagine her there—

in a fancy cage. He had to think of something else to do. *But what?*

When they reached the correct building, Wyll was surprised. It didn't look ready and waiting for a mass group of people to meet. "This is it? You sure?"

She chuckled. "Yes. I told you not to worry. We know what we're doing."

It didn't make him feel any better. They entered the building that had become storage at some point. There were tarp-covered crates and who-knows-what piled against the far wall. The thing he didn't see was all the dust he usually saw on the floors. He didn't spot any of the chairs, either. "Someone swept," he commented.

"Yes." She looked impressed that he'd noticed. "No dust, no footprints."

Sira led him to a door and a concrete staircase with red lights. They descended one level, two, three. What could be down here? He didn't like being underground and descending. He could feel the walls closing in on him. She opened a door on the left, and lights burned brightly from inside.

They entered a large conference room. Tall enough for Wyll to forget he was nearly in a cave. He started to sweat. Terrible things were going to happen here. They walked through the aisles of chairs and stepped up on the platform where Indigo leaned on the podium, talking to a few people. A great blackboard stood to the side, and colored fabrics hung on the walls. About twenty to thirty people milled about, pinballing between conversations.

"Hey, kids," Indigo said.

"Um, I wanted to know if you have a contingency plan? For Sira?" Wyll stood straight.

"What?" He turned to them directly.

Sira said, "He's gotten a little paranoid from you-know-where, and he's worried about an ambush."

"You feel she is in danger?" Indigo asked.

"I do." Wyll crossed his arms.

"Oh, come on, you guys. Nothing is going to happen." Sira dropped her shoulders and threw her hands up.

"Sira?" Malynda called from a table set with coffee and strange pots of something.

"Coming." Sira left to help her.

"Do you have any details about your feeling? Any idea what to expect?" Indigo whispered.

"No." Wyll knew he should just tell Indigo about the chip, but he couldn't wreck what he had going with Sira. So, he said, "When I was in the Reformatory, I heard the king say he would attack when the Resistance was in a large group."

"Does Sira know this?"

"I told her what I thought, but she doesn't believe me." Wyll watched her talking with two other women. She was so at ease talking to everyone. They all liked her; it was obvious.

"She still believes." Indigo looked over his shoulder.

"Believes what?"

"In innocence, and second chances, in lives that go on forever, and that nothing bad happens to the good people … in her father." Indigo looked into Wyll's eyes. "There's nothing wrong with it, but she's going to get really hurt one of these days by trusting the wrong person."

Wyll felt like he'd been kicked in the gut. He was the person who was going to hurt her, and he didn't want to. He wanted the chip out. Maybe he could find a tool to dig it out and throw it somewhere. Then, the king wouldn't be able to find either one of them. He made an excuse to Indigo and slipped out the door as more people arrived.

He checked the other floors, pointing incoming Resistance members to the right place. He'd earned their trust by getting shot the night before. His need to find something useful increased, but each floor had hallways and locked doors like offices. Standing in the hallway, he kicked a door open, but the room was empty. He went up to the warehouse. The tarps dropped dust everywhere, and he noticed his footprints. He wiped his feet off and brushed his hands on his pants. He saw a huddled couple enter the building, and he moved out of sight.

In the back, a rusty old toolkit sat hidden under a corner of the tarp. It looked like something that would have come from his grandpa's garage. Either the king created it, or it really was old and metal, covered in chipped army green paint with rusted hinges. It held a turn-crank hand drill, a flat pencil, and a metal tape measure, along with myriad wrenches and screwdrivers.

He pulled out a long, thin screwdriver that wasn't as dirty and sank down where he was in the soft light from a high window. He pressed the used edge of the screwdriver into his skin, but it only pushed the chip in the other direction. He tried gouging himself with it but barely broke the skin. Even when he firmly pushed the screwdriver into the bloody scratch and dragged, it didn't do anything, and *damn, it hurt!*

Holding the chip in place with a finger, he tried to use the other fingers to poke with the screwdriver. How could a piece of paper cut his skin just fine, but this thin tool was just mangling his wrist? The area was bruising, his skin was red and scratched, and he had a small bloody patch the size of a pencil eraser. If only he could get that spot to open enough to pry the corner out, he could squeeze it through. But it didn't look like that was going to happen. It was too deep, so he pushed in harder, gritting his teeth. A bubble of blood covered the screwdriver's head, and he was encouraged, but it didn't get him anywhere. He was still worrying the flesh when Sira came upstairs.

"Wyll? Wyll, where are you?" She sounded panicked, so he put down the tool, pulled his sleeve down, and stepped into the open.

"Yeah?"

"There you are. I've been looking for you everywhere. What are you doing?" She looked around wildly, but there was nothing to see but tarp.

"I was checking for other exits." Why hadn't he thought of that earlier? Now, he wished he'd actually done that.

"Very smart." She linked her arm with his and squeezed. "It's time to start. We must hurry."

He placed his clammy hand over hers. He felt sick. *What have I done?*

Chapter Nine
STARRY-EYED BETRAYAL

Wyll perched on the edge of his chair at the very end of the front row, near the place Sira stood on stage. His knee bounced like his heel was a spring, but he did nothing to stop the motion; it held him in place. He was hoping at this point that the soldiers wouldn't shoot Sira when they attacked, and perhaps she'd tell the Resistance to lay down their arms and— No. *She wouldn't.*

Small fans blew through the stuffy room, making the extra lanterns' flames flicker. Indigo spoke with a fancy microphone wired to a speaker box on the table. Wyll kept running scenarios through his mind, and they all ended with him sacrificing himself to save her. It was a great idea, in theory. He wanted to, but as much as he'd love to be that guy, he knew he couldn't do it. Not when it came down to survival. He couldn't deny the pull he felt toward her, though, and he *needed* to see what would happen. He wanted to know her, inside and out. He wanted to hear her thoughts, touch her face, inhale her scent... He shook himself. Nothing would happen between them if they all got captured tonight. He growled internally.

Paying attention to the speeches and pleas for ideas or solutions was impossible. Wyll heard a high-pitched squeal from the microphone and barely stopped himself from jumping out of his chair. He settled back on the edge of it. As far as he knew, there was only one way into this room: the door they came through in the back of the room. He couldn't see any more of it as undulating fabric blew against the walls, making waves of patterned silk flow in gentle ripples.

Indigo took suggestions from members, and Sira wrote them on the board. Wyll noticed several people had created "inventions" to somehow help them overturn the monarchy. They all wanted to be the hero. He chuckled wryly. People really were the same no matter where you went.

He swiveled his toe and tapped his heel rapidly against the leg of his chair. Every time the door opened, Wyll's head spun back in panic. Sira smiled at him from the front of the room and lifted her shoulders, mouthing the word *breathe* as she noticeably relaxed her body. He grinned at her, so proud of her for standing up there. He wouldn't speak in front of this many people. There had to be at least a hundred people in the room—though he wasn't great at guessing crowds. He'd been forced through a semester of debate and completely bombed it in front of the biggest audience ever before he could drop that class. *Public speaking.* He shuddered.

He'd pay attention when *she* spoke, but right now, it was some really tall and skinny dude who reminded Wyll of a train engineer. Maybe it was the hat. And all the black streaks on his skin. Well, at least that guy would have good camo later. They'd all be needed in the square tonight. They still had to rescue the people after this. He'd forgotten. Maybe that's when the king would attack. He relaxed, knowing the king couldn't know everyone was together *right now*. He'd wait patiently by the square for them to show up en masse. Finally, Wyll leaned back in his chair.

That's when the door swung open, crashing into the wall. Soldiers poured into the room, shouting directions Wyll couldn't hear over the screaming. The people rose and swung to face the intruders, many aiming weapons toward the door. Wyll's arm was nearly pulled from its socket, his shoulder screaming in pain as he looked behind him. Both Indigo and Malynda tried to pull Sira back, but her hands were wrapped around his bicep. As if it all worked in slow motion, he turned toward her when the electric lights went out and pushed Sira toward the couple.

"I'm behind you. I promise."

Indigo slipped behind the giant chalkboard, and Wyll understood its purpose. In the lamplight, the guards rounded people into a circle as Wyll disappeared behind the board and into a slit in the fabric. Indigo looked at Wyll and pointed over his head toward the corner.

"Sira," the voice of one soldier called out.

Sira spun on her heel, but Wyll grabbed her by the arms and clamped a hand over her mouth, shaking his head sternly at her. All the people got quiet. No one said anything.

"Princess Sira, we must bring you in if you are here. If you do not answer, you suffer the fate of those around you." The voice lacked emotion of any kind. It was a fact. Wyll heard the sound of guns powering up—many guns.

Sira opened her mouth, and Wyll wrapped his arm around her head and covered it with both hands. She struggled. He didn't want to hurt her. He wanted to protect her.

"Answer now, Princess, or die with your followers."

Die? Wyll wasn't sure what happened first. Sira started screaming under his hand, and Indigo pulled Wyll's arm because he held Sira. At the same time, gunfire rang throughout the room. He didn't know whose side started it, but the entire room exploded. Wyll wrapped his arms around Sira's struggling body and picked her up. He followed Indigo out a metal door leading to another set of staircases—one staircase rose from the landing, and the other set descended. Wyll shut the door behind him and leaned against it.

Sira sat on the second step, crying into her hands. Indigo paced the platform, running a hand through his shiny shoulder-length hair, which had fallen out of its tie. Malynda leaned against the wall. She had a hand on her chest like she was trying to calm her heart. They were still as they listened to pings and thuds. People screamed. Some were battle cries, some sorrowful, some painful, or shouts of anger.

When it was quiet, Sira whispered, "I need to check on them."

Wyll stayed flat against the door. "They could still be in there or calling for help. We need to go up these stairs and get you out of here."

"Don't you get it? I'm not the one in danger here." She threw her hands up and paced before him. "I can't believe he's turned this cruel. But he asked for me first. He wouldn't have them shoot the people if I was there. He wouldn't. I could have stepped out and saved all those people's lives."

"And then what? You would go back to the castle under your father's thumb. Do you think he would let you out again? Do you really think they would've let the rest of us go?"

"Well, they said—"

"They said they were taking you back; nothing about the rest of us." Wyll's pulse was still thumping against his neckband.

Indigo laid a hand on Sira's shoulder. "He's not the same as he used to be. The pen has changed him. I'm sorry, but Wyll is right."

"How did he know?" Her eyes narrowed as she thought, and she tapped her pointed little chin.

"Wyll said when he was in the Reformatory, he overheard the king plotting to invade when we met in one place. Right?" Indigo looked toward him, and he felt Sira's gaze as well.

"Why didn't you tell me this?" she asked.

"I just, um. I thought … ah. I thought I told you. I mean, I don't know. I just remembered. Today." *Wyll, you're an idiot.*

"Oh… You forgot about it? From the trauma? I guess I get that." She huffed out an angry laugh. "I thought you just didn't tell me. That's as bad as lying to me."

"I wouldn't do that." *Shit.* He couldn't tell her about the chip now. She'd hate him. What was he going to do? *Shit. Shit. Shit.* Okay, he would play it safe as long as he could. They wouldn't have another meeting this big, not after this. Most of them had been present. Maybe that would satisfy the king. Who would rescue the people in the square? They didn't have enough people to storm the square now, and they couldn't afford to lose any more.

But once the king realized Wyll and Sira weren't captured, what if he used the chip to find her? What if he knew where her apartment was?

"Hey, guys? What if none of our secret places are safe?" Wyll's brows raised.

"He's right," Malynda joined the conversation. She didn't usually say much but listened intently and studied people like she was completely invested in what they were saying. "We don't know how Rozam's men found this place, and we can't guess what else he knows. There's a chance you won't be safe in the apartment."

Indigo wrapped his arm around Malynda's corseted waist. "It's okay, my love. I know a place where they'll be safe. Leave it to me."

Malynda opened her arms for Sira and hugged the girl to her chest. "You're too special for this place, little Sira."

They had an emotional girl-moment and cried and whatnot. Wyll took a second to let his neck relax and dropped his chin to his chest. The pain was creeping up his neck and down his arm. The scorching energy around the bullet nearly cauterized the skin as it went straight through his body. He had a finger-sized divot in his shoulder now. The flask called to him, and he sipped from it—enough to take the edge off. It was beautifully comforting, and he didn't feel guilty anymore.

The foursome walked quickly to the apartment for their belongings; Sira had extra clothes in a trunk near the bathroom. Wyll grabbed his clothes and the medicine from the cabinet while Indigo gathered bedding, and Malynda packed the picnic basket on wheels.

They slipped into the night, and the scent of rain weighed heavy in the air. Malynda proudly pushed the basket like it was a baby carriage in front. They traveled the outskirts of town to get to the West side. Wyll and Sira carried bags, and Indigo followed with his arms full of blankets and pillows. The night was inky, and despite the cloud cover in lieu of a moon, an animal howled in the distance. When the roads turned to gravel, Wyll listened to the crunch of their boots, inhaling the sweet fragrance of freshly cut grass. Crickets sang around him. He momentarily wondered if they were also clockwork but decided it didn't matter. It felt like a chilly fall night at his grandparents' farm. He smiled.

They passed fields and fields. Poor Indigo's arms shook as they approached a small farmhouse with shingled gables and a stained-glass sunrise over the door. When they knocked on the door, someone flipped on the light, and the sun lit up. A face appeared in the frame of a screen door. "Do you youngsters know what time it is?"

Indigo stepped into the light. "Hi, Mr. Tungsten. Might we use your barn for a few nights?"

"For you, son, it's no problem. Just don't touch my equipment." The front door closed while a nearby cricket made a racket.

"This way." Indigo walked off the edge of the porch and around to the side yard. They passed a chicken coop and saw the barn standing like a red sentinel in a landscape of small green plants, gray in the dim light. It was mostly a bloody color at night, with a pulley reaching out from the peak. The open loft was stuffed with hay. They turned a big gear that worked as a door handle and entered the barn, flipping on the two hanging bulbs. Shadows clung to the corners, and dark shapes shifted behind the dirty, white-painted stalls. Wyll jumped as a monstrous kitten brushed up against his leg, tiptoeing around on its furry claws. He pushed it away with his foot, but it came right back.

"You'll be safest in the loft. Darling, won't you set up their bedding?" Malynda blew a kiss to Indigo, flipped the levers on the basket to ground it, and then opened the table.

Peanut butter sandwiches filled them up. Malynda had put them together while they packed. The sticky texture glued Wyll's tongue to the roof of his mouth. "These need jelly."

"What's a jelly?" Malynda asked.

"Are you serious? You don't have jelly? It's this gooey fruit in a jar that you spread on toast or peanut butter sandwiches. I can't believe you guys don't have it," he said.

"I think there are many things the king didn't make just because he didn't like them in the real world. Like, I remember toy stores. I remember miles of shelves with bright colors, textures, smells, and toys that made noise. But when we moved here, he said they had no toy stores. I was older when I figured it out." Sira shrugged one shoulder. "By then, it didn't matter anymore, but it made me wonder what else I'm missing?"

Indigo returned, his black coat flapping against his legs, and whispered in Malynda's ear. She laughed lightly, tapped his chest playfully, and then spoke into his ear. Her dress in grape satin matched the flowers on her hat. They were a striking couple, long and lean, fancy and refined, one pale and one olive. He wrapped his arm around her waist and tucked his fingers in her skirt's hip pocket. She brushed her whiskers on his cheek, and they laughed.

Sira watched them with starry eyes. Wyll knew he was on borrowed time. He watched her, drinking her in. Her hair gleamed when she stood under the light. He smiled. He could imagine it might not feel like imprisonment to care for someone else more than himself—for her, anyway—to sacrifice oneself for the other's good. The thought made him want to wrap Sira in a possessive embrace. He imagined protecting her, holding her... The scent of horse manure kind of put a damper on his libido, though. The mood wasn't right in the barn. As a girl, she would probably be averse to all this dirt and also upset about the meeting. Best to stamp out any hopes for now.

"We'll be back tomorrow morning to figure out how this happened." Indigo took Malynda's hand. "Ready, my love?"

The Clockwork Pen

"Yes." She smiled at him. They were treading a fine line between being a #couplesgoal and being nauseating.

When they were gone, Sira turned to him. Her cheeks glowed bright pink. "Should we, um, go up?" She pointed to the ladder.

He chuckled. She was adorable when she was nervous. "Sure. Lead the way."

Indigo had piled hay near the open loft window and covered it in a downy spread and quilts. It looked impossibly soft. He went to the side of their bed and shucked his outer clothing till he stood in his shirt and trousers. He wondered what she was going to sleep in. He peeked over his shoulder to see her standing on the other side, looking down at the bedding in dismay.

"What's wrong?"

She pointed to her outfit. "I didn't know I was coming here tonight. All my clothes are formal."

He unbuttoned his shirt and handed it to her. "I won't look."

Wyll turned and stared at the boards making up the barn walls, then the slanted beams that rose higher. A screech outside caught his attention, and he looked out through the loft opening. Hay scattered out and fluttered to the ground, twirling like helicopter blades. He heard the sound again and realized it was the squeaking of the barn door in the wind. It gave him the creeps. The yard below was mostly dirt and gravel, everything dark and yet moving. Chickens still clucked about in their pen, and Wyll heard other animals nearby.

"Okay. I'm good."

The lights from below made a soft glow in the loft, the moon lighting their bed. Sira stood in his oversized, ruffly shirt, wringing the lace between her fingers. The soft white material exposed the delicate skin of her open neckline and hung to her mid-thigh. He had to swallow twice to get past the dryness in his throat. With her hairpins removed, shining tresses tumbled down around her shoulders. She studied him like she'd never seen a shirtless guy before. Maybe she hadn't. Her curiosity made his core flare with heat. She still wore white stockings tied above her knees with a pink satin ribbon. He could feel the burn all through his belly.

She scanned his eyes and then glanced away. "Sorry. I didn't mean to make you uncomfortable."

"It's no problem. I'm fine." He *involuntarily* flexed his six-pack. At least, that's what he told himself. He liked that he affected her. It made him feel invincible—like he could jump out of the loft opening and fly. He sat down to remove his boots and looked up. As she crossed to the sheets, with the light behind her, he could see the outline of her curves like a silhouette of the perfect hourglass. He took a deep breath, and she ducked under the covers. It was cold outside, but the barn loft was warm and thick with the musky odor of animals from below them.

He slid under the quilt, and she chuckled nervously. The bed had appeared so comfortable he'd wanted to hold Sira in its downy softness. But the hay poked him mercilessly through the bedspread. He shifted, trying to stay on his side, but the blankets weren't much bigger than the two of them. She held on tight as he moved, trying to tamp down the hay.

"It's poking you, too?" she asked.

"Yeah. You okay?"

"Sure. I mean, I'm here, right? I'm glad you're okay. We both could have..." Her face crumpled. "All those poor people."

She might as well have stabbed him in the heart with a hot poker. The whole debacle was his fault. He didn't want to be a useless coward; he wanted to be the man of his imagination—the man of her dreams. But he recognized the irony as he desperately wished to be someone Sira deserved when relationships usually required trust he didn't have. Only he was the deceiver this time. Guilt lay like a heavy lead blanket across his body.

She continued to cry softly, and he gently touched her shoulder. When she scooted forward to press against him, he wrapped his arms around her body in a tight, comforting embrace. She sobbed into his shoulder, her bent arms tucked between them, and her fingertips rested on his pecs like bumblebees lighting on flowers. He pulled her in, his guilt a filter, making it bittersweet and ironic. He hated being the cause of her pain, and he tamped down his rising anger as she grieved.

He hesitated before touching her incredibly soft hair. It curled around her shoulders, laying over his pillow, and laced through his fingers. He exhaled at the feel of the silky texture. "Shhh. It's okay. It'll be over soon. We'll figure it out."

She sniffed, coughed, then took a few deep breaths. "You're right. I'm being hopeless again. I'm sorry ... I do that sometimes." She looked into his eyes, the blue glaciers melting into a shallow sea. "Do you?"

"What?"

"Ever give up because things look hopeless?"

"Yeah." He consumed the reality of his circumstances. He had to tell her. *But maybe not.* Now that the king had attacked, he didn't need to know their location anymore. Wyll was off the hook. If things remained the king's fault, she would never need to know it was him. Wyll swept a curl from her shoulder.

She stared at him with all the hope in the world. He wanted her in every way. Like a popcorn bag that was finally hot enough to start popping, his desire increased and built on itself. He kissed her lips softly and pulled back. He didn't want to overwhelm her or— She wrapped her hands around his neck and pulled him back to her mouth. He chuckled and kissed her again.

"I'm glad you understand." She sniffed again. "Sometimes I think there's something wrong with me. I'm so emotional. And I'm the only one who can't seem to find happiness here. It's like I'm defective. I mean, I don't think clockwork people can have mental illness; it would have to be a program, I think. Not sure how that works, but no one else seems to cry for no reason or think themselves into outer space, longing for something they know is there but can't touch. I thought I was crazy—that maybe it was genetic—but you feel it too, don't you?"

"Feel what?"

"That pull toward something better, far away." She squinted, looking at the ceiling.

"Yeah. I get it. I miss the real world now that it's out of reach. Not that I want to stay home forever, but I haven't made a concrete plan for my life yet. Before, all I could think about was hiding—no, leaving for some far place where I could create a new life. It's got to be greener on the other side, right?" He felt like he was sitting across the table from his prom date's father. His mom had asked him the same type of question months ago.

When he was little, he'd thought he might grow up to be an astronomer with a huge telescope, finding new worlds. He snorted. He'd managed to find a new world without trying.

"I don't even know my options," she said. "When I finally get there."

"You could do anything," he whispered, wrapping a tendril of hair behind her ear. She shivered. He bent closer to her ear. "What do you want to do?"

"I want—I want—" She leaned toward him and whispered against his lips, "For so long, my main goal has been getting out of here. Now I don't know *what* I want." She closed the gap, melding them together, lips and breath. She leaned over and kissed the bandage on his shoulder, whispering, "But I have an idea."

His blood was so hot it was evaporating from his pores. He was instantly in a sweet cinnamon fog, and he was going to rip that shirt off in about two seconds unless he could distract himself. "What—ah, are you trained for anything?" He worked on breathing steadily. "Do you have experience?"

"Experience?" She raised her brows at the double entendre. "Maybe I could be a doctor? Or a manager of some sort? I like helping people. At the castle, I take requests from people who need help and try to find their solutions. Though most of the time, I do random tasks my father gives me to keep the castle running properly." She sneered, "Keylin calls me Princess Problem-Solver."

He chuckled, working to reign in his desire. "I like that. You could be a social worker. They do something like that."

"I'll look into it when we get out of here. You said everything's still in our house?"

"Yeah. It's all covered by sheets, but it's there. Your clothes won't fit." He laughed. "We could just tell everyone you moved back. What about your father?"

"I don't know," she said. "I can't imagine him letting me leave—especially not coming with me—but he doesn't want to go. He associates the human world with pain. He got into some shady deals before my mom died. Right before I was born, he came across the pen, and I think it involved him with some ... unsavory people."

"Tell me how it happened?"

"How she died?"

"All of it," he said softly.

She posted her elbow and looked at the ceiling beams. She filled out his shirt better than he did. "My mom was always kind of sick, I guess. She was born with a chromosomal disease. She'd inherited a lot of money when her parents died, and my father had never had enough. He loved living like a king with their new money. They bought the house, and when her medical bills started draining the money, they paid it off. But the money kept dwindling. Mom was really sick when she was pregnant but wouldn't take the treatments because they might hurt me. That's when things got bad for her, and they found the cancer. Dad worked extra shifts to cover treatments until his company said they couldn't afford to pay it anymore, then he got involved in things that bothered her."

"Did she tell you that?"

"No. He did. Anyway, back then, Dad went out every night. He told my mom he would fix everything—I don't think it could have been anything legal. Once he won the pen set, he learned how to use it and discovered how to make his own dimension, so he made a world that we could escape to. He made doctors and gadgets to help her, but nothing worked, and Mom was almost too weak to go back and forth often. I remember hearing them argue a few times when I was little. We lived there most of the time. When I was starting preschool, I brought home a cold, and it compromised her immune system. They brought a hospital bed to the house."

"I'm sorry. You know it wasn't your fault." Wyll brushed her hair back.

"I guess. A few times, big men in vests showed up at the house looking for Dad, and Mom said he wasn't there. He was always so afraid. Mom fought with him about buying a gun. And then she didn't make it, so we moved here to stay." She was quiet, and Wyll waited patiently for her to continue.

"To Dad, the real world is just a mess of problems. It's full of fear, debt, and loss. By the time she was gone, Sepherra had been up and running for years. He made the world clean and bright for her. He made doctors to fix her, and he made a world for me that would never hurt me. But it hurts every day that I'm stuck here. It's not *real*."

He squeezed her shoulder. "It feels pretty real to me."

She chuckled. "I'm one of the few real things here. He just wants to protect me from a world he can't control. But putting me in a prison that he *can* control takes away all my choices. It makes him as bad as the men who forced him out of his own life."

"I wonder if those guys in the house knew your dad. Maybe that's what they were looking for." It made sense to Wyll.

"I don't like thinking there's someone in my house. What if we move in and they come back?"

"We'll take care of that when the time comes. Right now, we have a whole separate set of problems." He wondered how the Resistance was going to work. Obviously, large group meetings were not feasible, but maybe they didn't require as many as they thought. What they really needed was someone on the inside to tell them the king's schedule and weaknesses. Or find a way to use someone already on the king's side, as the king had done to him. "What's the original plan you guys came up with?"

"If I could have him teach me how to use the pen, I could—"

"No," he cut her off.

"Excuse me?" She looked at him with her brows raised and gave her head a little shake full of attitude.

"No. You *can't* learn the pen. You know what it does. Besides, he'll never let you use it if he knows it makes him crazy—"

She put her hand out. "That's just it. He doesn't believe it's the pen, even though everyone else can see it. He researched the pen when he got it, and one article said that the price to use it was your life. He assumed it meant he'd die early, so he uses it as often as he can, never knowing how much time he has. But it obviously takes pieces of his mind."

"I don't want to risk it. Don't worry. We'll think of something else." He spoke almost as much to himself as to her. "It's going to work out. No sense worrying about it now. There's nothing we can do tonight."

"Right. Nothing we could do…" She looked up at him in the moonlight, and her eyes glowed like liquid pools of cyan. She lifted her chin and watched him through half-closed lids.

He leaned toward her slowly and stopped when their lips were a breath apart. He smiled. She whispered against his lips, "Do you feel it?"

"What?"

"My fingertips are tingling." Her lips curled into a delicious smile.

He stared at her. "You are fearless and beautiful, but what could you see in me?" He suddenly really wanted to know.

"I didn't like you at all at first." She gave a throaty chuckle. "But you endured the Reformatory and don't whine about it, though I know it still affects you. You're sensitive, dependable, you make me laugh … and you think what I have to say is important. You're not too bad on the eyes,"—she ran her fingers over his shoulder and down his arm—"and you're here and real."

Wyll held her to his chest.

"What's home like?" she asked wistfully. "Is it a bad place? Is that why you always wanted to hide? My father told me horrible stories, but I don't know if they were true or if he just wanted me to hate it as much as he does."

"They were probably true. It's a mess out there. But I figure it has to be better somewhere new, where I can start over."

"Why?" She peered up at him.

"It's a long story."

"If it's a true story, I want to hear it."

Wyll warred with himself. Exposing his pain—his failures—would make him defenseless to her. He couldn't risk it.

Instead, he ducked his head and pressed his lips to hers, gliding along them with long, slow caresses. He rolled forward, pulling her lips with his, and their mouths melted together, working with and against each other. His lips traveled across her cheek, and he nipped her ear lobe. She gasped as he continued down the side of her neck, drawing small circles on the back of her neck with his fingers. Her hands gripped his biceps as he leaned over her. He flexed his arms in her grip and felt her fingers tighten around him. Power rushed through his veins, and he was intensely aware of how delicate she felt in his hands. He was every hero in every movie he'd ever watched, and she was the quintessential princess.

She allowed his exploration and gave a little sigh of pleasure. He pulled back a little to give her some room to initiate or gather her control. Her shy reaction to him reminded him that she was new to all this. He'd been on enough dates ending at remote locations around Olathe Lake, parked in a steamy-windowed car, to impress most girls, but he didn't want to overwhelm her. He peered into her eyes. "Is this happening too fast?"

"I don't know. It does seem fast, but then, it feels like it's taken forever to finally happen." She lowered her gaze, appearing embarrassed.

"Didn't you *ever* have a boyfriend here? Surely, they've asked you…" He pushed up and faced her on his side, his head held up by his hand.

"No," she said in a tiny voice, propped up on her elbow. "None of them are human. They can't have children at all. The last thing I wanted was to hurt someone. But I know what I want—and the future I dream of—and I can't fall in love with someone who can never make me happy. And I wouldn't be satisfied taking a clockwork person back to the real world. For years, I dreamed of a mystery man, a human without a face—I hoped the first person I met would be someone my age. I knew it was unlikely, but I hoped. I couldn't have imagined a person like you. I think you hide more than you know. And I want to know more."

"I don't mind being first in line." He smiled, slowly running his finger down the slope of her petite nose. "You're pretty great, too."

She laid her forehead on his chest. "Thanks. A few tried over the years, but I never considered them."

"Did it cause problems?" He inhaled her scent and kissed her hair above her ear.

She shrugged her shoulder. "One guy in the Resistance got pretty mad when he thought I rejected him."

"Did you reject him?"

"I didn't feel like I did because I wanted to be his friend, but it wasn't romantic for me," she said. "I can't help the way I feel."

"Anyone I've met?" He didn't know many of the names from the meeting.

"No. Jett is pretty busy in the castle staff…" They were silent for a moment, their bodies close.

"How was your life here? Were you happy as a child, or did you always want to leave?" he asked. He wanted to know everything about her, picture it in his mind. He'd seen the photo of her as a child, and he could imagine her.

"I was a carefree child. I had everything a girl could want in life—a big home with room to play, an adoring father, a pesky stepmother,"—she chuckled—"a best friend like a sister, and a bedroom suite full of my own things. The castle staff loved me and would just laugh and shake their heads when I careened down the halls in my stocking feet on the freshly waxed floors or when I would sneak treats while the kitchen staff was busy. Then I'd eat half and tease the milgen in the moat below with the rest. I always sang loudly through the family wing, and no one ever told me to stop. There was a phase where I loved to pester the staff with jokes during work hours. I had all I needed and mostly all I wanted… Except what I desired most—my mother."

"That sounds like you." He smiled softly and traced her face with his finger. "So, when did you decide to go?"

"When I discovered my castle was a cage and that it hurt others." She frowned. "It was both. I needed to be free, and I really wanted to help."

"Did something happen that changed your mind?"

Sira smiled softly. "When I was around thirteen years old, I noticed a change in my father. He became irrational in arguments, rash in judgments, and unstable in his moods. He forgot things and yelled at the family, accusing us of things we were unaware of. The more distracted he got, the more he insisted on protecting me like a small child. Naturally, I recoiled; I felt my independence slipping away. I vaguely remembered the old house and my bedroom upstairs—"

"It's yellow," he said with an enthusiastic grin. "I saw it. With little pieces of white furniture." He put his thumb and finger an inch apart.

"Right." She smiled at him like they had a secret, and he kissed her softly. Slowly covering her mouth with his, sealing their mutual feeling of desire. Slowly, he pulled back.

"Go on," he said with a chuckle. She'd lost concentration.

"Whoa." She exhaled. "Um... I still remembered my mother in the real world, where she was happiest. I remembered restaurants, toy stores, and going to early school with my friends. At first, we lived in both worlds; then, after Mom was gone, Dad had no reason to stay in that world. But when I asked my father about going back there, he would grow angrier each time, insisting that we were better off in the world he'd created for me. But I wanted to go home."

"That's the cage. But who was it hurting? Is that when the rebellion formed?"

"Pretty much." She looked excited for a second but then drooped. "It's a long story." She yawned. "To be short, I had a doctor who took care of my mother at the end, and he was my friend. My father was paranoid about my health when I went through—" She stopped and blushed deeply.

He was intrigued. "What?" He had a feeling he knew, and he grinned at her. "When you went through what?"

She realized he was teasing and poked his arm, her smile shooting to the side. "Puberty. There. I said it. Sheesh. Anyway, that's when my Mom got diagnosed with whatever illness she had, leading to bone cancer. So, Dad was crazy about my health. Well, when I was thirteen, Dr. Warton—I really liked him so much; he was like a father to me—anyway, he gave my father a perfect report of all my numbers and functions. But a few weeks after that, I got sick with a bad respiratory infection, and my father was livid at my bedside while I was burning with fever and coughing. He felt like Dr. Warton had tricked him or given me bad medicine and decided someone had to pay." She frowned.

He yawned and said, "Who got hurt?"

She slowly closed and opened her eyes. "My father had Dr. Warton's wife and child dismantled. My nurse told me. She was one of the first group that thought the pen was making my father insane … and I joined them."

He pulled her close. "We should get some sleep," he spoke against her temple.

"Yeah." Her breath warmed his chest.

"Goodnight," he whispered, but she was already gone.

The Clockwork Pen

He slept on his side, holding her tightly, his cheek against her forehead. A faint ticking sound came from the chip in his arm near his ear. It sounded like a ticking clock—a countdown, but a countdown from his deception to his demise.

He dreamt of home. Flashes of the dining table, his dad's elbow on the recliner clicking through channels, his mom at the table with her coffee and a book, and his messy bedroom floor all passed before his eyes.

He sat on his bed, looking at the floor.

"You should clean this up," his mother said from the doorway.

"But I know where everything is," he said in a challenging voice designed to drive her away.

"You must make good decisions, Wyll. It will be more important as life goes on." She leaned against the jamb.

"Yeah, yeah. I know, Mom. Dad's a broken record." His father was an engineer, like Derec's. He thought Wyll should have his life plan diagrammed by now since he had his life planned by age eighteen. In his eyes, Wyll had six months to make something out of himself. Up till now, he'd only been a disappointment.

Wyll had skipped Boy Scouts. He didn't know how to start a fire with sticks, tie a square knot, or sail a boat. He couldn't anchor a tent or hunt for food. To his father's generation, he was useless.

"He just wants to see you live up to your potential. He believes in you, in what you could be. When you get older and figure things out, it will get better. I promise." His mother came over to the bed and hugged him. She smelled like flowers; he inhaled.

"I'm trying, Mom."

Wyll felt a sharp pain in his back. He looked at his mother, and her fingernails dripped his blood. Why had she scratched him? He instantly recognized his dark cell in the Reformatory, and a guard was poking him through the bars with a long spear. It pierced the skin of his back, raking across his flesh. He reached for his mom, her voice trailing away as another lance shot through his back, pulling to the side. He screamed, but somehow knew it was a dream and no one was coming to help him.

The darkness closed in, and he heard his mom say, "A man of honor will always be the hero, Wyll. Do the right thing..."

The next spear cut so deep he cried out.

Wyll heard himself scream as he jolted awake.

Chapter Ten
NEW WORLD, NEW CASTLE

A knock resonated from the door of King Rozam's circular office, interrupting him. "Yes?" he called, his voice gruff with impatience. "Enter."

A man in a staff uniform stepped inside the door, appearing paler than when he'd left. He held his hands in front of him with a frown. Rozam couldn't remember what he'd sent the man to do, and confusion frustrated him.

"Well?" The king growled. "Don't just stand there. You are wasting my time."

The man cleared his throat. "She wasn't with them, Your Highness." *Ah yes. I remember.*

Rozam stood abruptly behind his desk, and the man shrank back. "You're sure?"

The man nodded.

"Hmmm. She was there. I assumed she and the boy would be taken with the resisters. Never mind. I will know where he is, and she's safe enough. You may go. Report to Orren; they'll need help in the Reformatory." He waved toward the door.

The man grimaced but nodded. "Yes, Your Highness." He backed from the room and pulled the door shut.

"I told you." Rozam's wife tossed him a gloating smile from her seat across from him.

"I don't need your commentary, my *dear*." Rozam crossed the room to a floating counter holding his squid-shaped version of a French press and poured a fresh cup of Sepherran coffee from a tentacle. He loved this blend. It had the texture and heady aroma of black tea and the flavor of rich Columbian coffee. His mind wandered to the mountains of Columbia and envisioned rows of bent workers collecting beans from leafy, green—

"She's becoming trouble. My sources say she is rooted in that Resistance. We should—"

"You forget yourself," Rozam boomed, and she shrank into her chair, patting her elaborate coiffure. *She has no business coaching me on my daughter. Where is Sira? She's grown into such a strong and loving girl. She'll love my plans.*

"All I'm saying, my love," she started again, sitting upright and crossing her dainty booted legs, "is that she's too wild for her own good. She has your adventurous personality." She smiled. "You would be right to assign her a punishment." At his scowl, she continued, "Nothing that will break her spirit, of course, but let her know her place is here."

He returned to his seat in the opulent room of nautical-themed furnishings. The corners of his mouth sunk in as he contemplated her statement. "Not a bad idea. Then you can keep a better eye on her." He scratched the red whiskers of his goatee, struggling to keep his mind on track. "This Resistance has everyone disconcerted and wary. Under my instructions to discover the members and stamp out the defective, my leaders have scheduled meeting after meeting with ideas and solutions. It's too tiring to be worried about Sira. And I've got some new ideas for another creation."

Her eyes lit up. "What creation?"

He laughed—a bit maniacally. "Something for you, my dear. And Sira. Something new—and big—to excite everyone and take her mind off that damned 'other' world."

She clapped diminutive hands, gloved in wine-red cotton with pearl buttons to match her skirt and hair ribbons lined with pearl strands. Her smile was genuine, and times like this reminded Rozam how happy he was in his own dimension—dominion—domicile? He could barely remember that horrid place he'd come from. His painful memories swirled in a black void of empty thoughts and flashes of his previous life that had ceased to make sense.

When he created his wife, she was made to be a good listener, a supportive partner, and a creative bedmate, but he hadn't made her to be a mother. He didn't want her to take the place of Sira's mother. No one could replace Giselle, and he knew that Sira would never have accepted a clockwork woman as a mother. She had some superstitious notions. Yet lately, she'd been admonishing him regarding the "humanness" of his subjects and her aversion to his decisions to disassemble the wayward rebellious characters. She just didn't understand. *Children rarely do,* he thought with a shake of his head.

"You're killing them, Dad," she'd said at the dinner table.

"Of course not. They have no right to life. They weren't born. I made them, and I can deconstruct them if they are inoperative."

"But you made them with free will."

"I made them to obey." He frowned. "Just as you will obey me and cease arguing about this subject forthwith."

She'd sulked for days. He loved her spirit as well as her caring heart. Surprisingly, even without her mother, he'd managed to raise a wonderful child. But there was still so much she didn't know. He decided—to take her mind off things—he would soon teach her how to use the pen. Eventually, she would rule this land. Maybe she could help him with his new creation—a new land to explore on the other side of the mountains. It would be just the two of them again.

The Clockwork Pen

His wife brought him back to the present with a sobering thought. "What will you do with the boy?"

What boy? Rozam remembered the chip and the tall boy but had no idea what to do with him now. "What are your thoughts on the matter?" He studied her.

"He cannot stay and disrupt things. No one would know if you took care of him." She sipped from her teacup.

"Yes. My thoughts exactly."

She nodded, then said with distaste, "Of course, she is always babbling about the inferiority of our men because they can't make humans."

"Hmmm." He stroked his chin. "Maybe keeping him as her mate would take her mind off the need to leave. She would be happy here with him. My spies say she appears to like him. Though he'd better not be taking advantage…" He growled. "Best to marry them as soon as possible."

"How are you going to make *him* forget the other world? Can you make a creation for that?"

"I don't know. It's a good thought, Dear. I shall have to think on this. How to make him forget? He must be convinced that Sira belongs here and that they are happiest together in this world. Maybe I can create a small castle for them in the new land."

"You are making a new land?" Her eyes widened with joy.

"Oh. You made me spoil the surprise." He pouted with a grin.

"Darling, I shall reward you handsomely after supper." She winked at him with long, dark lashes fluttering, and the bottom of his stomach fell out. If he could have written the sun to set faster, he would have.

Chapter Eleven
Even Humiliated Moles Have Hope

Wyll and Sira slept facing each other, bodies pressed together. She was startled awake by his scream and sat up as he jolted into consciousness. "Shoo! Get off him!"

He roused. "What?"

She laughed. "Oh, I'm sorry. I know it isn't funny, but they must really like you."

He opened his eyes and rolled to lay on his blazing back and found it hurt worse in real life. Then he noticed the ring of creepy cats that circled him with big eyes and steady mewling. They pressed into him, and one reached out to pull its claw across his leg, scratching a tear in his trousers.

"Hey!" It was the only pair he had. He sat up. "Get away."

He leaned forward and pushed the one away, but three more cats edged forward to brush against him with their massive heads. They were all colors, but not rainbow hues, normal animal shades—gingers, browns, greys—they were covered in spots and stripes.

Sira gasped.

He was instantly alert and looking around for the threat. "What?"

"Your back."

"It hurts." He put a hand on his arm as if he could turn it around to see his own back. He looked over his muscled shoulder to see if he could make out anything.

Her touch was cool and gentle on his side. "They scratched you up fairly good. I'll have to see if Malynda has any ointment. We need to change your bandages anyway."

They got ready, brushing cats aside as they changed and folded the bedding.

"Should we leave it here?" he asked. "Since we don't know where we'll be tonight?"

"I think that's a clever idea. We can always come back for it."

They were finishing up when the farmer's wife called up to them. "I have some breakfast for you two."

"Thanks," Wyll said. "Be right down."

"Mrs. Tungsten, you shouldn't have." Amid the stalls, Sira accepted a big basket from the woman who wore a grey apron covering her clothes and a floppy hat over her hair. Her dark-lensed goggles wrapped around her ears, and she smiled a lot, so all you could see was the tip of her nose and teeth. She could have been anyone,

The Clockwork Pen

even his own mother, and he wouldn't be able to recognize her.

They sat in the yard, in a reclining rocker for two, made of lead piping and gears, eating while they watched the chickens peck the ground. The basket was loaded with biscuits, butter, fruit, and two bowls of scrambled eggs. It was farm-fresh and delicious. In the early morning chill, frosted blades of grass twinkled in the sun rays that warmed their faces. When they finished, Sira took the basket into the main house for Mrs. Tungsten.

Wyll stared out at the trees. Beyond them, he could hear the rush of the river and see the shimmering specks of light bouncing off the waves. If he looked far enough South, he could see the mountains' hazy form towering over the landscape.

"Beautiful, isn't it?" Indigo walked up and sat next to Wyll. "Malynda's in there having girl time." His rich laughter was soothing.

"Yeah, it is. I can see why he wanted to create it. I just imagine him drawing it on a map and the buildings popping up across the neighborhoods. It's wild. I wonder what I would've done if it had come to me?" It was a dangerous thought, though. You'd get everything you ever wanted but lose your mind in the process, so you couldn't enjoy what you'd made. Could you even stop yourself from using the pen once you'd started?

"I tell you what I *wouldn't* do." Indigo sighed. "I wouldn't make people without allowing them to use their own will. He can't play at being a Creator—even if he did manage to create life. Once people are given a life, it belongs to them. You can't just torture them to find ways to improve them. One of the recent people he 'made' came out crazier than he is. We had to put her in a room in the community building for constant supervision."

"Yeah." He could relate. His father thought Wyll was an extension of himself, and everything Wyll did or didn't do "reflected on him." Wyll was an embarrassment. His father didn't think Wyll had a mind of his own or that he had any right to one.

It was always, *"This isn't your best."* Why would he want to try any harder? It would never be good enough. He'd rather not try at all and live with the disgrace and the disappointment than try to please the man by doing his absolute best and have it considered not good enough. That would be too much for Wyll's psyche.

They talked about the colors in the flowering trees and the scent of water in the air. It was bright and sunny, but dark clouds were listlessly pacing the horizon, waiting to strike. The sun was starting to warm things up. They were laughing when the ladies joined them.

"We've been talking," Sira said, pointing to herself and Malynda. "And we think there must have been a mole. I mean, the king had no idea we were meeting, but even if he guessed, he wouldn't have known where. I vote on an inside man. Which isn't a bad idea for us, really."

The Clockwork Pen

"Yes," Malynda continued. "If we had someone on the inside, we could find out where King Rozam keeps his magic pen when he's not carrying it. And possibly get the details we need to take it."

"I agree. An inside eye would be an asset." Indigo rubbed his chin.

"What do you think, Wyll?" Sira asked.

"It's a promising idea. Let's get moving on it." He wanted to point the direction toward what they could do and away from whom they thought the traitor was.

"Who do you think we should use?" Indigo asked Sira.

"There are several to consider who are in positions to help us," she said. "But I think the best thing is to tell our remaining people and see who wants to volunteer. After the meeting, the remaining people will be reeling. Let's give them some hope and give them something to step up for."

"But what about the king's mole?" Malynda chewed on the corner of a fingernail. "How are we going to figure out who it is? No one is going to admit to doing it. And what if they volunteer to be *our* mole? We can't afford to have a double agent. We must use drastic measures."

"What do you mean?" Wyll asked.

"If we feel someone is lying, we can use a device Kipper invented to hold the hand and snip off fingers at each joint. With fourteen joints on each hand, there are plenty of options," Malynda said with distaste, and Indigo made a face like he had a mouthful of something slimy.

The blood rushed from Wyll's head, and he felt faint. There was no way he could watch them snip off even one digit, knowing it was his fault. He had to tell her. Maybe if he said it in front of all of them, she wouldn't kill him. He steeled himself. *Heroes are made of men with honor.* He had to do this. He coached himself. *It's better now than later...*

Before he could stop himself, Wyll cleared his throat, took a huge breath, and spoke, "Um, guys? I know how the king found us."

Silence enveloped the yard as everyone looked at him. A nearby chicken clucked, sounding like a clanging cymbal to Wyll. *Maybe this isn't the best idea.*

"Well? What do you know?" Sira smiled. *Oh crap.*

He hesitated, wishing he could take it back. *Say it fast.* "It was me."

"What?" the other three echoed each other.

"What are you talking about?" Malynda laughed nervously.

"That's not possible. You were with me." Sira's confusion contorted her features. She squinted at him and backed away a few steps, shaking her head.

Wyll turned over his forearm and touched the corners of the chip with his fingertips. He moved it around so they could see the square shape.

"When?" Sira's dead calm frightened Wyll more than if she'd screamed at him.

"In the Reformatory. I didn't want him to. I couldn't stop it. I tried to get it out." He ran his fingers along the scabbed scratches on his wrist.

"All this time..." Sira began. "You have been betraying us all this time." She spun on her heel.

"No, Sira! Wait. I didn't want to; I didn't mean to!"

"No." She whirled to face him. "You don't get to defend yourself. You gave my father the location of my apartment, lied to me, and let the soldiers shoot at those innocent people like lame ducks in a pond. What part didn't you mean? The revealing, the lying, or the killing? You know what? Never mind. I don't want to hear it. I thought you were ... more."

She turned her back on him and marched back into the house.

Malynda cleared her throat. "Let me go check on her."

The two men sat quietly for several minutes, each lost to their own thoughts. But after a few minutes, the silence grated on Wyll's nerves. "Do you think she'll be okay?"

Indigo looked at him and shook his head. "You really messed that one up."

Wyll knew he'd blown everything he'd built with Sira so far. "I know. But I want to fix it. I couldn't let it go on. I've never cared this much before."

Indigo shook his head, lowering his forehead to rest in his palm. "If you'd come to us straight away, we could have helped you. Actually, we should probably get rid of it now. We don't want Rozam to hurt these farmers for helping us. When Malynda comes back—"

"I'm back. What do you need?" She breezed up in her red and white pinstripe dress and matching jacket with puffy sleeves, like she was on a social call. Her tall frame took up the doorway.

"Where's Sira?" Wyll asked.

"She's gone back to the castle. I think she needs some time to cool off."

"Won't the king hurt her for being gone so long?" Wyll wondered if he should go after her.

"No. He doesn't believe she'd cross him. Which is going to be hard for her when things are finally fair." She sat in a complicated lawn chair. "So, what do you need?"

"We need to cut out the chip," Indigo said.

They asked the Tungstens for their sharpest knife.

"Come in the kitchen; it's so dirty out there." Mrs. Tungsten waved them in.

The kitchen was homey, with a maritime theme. On the wall, a big wooden steering wheel hung among a tangle of nets. The dark woodwork on the cabinets, floor, and table shined like they were freshly waxed. The walls deepened the feel in navy blue with crimson and white trim.

"Sit, sit." Mrs. Tungsten directed Wyll to a chair at the table and laid out a white cloth with a wicked-looking knife. His stomach dropped at the sight of it. She left to collect bandages.

Indigo sat next to him. "Do you want some help?"

"Yeah." He nodded.

"Take a deep breath," Indigo said, holding the knife tip over his wrist.

Wyll inhaled, and Indigo pressed the blade into his flesh. It made a pop feeling when it broke the skin. He didn't want to watch, but he couldn't stop himself from being fascinated by the line of blood that pooled when the knife dragged from one end of the chip to the other. It stung, but not too bad.

"Okay, here's a pair of tweezers. See if you can pull it out." Indigo took tweezers and a needle from the farmer's wife.

Wyll dug into the incision, plucking at the corner. The tweezers slipped off with a click. He tried twice before getting a hold of it and wiggling it out. His head floated above his shoulders like a balloon full of helium. The room spun.

"Don't pass out." Indigo put a hand on his shoulder to ground him.

"Here, drink this," Mrs. Tungsten said, bringing him a glass of orange juice.

He accepted it gratefully, its sweetness lingering on his tongue.

"Do you think she'll be okay?" Wyll asked Indigo again.

"I'm sure she'll be fine. It would have been better if you'd told us right away."

"I know. I just didn't think there was anything I could do. And I didn't want to piss off Sira, but I think I ruined all of it."

"I'm sure it will blow over." Indigo squeezed his shoulder, making him wince. "Oh, sorry about the shoulder. How's it healing?"

"It's okay. Sira said I needed to change my bandages, but I don't—" He almost got choked up thinking about her. All he could remember was the face of horror she'd made when she looked at him and realized he was the one responsible. It was eating him up—the way he felt, the guilt of feeling it. The situation was an additional absence of light in this dark, mechanical world. He wondered if it made him feel like he wanted to go home. He weighed his thoughts. As awful as his experience with Sepherra was so far, Sira shined like the sun—her eyes, her bright white smile, her wild laughter. She was somebody to fight for. He needed to earn the right to her trust again. The thought of having her in his arms again, knowing they had no secrets, stirred his spirit—his heroism—hell yeah, he'd rescue his princess from her cage.

"It's okay. We'll help you. There are supplies here." Mrs. Tungsten stepped into the room. "Oh, my mouth. I'm sorry. I was listening. That's one girl who won't let anything stop her. You're going to have to work for it."

"What will she do?" Wyll asked Indigo. "You seem to know her the best."

"We are back to square one, as the saying goes, only with fewer members. We will have to find out who is still alive and where they are."

She would need his help. What if she was so mad she left him out of the entire escape plan and left him behind, stuck in Sepherra? He couldn't afford to be left out. It was time to move.

"What can I do?" he asked.

Mrs. Tungsten brought more gauze, medical tape, and a pot of ointment. She picked off the edge of the dirty tape on Wyll's shoulder and unwound the fabric.

"There's not much you *can* do now." Indigo took the wads of cotton fabric and threw them in the trash. "I'll give her a day and then see what she wants to do. It'll take a few days to get a good head count of who's left. Hopefully, the display of prisoners in the square convinced some more people to join us. The trick is making sure they are authentic."

"Not a traitor, like me." Wyll hung his head. "I'm so sorry, man." *Looking out for number one* had always kept him ahead of everyone else. He had to learn to trust a team. *Meeting Sira is going to change my life*, he thought, amused. She was magnetic, and they were just reaching the part where he wanted to hear everything about her life. Now, he couldn't even talk to her.

"It may work out," Indigo said.

Mrs. Tungsten gently applied the ointment to his shoulder with her fingers. They were soft and delicate, but he couldn't stop wondering how it would have felt to have Sira's hands patting on ointment, brushing along his shoulder. He remembered her kissing his shoulder and felt a stirring ache in his belly.

Indigo put the lid on the pot. "When Sira and I figure out the plan, I'll come here to explain what's going on. I will try to convince her to give you another chance."

"Indigo, I need to be close to her. She'll never trust me if I'm out here alone." He'd only known her for less than a week. *Can you feel this much for someone you've only known that long?* It was irrational.

"I don't know where—"

"Please, Indigo. I don't have anything else here. I don't have anything to do to take my mind off her. You don't understand," Wyll said.

"Yes, we do." Malynda brushed Indigo's arm. "Right, Indi? Remember when we first moved into our house? We were so afraid and so excited to get to know

The Clockwork Pen

each other. We always wanted to be together—couldn't wait to get home from work and stay in… Not everyone has a partner tailor-made to suit them … but we do."

Indigo sighed. "All right. Let me see what I can do. I might know someone—"

"Thank you. Thank you so much." Wyll winced as Mrs. Tungsten finished pulling the bandage tight and secured it with tape.

Indigo left, and Wyll helped the farmer with his chores all afternoon. He didn't have much difficulty using his shoulder, though that side was weak. He spread the chicken feed and pulled the brittle brown weeds in Mrs. Tungsten's vegetable garden, preparing the soil for seeding. His cheeks and ears tinted pink in the sun. The tall chickens' long legs and breasts were twice the size of typical chickens, with tiny golf ball-like heads. He chuckled as they pecked at his boots and his belt and one bit his finger.

"Shoo." He waved them away. He thought of all those people in pain. His betrayal of Sira burned like a tongue of fire, but the guilt of saving himself from their fate *and* causing it scorched his heart. Was it stupid to think she might forgive him?

He was a sinking ship of rejection. He wasn't used to feeling that way for girls, and it affirmed he was right to keep his secrets last night. It was too risky. Wasn't that the whole point of wearing his arrogant armor? *Don't let anyone wound you ... look out for number one and screw the rest.* But he didn't want to be like that anymore. Somehow, knowing how it felt to see faith mirrored in someone's eyes, then disappear, made him consider changing the way he did things. He might have blown it, but he coached himself to remain positive. They'd had a connection, he knew it—her fingertips even tingled. All of him hoped that was an essential step toward winning her heart. At least, good enough to remind her of how she felt about him then.

He checked for any ripe winter berries and tossed them in a basket Mrs. Tungsten brought him. Any veggies left were withered. He weeded the flower bed as well. It was too much time alone to think, and the guilt of hurting everyone he knew in this world ate away at his confidence.

He was glad he'd only been momentarily tempted to say *screw you*—if she was going to be like that, he didn't have the energy to care for her fickle emotions. When he let himself go down that rabbit hole, a few thoughts did upset him. *How could she not see that I was manipulated? She didn't even give me a chance to explain.* Had she been waiting for a reason to give up hope—to lose faith in him? It was the same way his father made him feel.

Hot, sweaty, tired, and bitter, Wyll sat at the Tungsten's table for dinner. They talked about the farm and rainfall. Wyll mostly followed the conversation and

The Clockwork Pen

nodded when appropriate. They were finishing when there was a knock at the door. Indigo stood outside in his top hat and coat, holding a sapphire cane in front of him.

"Come in," Mrs. Tungsten called.

"Obliged," he said, entering the shadowy kitchen. He sat at the table, pushing his long legs out before him, and rested his cane on the wall.

"Did you talk to her?" Wyll asked, not sure if he would like what she thought.

"Yes." Indigo nodded.

He warred with himself. Would he look desperate chasing her? Could his ego afford to care? He sighed. "She's still mad?"

"Yes. It will take time. She protects herself. I was a little surprised she let you in so quickly. You've broken trust—I don't know." Indigo put a hand on the back of Wyll's chair.

"I've really farked this one up." Wyll was defeated. And in his pensive mood, he hated that it mattered to him. He wasn't sure why *she* mattered so much to him when none of the others had.

"But I have good news."

Wyll looked up. "What? Will she see me?"

"No. I'm afraid not. But I got you a job in the kitchen. I know a guy. Maybe you'll be able to talk to her—or at least see her," Indigo said. "That's all I can do."

"I can figure it out." Wyll imagined putting a note on her tray, sneaking to her bedroom, or—

"When you've eaten, we can go." Indigo pulled the top off a biscuit and folded it into his mouth.

"I'm ready. Let's go." Wyll wiped his mouth on the napkin beside his fork and dropped it on the table. He stood and turned to the farmer and his wife. "Do you need help cleaning up?"

"No," Mrs. Tungsten said with a smile and tilt of her head.

"Thanks for letting us stay and feeding us."

"Yes," echoed Indigo. "Thank you for providing for us."

They stood and hugged them both, talking over each other, "Bye, Wyll."

"Nice to have you."

"Thanks for coming."

"You're a good boy," she said.

"She'll see," the elder farmer said.

"Come again."

Wyll tried to keep up with who was speaking, but it didn't matter. He embraced them both and followed Indigo into the evening air. The pink and orange clouds blazed across the sky like flames in a deepening blue sea of stars.

They followed the cobbled streets to the castle. Wyll's breath fogged in front of him in plumes of white. He smiled and felt his nose numbing in the cold. It didn't matter. Emotions churned within him. The clicking of his boots on the stones matched the ratcheting of his nerves, his heartbeat thumping along.

The castle was magnificent, flashing reflections of the fading hot pink sunset. They climbed the stairs. The final staircase rose to the massive porch and front doors, but they still didn't go that way. He wondered if anyone used those doors. Stone archways adorned the lowest level around the castle in white brick.

As they followed the sidewalk around the castle, the light quickly dissipated, and Wyll had trouble following Indigo through the shadows but heard him say quietly, "This way."

They stepped into the light of an archway and then another and another until they were behind the castle. It smelled delicious. Wyll was sorry he'd already eaten. A wooden half-door stood open on top, pouring golden light onto the stone tiles. Indigo approached it and rested his hands on the heavy wood, leaving room for Wyll.

A man approached the door, and Wyll recognized him by his bowler hat and goggles. Because of a last-minute problem, he hadn't made it to the meeting, thank goodness.

"Hey, Nally," he said.

Nally came over and shook flour-covered hands with them both. "How's it going?" he asked.

"Good," Indigo said.

"I didn't know you worked here." Wyll gripped the door.

"I work here part-time and then run my own shop. My wife works the hours I'm here."

"I told you I knew a guy." Indigo smiled at Wyll and crossed his arms.

They barked out a short laugh.

"Okay, you'd better get in here. There's a lot to do." Nally waved for Wyll to come in.

He held up a hand toward Nally and turned to Indigo. "Thanks, man."

Indigo tipped his head in acknowledgment.

"The first thing you do in this kitchen is put on an apron and go wash yourself." Nally looked at Wyll's hair through a squinted eye. His cut was longer on top. "The sides are short, at least."

Wyll smiled; but realized everyone else was frowning.

He stood in a glowing kitchen with an arched ceiling in red brick housing two massive stone ovens burning bright. Four workspaces were stationed around the room, rectangle tables lined with benches. Sitting at the nearest table were two women and one boy, who pet a small barking animal.

"Hi," he said, smiling with his dimples to appear his friendliest. "I'm Wyll." It was the smile that made girls gasp, giggle, and blush.

The older woman "Hmphed" and crossed her arms over her chest, completely unaffected. The younger woman, though, had admired his smile to its desired effect and grinned back at him, giving a little wave that made the woman grunt again.

The boy was brave enough to speak to him, however. "Are you working here now?"

"Yep."

"Why are you here?" The boy planted his hands on his hips and tilted his head.

"Ah..." Wyll scratched the back of his neck. "I'm kind of a friend of the, ah—princess—I guess. But she hates that." He raised his eyebrows and shrugged.

"Why aren't you out there if you're a friend?" The boy pointed down a hall.

"Because I'm not a prince." He ruffled the boy's hair, and they smiled at each other.

The older woman "Hmphed" again and stood up to walk to the sink. "Break time's over. Get back to it, you two. *You.* New boy. Come here. Ya know how to wash a dish?"

He stared at her. "Of course I do."

"Good. Do 'em." She pointed to a towering stack of dishware that he hadn't seen, and he groaned but plunged his hands into the hot, soapy water.

When he finished the dishes after a little more than an hour, only miniature flames and embers glowed in the red brick ovens, pulsing and fading. Shadows chased each other around the room like sprites. The younger woman swept the floor, and the boy sat at the table, his head on his arm, drooling into a puddle. The older woman came into the room and looked at Wyll.

"Follow me," she said, turning to go the way she'd come.

He watched her go down a hall lit by wall sconces, then jogged to catch up. She turned right at a similar hallway and opened the second door, waving him past her. He entered a small room and sat on the iron-posted bed, giving it a small test-bounce. Next to him, the bedside table held a clock with an unusual rhythm, *tickety tickety tickety*. It sat under a curling lamp shaped like a flower of some kind, made of stunning glass art. He yawned as he watched the woman cross to a gear-knobbed chest, open a drawer, then place a bundle of folded, simple clothes and an apron on a plain wooden chair. The space was smaller than his bedroom at home, but it would work for now. He was going to sleep like the dead.

"Thanks." He looked at the woman in the doorway. "Will you tell me your names, or should I just poke people?" He smiled, but she wasn't amused.

"I'm Eleeda. The girl is Lyri, and the boy is called Pyne. Have yurself in the kitchen by five. Goodnight." She pulled his door closed as she walked out.

A lump on his bed had a note, *"From Indigo and Nally."* Under it were a soft nightshirt, extra underclothes, and another outfit, complete with hat, coat, and cane. With a swell of gratitude, Wyll shucked his clothes and crawled into bed in his soft shirt. Under the crisp, clean sheets, he

The Clockwork Pen

felt like himself for a moment. When he closed his eyes, he could imagine he was home. He reached over to turn off the lamp and realized it was late by the aberrant clock. He barely chuckled as his head sank into the pillow and was immediately asleep.

Wyll was jarred awake by screaming. Well, he thought it was screaming, but it turned out to be his shrill alarm. As he dressed, he heard Eleeda blaring instructions to everyone in the kitchen, already causing one of the girls to cry as she ran past his door. He rushed to the kitchen and tied his apron behind him as he entered the bright room. People rushed in and out, but the kitchen was always full of at least fifteen people. The energy was high, and staff argued, some shoving before others. There appeared to be considerably more people and activity than he had assumed necessary for a routine breakfast.

"What's going on?" Wyll asked when he saw Lyri.

Her eyes were round, and she nearly tiptoed in place while she talked. "The king is—!" She took a deep breath. "The king is going on the Zamboni today. He wants us to make his favorite food here. Ooh, some get to go with them. I hope it's me!"

If it was Wyll, he might have a chance to talk to Sira, and she wouldn't be able to get away. They needed to talk. He was determined to get on that ship.

Chapter Twelve

ZAMBONI IN THE SKY

It took some haggling and one girl's tears, but finally, Wyll stood in line, dressed in a leather apron and hat, holding a covered platter that was making his mouth water. They were the last to board with the hot food. The ship loomed above them, and a canopy of gold and cream floated even higher in the biggest balloon he'd ever seen. These things were supposed to be notorious for blowing up, right? He was rethinking his plan when the woman behind him pushed her tray into his spine.

"Psst. Get moving."

He followed the stout man before him, and they shuffled up the gangplank into the servant's quarters. They passed the open doorway to an opulent ballroom where mirrors hung between swaths of rich burgundy fabric draping the wall, all gilded in metal frames, some with intricate filigree and others chunky and mechanical.

"This way," a gruff man with a salt and pepper beard called to Wyll.

He caught up to the guy in front of him, and they bypassed the kitchen to enter a narrow hallway that led directly to the king's dining room. They entered the wood-paneled room, lining up against the wall. People dressed in their best finery crowded around the twenty-foot table. Feathers, goggles, and skulls decorated the hats. Gun belts and gold buckles adorned the men, many of whom carried pocket watches in their vest pockets.

The decorations were over the top to impress the patrons of the expensive luxury air cruise. The men had obviously checked their hats with their coats and sported pomaded hair—longer and parted in the middle, parted on the side and swept over, or pulled back and held with a manly leather tie, like Indigo's.

The women still wore their hats—pink ones loaded with flowers on the brim, deep violet top hats piled high with matching tulle that hung down the back like a veil and crimson wide-brimmed hats holding an assortment of objects like pocket watches, metal gears, black feathers, buttons, and even a small book. One woman's hat lit up with tiny white lights weaving in and out of the feathers, flowers, and tulle decorating the top.

He searched the faces at the table. Some guests had donned masquerade masks, making their faces difficult to see. Ladies wore black lace that climbed their temples like a vine and wrapped around their eyes, creeping to the jaw on the other side, like a half mask. He bounced his knee, knowing he didn't have much time. The servants stood in line, each holding a covered platter of steaming food. His eyes scanned each passenger.

There. She sat looking across the table. Surely, she didn't know he was there. He laid his platter on the side buffet and plucked a glass from the water tray. He took it to her, ignoring the hushed orders from his supervisor. He leaned over her shoulder to set the glass on the table and lay his corded forearm next to hers, feeling the warmth of her skin. He felt her soft gasp low in his belly. She smelled like a cinnamon cloud.

When he inhaled without moving, she turned toward him but frowned.

"What are you doing?" she whispered.

"I wanted to talk to you."

"Well, I don't want to talk to you." She returned her attention to the table. "Go find someone else to betray." *Ouch.*

He stood up to see his supervisor waving wildly, motioning him to come back. He shrugged and joined the crew. After a few moments, the servants placed their dishes on the table and filed out. Windows lined the far wall, framed by gauzy curtains. Wyll touched the cold glass as he passed.

The ship was rising, and he glimpsed the surrounding area. It fascinated Wyll, and he wanted to see how much of Sepherra he could view, but someone tugged his sleeve, ripping him away from the sight.

When they entered the gray metal kitchen, they gathered in a circle.

The Clockwork Pen

"You cooked ahead of time, so there's not much for you to do now but wait. You'll go out and fill glasses and take empty plates in a few minutes." The man in charge was tall and thin with gaunt cheeks, a narrow black goatee, and a mustache. He wore rectangle glasses and simple clothes under an apron.

Everyone dispersed to enjoy their few minutes of reprieve. But Wyll needed to get back in that dining room. He stood by the door, looking through the small opening. It was stupid to do this without a plan. *What did I expect her to do? Swoon at the sight of me?*

"You're new around here." The lead man stood behind him.

"Yeah, I'm Wyll," he said, distracted. He tried to think of something covert. How could he change her mind?

The man shook his hand. "I'm Hark. You work at the castle?"

He didn't turn. Sira was laughing at the man next to her, and a scarlet wave covered his vision. He tossed out words without thought. "Kind of. I found the place by accident. I'm from the *other* world, but that wouldn't make sense to you. Anyway, I can't get back 'cause of the nutty king—" He stopped quickly, remembering where he was and wondering if the man would turn him in for treason. *Damn.* He felt the sweat gather on his neck as Hark watched him with narrowed eyes.

Wyll and Hark spoke in hushed tones. Hark was interested in Wyll's true feelings about the king. Wyll considered keeping his secret, but he had an agenda on the ship, and Hark, as his supervisor, would only let him see Sira if he knew the depth of the problem.

"You're not joking me? Pulling a prank?" Hark squinted in doubt.

"What? Why would I—? No. No. I'm not clockwork. I'm like the king. But my experience with him hasn't been particularly great. I was stupid even to hope he ever planned to send me home. I'm pretty sure I was never a threat to him at all." He huffed a laugh.

"I don't know the other place you speak of, but there are many places I have not been to in Sepherra. If the king made you any promises, though, I doubt he meant *whatever* he said." Hark looked ill just saying it out loud. His complexion paled. "He's become ... unhinged." He looked around them and whispered in Wyll's ear. "I might be able to help you. I know a group of people who gather in private to protest."

"Like the Resistance?"

"What's the Resistance? Does that have anything to do with the square?"

"Yes. It was a group run by others..." Wyll was already deep in this; he might as well be completely honest. "The princess was involved. Then, I accidentally got everyone killed. I was trapped. Now I don't know. She won't speak to me." Wyll grimaced. "He used me."

"Who?"

"The king."

"I didn't know Princess Sira was—" Hark began.

"On the other side?" Wyll asked.

Hark nodded as a girl passed them with an arm full of plates. She scowled at them.

"I made a mistake and led the king right to our group. We shoved out a side door when the soldiers started shooting." Wyll was hollow on the inside. An anvil sat on his chest. He wanted to disconnect from the guilty feeling of remorse. Saying it out loud to Hark seemed to relieve some of his pressure. Maybe Hark could help him solve this. He needed help. It was too big for him to solve.

"She blames you," Hark said like a fact.

"Yeah, I guess so. She's right." He shrugged one shoulder. "But you should tell her about your group. She'd be so pleased to have allies."

Hark smiled with a wink. "You could introduce us. Be part of the solution instead?"

Wyll felt a stirring of hope and smiled. "It probably won't matter, but I'm willing to try it."

Soon, the guests moved to an observatory. He saw her standing next to a window reaching from the ship's side to the floor, where guests could literally stand above the city. It was afternoon, and she stood in the sun, sparkling in a gold dress that hung from her shoulders like a Roman gown and draped from one hip to the other, falling in ruffles behind her like some modern Victorian goddess. Crystals sparkled among her red curls. He wanted to sweep them away from her neck and lay his hand there to pull her toward him…

"Ahem," Hark said next to him. "She's not going to be happy you're staring."

Wyll snapped out of it. "Stay in the dining room. I'll bring her to you."

"That's the spirit." Hark smiled widely and punched Wyll in the arm. "I'll be waiting."

Wyll shook his arm as he walked up to her. "Excuse me."

"I already said—"

"No, not me. You need to speak to someone in the dining room." He hoped she wouldn't argue.

"Who is it?" She raised her brow.

No such luck. "Someone you want to meet." He could tell she was curious by the tilt of her head. "I promise." Regret filled him, the pressure causing a residual headache. His forehead wrinkled as a bolt of pain stabbed through his temple.

"Are you okay?" she asked in a soft voice. "I mean, I just left you. I shouldn't have done that. But you… you…"

"I know," he said. "And I'm so sorry. It was imbecilic. I never meant to hurt you, but I knew it would eventually. I just didn't know what else to do—"

"Wyll, I can't. I hope you're taken care of, but I can't be your friend right now. You took *all* my friends from me. You took away my purpose, my advocates." She left him and strode to the dining room, looking every bit a princess.

He'd been hoping to take her there himself and introduce them. Then, when she was so happy, he would say, *"See? I am sorry. I'm trying to help."* But she was nowhere near forgiveness. He was no longer in the mood to see her, so he found his way back to the kitchen.

"Oh, thar he is." One woman stood nose to nose with him just inside the door. *"Prince of the kitchens.* Too high and mighty ta do the work like the rest o' us." A tile wall was about a foot from his left side, and he marveled at the design as she spoke. When she finished, he walked around the island to the sinks, but everyone, even those who didn't need to, turned their backs on him.

One man spoke to Wyll as he walked to the closet. "You wait. You don't work, you don't get paid, or have a warm place to sleep." He grabbed a broom and threw it at Wyll's chest. The end conked him on the forehead, but he caught it. Something told him he'd never live it down if he hadn't. It hurt his head, and Sira had taken the pain medication with her.

He was nearly done, and his shoulders ached when Hark joined them, but no one dared to chastise the ship crew's captain. Wyll chuckled wryly to himself. Hark came up to him and took the broom. He started sweeping between them and quietly said, "She's extremely ambitious—a lovely person. Thank you for introducing us."

Wyll listened while he rolled his shoulders and pinwheeled his elbow slowly, holding the shoulder joint. "Did it work? Was she excited? Did she appreciate my attempt?"

Hark looked down and swept around him. "She was quite pleased. And she wants to meet my people soon because she has a plan. We're going to talk more later." He saw Wyll's expectant gaze and winced. "I forgot to mention you."

"Ah, great!" Wyll glanced to see everyone looking his way. He waved at them, and several rolled their eyes as they returned to their tasks. "I needed her to know I was trying to fix things. So, what's her plan?"

"Well..." Hark swept around himself. "I guess since you put us together..." He turned back to Wyll. "For good faith, I told her about our ideas, and she told me they're choosing someone to work on the inside. They were focused on rebuilding, and now we will merge our people. She's planning to learn about the pen from the king, so we'll think of something there."

Wyll hardly cared about the pen right now and going home. Gaining Sira's trust must be accomplished first. He'd never experienced this heavy, sticky, black feeling before. He'd been upset before, unliked, and selfish, but it had always been about him. Then, when he was ready, he'd brushed the emotions away. But when he remembered betraying Sira, the darkness pressed against him, pinning his lungs and forcing out his air. White spots danced in his vision, and the air tasted sickly sweet. For the first time in his life, he needed to redeem himself, possibly at his own expense. This time, he'd do what she needed instead.

"How can I help her?" Wyll whispered intensely.

"I don't know if you can. She'd never let you volunteer. And short of finding an answer or stealing the pen yourself, I doubt there's much she'd be impressed by. She is quite dignified."

He didn't like the look in Hark's eye, but he had no claim on Sira. He knew, though, that she wouldn't return Hark's affection—if indeed that was what he saw—because she wanted a human mate. Should he mention it? He did know that if he didn't fix this by the time she got to the real world, he'd lose her to a whole planet of human choices.

Hark lifted his broom, smiled, and patted Wyll on the back. "Let's go do something else. I think you've slacked off enough in here. I've got more work for you to do."

They cleaned the dining room, removing the linens and decorative table assortments of flower-laced lanterns entwined with waves of stiff lace. The table polish smelled like lemons. He wondered if it was the same stuff they had at home. Was it imported, or did one of the factories make it? He gave up. Only the king would know. And he didn't want to see the man again unless it was to wave goodbye.

The guests of the airship watched a movie in the elegant theater. Staff brought them champagne when anyone raised their glass. It was some movie from the eighties that his parents liked, but he had no idea what it was—must be one the king liked. He wondered what media the king had made available to them. When they finished, the guests stretched their legs and arms, playing a sort of pickleball. No matter where they went, he saw Hark talking to Sira. She looked down, chuckling, and placed a slender hand lightly on his arm.

By the time they landed, Wyll was fuming, and the sun was setting. He really wanted to get out of there. If he were home, he would get on his bike and ride to Derec's, and they'd go get shakes and sit by Olathe Lake. It took a while to get to the restaurant, then the lake, and the ride was hard, but whatever was eating you was mainly forgotten by the time you got back home. So, it was effective.

But this wasn't home. It would be easier if it were—in most ways. He scrubbed every spot off every dish and fell into bed that night, exhausted and broken. He saw Sira in his dreams, twirling around and around. She wore brightly colored silk scarves, flowing from her like a liquid rainbow, spinning round and round. She laughed with her head thrown back until she saw him and frowned.

"What do you want?" she asked.

"I'm sorry," he said. Did he want forgiveness? His brain was fuzzy.

She looked intensely into Wyll's eyes and said, "Prove it."

He woke thinking it was strange, but in the time it took him to think it, he was already forgetting the dream. He awoke with an instinctive drive to make up for his mistake.

Wyll rose early and helped Eleeda with braiding the bread dough. It turned out to be really simple. Take three ropes, left to center, then right to center, and repeat. They smelled so delicious when baked into cheese braids, cinnamon raisin buns, fruit and nut loaf, and breakfast biscuits. He set a basket of hot, fresh buns on each of the servants' tables and jumped as he noticed Lyri at his elbow.

"Geez!" He shook his head. "You scared the crap out of me."

She smiled and looked up at him with huge, blinking eyes. "Hi," she said. Then, her face grimaced in pain as someone twisted her ear.

"Leave him alone and go eat your breakfast." Keylin faced him, letting go of the poor girl's ear. "Surprise. Staying home with Mom turned out to be a good thing after all."

"How is she?"

"She's hiding out at her cousin's, though Rozam doesn't appear to care about her at all now that his girl is home."

"Careful, your claws are showing."

She laughed. "It's not like that. I don't resent her. It's him. Do you have any idea what a head trip it is to realize you came from a pen and your insides are mechanical? What am I?"

"Just a girl." He smiled, and she returned the gesture.

"You have breakfast yet?" She played with a brooch on the corseted bodice of her dress.

"Nope. I was just about to sit down. Join me?" He motioned to the seat next to his place at the table and wiped his hands on a towel looped through his apron.

"Sure. So, you're in the kitchen all day?" she asked.

"Yeah. You?"

"I *was* learning with Sira during the day, but since Ole Roz threw the tutor out, we thought I should lay low and do my other chores. Mostly laundry, but I'm in the kitchen today. Best not to rock the boat, right?" She laughed.

An hour later, a message arrived in the kitchen. The princess requested a breakfast tray in her room. *Is it a message?* Did she want to talk to him?

"Please, Eleeda. I need to do this."

"That's exactly why yar not. It ain't appropriate to be goin' in a young lady's room." She put her hands on her hips and turned to Lyri. "You take the tray up ta the princess."

Wyll sighed in frustration. He didn't even know where her room was. He told Eleeda he was using the bathroom, then circled back and followed Lyri down the polished wooden halls covered with thick, velvety rugs.

He paused when he came to a tower-like atrium where the stairs boxed the opening to many floors. He followed her up a flight of stairs. Over the balcony, he was even with the tall mechanical sculpture spouting water several feet high. Lyri was already one more flight up. He ducked back as she peered down. The five-second wait was killing him. Finally, he turned and jogged up the stairs.

He turned, hunched over so he was lower than the railing, then crossed the landing and started up the next flight.

"Hello, William." The king stood on the stairs above him in a coat with tails, watching him and leaning on a black-marbled cane.

He stood up. *This does not look good.* "It's just Wyll." His voice shook.

"I heard you were in my castle. Oh, don't look surprised, my boy. I hear everything around here. Thank you for gathering all those resisters. Because of you, we have them all in custody. We can study them and identify the design flaws. Make better people. Find out where I went wrong…"

The lie incensed him. "The soldiers killed them. I heard the shots."

"Stunned them is all, my boy. Can't study them all at the same time." He laughed, genuinely amused by himself.

Wyll could see his mind had unraveled even since the first time they'd met, but it did nothing to ease his fear of the man. It only made him less predictable and more dangerous.

"I did wonder about your motivations, though." The king looked at him pointedly. "I thought you wanted to go home, but instead of turning yourself in, here you are, slinking around my domain. I was going to send you there myself, but I heard my daughter quite fancied you before the subversion. Tell me, were you trying to impress her with your deceit? Make her believe you are anything but a liar? Thinking it wouldn't matter when you removed

The Clockwork Pen

the chip? If you'd sell out my daughter, what's to keep you from double-crossing me? Did you tell her about the chip to turn her away from me?" His voice rose in volume.

Indignation filled Wyll. When they were younger, Derec would jump out and try to frighten him, but Wyll's first reaction was generally not fear when threatened. Many times, it was to strike out. Poor Derec had been punched, kicked, and tackled before he stopped trying to scare Wyll. In the same irrational way, he lashed out at the king. "I only listened to you in the first place because I was afraid—and I had to get out of there." *I'm not as scared anymore; he's just a man.* "You're the one who lied—you were never sending me home. It was never about me, though, was it?"

"If you're thinking of being a hero, just remember what lies below us."

"I did what you said. You told me you'd send me home if I did what you asked. I'm here now, so send me back ... and let Sira come with me."

"You really thought I'd let you go back, knowing about Sepherra?" The king boomed with laughter. "You are thick. You're not expiring in a cell right now because my daughter wasn't ready for me to dismantle you. It seems she doesn't think it's worth my time to eliminate you. She dreams of your redemption—I can see it on her face. I know that child like my own reflection. Eventually, she'll change her mind about you, and I think I can still use you to my advantage. I want you here for her. She's just rebellious; it's a phase.

"She'll eventually settle down when—and with whomever—I choose. But she'd never forgive me for permanently breaking her human. Yes, I know how she feels. So, I'm glad you're here where I can keep an eye on you. And if, who knows, you become a prospect, I want to know I control your actions."

"If you think that you—" Wyll began, veins flushing his skin and heating his face.

"There you are! Cook needs you." Keylin skipped up the last few steps from the floor below as she crossed the landing and passed under a stained-glass window above them, fractals of red, blue, and green reflected on her face. She grabbed Wyll's elbow and plunged into a quick curtsy for the king. "Sorry, Your Highness. It's important."

Rozam waved his hand dismissively and spun on his heel to ascend the stairs.

"What are you doing? Are you a moron? You can't talk to him like that," Keylin whispered, dragging him back toward the kitchen.

He growled after her. "What does she want?"

"You *are* an idiot. She doesn't want you. I was saving your butt." She stopped in the hall and let go of him in disgust. "You are either entirely self-preserving or not at all. There's a balance, Wyll. Know when to be the hero, jackass. And if you're wondering, yes, she told me it was you."

Her behavior made sense to him in the span of her last comment. "I'm sorry."

"Yeah, well, what's done is done. If you stay in the kitchen and do whatever Eleeda tells you, I'll keep you informed on what Sira's doing. But you can't just walk around the castle sassing the…" She looked all around them and barely whispered, "Crazy king."

"I need to talk to her, Keylin." He stopped in the hallway abruptly. When she turned to see what kept him, he put his hands on her shoulders. "I need to tell her I'm sorry. She has to know I didn't mean—"

"She knows." Keylin sighed. "She knows everything. It's just going to take time, Wyll. Unless you could solve one of her biggest problems right now, you're just in the way of the Resistance's plans. It's better if you're not informed. Especially if you can't keep your mouth shut around the king."

"You have to tell me something, at least." He held his hands, palms up. "Has she gotten the king to agree to let her use the pen?"

"She is currently grounded to her suite. The king won't want you talking to her. She's working on getting him to show her how he uses the pen, but he told her *not yet*. I think he doesn't trust her after they recognized her in the square, but I said she was out with me the night of your … snafu, so his precious princess is innocent."

"I have an idea, but I don't know if it will be enough for her to forgive me. How do I fix it?"

An older woman with a severe bun and gray Victorian-type dress walked past them with a tray, so they stepped to the side.

Keylin whispered, "Get her out of here. That's the only way to right what you've done. Killing all her friends is not usually the way to a girl's heart."

"But they're not dead. The king just told me that he has them in the Reformatory... I must get them out. That could resolve it, don't you think?"

"I don't know. She's been so obsessed with leaving that she's only had one agenda: getting that pen. She thinks it's the answer. Besides, he could have any reason for telling you that."

He waved away the suggestion. "And you don't think the pen is the answer? Any ideas? What about our mole, any luck there?"

"Personally, I don't know anything but my life here. Like the king or not, I depend on him, and I have a home. I can't imagine a new government changing my life. And I don't see a need to escape to another world with different problems. Somewhere that's unfamiliar and strange? I think I'd just want to visit and come home. But I try to understand."

Wyll looked at Keylin in her rose-colored satin dress with the bustle that fell in waves to her white- and silver-laced ankle boots. He noticed how well she wore

The Clockwork Pen

her hair up in the Victorian style and the delicate drop earrings that climbed up the shell of her ear. She fit in here perfectly. She was *made* to fit in perfectly. Did any of these people want to leave this world? How many really cared? He nodded in understanding. "We do have a mole, though, right?"

"You're like a kitten with a toy. Yes, they chose someone." She grimaced as she looked up and down the hall. They heard footsteps clicking on the atrium tile, but they faded away down another hall.

"You don't like them—whomever they chose. Do I know who it is?" Wyll was wary at the idea that Sira might be forced to use people she didn't fully trust now that everyone important and faithful was captured.

"No, you don't know him." She exhaled slowly. "He liked Sira for a long time before he ever asked her... You know her stance on dating here. I'm sure she's told you. It's no secret now, but before him, no one had a clue that she didn't want to be here or thought she had no future with a clockwork man," she sneered.

"Aaah. You think she's stuck up. Why would she pick him for a mole, then?"

"Because he's one of the only ones left. And his devotion to Sira might keep him loyal." She cocked her hip to the left and rolled her right foot in little circles, her toe never leaving the floor. "And his allegiance to her father puts him in a great position to help us."

"What has he discovered?" He didn't fancy the idea of someone else admiring Sira, especially a man in the position to get her out of Sepherra. That would make *him* her hero and not Wyll. Every drop of testosterone in his body desired to be the man she sought. He needed to get on the ball with rescuing the Resistance.

"He just got situated in his new position yesterday. The king is always guarded when he gets fresh staff. He doesn't let them know his secrets. But we do know now that he has decoy pens all over the place. His office is full of pens that look exactly like the magic one. Apparently, he tried to make more magic pens, but it didn't work. I think when he was saner, he may have had an idea of what the pen was doing to him and thought that if he used each pen very little, he could slow down the insanity. That's what I think. Or he made a crazy number of decoys, which … who knows?"

"But magic doesn't make more magic?" Wyll pondered the idea.

"Apparently not. Look, I've got to get to work. I'm carrying trays today. I'll keep you updated. Just stay in the kitchen and don't mess anything else up." She smiled at him and walked down the hall. Turning back, she said, "It's never over, Wyll."

"What's not over?"

"Anything of great importance. Don't give up. Life, love, trust, clockwork … unless you're dead, it's never over. Keep trying. Just—" She looked into his eyes.

"Just think about what she really wants. Her father loves her so much; he made her a world apart. But all she wants is to be free from it. Even if she fights it until she's dead, it will never be over for her. She might not find happiness when she gets there, but you help her get out, and she'll love you forever."

"I hope so." He grinned. "Thanks, Key."

She chuckled at the nickname. "I think you can do it."

She turned the corner, and he watched her tiny waist, encircled with a loose belt of pink roses that swung when she walked. He could appreciate the beauty of this place and begrudgingly thought that he might have made the same choices if he had come to own a magic pen. It made him wonder if he was as evil inside as the king.

He certainly wasn't any good for anyone so far. He'd been in Sepherra for days, and he'd already managed to both find and wreck the best thing that had ever happened to him. He'd almost had the first relationship where he liked her as much as she liked him. She was unlike any girl he'd ever met. Not whiny and giggly, she was beautiful and headstrong, yet passionate and hard, deep and honest. She was an enigma to him. He desired to solve the puzzle that was Sira, to be part of her life. He slowly walked back to the kitchen, his brain a million miles from his feet.

He met a wave of activity in the kitchen and made a direct line to the sink, filling it and washing dishes while

Jennifer Haskin

his brain spun. How would he accomplish his goal of releasing the prisoners? Nothing came to him, so he let his mind wander into fantasy, but it frustrated him. Why couldn't he come up with a solution?

"What's wrong with you?" Wyll's dad yelled at his mom. Wyll was in his bedroom, sitting on the bed. He didn't mean to be listening, but it wasn't hard to hear when they were shouting, and it was about him, so he had a vested interest.

"He's just a boy!" his mother said. "He doesn't need to have a job, as well as school. He's not the brightest kid. He needs to focus."

"Exactly. He's never going to get a real job in the real world if you let him sit around and play video games and footsie with every cheerleader. He needs to be a productive member of society. Fantasy is for sissies. He needs to be able to use his math skills and do some challenging work first, and some manual labor to straighten him out, make him like—"

"Like YOU? Is that what you mean?" his mother shrieked.

"What's so wrong with being like me?" he boomed.

"Oh, let me tell you..."

That's when Wyll got up, shut his door, and turned on his laptop. Putting on his headphones, he drowned out the noise with lilting music. He could escape into a web serial and let his mind wander. He hated being the cause of their fights.

It was usually, "You're too hard on him!"

And then, "You're too soft, so I have to be harder. It's like you don't want to make him do anything. He needs discipline..."

They didn't fight over the important things you heard about in magazines: money, church, sex (ewww), whatever. They fought about Wyll. It was breaking up their marriage, and it was Wyll's fault. He had already tried being a perfect son, but not only was it exhausting, they expected him to do it all the time, which was ridiculous. To say that teens aren't going to mess up—frequently—was ignorant.

The smell of fresh bread broke through his memory, and Wyll decided his parents needed a reality check. He was a good guy. Maybe he did need a job. He was good in the kitchen. And he could use the money—if he ever got out of here. But if he escaped, hopefully, that would mean Sira was leaving as well. Would she live in the mansion? Would she go to his school? He was instantly possessive. No other guy would talk to her if he could help it. She would walk into his school like a hurricane, blowing everyone away with her beauty, wit, and charisma. He smiled.

"Not everything is my fault. And I can fix one of the biggest things." He dried his hands.

"Just what do you think you're going to fix?" a heavy male voice asked behind him.

Chapter Thirteen
Hark Joins the Team

Wyll turned abruptly, his attention drawn to a man wearing a flour-covered apron, sporting goggles, and a pageboy cap. "Nally! When did you arrive?" Wyll exclaimed.

"Hey, buddy," Nally replied, carrying a tray of buns as he clomped across the room in what looked like Derec's vintage Doc Martens. While Wyll had been engrossed in cleaning the morning's cookware, he hadn't paid much attention to the others. "I greeted you when I came in. You seemed lost in thought."

Nally bent forward, placing the tray inside one of the room's four large ovens. Two kitchen tables provided seating for meals, while taller tables with shoved-in seating were primarily used for food preparation. Massive stone fireplaces stood at the far wall, with roaring fires and black pots suspended above them, slowly cooking for a future feast. The heat was stifling, but the back door's top half was open, allowing an icy breeze from the moat to offer a refreshing and crisp sensation against Wyll's cheeks. It evoked memories of winter at home, although things were different now.

Wiping his hands on his apron, Nally asked, "So, what's your plan?"

"For what?" Wyll asked, perplexed.

"You mentioned wanting to fix 'things.' If my intuition is correct, I believe I understand. What's your plan to fix it? I'm genuinely interested." Nally grinned, revealing a gold molar.

Wyll briefly wondered if the tooth resulted from a dental visit or if the king had made him with a gold tooth. However, he dismissed the thought and replied, "First, I need to talk to Indigo. Once I've done that, I'll have a clearer understanding. But I don't remember how to find his house. Does he work nearby?"

"Not too far. He's employed at the Office of Credit," Nally said.

"Ah, he's a banker. That makes sense." Wyll joined Nally near the stove, where he shook a pan of cubed meat searing over the flames.

"What's a banker?" Nally asked.

"It's the same thing. Someone who handles money, I mean, credit. What can I help with?" Wyll asked, re-tying his apron.

"Cut up those carrots, if you don't mind."

Before Wyll could respond, Eleeda interjected, snatching a canister from the counter. "O' course he don't mind. It's his job; he'll do it if he wants a place ta sleep tonight."

Wyll waited until she departed before sticking out his tongue at her. He contemplated flipping her off but refrained, unsure if such gestures would be understood in this world. Nally chuckled at the exchange.

"Where exactly is the Office of Credit?" he asked, holding a carrot in one hand and chopping it with the other.

"It's located past the warehouses. The king had all the offices of Community Needs situated in the grandest building he constructed. You'll find credit, doctors, hospitals, legal services... Have you seen it?" Nally poured a brown sauce over the sizzling meat with a flourish, its aroma making Wyll's mouth water.

"Yeah, the high-rise. I spotted it. What are you making?"

"Roll-ups."

"What now?" Wyll was learning that whatever name the king gave something, it was used without question.

Nally looked confused. "They don't have roll-ups where you come from?"

"They have a lot of things where I come from, like jelly. And we have fruit roll-ups—"

"Jelly? A fruit roll-up might be good if I did it right. Hmmm." Nally thought. "What would you use for the filling?"

"Probably jelly." Wyll laughed at his own bad joke. "But real fruit roll-ups are just mashed-up fruit and sugar in a thin slice, dried, and rolled up with a sheet of plastic."

"Ooooh." He nodded. "We spread out dough and layer in savory meats and vegetables, then roll it up and bake it. Sometimes, we use red sauce, sausage, and cheese; other times, we sprinkle in oregano, basil, and garlic with chicken. There are many variations. But you've got me wondering if I could make one with berries or apples and cinnamon?"

"That's pretty much a cinnamon roll. Cut it into thick slices after you roll it up and lay the slices on their side to bake." Wyll felt like Wiki, telling the baker how to cook. "When should I go see Indigo? I wanted to talk to him soon, but Eleeda would kill me if I left. I have no reason to go over there." Wyll scrunched his brow in thought.

Nally looked up with a twinkle in his eye. "Hang on, and I'll make up a delivery for the office. Bring me those scones."

Wyll hesitated. "Nally?" He picked up the platter and brought it to the baker.

"Yeah?" Nally stirred a milky mixture in the pan before turning his attention to the platter.

"I really expected you to hate me," he confessed, a hint of vulnerability in his voice. "I'm sure the captured Resistance members do, but I figured everyone would feel

The Clockwork Pen

the same. Why are you so nice? Sira won't talk to me, and Indigo hasn't been the same. I see the uncertainty in his eyes. I mean, he's still not mean, but he doesn't trust me either."

Nally paused momentarily, cocking his head in thought as he loaded a basket with scones. "I suppose it's just my nature," he replied, his tone filled with understanding. "Some people have so much in their lives that they can afford to throw people away. I don't have much. I was made a single man and found my wife five years ago. She is young and wanted children, but I'm too old for that. I've learned not to wallow or blame others. And I'm not your judge. Bring me that towel."

His words humbled Wyll. He didn't deserve such forgiveness, and he was grateful. He did as he was told, fetching the towel and handing it to Nally. Soon, he walked out the back door with a covered basket under his arm, knowing that Nally would take care of Eleeda.

"Go south at the square until the road stops, then go east. You can't miss it," Nally instructed. "I hope you have a good plan. I want revenge for Kipper..." His voice trailed off, and Wyll noticed the tears in Nally's eye as he lifted his goggles to wipe them away, revealing red rings from the rims.

"Kipper's not dead," Wyll whispered, his voice filled with determination. "I'm going to help him escape the Reformatory."

"How... How do you know he's there?" Nally stuttered, his mouth malfunctioning from shock.

"The king told me," he said. *"I have to bring them back. It's the only way to fix things."*

"If the king told you, he's expecting you to attempt a rescue. He's set a trap for you."

"Or he doesn't know what he's saying—sometimes it's obvious. I can't not try," Wyll said resolutely when Nally looked ready to object. *"It's a shot we have to take. Plus, it's the only thing I can do. I can't walk around wondering if they're suffering down there."*

"One thing, Wyll." Nally's gaze was steady like a wise wizard. *"Don't expect a ton of thanks from the Resistance, even if you do rescue them. People are skeptical by nature. I just mean, don't let it surprise you."*

Wyll's mind raced. The idea that the king wasn't merely rambling deserved extra consideration. Relying solely on his information was problematic. What if it was all a ploy to lure him back to the Reformatory? What if the Resistance members weren't there at all?

Sira's face flashed before his eyes, a mix of shock, disillusionment, and sorrow—just as it was when he confessed his deception. It didn't matter if it was a trap. If he ever wanted to change her mind, he had to go. He had no choice but to face the terror.

Wyll walked all the way through the main street of commerce and past the warehouse district. When he turned east and walked another block, his shoulder began

The Clockwork Pen

to ache from the basket. He saw the building and remembered what Nally said about it being the biggest building. He chuckled. It wasn't that big, nothing you couldn't find in downtown Kansas City.

The main floor was the hospital emergency room. Mechanic surgeons ran around, ready to perform inner or detailed repairs on people, and nurses gave bandages and pain meds to those with occasional cuts and regular injuries that didn't need wire repair. The thought of pain meds made the wound in Wyll's shoulder throb. He would give his left toe for some more of that water. Briefly, he considered going to the apartment and looking for it, but he would feel like he was breaking and entering someone else's property. He knew she wouldn't want him there right now.

"How may I help you?" a pretty nurse asked. She sat at a desk facing him in a white corset over a white lace top with a high neck and poufy sleeves to her elbows. Her hair was done up like she was going to the opera, and a white nurse's visor with a red plus sign perched in her bouffant. *Sheesh.* If nurses looked like that at home, men would be getting hurt on purpose. She smiled at him as he came to the realization that he was staring.

"Oh. Sorry. I'm looking for the credit offices?" He motioned to the basket as if that made any sense to her. He wanted to face-palm. "I have a delivery."

"Great." She smiled at him with even, white teeth, easing his tension. "Take that elevator up to the sixth floor, and you'll be there."

"Thanks."

He got into the elevator with a doctor as she pushed a button, and he pushed the button for the sixth floor. Her outfit was different from the nurse's. She wore a simple, dark, wine-colored dress with long sleeves and black gloves to her elbows. She stood in black lace-up boots, and a stethoscope hung from her neck. Definitely not modern-day medical practice, but he remembered with a chill *they're not really people*. She smiled at him, and he returned the gesture.

"Smells good," she said.

"Oh, ah, yes. They're from the castle baker. They're delicious. Want one?" He lifted the corner of the towel covering the scones.

"Thank you." She plucked one out. The elevator dinged at the second floor, and she left.

Next, the elevator stopped on the sixth floor and opened into a lobby—the kind you see in movies—with a semi-circle-shaped room, a receptionist at a desk facing the elevator, and offices on either side. He felt like he was on TV. Maybe he was. The king probably had hidden cameras everywhere. *He* would if it were him. Wyll shivered, then walked up to the desk where a woman sat typing on a device that looked like his laptop. "Hey, is that a computer?"

The Clockwork Pen

She looked up at him in confusion and annoyance. "Can I help you, sir?"

Wyll couldn't answer right away. She was drop-dead gorgeous but also looked like the biggest bitch he'd ever met. Her jet-black hair was short and teased into spikes shooting out of her head—held back by a pair of goggles—and her eyes were lined heavily in black with feathery lashes, tinged bright purple on the ends. He knew he didn't like her, but man, she was stunning.

He smiled and held the basket forward, saying with all the enthusiasm he could muster, "I brought scones for the office from Nally, the king's baker." He said it excitedly as if she'd just won the Publisher's Clearing-whatever.

Her narrowed eyes lit up. "Really? That was ... nice."

"Yeah. He's very thoughtful. Can I talk to Indigo Porra?" Wyll looked at the offices on either side for a glimpse of him or a sign with his name.

She narrowed her eyes once more. "Why?" She crossed her arms, covered in detached purple and navy stripe sleeves. It only highlighted her perfect chest, popping over her corset. He forced himself to look into her eyes—which were wide open under raised brows now.

Stop being a typical seventeen-year-old guy. "He's a business associate. I need to speak to him about business matters." He cleared his throat nervously. He'd overheard his father do business from "the office" at home. One thing was for sure: his dad knew how to get things done. Maybe he had a point. Wyll didn't know how to survive alone in the real world. He'd be eighteen soon and leaving home and didn't have experience with anything. All the working kids around him weren't getting ahead. He was falling behind. He vowed to find a job when he got home. His dad would certainly teach him to be a jerk and get things done if he asked. Wyll quoted, "Is that a problem?"

The receptionist said deadpan, "Not at all. I'll go get him for you."

What's the saying? *I hate to see you go, but I love to watch you leave? Yeah, that was it.* Indigo peeked his head around the semi-circle wall and motioned for Wyll to come back. He set the basket of goodies on the receptionist's desk and followed Indigo to his office, decorated in the Steampunk style, meshed with an early '80s corporate office feel. Wyll crossed to a wall of floor-to-ceiling windows, looking over an expanse of treetops.

"Have a seat," Indigo said, motioning to the chair facing his desk. "How can I help you?"

Wyll's feet sank into the pile of a patterned rug in crimson, ochre, and teal and sat facing a dark wood desk surrounded by built-in shelving.

"I know I messed up, Indigo, but I found out from the king today that the Resistance didn't die. They are in the Reformatory. We must bring them back. Well, I plan to liberate them, but I need help." A golden floor lamp stood to his left, open-geared, parts moving in conjunction—little wheels turned and fit flawlessly together, teeth sliding into grooves.

Indigo sat with his elbow on the desk, chin in his hand. "Go on."

"I need someone with a cell key, a diversion, and a place to take them." Wyll sat back. "That's what I've come up with."

Indigo thought for a minute. In his silence, Wyll looked for more tech. Everything he considered normal and boring in his own world was multi-functional here and decorated with cogs and pulleys. Looking at all the eclectic gadgets lining Indigo's shelves was interesting.

"You found out from the king, you say?"

He sighed. "Yeah. I know. It's complicated. He told me he would find out what's wrong with them to make new people."

"So, they could be down there, or the king lied to you and set a trap for the remainder of the Resistance."

Wyll grimaced. "That doesn't sound very convincing. But if they *are* down there, someone has to go, even if there's only a chance. I can't let him destroy those people if he hasn't already. It's my fault they were captured, and will be my fault if he kills them. Can you help me?"

"When do you want to do this?" Indigo rummaged through his desk.

"Tonight. As quickly as possible. He said he couldn't take them all apart at the same time. I don't want even one more person to suffer. He's so crazy. Maybe he doesn't even realize what he told me. If he's holding them, I don't want to give him time to set a trap. Who knows what he'll do? We don't have time to waste."

Indigo looked up from his writing. "Sira told me you introduced her to Hark. He's been greatly beneficial—helped us with the members in the square. I can see if he has anyone who can help with a key and a diversion. As for a place to take them, they will probably want to go home to their families."

"Oh yeah." Wyll felt dumb for worrying about it. Indigo looked at his watch, and Wyll saw a fancy-looking laptop on his desk. "Is that a computer?"

"No, it's called a *Laptop*." Indigo turned it around to face Wyll.

"Yes, I know it's a laptop. Does it have internet?"

"What?"

Wyll leaned in to look at it. He recognized the spreadsheet; it was a budgeting software installation. The entire office was wireless. They *must* have a connection. Unless the king had it set as "restricted" and didn't tell anybody about it. *Hmm.* Could he get a message home? What would he say? *Hey Derec, go back to the basement of the house we broke into and open the damn door?* Derec could think he needed help and come for him just to get caught by the king. Then, Wyll would have another person to rescue. "Never mind."

"Okay, well, I'll tell Hark—if he has a group—to meet you outside the kitchen at eleven tonight. Will that work for you?" Indigo scribbled quickly on a piece of paper and rose.

Wyll stood, too. "Sure."

Folding the paper, Indigo made a small square and pressed it into his hand, saying, "Give this to Kary on your way out."

Wyll smiled and waved, though he was disappointed Indigo was being so removed and business-like with him. He'd hoped they were still friends and Indigo would have wanted to join him on his new quest. Or take over. He really didn't want to orchestrate this whole rescue, though he knew he needed to be the one who did it if he ever wanted to earn Sira's forgiveness. She was not going to accept a simple "Sorry."

He stopped at the door and looked back at Indigo. "Thanks, man."

"See you tonight." Indigo winked. It would have seemed like an uncomfortable come-on from any other man but from Indigo? It was suavity in action. Wyll chuckled at the thrill he felt over the possibility of not completely destroying a friendship.

The rest of the day, Wyll operated on autopilot. It was like being in a dream. His senses seemed beyond his reach while he ate and washed the dishes. His mind ran like a hamster in its wheel as he diced and kneaded. He knew they would be expecting him to have a plan, so he thought about how he would get in and out as swiftly as possible. Would the king anticipate his arrival so soon after telling him about the prisoners? *Of course he would.* They'd have to prepare and be extra careful. There was no one left to rescue them if they failed. Since they didn't usually meet until midnight or one, he worried that meeting earlier might throw off the plan. It didn't fully make sense, and anxiety ate him all afternoon.

At ten till eleven that night, Wyll stood, shrouded in darkness, outside the kitchen's back door, just behind a square of dim light cast on the stones. It grounded him like a beacon in the night. Everyone else from the kitchen slept in their beds, leaving the fires to die, the light flickering into shadow. He waited impatiently with his back pressed to the wall.

A pair quietly passed through the kitchen door, and he was about to call to them when he noticed their linked hands and heads close to each other. Just a couple of lovers looking for some privacy. Probably Lyri and her boyfriend. Eleeda frowned on relationships, and the poor girl wasn't in a position to rebel.

The town clock struck eleven. Several minutes later, Wyll wondered if he'd been left to his own devices when he heard voices whispering in the dark. "Who's there?" he called softly.

The voices paused.

"Who are you?" a deep-timbered voice asked ominously. "We are armed."

Armed? Were they guards? He hesitated for a moment. "It's Wyll. Who's there?" he repeated.

Silence.

He stepped into the patch of light from the kitchen doorway.

"Get out of the light, imbecile," a voice hissed.

He approached the voices warily. Under a nearby arch, he found Hark, a coil of rope on his shoulder, with a small boy and a girl, no, a small woman in her twenties or so. What was it with all the beautiful women? He thought about it for just a second and decided if *he* was going to make an entire race of people, he wouldn't make any ugly women, either. Again, he wondered at his similarities with the mad king, which scared him.

"Would you like a picture?" the woman asked.

"What?" He was about to apologize for gawking when he heard pebbles hit the water. They each stepped back, watching for trouble.

"I hope I'm not late," Indigo jogged stealthily up to the group, dressed down from his typical formal attire. Seeing him in a gray shirt with a black vest and his dark trousers covering his boots was strange.

"No, we just got here," the woman said. She pointed her thumb at Wyll. "This one of yours?"

Damn. No need to get snippy. When instigated, Wyll knew he had a small temper problem, and he snapped at her without thinking. "I'm the one leading this operation. I don't know who you are, but this is a big job, and it won't be easy. Are you sure you're up for it?"

"I'm here, aren't I?" She narrowed her eyes at him.

Ah, doesn't like being challenged, huh? "It could be a trap. You might get caught."

She pulled up a black hood and crossed her arms over a black jacket with sets of silver buckles strapped across her chest. "I volunteered for this job, toddler."

"You are—"

"Wyll, you know Hark." Indigo nodded toward Hark. He affectionately ruffled the boy's hair, and the boy grinned up at him like a hero. "And this little guy—"

"I'm Juke," the boy said, sticking his hand out for Wyll to shake.

"He's Kipper's boy. He came to help us with the distraction." Indigo clasped Juke's shoulder.

Confusion clouded Wyll's mind. He pointed to the girl, ah, woman. "Then what's she here for?" He had to admit—he relished watching her come so close to losing her shit while simultaneously being required to keep quiet.

Indigo gave a little cough to cover his chuckle. So did Hark.

The Clockwork Pen

"This is Mandalyn," Hark said. "She's my lock expert."

Wyll looked up at Hark in shock. "No one has a key?"

"First of all, I'm better than any farking key, and you can take this job and—"

"Manda," Hark said her name with authority. Maybe they were related. "You two play nice."

She thrust out her hand to Wyll. "Call me Manda."

Not that he had a thing for older women, but he'd call her anything she wanted, fiery temper and all. *Wait.* What was he thinking? Compared to the fire in Sira, Manda was the cold bite of dry ice, but he needed all the help he could get right now. "Glad to have you."

"So, what's the plan?" Manda asked.

"I'll tell you as we go. First, Indigo, do you have the codes for the reformatory entrance?"

Indigo nodded.

"Good," Wyll said. "Everyone, follow us."

They traveled around the sidewalk, hugging the castle walls, and slipped through the main entrance ala Indigo, then descended, single file, down the interminable, winding staircase. When they reached the bottom, Wyll held his hand up and stopped. The group held still while he inched his head around the opening and peered through the red light from above the door. The silent blackness magnified his anxiety. He wasn't as afraid of seeing the soldiers as being caught off-guard by that wordless terror machine. It seriously creeped him out.

The idea was to get as many people outside as possible before alerting anyone of their presence. With only one way in or out, Wyll stood guard near the doorway, waving for the others to pass him. They crept along the wall opposite the cells, diligently aware. There was no sign of the soldiers ... yet.

Indigo pulled his goggles off his hat, put them on, and then handed a pair to Wyll. His face all googly-eyed, Indigo grinned, white teeth nearly glowing in the dark. "Put 'em on."

Wyll stretched out the elastic and pulled the dark lenses on, not expecting to see anything, only to find he could clearly see the people in their cells. Not necessarily night vision, but not heat vision, either. The prisoners' dejected faces peered sightlessly in the dark. The group prowled in silence. Wyll wanted to set them *all* free but knew it wasn't possible, so he followed the wall, not alerting anyone to their presence. When they came upon cells filled with small groups of elegantly dressed occupants all in disarray, he knew they'd found their party.

Despite the chill, Wyll could feel the sweat roll down his temple. He didn't know if he should feel fortunate they'd had no need for a distraction or not. Part of him was just waiting for someone to sound the alarm. He turned to little Juke and gripped his shoulder,

The Clockwork Pen

whispering, "Can you go back to a place near the door? Look for the red light. If any soldiers come, just start crying loudly and say you're lost. You shouldn't be here—and they know that—but hopefully, the confusion will give us some time to know where they are and manage to sneak out as many as we can. Once you get everyone's attention, run." He felt the boy's body jiggle when he nodded vigorously. Wyll patted his shoulder. "Okay, go now. Stay hidden if you can."

He cringed as Manda's tools ground into the corroded metal, scraping the lock. The people behind the bars murmured, and he heard Indigo's whispered platitudes. Wyll's knee shook. *Hurry, hurry.* The energy in the small space ramped up until he could feel it like static electricity on his fingertips. He felt like he could shock anything he touched.

Hark led the first group to the door and out without a problem and had already gathered the next huddle of bodies. *It's too easy,* Wyll thought. His heartbeat picked up speed. Where were the guards? Where was that machine? Rather than feel fortunate at their luck, he was sure the soldiers lurked behind the shadows, lying in wait. Indigo led out the next group and came back with Hark.

"Where'd the people go?" Wyll whispered. It felt good to think of someone else for a change.

"They've gone home for now. We don't know if the king will decide to pursue them or not," Hark said.

"Just in case, we're planning to meet outside town in the morning, so they are hugging their families and packing."

"How many groups are left?" Indigo asked.

"Just the two—" Wyll was saying when Juke raised a ruckus, crying and pleading for someone to take him out of the unfamiliar place. The soldiers must have been on a break of sorts. Maybe coming down here earlier than normal had been the best idea. Random shouting prevailed as the guards realized they were under siege and came down the cavernous corridor, their boots clomping on the rock floor.

Something whizzed by Wyll's ear, and he realized they were being shot at. His ear immediately began to throb, and his shoulder decided to cause sympathy pain. He ran toward the soldiers, pumping his arms. He ducked his head, leaning forward like a tackle drill, aiming for the guard's center with his shoulder. *This can't be a failed mission.*

"Get the next group out!" he yelled, barreling into the first soldier. He could have never brought a soldier down, but the darkness was good cover for his surprise. Maybe the technology in his goggles trumped their night vision because the soldier he barreled into did not appear to see him coming. Wyll rammed into the metal body and flew forward, on top of the soldier who grappled for his neck. He could hear Hark and Indigo combatting the other two tin men. Someone grabbed a guard's shooting arm, and bullets flew everywhere.

The Clockwork Pen

"Watch it!" Wyll shouted as he felt a burning pinch in his calf. He held back his opponent's gun arm as the man hadn't decided yet if he wanted to let go of his gun to strangle Wyll or shoot him. Wyll shifted his weight, rolling the soldier, and bent the man's arm back.

The soldier's elbow went far enough in the wrong direction to lose the wrestling match with a loud crack and a scream, and he dropped his gun near his shoulder. The guard tried to buck Wyll off, but he picked up the gun and hit the soldier's head with the stock until the lights on his vision panel faded and blinked out.

The other men were subduing their adversaries. Like yarn art, Hark tied up his opponent with the rope and joined Indigo in his own struggle. The three wrestled with one gun, grappling for it as it fired, and they all fell. The terrified prisoners huddled, waiting for directions, and Wyll dove for his friends.

He rolled over the stunned men and found the guard on the bottom, with his face panel open and gasping like a fish on the shore, a bullet hole in his neck. Wyll felt strangely sad for him. He was not a man, but he had a soul, not from his choice but from the mind of a king who thought himself God. It wasn't fair. The guard hadn't asked to be there. He'd been built for the job. Wyll shook his head.

"Hark," he said, "take the Resistance members out. Indigo and I will grab the last group."

Jennifer Haskin

In the firing, a few prisoners were hit and were dealing with injuries. Hark held up a man who'd been shot in the hip and couldn't move his leg. "I'll need Indigo to help me get these people out," Hark said, "but you've got Manda. She's back there working on the last lock."

"Perfect." Wyll walked into a cobweb, brushed it off his face, and spat the strand out of his mouth, plucking at it with his fingers. "You guys go. We'll be right behind you."

His heart pounded with adrenaline as he jogged down the long corridor to the last cell. Every instinct he had told him that this wasn't over. Manda had the door open and supervised the group as they trudged, single file, through the small cage opening and grouped against the wall. Wyll smiled brightly at Manda. "We've got the guards subdued." He could hear the one conscious guard yelling but couldn't hear what he said as sound echoed off the rock.

She turned to him and stopped. Her eyes moved past him and widened. She was so stiff he could see her shaking. Instantly, he knew what was behind him, and it raised the hair on the back of his neck. He turned to see the terror machine about a foot behind him, and he jumped back with his fists up, punching out with one. It stood there bouncing on its spindly legs, its knobby knees bending and straightening. It waited like a dog expecting a treat or a pet.

Chapter Fourteen
MANDA

Wyll stammered, "G-good boy."

The terror machine lumbered closer to him and stood expectantly. He didn't know what to do. He called over his shoulder to Manda, "Can you get them out while I occupy this ... *thing?*"

Manda tried to steer the people around him, but the machine stomped its foot, and the people began screaming, each in their own terror.

"Stop!" Wyll held out his hands toward the machine.

The people stopped their howling and huddled once more, a few still crying.

"What are we going to do?" Manda asked from behind him, her voice near his ear.

"I'm trying to think. It's in between us and the only way out."

"Um—" She was hesitant, and Wyll could tell she really didn't like what she was thinking. "That isn't the only way…"

"What is it?"

"Behind us, at the end of the corridor, is a drain that opens to the moat. You and the others could get out that way." She touched his shoulder as she spoke into his ear only.

"What about you?" He ventured a small turn of his head to see her pinched expression.

"I can't swim."

"Okay, then that idea is out. I'm not leaving you here. I'd just have to come back and rescue you tomorrow—and it isn't that simple."

She chuckled. "Okay then, how are we getting past this thing?"

The machine pressed closer to Wyll. "I'll ... I don't know, play with it? I guess. Distract it while you lead the others out."

She nodded. But then they both heard shouting. More guards were coming. They were running out of options. He didn't know how many soldiers would be down here, but he and Manda couldn't subdue more than one or two of them. They couldn't take the chance.

"We're gonna have to go down the drain if we want out of here," he said. "Together, we won't be enough this time."

"I *can't*."

"A strong, capable woman like you? With your skills?" He smiled at her. "I know you can do it."

The Clockwork Pen

Wyll pointed down the corridor behind them. "Go that way, everybody. Keep calm, but go quickly. I'll stall for time."

He stood in front of the machine and touched it with a shaky hand. When his fingers brushed the metal surface, the thing started really bouncing, like it was excited. It took all his willpower not to pull his hand back and run from the monster. He didn't know what it could feel, but he scratched the surface like he would behind TeaCup's ears. The machine appeared to shiver and nudged closer to Wyll.

When he knew the people had gone, he said to the machine, "Okay. Nice boy. I have to go with my friends now." He could hear the guards questioning the ones they'd disabled. He didn't want to wait to be caught. However, when he turned and took a few steps, he found himself at the edge of a very tall cliff. Water beat the jagged rocks at the bottom with the force of a Mack truck, shooshing and spraying high enough to dampen his face, then swirling back to sea. He stopped and teetered at the very edge, throwing his weight back on his right leg.

Sweat beaded his brow. He tried to tell himself it wasn't real, though his brain told him this was very real. *If you go over the side, you* will *fall and die,* his brain said. He stood paralyzed. Though he heard noises around him, people shouting over the noise of the ocean waves, the spray on his face convinced him he was on the cliff.

Suddenly, a hand gripped his arm and pulled as the voices became louder. He couldn't see anyone and his terrified mind was panicking. But as he stumbled forward, he stepped over the edge and hung in the air. *He didn't fall.* His arm nearly popped out of its socket, and he shook his head to see the Reformatory cells.

Manda tugged his hand. "Let's go!"

He ran with her, not looking behind him to see who was following. He could only press forward. If he didn't get these people out, he would be a prisoner again, and there was no way the king would come down and shorten his sentence like last time. The thought of hours with the terror machine before he could be rescued stiffened his muscles. *IF they came to rescue me*, he reminded himself. He'd caused plenty of trouble, and Sira didn't care if he was in there. All he knew for sure was they had to keep moving.

They propelled down the slight decline, passing empty cell after cell. When he was almost upon them, he saw the last few people standing before a three-foot circular hole in the ground, the grate pushed to the side. *Looks pretty big for a drain*, he thought, but then realized how small it would seem with his body in it. The hole was black and dry, except for a trickle of water that collected and dripped down the drain. Where was the water of the moat? When did it start? How far was the swim?

The Clockwork Pen

"I cannot do this." Manda shook her head wildly, both fists pushing together on her chest, her eyes wet and shining.

Wyll grabbed her closest hand. "You must. Or you'll belong here. You don't want that, do you?"

"I never expected to have to go this way."

"I know. I'm scared, too. Manda, look at me. I'm petrified." He stared into her wide-eyed gaze. The grate sat under a red lightbulb that buzzed and blinked off occasionally, and they watched the last prisoner jump. The Resistance members wanted out any way they could find. The two looked at each other. He took her hand. "You'll be okay. I promise. Together?"

She squared her shoulders, and he saw some of her fire return as she stood straight. "Together," she said with a nod.

"We can do this, Manda."

They had to go one at a time, so she sat, and he lowered her until her body was hanging in the hole. "I'll be waiting at the bottom," she said, her lip quivering and a tear rolling down her cheek.

"I'm right behind you." He promised, then let go.

She shrieked, and he heard the guards pounding down the hall, nearly upon them. The terror machine came running into his view as he perched on the edge of the drain. He began to see a picture of the world from the rooftop of a skyscraper, but before the vision became clear, he jumped into the black hole.

Wyll's arms flew above him, and his feet flailed, hitting the sides of the hole. How far down did it go? When would he hit the water? When should he take a deep breath? He began to inhale and immediately plunged into frigid black water. It was one of his nightmares, swimming in dark water. He didn't want to know what living things were in the moat, and he didn't want to learn how big they were in person. He didn't want to open his eyes in case he saw a black fin…

Then he felt something grab his clothing. He began to panic as his shirt pulled, then a pair of hands gripped his arms. He remembered. *Manda!* He took her hand and felt the floor of the reformatory above them, so he kicked with all his strength, every so often, feeling the stone with his hand to see if they were clear yet. His clothes were so heavy, and Manda was slowing him down. But he couldn't leave her. So, he pulled and kicked and kept his eyes tightly shut.

When the rocks gave way to open water, he tugged Manda's hand and began to kick upward. Manda's hand was shaking in his, and he worried about her. His lungs were on fire, and with every kick, the exertion of his muscles demanded more air. He was tingling and light-headed. He pushed himself and felt Manda's hand squeezing his so hard he thought his bones would break. Then her grip went slack, and he almost lost her. She slipped out of his hand and began to fall. In a split second of despair, he reached down, struggling to find her, and

The Clockwork Pen

pulled her up by her hair, then her shirt. She floated motionless, and he kicked as hard as he could, pushing the water down with one hand, the other pulling Manda.

He broke the surface with a huge inhale and gasped a few times, coughing, before he realized he was holding Manda's body. People on the shore were recovering in the dark night, and he could see the moonlight shimmering off their wet bodies. They would need to move soon before the guards came looking for them. He sluiced through the water to the abrupt edge, like at the swimming pool.

"Help me," he cried. "Manda needs help."

Several men and women came to help him hoist her body out of the water. He only knew the CPR he saw on TV from that doctor show his mom watched with the totally unrealistic hunky doctors and hot nurses all having affairs with each other. He leaned over her body and pushed on her chest, trying to coax the water out. Nothing happened, so he tilted her head back, pinched her nose, and blew into her lungs. He could see her chest inflate, and it gave him hope. He pressed on her chest hard, giving it several thumps before breathing into her again.

After a few minutes, nothing had changed. The last few people murmured, and a few touched Wyll's shoulder, telling him how sorry they were and how grateful ... but they couldn't stay. And *he* couldn't stop the CPR. What if he stopped before the last breath that would bring her to life? What if it was only one chest compression away?

The people around him shifted. Indigo appeared next to him with Hark.

"I don't think it's working," Indigo said gently, placing a hand on Wyll's back.

Wyll shook his hand off and ignored him. *This was the last one; no, this one ... just one more...*

"Son," Hark said, his voice full of emotion. "Let her go now."

"I can't," he cried out. "She was just with me in the cave. She was just *here*. She told me she couldn't swim, and I promised her it would be okay—" His voice broke off. He wanted to shake her body or punch her heart as they did on TV sometimes to see if the force would awaken her, but he didn't want to abuse her body, either. Wyll sat back on his heels, dripping water and shivering. He looked up helplessly at the men.

"We came back and heard them chasing you to the drain, so we figured this was about where you'd come up." Indigo reached down to offer Wyll a hand up. All the other prisoners were gone.

"They'll figure it out pretty soon," Hark added. "We should go."

"You did good tonight." Indigo patted Wyll's back.

The Clockwork Pen

"Good? This is good?" Wyll cried, his words catching in his throat as he motioned to Manda, lying in the grass. In his desolation, he fumed, teeth chattering.

"It's one for the many. She knew that." Hark looked down on her with fondness. "Who knows? Maybe he can recreate her?"

"But ... a soul can't be recreated." Wyll slicked back his hair, feeling the top curl as he let go.

"How do you know?" Hark asked.

"People have been trying that since the dawn of time."

Indigo interjected, "We really should go."

"What about Manda?" Wyll asked.

"There's nothing more we can do for her." Hark touched her forehead with two fingers. "She must stay here. The king's men will take care of her remains."

"Don't you guys have a cemetery here or anything? Don't you want to bury her?"

The men both looked shocked. "Why would we cover her with dirt?" Hark asked for them both. "Her parts would go to waste."

"That's what happens when someone dies. You pump them with preserver and bury them in vaults in the ground, and after a billion years, their body decays into kibble." Wyll was fairly sure about his science on this. He'd just aced a test about embalming and burial in biology three weeks ago. It seemed like a lifetime had gone by since then.

Both men shook their heads at the idea. Wyll reluctantly let go and let them pull him away.

Coming out of his daze momentarily, he found himself alone in his quarters, stripping off all his wet clothes and dropping them on the floor. He left the lights on and collapsed into bed.

Wyll woke with a sense of finality. He was done with this place; screw it. He figured he had already jumped ahead to the anger stage of grieving. He'd never dealt with death so closely before. He floated in outer space, powerless to control himself. It could have just as easily been Wyll who ran out of air last night. The thought made him miss home. When he returned, first, he would hug his mom. He wished she was here now so he could—not necessarily because he was afraid but more because he was sorry. If life could be so short, he couldn't afford to waste it hurting people on purpose, out of spite, or anger, or just because he felt like bringing someone down to his level of disillusionment.

He'd been oblivious to his parents, utilizing the excuses of hormone surges and teen angst. To deal with his insecurity and wounds perpetrated by bullies at school, he channeled the emotions into stubbornness and a rebellious streak, but it was time to turn it toward someone else. *Rozam.* If Wyll had any value to this king, he would discover and exploit it somehow to escape Sepherra. *Time to go home.* But he wasn't leaving without Sira. He wouldn't doom her to deal with a madman she couldn't control alone. The king must be dethroned for the good of an entire world, and if Wyll did it, that would put the king in his power, and he'd take her back. *Because you're falling for her,* his subconscious seemed to plague him. *Shut up,* he told himself. It didn't seem right to be happy after Manda's sacrifice.

"You're off'n outer space," Eleeda said as they stood shoulder to shoulder, peeling new potatoes.

"I'm hatching a plan," he said, his eyes on his hands, then he grinned at her.

"Aha. What kind o' plan? Is there a princess involved?" She winked.

He smiled. "She hates being called that."

"Aye, but the King' d skin us all alive if we didn't." She tilted her head to the left and knocked it into his shoulder.

"Yeah, I can see that." He was quiet for a minute. "Hey, Eleeda?"

"Yeah?"

"Can I take Sira's lunch tray today? I won't be long, I promise. Keylin can show me where she is and be a chaperone." He raised his eyebrows and gave her the dimpled smile that made girls blush and giggle into their hands.

"Och." She hit him on the arm. "Fine, but don't go makin' lovey-dovey eyes at me."

He laughed, and she cleared her throat, adjusting her funny little hat and leaving a potato peel hanging in her fuzzy hair. He knocked it off and watched it fall to her sweater, then her full skirt, catching in the ruffle by her apron, where he noticed about ten more peelings. He laughed and went back to work. She'd shake them off later.

When it was finally time for lunch, he gathered Sira's tray from Eleeda. "Lead the way," he said, nodding to Keylin.

"Okay," she said in a singsong voice.

They walked all the way to the main entry in silence. The king and his family sent a note to the kitchen if they wanted anything for breakfast or lunch, delivered anywhere in the castle. However, they ate supper together in the dining room. Today, Sira was having lunch in her room rather than her office, where she usually studied or worked on things for her father during the day. Wyll wondered if she was ill. Keylin must have been thinking about something else.

"Did you really drag a dead girl from the water last night?" she asked softly.

He stopped. Of all the questions about last night that he thought she might ask—*did you really rescue all those people last night? Were you scared? Were they okay? Did they all make it home?*—she almost made it sound like all he'd done was kill a woman. "Where did you hear that?"

"Oh, Indigo met with Sira this morning—early. Before he went to work, I'm sure."

"Is that all he said? That I pulled a dead woman from the water?" He frowned.

"No, he told her everything. I was just wondering, what did she feel like? When she died. Did her skin change? Did it look different, feel different?" Her voice held a tremor.

It registered with Wyll that she was simply concerned with death. Why wouldn't she be? He smiled sadly at her. "No, it doesn't feel different right away. They look like they're sleeping at first. Once you make sure their eyes are closed, of course. It's too creepy with them open. But after so many hours, they get stiff. I don't know about clockwork people, but I assume it's the same."

"Where does she go? After she dies."

"Whoa. That's a *big* question. Maybe you should ask your mom."

"She wants to know, too." She looked at him with bright-eyed innocence, and he told her about what he thought as they walked up the atrium staircase toward the royal family's living suites. All he knew was what his mom had taught him about Heaven from church, but he wondered if he should even get her hopes up. Did God have a Clockwork Heaven?

Jennifer Haskin

They climbed the stairs to the fourth floor. Outside the family quarters, the landing housed a lounge of sorts, and the king sat reading a book. He looked up as they entered the room and met Wyll's eyes. "Hey, boy." He rose. "I know you," the king stated, his voice filled with a mixture of familiarity and detachment. Despite his apparent pleasant mood, there was a sense that his full presence was not completely there. Wyll seized the opportunity to challenge him, realizing that the king must have been informed of his presence in the Reformatory the night before.

The terror machine was undoubtedly aware that Wyll had been there, but could the thing talk? If the king was aware, Rozam had every reason to return Wyll to his cell. However, the king had expressed his desire for Wyll to remain in Sepherra, emphasizing Sira's concern for his safety. If Wyll didn't take action now, he might not get another chance. He noticed the absence of guards, reinforcing his hope that he wouldn't be immediately apprehended. Wyll banked on this temporary advantage.

"Wait here," Wyll whispered to Keylin, handing her the tray before striding purposefully toward the king.

"Yes, you know me," Wyll addressed the king directly, his voice steady and assertive. "I'm Wyll."

The king responded with a hint of jest in his tone, "You been up to something?"

"I have," Wyll replied, pausing briefly. "Are you missing anyone?"

The Clockwork Pen

"You let my subjects go." The king growled briefly before bursting into laughter, treating it all as if it were a mere joke. The king's grasp on reality was visibly slipping, a development that pleased Wyll.

"You were already aware of that. The truth is, I will continue to liberate them, again and again, until you send me home. And I won't leave without Sira," Wyll declared, a confident smile gracing his lips.

"Oh no, you're mistaken. I have plans for you, and Sira will never leave me," the king countered, returning the smile and projecting an air of unwavering self-assurance.

"Plans can be broken. What is it that you truly desire from me? What is your game?" Wyll's mind brimmed with suspicion and a determination to uncover the king's ulterior motives.

"You? You're merely bait," the king lowered his voice, his words filled with a dark undercurrent. "You will lead me to the last remnants of the Resistance fighters."

"You'll never find all of them. Their number grows every day. Your cruelty has turned them against you, and they will continue to resist. It will only get worse until you are overthrown," Wyll boldly predicted, his voice resonating with unwavering conviction.

"I am not cruel!" The king's voice rose in volume, his frustration evident. "I am a kind and loving father, a benevolent king, and a scientist tirelessly working to perfect my methods. I mean, only through absolute obedience can... I mean..." Frustration flushed the king's face, exposing the cracks in his composed facade.

Wyll waited for him to continue, but he stopped speaking and looked over Wyll's shoulder. Wyll had accomplished nothing—he had to press harder. "If you don't mean to be cruel, why don't you let me go? Let Sira come home."

His glassy eyes narrowed. "She *is* home. It is you who needs to get used to your new place. My daughter's just angry. She will come around. She always does. She will forgive me, and things will return to how they've always been. Then, before long, she'll miss her pet human—she'll appreciate my plans and be so happy I kept you here. I'm doing it for her. Don't you see? Everything is for her."

"What if she doesn't want me here?"

"She's set on being a mother. She will have a human no matter what I say. It's the only thing I can't make for her. And you're here now, so you'll have to do. No one else can know about Sepherra. It's more than your destiny; it's your new cage, little bird."

The man had lost his marbles, like an overturned box of monster-kittens. Did he have these lapses in sanity often? How could they capitalize on this?

"Yeah. Sure." Wyll turned. "I'm gonna go." There was no use trying to have a conversation with the man. He obviously hung his hopes on the idea that he couldn't lose Sira or turn her away. Wyll might as well see her and plan their exodus together—if she'd ever give him another chance.

"Proceed." The king yawned and sat back in his chair, reopening the tome, something about a boat.

Wyll strode back to Keylin with her mouth hanging open. He lifted his tray from her arm and waved for her to keep up.

"Why would you talk to the king like that? Are you a complete moron?" Keylin whispered when they'd entered the family's quarters through the double doors. "You know he could do literally *anything* to you?"

"I needed to see how much value I have to him. To see where he thinks I fit in, now that Sira doesn't—"

"Like you anymore?"

"Thanks for that," he said, curling his lip at her. "Basically. If he wants me alive and sane, that means I have value, and *that* means I have power."

"Power for what?" She came to a stop next to a closed door.

"I don't know yet." He nodded toward the doorway. "Is this it?"

She rapped on the jamb and gave him a sassy smile. "Yup."

He'd expected her to leave and give him some privacy to apologize to the—to Sira. He really didn't want to grovel in front of an audience. "Why don't I meet you back on the stairs when I'm done?" he whispered quickly.

"Keylin? Why are you knocking?" Sira opened the door and froze, her eyes as round as her mouth.

"How about I don't?" Keylin whispered back with the biggest smile.

Chapter Fifteen
The Slimeball and the King

Jett heard the king bellowing at someone down the hall and quickened his pace toward the royal office. He brushed dust from the front of his uniform and smoothed his short, styled, black hair. He'd just finished cleaning his closet-sized office. Happy to give up his position overseeing maintenance, he was applying to be the king's aide and supervisor for a project "off the record." Not every staff member knew about it, but the king had petitioned his existing managers for the task. It was perfect. He could be Sira's mole and play both sides. The more the king liked him, the easier it would be to complete his own secret plans. No one would know his agenda. He smiled.

When the remaining Resistance managed to overthrow Rozam and free the country, Jett would be in a perfect position to campaign as the new leader. And with the pen, it would be easy. He knew the suspected cost of using the pen. That's why he would create staff to scribe his ideas as he dictated. He would rule without ever facing the consequences of the device. He needed only to watch the king use it and learn the procedures first. Then he'd deal with Sira.

He turned into the last hallway and replaced his smug grin with a mask of humility. He was proud that no one knew exactly who he was or what he wanted. They'd never expect his machinations. Just as he got to the doorway of the king's office, King Rozam barreled through the opening and ran into Jett with a grunt.

"What are you doing here?" Rozam growled.

"We had a meeting, Your Highness. Ten o'clock?" Jett smiled.

"Oh. Yes. I need some air. Walk with me, and we can talk in the pavilion." King Rozam waved in the direction he was heading.

Jett fell into step with the king, and they descended the back stairs to exit the building. The guards stationed there held the door for them.

"Lovely day," Jett said as the sun poured down, unheeded by clouds.

The king grunted. Then he took a deep breath and let his shoulders drop with his exhale. "Quite so. Just what I needed. Keeping a kingdom can muddle the brain."

Your brain is more than muddled, Jett chuckled to himself. "I'm sure your vast wisdom is occasionally taxing."

"Yes. Very astute of you, young man."

They traveled around the turret on a covered walkway to the west tower. Its first floor was an open courtyard held up by multiple support columns, with scattered groups of furniture used for informal gatherings in pleasant weather. A chilly breeze ruffled Jett's hair, irritating him momentarily. He followed the king through the courtyard, called the pavilion, to a set of chairs in a slant of warm sun. He waited for the king to sit and took a place facing him.

King Rozam peered out beyond the moat to the gently swaying trees. He appeared lost in his thoughts, so after a few minutes, Jett cleared his throat, startling the older man.

"Remind me, young one, of our meeting."

"Of course, Your Highness. We are discussing your newest project. And I am interviewing to oversee construction. Could you tell me what the job will entail?" Jett was gentle and polite, with a gracious smile.

The king appeared pleased. "Yes. I shall be constructing an expansion. Do you have experience with leadership?"

"I run the maintenance department in the castle. Where would this expansion take place? Are we building new homes, stores, or offices?"

The king flashed a conspiratorial smile and waggled his eyebrows. "We will build a new land on the other side of the mountains to the South."

Jett leaned forward in interest. "An island?"

"Precisely. Something new to explore—and enrich the kingdom. Maybe an attraction to renew the people's spirit—give them something pleasant to focus on and quell this ugly struggle of opposition." The king made big gestures with his hands, fluttering ringed fingers, his smile broad. "What think you?"

"It sounds creative, Your Highness. But ... have you considered going bigger? Instead of an island, maybe a sister country? You could make a new people group. Would you make them a new language to learn?"

"Fascinating idea. Hmmm." The king ran his fingers down his goatee in thought. "That would mean new language classes and cultural differences. You believe you could oversee such a substantial design?"

"I am confident of it, sir." *And it would hopefully be enough pen usage to send you over the edge.* Jett flashed a broad grin.

"Are you a keeper of confidences? This would be an inconspicuous production until it is complete. And I would require preview diagrams of your construction before establishment."

Can I keep a secret? He has no idea. "Your Highness has no cause to worry. I am unfailing in confidentiality."

"The other staff never suggested broadening my design to make it better. I need a man with initiative. You are hired." The king stuck his hand out, and Jett gripped it.

"Thank you, Your Highness. You will not be sorry."

The Clockwork Pen

"I trust you are right—and one more thing. You will be required to construct a small castle for Sira. A honeymoon gift."

Jett managed to keep his jaw off the floor. "Is she to be married soon?"

"Not soon, I hope. But she will be grateful. She will be so busy with her new human husband and running a castle that she won't have time to be rebellious. I shall make her the leader of the new country. She was adept at learning the language here; she can learn a new one. And there may even be grandchildren to toss about in a few years." The king looked ecstatic, with raised brows and open joy. He clapped his hands together. "Yes. That will do nicely."

"A human, sir?"

The king's expression darkened. "The boy she found. She likes him. He will require some convincing to remain, I'm afraid. But if he makes her happy, I will overlook his many faults."

Wyll was what she called him. He'd heard there was a boy there—sold out the whole group. Jett was lucky he'd been too busy for the meeting. It would have ended his job and life in the castle. He was immediately apoplectic—he'd thought that without any human males in Sepherra, Sira would learn to compromise in time. They could have petitioned the king for a child made of their combined DNA. She could still be a mother. He gritted his teeth. "That is fortunate," he said with a broad smile. "I'm sure she will appreciate your gift."

And if it drives you past the point of reason, I can do anything I please to them. Without the boy, the plan may still work.

"Yes, you are right. Of course, she will finally be happy here with me. Forever." The king rose, and Jett followed.

"I will get right to work on the designs, Your Highness. I will be available whenever you need me. I am at your disposal." Jett bowed to the king.

"You are excused. I will wait expectantly for your blueprints."

"Thank you." Jett exited the pavilion, his mind running scenarios of what he could do with this latest information.

Chapter Sixteen

THE COMPANY OF MILGEN

Sira stood as a statue in the doorway to her room. She scowled at Keylin. "Why did you bring him here?" She didn't appear to be ill. Then Wyll remembered her father's banishment to her quarters as a punishment.

Keylin had the grace to blush and bow her head.

"I, ah, brought your lunch. Since you're grounded and all," Wyll hoped he didn't sound anywhere near as lame as he felt at that moment. He tried his panty-dropping smile. "It's good to see you."

She stepped aside, her mouth in a firm line, and nodded to him. "Come in." She looked at Keylin. "Just stay nearby."

"Aaawww," Keylin said, drawing the sound out. "You know I'm just going to listen at the door."

Sira sighed. "Yes, Keylin. I'm aware."

She pushed the door shut and turned back to Wyll, who stood behind her with the tray. He waited expectantly for directions, but she stood staring at him for a moment. Her attention warmed him in unexpected places. Of course, some places were bound to be sensitive, but he didn't expect to feel a clutching in his chest. It was deliciously painful, and he soaked in it for just a second. Then he felt awkward and didn't know what to do. He wondered what she thought of him now. At least she hadn't slammed the door in his face. Sira was obviously lost in thought, so he cleared his throat.

"Ah, where do you want this? It's kind of heavy."

She jolted and pointed to a side table with two pipe legs curved in a figure eight against the wall and dark, polished woodwork. "Over there … thanks."

He passed a plush velvet couch with curling wood trim. A giant clock leaned on the wall, and picture frames were everywhere, some with deeply colored mirrors. The room had no bed, and he realized she must have a suite with an attached bedroom. He chastised himself for even imagining her in bed. They had taken such an enormous step backward; the distance between them was tangible.

He set the tray down carefully not to scuff the polished grain. The table's hind legs seemed to hold all its weight, but a pulley mounted on the wall above it attached to the tabletop with heavy rope. He wiped his hands on his pants, not sure what to do. "Do I serve you? Or—"

"Oh no. You don't have to do that." She chuckled. "You should know I wouldn't let you even if you were supposed to."

He smiled at her. "Sira, I know you're mad. I tried to make up for it. But—"

"I know what you did." Still no expression on her face.

What does she think?

It was so frustrating. He was walking on eggshells and knew that she wasn't. It was one part each: galling, humbling, and humiliating. He needed to talk to her before he got angry. He was there to tell her, *I'm getting out of here, and you're coming with me.* And then he'd grab her and dip her back and kiss her while his other hand held up a sword... No, that was the cover of some movie he'd seen from the vintage store. *Try again...*

"So, you doing all right? Keylin said Indigo came by this morning. Is there any news?" He watched her expression sour, and suddenly, he wasn't sure she was willing to forgive him. "I mean, if I'm allowed to know and all. I just—I'm sorry, and I want to help."

"But you said yourself, *'I'm no hero. You can't count on me.'* Yada yada yada." Her fists perched on her hips.

"I know. I know what I said. I messed up, okay? I didn't get it." He glanced up at the glorious map that filled her ceiling. "Life isn't a dream—you have control. It is what you make it. I thought I was existing by reacting to things that happened to me, but then I met you, and you don't do that. You choose everything about how you exist, from how you look to what you believe in. I just want you to believe in me again."

He'd been looking over her head at the thin, floor-to-ceiling fish tank that doubled as a large window. Looking down at her, he didn't know what he expected. He hoped for a tear in her eye and a big hug. But she stood in brown leather pants, with her hip out and her arms crossed. Her head was lowered, so he couldn't see her face—just her hair. It was so shiny and silky, and he remembered how soft it was and how good she smelled...

She looked up at him. "We were so close," she whispered. "I thought we were. But you let all those people get hurt. My people. OUR people. Without any conscience. How can I trust you again?"

"Don't give up. Please. You didn't like me when we first met, right? You got to know me. You learned about me. So, find out how I've changed." He hoped she'd give him a break. It hurt to know he didn't deserve one, but he'd tried to fix things. Of course, he murdered someone. *Oh shit, right.* He had forgotten all about it when he saw Sira. Now he saw Manda's face, and he frowned in agony.

She watched him closely and wrinkled her brow. "I can see you're sorry. I can read the pain in your face. It makes me feel something, but I don't know what. My head doesn't match my heart when it comes to you, and I'm afraid if I don't lock up my heart, you'll find a way to steal it. And we are nothing alike."

Wyll wasn't sure if he was being let down, but he didn't get the feeling things were going well for him. He had a great idea. "You, of all people, should know that couples don't have to be anything alike to make a great pair. Look at your parents—at every couple in Sepherra." He pointed at her and smiled. "I know you believe in that. In differences not mattering when it comes to—"

She smiled slightly, with her arms still crossed. "What, Wyll? Love?"

He shifted uncomfortably. "Maybe? I don't know. Why does it have to *be* anything? Why can't it just *become?*"

She shifted her position as well, this time cocking out her other hip and threading her thumbs—in fingerless gloves with a silver buckle—through her belt loops. "I don't know if I can change like you can, apparently. Maybe it's the pressure I'm under. My father won't let me use the pen, which frustrates me. Indigo and I think that if we could get him to let me use it, once he shows me how, I could make a quick decoy pen and give it to him instead. We'd be long gone by the time he figured it out."

"Well, what can I do?" He spread his hands. "Do you need me to find anything? Talk to anyone? Be a distraction?"

"You're already a distraction." She chuckled. "I'm afraid there's nothing you can do. Jett is already shadowing him as his new page of sorts, taking notes."

"Isn't that the guy who liked you? What if he's just trying to keep you here?"

"What? He's a little weird, but I don't think he'd betray us. I mean, he would have freedom with a new government or be free to go with us … if he wanted." She appeared to be thinking about it but then shook her head. "I don't think he'd do it, but a good leader considers all possibilities."

The door flung open, and a woman in a black and gold ensemble breezed in, with black lace dripping from her elbows. She was dragging Keylin by her sleeve. "Oh, hello," she said, apparently faking her politeness. "I figured something was happening since Keylin had her ear to the door."

"I did not!" Keylin said, though her cheek sported a red circle where it had been pressed to the wood.

"We haven't met." The woman held her hand out to Wyll and narrowed her eyes at Sira.

"This is my stepmother," Sira said with all the excitement of a three-year-old receiving a head of cabbage for their birthday.

"Shendy Sepherra. It's nice to meet you, finally. Rozam has said so much about you."

Wyll shook her tiny child-sized hand.

"Oh, I'll bet he has." Sira tilted her head to the side, mocking her stepmother's fake interest. "What's he said, Shendy?"

Shendy frowned. "You know I don't like that."

"We're not in public, and you're not my mom. So, I'm calling you Shendy. Plus, Wyll knows."

"Knows what?" The woman narrowed her eyes to slits.

"He knows Dad only created you for two things: warming his bed and spying on me." Sira's hands were fists again. Wyll could see both sides, but he loved watching the fire in Sira ignite and roar. *Team Sira,* he thought.

Shendy raised her hand like she would strike Sira, and the hackles on the back of Wyll's neck stuck up. His spine stiffened, but Sira only raised her eyebrows at the delicate black-lace-gloved hand hanging in the air. Shendy dropped her arm.

"You'd just love for me to give you another reason to hate your father and me," she said in disgust.

"Nah. Just you."

If Wyll had said that to either of his parents, there'd be a funeral in about two or three days. Shendy inhaled with her other hand on her diaphragm, somewhere in the ruffled flounce of her skirts with vertical black silk panels between the gold stripes. She turned sharply, zeroing in on Keylin.

"When is your mother coming back? You two should be in school and having class. *Or serving people,*" Shendy sneered.

Keylin looked down at her hands, playing with her apron strings. Wyll knew she worked a lot. She was basically a kitchen wench when she wasn't a laundry maid. He wouldn't be surprised if she had brought him food when he was in the Reformatory. She was obviously uncomfortable.

Sira answered for her. "Well, tell Dad to promise that he won't beat her up or imprison her anymore. Geez, Shendy. Don't you notice anything? He put her in the square. Why would she come back?"

Shendy looked a bit confused. Wyll wondered if the king kept her from understanding certain things, so she remained loyal. Yeah, knowing this guy, he was sure that was it. It's what he would have done if he'd made himself king.

"Well, I have things to do." Shendy smoothed down the front of her bodice. "I'm sure you were leaving, right, Keylin? Good day, Sira." She breezed out as lightly as she had come in. Not a care in the world. If he could make a woman any way he wanted, would he make a docile sex machine that would be his spy? He imagined the current Playboy model of the month as a clockwork woman in his bed, and he thought that might work. But then, he imagined what Sira would say, and his mind transformed the images—Sira's face on the playmate's body. He felt suddenly inappropriate and needed to escape.

He shifted uncomfortably, trying to think of things like ice water and cows. He had no idea why those were turn-offs for him, but it worked. Keylin grabbed his elbow. He could feel the tremors of her fear and was awash in sympathy. She really had no place to be. Her mother was hiding out, and she'd only ever lived in the castle. If they decided to kick her out, they could do it on a whim, and she'd have no home to go to. She was best off not being seen or heard.

"Let's get back to the kitchen," she pleaded. It was warm, inviting, *home* ... and had become that for him. Eleeda was right. If he got up when she said, went to bed as she said, and did everything she said, things went well for him. It was a hard job but an easy rhythm. The kitchen staff was a family, and they'd been welcoming and accepting.

"Yeah." He looked at Sira. "I'll see you later?"

She appeared to deflate before his eyes. "I don't know, Wyll. I really want—I just... I don't always get what I want. I can't promise you I'll change."

"That's okay. I'm leaving. Just work with me, and I'll get you home." He looked around and saw her luxurious bed with a curved canopy and fireplace through another doorway. "Your real home. But I'll warn you; it isn't anywhere near this cool where the humans are."

She chuckled. "I'll take that chance."

He felt the weight of Keylin's hand on his arm, so he squeezed it to his body. "And you, too, Key. I think your mom should come back with us to watch over you two." He smiled at Sira, who frowned slightly.

"Why would we need watching after? We are almost factory-ready."

"What's that?"

She rolled her eyes as if he'd asked the dumbest question ever. "When you are old enough to quit classes and work exclusively. Then you get a marriage license, a partner, a house, a job assignment, and you plan when to have kids, yada yada yada."

"Oh. Well. In our world, you are still a kid. And you don't get a marriage license when you reach a certain age or get your partner from the government ... or a house. Geez, that would be nice."

Now Sira looked as confused as she apparently thought he was. "How do you—? Oh, I'll ask later. You guys go before the eminent spy comes back." She smiled at Wyll, but not in a "*bye, it was good to see you*" way. It was a pity smile. She knew he had it bad for her, and she didn't feel the same. Maybe he'd wrecked it before she even got there.

He gave her a tight smile in return and patted Keylin's arm. "Let's go."

It was another week of rising at dawn and working until he fell asleep, dead-to-the-world exhausted, before he heard anything about the plan. He'd never worked so hard in his life. His mom would be so proud of him. But really, he was trying to scrub away the image of Manda's panicked face under the blinking red light.

I can't, Wyll.
Trust me.

The Clockwork Pen

How long had he even been here? In some ways, it seemed like forever. He'd received a week's pay of credits and had no idea what to do with it. He thought he'd probably make a credit system if he created a world himself. But every time he admired something the king did or thought *Awesome job, dude*, he cringed inside. If the pen had fallen to him in the same circumstances and he had the same threat of losing Sira, he was surer and surer that he would have done exactly the same thing. Did that absolve Rozam from being a monster? Or did it condemn Wyll?

He strolled around the pathways of the castle grounds with his hands in his pockets. His killer pocket watch hung from its chain in the breast pocket of his vest, and he held the hard metal object in his palm, warming it. He thought as he walked, mulling over the same problem as he did every evening in the crispy cool of early night. How could he free them? Short of killing the king and causing Sira to hate him, there was no more solid plan than the one she already had. He hated leaving it up to the king's timing and hated that he wasn't in control of the circumstances or any variables at all.

How could he be the one to rescue her if she was in control? Did it make him less of a player in his own story? He wrestled with his need to win and the guilt over making it all about himself. If they both got home, that's all that mattered. *Right?* His masculinity disagreed.

Wyll leaned over the balcony railing and watched the water below him. Black and ominous, he couldn't believe he'd come up through that churning, sloshing deepness. It made him shudder, and he stiffened.

"Come here, you little freaks," he called, holding a loaf of stale bread out over the water. A flock of creepy-as-shit duck-like things floated over, honking excitedly. They weren't far away; they knew he was coming.

He refused to be a slave to his fear. The reformatory had taught him that he had more fears than he knew about, and since his stay there, he'd had so many new fears enter his mind at the most random times. He'd be washing the pots when he'd think of something terrifying and think, *Thank God I didn't think of that while I was in there.* He dropped a plate once from the anxiety of imagining himself being held upside down by the king and having hot wax poured into his nasal cavity. You wouldn't die, but it would feel like you were drowning, besides hurting like hell.

Wyll tossed hunks of bread into the air, and the ducks' accordion necks all bobbed and ducked, trying to get the pieces, some of their necks tangling, and then they tried to peck the ducks who'd caught the morsels they wanted. He was no closer to being healed than he was to leaving. He'd been told to stay where he was, and any word would come to him.

He'd seen Jett twice and asked how the plan was coming to feel the guy out.

"I'm working on him," Jett said in a hallway alcove near the kitchen when he'd come to fetch a snack for the king.

The guy was about as vague as he could be. With his parted hair and a bowler hat, he was good-looking enough, self-assured, but he knew it. *Yeah, that kind.* Wyll knew instantly why the guy had gotten mad when Sira turned him down instead of being heartbroken. Jett would have thought she had absolutely no reason *not* to be with him. Why wouldn't she?

Wyll wondered if she had actually explained that it was because he was clockwork. Knowing Sira, probably. *Ouch.* It solidified in his mind that this guy was one to watch. He had reason to strike back at her—and to keep her here. That also made him a threat to Wyll. The inner circle—including Jett—knew Wyll was human and desired to leave with Sira.

The ducks were wildly honking a racket. "Hush, little beasties. You're going to get me caught, and no more food for you." He shook the loaf, and crumbs flew everywhere. The duck-things went psychotic. He laughed as he tore off a bunch of small pieces and threw them into the air at the same time. He didn't know why it cracked him up so much to watch their necks get all twisted in their fight for flying bits. His belly was sore from laughing when someone touched his shoulder. Wyll jumped around with karate hands out. Not like he knew any karate, but other people didn't know that. He froze, not recognizing the hooded figure at first.

"Indigo! How are ya?"

"Good, good. I thought I'd find you here. The milgen love you." He looked down at the ducks, honking again.

"You guys have some of the strangest names. I guess it is another language, but ... weird. So, what brings you here tonight?"

"I'm here to see you."

Wyll's brows rose. "What for? Let's go somewhere else. These crazy things are too loud."

"I can't stay long. Malynda's going to be worried as it is."

"I'll walk you home," Wyll said. "Kill two birds with one stone."

He frowned in confusion.

"It's just an expression for doing two things at once."

Indigo smiled, his shoulders relaxing. "Great. She'll love to see you."

When they reached the bottom of the steps, Wyll said, "I'm dying, man."

"Jett said the king keeps the pen in the safe in his desk. It has a digital six-number code lock. The king has told Sira he will show her how to use it tomorrow. She has convinced him that she must learn before he loses touch or forgets who she is. He swears that will never happen, but at this point, even *he* knows he's not what he used to be, regardless of the cause."

"How can I help?" Wyll said.

"We're forming ideas on what she should do. She won't be able to run far with the pen before she's caught. The king knows all our other hiding places now, unfortunately, from the poor people who were in the Reformatory. Some are still struggling. Anyway, Sira wants your opinion."

Wyll felt his chest immediately swell, along with his heart. "She wants to know what I think?"

Indigo stopped and put out a hand. He smiled broadly at Wyll. "She does. She won't say so, but she does. Just take it slow. She hurts from things you had no control over. And she knows it was only partially your fault, but Sira doesn't trust easily. And she doesn't like hurting people."

He nodded. "Right. That's the plan. And I know what she should do."

They started walking again, entering the neighborhoods. "Do tell." Indigo cocked his head.

Wyll made unrecognizable shapes in the air with his hands. "I saw this in a comic once. She should make a tranquilizer gun when he's not looking. I mean, after he shows her how to use it, have Jett call him with a message or some distraction while she draws it. I can show you what it looks like. So, then she can shoot him with the tranq gun and then take the pen."

"She will not kill her father."

"I know. That's the beauty of it. A tranquilizer gun will shoot you with a dart that makes you fall asleep. So, he'll be knocked out in his office. We can lock the doors and go. By the time he wakes up, we'll be long gone."

"I like it. I'll tell Sira and see what she says. Be ready to go by lunchtime."

"I will." He opened the gate and let Indigo through first.

Indigo jogged up the stairs to his home and opened the door. Wyll stood behind him on the porch. The smell of roasting meat tempted Wyll's nostrils. Not knowing he was there, Malynda flew into Indigo, wrapping her arms around his neck and smothering him with kisses. Softly rubbing her cheek up against his. Indigo put his hands around her waist and pulled her back, clearing his throat.

"Sweetheart, Wyll's with me."

"Hi," Wyll said as he peeked around Indigo and waved.

Malynda blushed crimson and smiled. "I'm sorry, Wyll—"

"Don't be sorry for being in love," he said. "I just walked Indigo home so we could talk. I've got to get back and, ah, probably wash something." He pointed over his shoulder.

She laughed. "You are welcome to stay for dinner."

The Clockwork Pen

"No. I'm good. Already ate. You guys have a good night. I'll see you tomorrow if all goes well." He smiled, but Indigo frowned.

"This can't go wrong, Wyll. She's got one chance at this. He will ensure she never sees that pen again if it doesn't go according to plan. He doesn't believe she's with the rebellion, but he won't be able to lie to himself anymore if he catches her trying to steal it. We must be incredibly careful."

"It's okay, man. Sira's got this. I'll draw the tranq gun. Have somebody get it from me and give it to Sira. Make sure she knows and thinks of its purpose when she draws it so she doesn't draw a real gun."

They stepped outside the door before they let all the heat out. Indigo stood on the porch as Wyll stepped down, Malynda draped over his shoulder. "Don't you see her yourself?"

"I do, but it's not till lunch, and her stepmother always needs something at that time or accidentally forgets where the bathroom door is or has something important to say when I'm there. It's like they allow me to see her as long as we're chaperoned. We can't even have a decent conversation. It's all chitty-chatty small talk that girls can do like they were born for it. I can't talk about that crap and pretend I'm interested. I just want to get her alone." Wyll said it with such yearning that Indigo chuckled, and Malynda clutched her hands over her breast, pushed up by a deep blue velvet corset detailed in swirling silver stitches.

He realized immediately what that sounded like and bumbled, trying to get the words out of his mouth. "Well, you know what I mean." His face and neck were nearly steaming in the night air, and he was glad for the dark. Wyll backed up. "I'll see you tomorrow."

He clicked the gate shut and saw them through the oval window in the door, Indigo cupping her face and kissing her. He thought of Sira. He really did want to get her alone. The echo of her kiss drove him wild. He remembered her in the barn, her hair falling and curling around her face, her eyes half closed, and how she looked at him when she smiled right before he claimed her mouth. *Whew!* Wyll stopped himself and took a deep breath. He jogged all the way back to the castle. The brisk, fresh air did wonders in cooling him down.

Wyll stayed up late drawing a detailed picture of a tranquilizer gun and a sedative dart, or the best he could do from memory, but he had read this comic a lot and had an inkling he was right. Since they needed the item to be functional, he sketched and erased parts repeatedly, gripping the pencil tightly to get the proper proportions. He didn't know how late it was when he finally crawled into bed, his eyes puffy and his fingers sore.

He woke so late that he missed the royal breakfast completely, and Eleeda laid into him for being lazy. His punishment was a full list of chores that she would

The Clockwork Pen

supervise. Nally took his drawing up to Sira while he worked. Anxiety chased him all morning like a rabid dog, and his heart thumped with a panicked beat. When lunchtime arrived, Eleeda sent Pyne to Sira's office and made Wyll scrub the floor. The task wasn't easy to begin with, but people incited his rage when they kept walking across his clean, wet floor.

He forgot all about the plan, realizing at dinner time that no one had sent for him at all. He was chomping at the bit to hear what news there was. He waited around the royal suites, but he never saw Jett. Nally left early with two huge baskets full of food. Eleeda tsked at him and shook her head, but she turned her back and let him leave, no questions asked. Wyll didn't even have time to ask him what he'd heard.

He fed the ... whatever the freaking ducks were called, waiting for Indigo or *someone* to bring him news. When he was chilled to the bone, his thumbnail chewed down to a nubbin, he pushed away from the railing, disgusted. He didn't even know if Sira liked his idea. He went to his tiny room, stripped, and flopped onto his bed. He nestled under warm covers. Since Keylin lived in a little room off Sira's in the royal suites, her room was plush and very well financed. She'd given up one of her feather blankets, and Wyll told Lyri she could have the other half if she sewed it to fit his small bed. He smiled, remembering her delighted face when it lit up as if he'd given her an actual gift.

He kept his eyes open in the dark, watching the ceiling, his hands folded over his chest. Normally, he'd flip over to lay face down on his pillow, drooling on the pillowcase. But too many thoughts crowded his brain. *Has anything happened? Did it go well, and no one told me? Maybe they're already gone? Or did it go badly, and they're all in trouble? Is Sira locked away in her rooms again? Or worse? Will they come for me, too?*

If he fell asleep, it was deep and dreamless because it seemed as if the minute he closed his eyes, he was shaken. The first semi-formed thought flashed through his mind, shouting that the soldiers were taking him away, and he flailed his arms. Jolted fully awake, he realized Sira gripped his shoulders, her face even with his. She leaned over him, her brows drawn, but he couldn't read her expression.

"What's going on?" he asked, rubbing dry, sticky eyelids.

"Come on." She stepped back, grabbed his clothes from the chair, and tossed them on the bed. "Put these on. Let's go. We're getting out of here. Now."

Chapter Seventeen
BETRAYAL ON THE BEACH

Sira tossed Wyll's belongings into her duffle bag as he threw on his clothes. He pulled on his boots while she stood with the bag in both hands, tapping her foot impatiently. They were silent as he rushed to push his heel into place. He trusted that if they were leaving in the night, something important was happening, and he'd be brought up to speed as soon as she had time. They didn't speak as they left the castle, nor through the square, or even past the warehouses. They sped South down the dark street, their breath whooshing out clouds of vapor trailing behind them like steam engines.

"Are we ... going ... home?" He breathed deeply. His hard work in the kitchen had kept him in shape—built up his arms and sculpted his legs—but his anxious heart beat faster every minute that Sira kept him in the dark.

"Not yet. But we're out of the castle and *not* going back until I know what to do. You're one of the few people I have left who knows my goal. And you're the only human I can trust now."

Wyll slowed. "You don't trust him? What happened?"

"He said some … things. I know he didn't mean it—he couldn't. And I know he was in a mood, but if he ever followed through on making—" Sira emphasized a shiver. "I can't even explain it. He thinks he can make a game if he creates a predator to roam the streets and eat the dissenters, then he may not have to cull his own society. He wants to … no, I can't."

"It's okay."

He turned toward the building with the secret apartment as they approached it, but she didn't veer from her course. He nearly tripped, following her. "Where are we going?"

"Where the Resistance is. Many people didn't feel safe anymore, even at home. So, they've made camp at the beach until I can find a solution. The hourglass is emptying quickly."

"Hey." He stopped and gently pulled her shoulder around to face him. "What's going on with the Resistance's plans? What else happened today? Did he teach you? Are we leaving? I've been worried sick all day."

She looked down, her curls falling forward. Her eyelashes dusted her cheeks, and he wanted to tip her face up to see the moonlight glow on her skin. It was killing him that he couldn't just kiss her right there. *Go slow*, is what Indigo had said. *She's like a wild animal. If you spook her, she'll run away.* He waited while she formed her words. He'd never had to be so patient before.

"I was sitting in my dad's office. He has a little desk off to the side of the room. I used to sit there and do my homework just to spend time with him. We'd be working, and both happen to look up and see each other, and we'd smile like we had a secret. We were working *together*. Now, his wife sits there and does whatever she does. Probably takes notes for him. I don't know."

Wyll nodded to encourage her. He knew it would be a long story, but her voice was a balm to him; he could listen to her for hours. The wind howled between the buildings, and he shivered. He opened the duffle, pulled out his cloak-like coat, and swung it on. "Let's keep going; it's freezing out here." They were alone this far out of town, and he ached to feel her close. He offered his elbow as men there did.

She took it, threading her hand over his forearm. He leaned into her, and she smiled, leaning back. They walked slowly, pressed together, and she picked up where she left off. "Anyway, when I sat down at the little desk today, he told me a secret. I can't believe I didn't know this until now. He said the pen is only a *conduit* for the magic ink that goes inside it. The ink makes life. He said he never goes anywhere without the real pen and must be present when I use it. He can either write or draw with the ink. Drawing a picture can create things, and writing produces life."

They were silent while he processed the information. "So ... it's not the pen? It's only the *ink*? Well, why does he tell everyone it's the pen?"

"It's a secret, I think. A diversion. No one can overthrow him with the pen because it's only a conduit."

"Huh." He would have to rethink his whole strategy. "What happened then?"

"He got an important message a la Jett, and I traced your drawing. The paper's not magic, just the ink, so I traced over your lines." She held open her coat to show him a righteous pistol, resembling the one he drew but with steampunk accouterment. Knobs, springs, and things—absent from his design—covered the piece. A pearl-inlaid handle gleamed in the moonlight. He was proud to have drawn it but curious about the pen's unexpected alterations.

"So, did you shoot him? I'm guessing not—since we're here." They entered a small copse of evergreen trees. Plant life on the ground was sparse, the needles crunchy. They rolled and popped under his boots as the couple headed toward the beach. A faraway campfire glowed through the scattered trees.

"No. I didn't shoot him. I couldn't do it while he was looking at me. I just couldn't. Maybe it would injure him ... and I couldn't bear the look in his eyes if he saw me point the gun at him, not knowing I didn't mean him harm... He left then because he had a real problem that he needed to solve—some technical emergency with one of

The Clockwork Pen

his mysterious 'building' projects. So, he took the pen, and I hid the pistol under my skirt. I watched him put the ink in his safe. Oh, and there are decoy pens all over the office. If he put his down, I don't know how he'd find it again ... maybe that's why he doesn't."

"It's another way to throw people off the trail. If they come looking for the magic pen, they won't know which one it is. Or maybe he can use any of them. It's the ink that's magic, right?" Wyll stopped. "I wonder how he's been able to use it all these years and still has any ink left? I guess if it's magic and life-giving, it could just replenish itself." He needed to finish the conversation before they melded with the group of resisters, and everyone else had Sira's attention—if they were still awake. He realized he finally had her all to himself. *Alone.* And he wanted to keep it that way, at least for a little while longer. They had almost reached the bank, jutting out north of the beach, when he stopped again.

She turned toward him, curious brows raised. "No idea about the ink. Why are we stopping?"

"I don't want to go just yet. Finish your story," he said in a deep timbre.

She chuckled and leaned back against the trunk of a tall pine with her hands behind her. "You know? Me either. What was I saying? Oh, yeah. When he put the ink away—and it was full—I heard six beeps. It could be a date?"

"It could be anything." He stepped close enough to feel her body heat radiating between them. Still as stone, Sira gazed up at him, her eyes sparkling in the moonlight reflected off the water. "Then what happened?" He lifted a curl that caressed her cheek, running it through his fingers like a silk ribbon.

"He rushed me out, but I got the pistol into my holster before he saw me. We need to tell Indigo we had it wrong," she said breathlessly.

"You haven't spoken to him yet?"

"No." Her eyes lowered to his vest, and she lightly traced the pattern with her finger. His breath caught when she rolled her lip between her teeth. He wanted to pull it out with his own.

"Why not?" he whispered. He traced her jaw.

"I had to babysit the step-clock while she ate because she doesn't like to eat alone, and Dad was busy. I think it's her way of watching me when he's gone. As long as I'm with her, I'm not out causing trouble until he returns." Anger flushed her cheeks, and the blush heated his blood as well. "When I could finally escape, I came right to you."

"Thanks," he said softly. Though no one was around, the night encouraged silence along with the lapping waves on the shore. The fresh scent of pine enveloped them. She peered up at him, and he leaned forward, effectively pressing her against him. He wrapped an arm around her, smiling as the cloud of her breath

The Clockwork Pen

warmed his chin. "I've missed you. Being so near you every day and never being alone is torture."

"Wyll." He could see her drowning, holding onto his arm as if she was slipping under the water's surface. Her chin rose high, and her breathing was shallow and quick. She looked so helpless. He wanted nothing more in that second than to protect her. Belong to her. Not like a possession, but the way you bond with someone and admire them, knowing you belong to each other. It's two against the world, back-to-back, guns out. He wanted her, and he wanted her with him every moment. She gripped his biceps, borrowing his strength, then succumbing to the deep water.

He was treading the icy blue ocean in her eyes and watched them slowly close as he dipped his head. Tipping her jaw up, he gently skated his lips over hers, testing her, tasting her. She responded, thankfully, not with a slap but with a slow grin. He looked down at her curls, so rich in the darkness, framing her face like a decorative vine.

She opened her eyes and raised her brows in question. "What?" she whispered.

"You sure you're okay with this? I don't want to rush you."

At his words, she stiffened like she remembered something unpleasant. Water slapped the shore, and she turned to the sound. She frowned, and he needed to know what was making her scowl.

"What?"

"It's nothing," she said, her voice sharp as a blade. "We should go see the rest of them. Indigo is waiting for us, I'm sure."

"Sira?"

"Hmmm?"

"I know I messed up, and I'm sorry. I know I have nothing to offer you. You have no reason to like me, but—"

Sira shushed him with a slender finger to his lips. "I think you're foolish but brave, opinionated but curious. You want to see and experience everything for the first time. You're astray but not misplaced. You don't know what you want, but you're willing to take what comes and make the best of it until the answers reveal themselves. If I could do that, I'd be happy here. You're a good person deep down, Wyll, and you make me feel like I matter—like my fight matters—and I'm not just a spoiled brat who can't appreciate all she's received. You're the only one who understands my need to be free."

"I don't think you're a spoiled brat." He ran through everything she'd said, trying to memorize it to play back later, but the tear streaking down her cheek washed his mind clean, replacing it with the need to comfort her.

Before he could *gather her in his arms* and kiss away her troubles, she sniffed, pulling her shoulders back, and said, "Let's go find the others."

The Clockwork Pen

Once again, he offered her his elbow. He didn't mind if she wasn't quite ready, she could set the pace, and he'd be whomever she needed him to be for the moment.

They walked the pebbly shore to a smooth beach area. The remnants of several cookfires glowed in the sand, and tents stood erect all along the tree line. It resembled a neighborhood of townhouses—tent, tree, tent, tree, tent, tent, tree, tree, tent... Blankets hung on ropes tied to tall branches.

Gadgets unfolded into beds and dinner tables, and all manner of fancy folding chairs dotted the area with designs tooled into worn leather seats. Screens stood sentinel around assorted families, almost all of whom were sleeping. A chorus of snores, groans, and farts played around him, joining the song of the crickets. *Cree, cree, cree.* Three lone figures sat around a dying fire, involved in their conversation.

As they approached the men, Wyll recognized Indigo, Kipper, and Nally. Indigo looked back at them with relief. "Thank goodness you two are safe. We didn't hear a word, and the people were getting restless. We had to do some damage control, promising them you'd be here in the morning. We were just trying to figure out how to do that."

"Aye, Missy, we're glad to see ya." Kipper looked at Wyll, and suddenly, his eyes were shining. "Thank ya for bringin' my boy to rescue me, Wyll—and for gettin' him out."

Wyll strode to Kipper, shaking his outstretched hand.

"Join us," Nally said, relaxed in his chair. His folded apron and top hat sat on his lap, and he held something like a thermos. Kipper sat back in his seat, the black satin stripes on his matte black pants shining in the firelight. Indigo reclined, as well, one slim boot resting on his other knee. He unbuttoned his coat as the fire heated them, exposing a ruffled white shirt under a navy leather vest, a hat perched on his lap as well.

Wyll was glad to have friends again and hoped the people of the Resistance would soon forgive him. He knew it was a lot to hope for, seeing as how they'd suffered due to his stupidity, but he still yearned for their clemency. At least this small group gave him absolution, and it comforted him.

They pulled up chairs and sat with the men. The words warbled as Wyll listened to them talk. Sira explained to the men her story of the magic ink while he half-dozed. It was *oh-dark-thirty,* after all. He struggled to rouse himself when he heard words like *plan* and *together*, trying to wake even as he realized his head was falling slowly, jerking upright every few seconds.

It's okay, he told himself, *she wouldn't leave me out, she'll take me back with her*. But he wasn't sure he understood *why*. She'd said all those things about him, but was that a sufficient reason to risk yourself even if it was true? Would he do it if the situation was reversed? Or

The Clockwork Pen

maybe she was just a "good" person who knew he didn't belong here? Were there other reasons? It bothered him that he didn't know. It shouldn't matter as long as he got home. But part of him needed to know if there was more there. She'd nearly admitted to liking him earlier, but was that enough?

"Come on, sleepyhead." Sira's light laugh doubled the warmth of the fading fire. She reached her hand out to him.

Gripping her long, slim fingers, he could feel fur poking out from her leather fingerless glove, rubbing his palm as she hoisted him upright in the hi-tech folding chair. Then she pushed a button on the arm, and the chair rose, dipping him out remarkably close to the right height. *Impressive.*

"Where we goin'?" He stretched his back with a yawn.

"I put our stuff over there." She pointed to the far end of the encampment, to a gap in the trees.

The air was remarkably colder away from the fire. He shivered. It would be a wintry night. He remembered who was sleeping next to him, and memories of the last time heated his whole body. It may not be that cold after all. He smiled in the dark.

"Do you have beaches like this where you come—I mean, where *we*—come from?" she asked softly.

He swung her hand in between them like a pendulum. "There are. Cold beaches and hot beaches, and you can see the ocean going on forever. Sunsets on the beach are the best. My mom likes to jog in the sand toward the sunrise when we're on vacation. Sunrises are brilliant but lack the depth of sunset's colors because of the shadow."

"Wow. I picked the right subject to talk about." She chuckled.

He cleared his throat. "Sorry. My grandparents lived in Florida. We would go to see them all the time. It's where my mom came from, so when they passed away a few years ago, she couldn't bear to sell the house. We kept it, and we take all our vacations there. I love the beach. I go to Olathe Lake sometimes and just pretend—"

"Will you show me? I mean, when we get out of here." She whispered as they passed the other camps and stopped beside the tree gap.

He faced her, placing a hand on her cheek. It was cold but smooth as polished pearl, her skin translucent. His voice husky, he said, "I want to show you everything."

She shivered, but from the look in her eyes, she wasn't cold at all. Twin pools shined in wonder, then slowly closed as he came nearer, nearer, until her lips touched his. They just ... fit—like puzzle pieces that had been too far apart. Their mouths melded perfectly. He pulled her lips with his own. Gently and then with an urgency leading him toward ... wait a minute.

Slow down, Wyll. He pulled back to look down at her upturned face, her cheeks flushed and her lips swollen. God, he wanted to dive into her like she was the ocean and drown.

He pushed a curl behind her ear, and she licked her lips. He gazed at the moon for a few seconds to avoid devouring her. "We should get set up," he whispered.

"Oh yeah," she said in a daze.

He chuckled. Wyll loved the way girls looked at him post-kiss, with their eyes halfway closed, framed by long dark lashes, their mouths half open, and almost smiling. He got high from it. Maybe he was a little cocky, but he wasn't a novice.

When he was little, the girl who lived next door to his grandma's house taught him how to kiss girls "the right way." Sure, it was only a peck at first, but when she got older, she became more … aggressive—and knowledgeable. He started out shy, but it wasn't long before he knew what he was doing.

Nothing else happened—just a hands-free makeout. Thanksgivings and Christmas, they'd hang out in the basement of Grandma's, with holiday specials playing on the TV. Only "kids" went down there. As a teen, she smoked pot and offered it to Wyll, but he had no interest. He just liked watching her blow rings out the basement window. His mom said she was troubled and told him to be nice to her. Shaking the girl from his mind, he kissed Sira quickly and stepped back.

"Where's our stuff?" He looked around.

She scrunched her eyebrows. "Over here." She pointed to a small pile of cloth and a broomstick pole next to a basket like the previous wheeled picnic basket.

"What are we going to sleep in?" He motioned to the other camps. "They all have blankets to sleep under."

She chuckled. "The blankets are for privacy. We all have tents. Indigo has extra; they're easy to carry, and we didn't know how many we'd need."

"Where's ours?" He wasn't following, and she looked just as confused as he felt.

She pointed to the pile. "It's right there? Are you okay?"

He wasn't sure. Maybe she knew something he didn't because there was no way to make them a shelter with some thin cloth alone, but he'd try. He went over to the cloth and picked it up. It was strange. It felt slick, like polyester fabric or something, and it was layered. The bottom was heavy, and he pulled it up to see a round metal circle sewn into the fabric with a circular lid. What the hell was it? He laid the cloth over the pole and looked for peg holes.

"Here. Let me. Our things must not be the same."

"No kidding." He stepped back as she reached for the metal broomstick. She unhinged a clasp at both ends, and it fanned out into a tall, thin, vertical accordion of shiny cloth with metal edges. Then she slid a lever up the shaft of the pole, and the whole thing popped up and opened into a standing tent big enough for two or three adults. It had a metal frame and some strange, stretchy fabric that was thinly layered and slick, like the blankets.

He pointed to the blankets. "So, what's with those?"

"You don't have these, either? I wonder if anything in your world will be familiar to me." She looked upset, but he was really interested in the hi-tech blankets. He'd hold her later.

"How does it work?" He reached for the round cap.

"Wait! Don't open that till we're in the tent, or we'll never get it through the door."

He was confused, curious, and excited. Grabbing the other blankets, he realized they were even thinner and very silky. He hurried into the tent after her. She laid the blanket down, flipped a little button he hadn't seen on the hem, and opened the round cap. A whirring sounded in the small space, and the blanket sucked air into the big hole rapidly, filling it up in a matter of ten seconds. Sira capped the hole and flipped the switch back. Instantly full air mattress. It looked comfy; all pocketed air, it resembled a fluffy cloud.

"What about these?" He handed her the soft blankets.

She did something similar to the air mattress, only on a smaller scale, and the blankets filled with a small amount of air between the layers, enough to feel like a down comforter. The picnic basket had food, but he wasn't hungry. He was exhausted. The only thing he was interested in was lying down with Sira.

She faced the tent's wall with her back to him and shrugged off her coat. *Oh yeah, I guess we're not sleeping in our coats.* He took his off and cringed at the frigid temperature. Being nervous didn't make sense, but sometimes she really shook his confidence. She was more than any other girl he'd known—more beautiful, passionate, angry, more … alive. He chuckled too quietly for her to hear.

Wyll put his gloves in his coat pockets and his scarf in his hat. He shucked his boots, folded his vest, and laid it all together. When he turned around, she was sliding under the covers in a billowy white shirt. He couldn't see much more than her leg in a white stocking as she tucked it under the blankets. He stripped down to his loose trousers and white shirt and slid into the bed.

Immediately, she rolled to face him. When she lifted her head, he laid his arm on her pillow, and she rested her head on his bicep. They lay pressed together, shivering in the night.

"Sira?" *What are you doing?* he asked himself. *Shut up. You are tired and speaking without permission.* "Thanks for pardoning me. You do understand, don't you? I didn't mean to get those people hurt. I can be— I've been a real jerk, but I didn't want anyone to get hurt because of me. I'm really sorry."

She tucked her head under his chin, with her ear to his chest, and his heart thumped. "I know," she said in a small voice. "Sometimes it doesn't matter. It hurts anyway. I was more disappointed that you'd been telling the truth when you said I couldn't count on you. That hurt. I wanted to believe in you."

The verbal arrow pierced his heart, not only because of what he'd done but because it was so close to what he'd heard at home when he was struggling. Pep talks while growing up, always focused on how much faith his mom had in him and how, if she imagined hard enough, there was nothing he couldn't do. *Moms have special power*, she said when he was little. *It's like fairy dust.* He took it as gospel. He totally bought that she could believe him through anything. Lately, it had turned into how much she wanted to support him, but it seemed he constantly disappointed her. Where did he go wrong?

When Sira said she had faith in him, he felt like he had as a kid—his chest wanted to swell—but then he realized she was speaking in the past tense and deflated. "I can't tell you who to trust, but I'd never do anything to hurt you. Not on purpose. Never again." He kissed her forehead, whispering against it, "Sira, you've got to understand how sorry I am."

"Mmmm."

"What?" He chuckled at her odd response to his serious attempt at an apology.

"I like the way you say my name."

He smiled into her hair. She'd taken down the rest of it, and mountains of curls lay draped over his arm. Silently, he inhaled her scent—spicy cinnamon. "You didn't listen to what I said."

"Yes, I did. It's just too hard for me to begin again. Depending on you came so easily the first time. It was almost detrimental. I have no problems relying on people—even the wrong people. But once my trust is broken, I seem to be unable to change. I would rather give a perfect stranger a chance."

"So, there's no hope for us?" He rolled into her, nudging her shoulder with his own. "Then what are we doing here together?"

"*Hoping.*"

There was nothing else to say, so he threw his arm around her and pulled her body as close to his as he could. She slid her thigh on top of his, hooking his leg with her dainty foot. Laying there, pretzeled together, he watched her fall asleep, safe in his arms. The future would be unbearable without this view. Reluctantly, his eyes closed, and Wyll succumbed to the heavy blanket of sleep pressing on him, holding his limbs in languorous paralysis.

The aroma of coffee brought Wyll straight out of dreamland. He opened his eyes to see Sira's relaxed face on his pillow, her eyelashes dusting her high cheekbones. She lay on her back, he on his stomach, with his arm and leg thrown over her like a body pillow. She roused as he shifted his stiff limbs, rubbing her eye with a yawn.

"Good morning," she said with a small smile.

He grinned dimples at her. "How you doin'? Sleep well?"

"Mmm hmm. Very warm and cozy. You?"

"Yeah. I smell somebody making coffee. Do we have anything to eat? Let's go find Kipper and Nally. Maybe they'll trade. I'd rather have my coffee than breakfast if I only have one option." He sat up and stretched his arms above his head, immediately missing the warmth under the covers.

Sira sat up and nodded sharply. "Let's find out."

Once dressed, they followed the beach down the tree line to Kipper's camp. Along with a few early risers, he was awake and making breakfast with Nally. Juke's snoring carried to the fire from their tent. It was surprisingly loud coming from such a little guy. They chatted over steaming cups and toast while eggs sizzled. Wyll and Sira pooled their food.

"I've got berries and oranges." Sira handed her basket to Nally.

He whipped up a breakfast of fruit, eggs, sausage, and leftover pastries. A baker-extraordinaire, his pastries were the best Wyll had ever tasted. Light, buttery, and flaky, they melted on your tongue.

Sira and Wyll washed the dishes in a steaming hot pot of soapy water, then they talked around the fire, waiting for the other camps to finish waking and eating.

"Hi, all. What are we up to today?" Indigo entered camp with Malynda on his arm.

"What's the plan?" she asked. It was the first time Wyll had seen her without a dress. She wore black leather pants with suspenders that called attention to her chest. Her black hair was piled in a messy style on her head, dirty bronze goggles perched above her forehead. Around her neck was a stunning piece of jewelry in iron filigree, the swirls dangling deep red crystals like drops of blood. It was high society, just like her.

"I want to confirm changes in the plan from last night," Sira said. "We need to make sure everyone is on the same page."

Wyll listened to them ask questions, wondering aloud who would best explain the process for disabling the alarm in the king's office, but they were tossing around unfamiliar names. He wished he could contribute to the discussion, but he didn't know anybody here, nor would they work with him. He had no resources. It appeared that Wyll would be helping Sira with the ink heist. Indigo and Malynda would be their lookouts and clear the way for them. Even Keylin had a job. They were discussing the order of events when suddenly their words sounded like a garble of sounds.

The Clockwork Pen

"What's going on?" He squinted at their confusion while they continued to speak, facing him, but he couldn't comprehend them at all. He frowned and shook his head. "I can't understand you."

Sira's eyes flew open. Then she spoke in English, "Your translator. It's solar. Step into the sun and let it shine on your ear for about five minutes. That's all it takes."

"Should I take it out?"

"No. There's a little button on the surface. Press it, point it toward the sun, and that's it."

He stood with his ear cocked toward the sun and counted for a while, then his mind wandered to Sira's face in the moonlight and how delicious the ache was... *Yeah, that's about five minutes.* His boots kicked up sand as he crossed into the trees' shade, immediately feeling a chill, only partially relieved by the fire.

"...the agenda and agree that it must happen that way. From today, if anything unexpected occurs, the procedure goes on. No matter what. We substitute and move forward." Indigo was speaking when Wyll walked up. He smiled and continued, "Ah, Wyll. We were just laying out the details. The mission is in three days. We will schedule meetings, and everyone will know their parts as we do. We will attain all the information we can on guard schedules and codes. It must transpire regardless of happenstance. All in agreement?"

They scanned each other's somber faces, searching for agreement and camaraderie with their partners in crime. *This is starting to feel real.* He met their eyes confidently and realized he was part of the core group. They trusted him—depended on him—again. It felt so good. "Agreed," he echoed the others.

"Princess Sira! Princess Sira!" a little girl shouted as she ran up to them. "There's king's men after you! I heard 'em myself and saw 'em comin', too." She stopped and dropped her skirts, her little boots a miniature version of Sira's.

"Thank you, Debecka." Sira rose. "I've got to go. He can't find me here."

She took off for the tree line, and Wyll didn't know if he should follow her. He stood in indecision for a fraction of a second, then ran after her. Sira was passing a tree about ten feet ahead of him when a tent pole swung out toward her. Wyll watched it connect with her chest and throw her to her back. He pumped his arms. "Sira!"

Diving to his knees, he lifted her head. There was already bruising around the red and white line crossing her shoulders. She blinked her eyes and gasped—the wind knocked from her lungs. He reached out to touch the bruise when someone suddenly hauled him up by the back of his jacket. He came up swinging, and the soldier held him out at arm's length, his punch glancing off the man's metal body. The soldier laughed at him. "Don't waste your strength, *boy.*"

The Clockwork Pen

"I'll *boy* you, you son-of-a-bitch." He stretched out a foot and kicked him in the side of the knee. "Freakin' grandfather clock. I'm a man."

The soldier let go with a yelp, and Wyll grabbed Sira's hand, pulling her up, his other arm out to steady her. A hand crushed his shoulder, and he turned back toward his friends to see a fist flying at his face. Wyll's head snapped back with the blow. One of the men he'd seen around the Resistance stood before him, breathing great, heavy breaths, one hand crushing his shoulder. His face, red as a stoplight, wore a livid expression. Soldiers flanked him, leering with menace.

"Here he is. The traitor." The man shoved his sausage-like finger in Wyll's face and spat on his boot.

Wyll raised his shoulders, not comprehending. "What?"

The soldier walked around the man, smiling viciously, and clasped Wyll's shoulder. "Good work, William."

"It's Wyll. And what for?"

"For helping us capture this camp." The soldiers smiled slyly at each other.

"But—" Wyll spun to look at Sira, his eyes full of desperation. She frowned, and her brows bunched in uncertainty for just a moment—but that was enough to make him panic. "I didn't—I swear, I would never—I mean, you know I did. But I wouldn't do it again—"

"Take him away," one of the women yelled.

"Lock *him* up this time," another Resister shouted.

"Traitor!" many called out.

"Round them all up, guards. These two have special orders." The soldier smiled at Wyll and Sira. "Let's go."

Chapter Eighteen
Head Trip

Wyll wasn't worried about the coming consequences or whatever the soldiers had in mind. All he cared about was making sure Sira knew he hadn't sold her out. Again. It was so shameful. He could barely face the people glaring and shouting as soldiers marched him down the beach. The Resistance members screamed horrible things as he passed. Maybe not the worst he'd ever heard, but the verbal daggers thrown pierced their mark and hurt, nonetheless.

"Sira. Sira, look at me." He panted, trying to keep up with the long strides of the soldiers. "I didn't do it, Sira. Please believe me. I didn't bring them here. How could I? I was with you!" He ended up shouting as the soldiers dragged her off a different path.

"Damn." Wyll twisted to look at the soldier who held his hands behind his back. "Where's she going? Sira! Sira!"

"We're going this way. No, this way!" The guard struggled to corral Wyll as he fought to follow Sira. Wyll heard him calling for help, but he was concentrating too hard on reaching her, and he was gaining. Grunting, he pulled the soldier along with sheer anger, frustration, and adrenaline. He never noticed the soldier who hit him in the head, but as soon as he felt the blow, his head flew forward, and everything in his sight was sucked, like a straw, into a pinpoint before it went black.

Wyll kept his thick and heavy eyelids shut. He didn't want to know where he was. His mouth was painfully dry. He tried to swallow, and his thick tongue crackled in his mouth. His Grandma had a trick when he was little, and she ran out of mints in church. She'd plop a button in his mouth to suck on, and he wouldn't be thirsty anymore. It was probably illegal nowadays to put a button in a kid's mouth.

Miserable, he wondered if he had a button on his sleeve and wiggled his fingers but realized his hands wouldn't move. *What the—?* He cracked open an eye and lifted his chin from his chest. The windowless room was shadowy and made him think of evening. He didn't think he'd slept all day, but one couldn't be completely sure. The leather straps holding his wrists out to the side were soft but held tight. Similar leather strapped him to a chair inside an orb of metal bars arcing from floor to ceiling, connected to a frame by pulleys and gears. *What is this*

The Clockwork Pen

thing? He had no idea what it did, but knowing the king, he wouldn't like it. He felt like a huge hamster in an enormous ball. He expected it to move when he rocked forward, but it didn't. The room around him was small; only space for his cage, a wooden chair facing him, and a table by the door holding a lamp and a few small remote-like rectangles.

After a few hours of utter boredom, Wyll realized he needed to pee. He began to shout, calling anyone who could hear him. Not that he wanted anyone to come and turn on the contraption he was in, but someone was going to come for him eventually, weren't they? Or was he doomed to starve in this chair? Whether his ankles were bound to the chair legs or the floor, he couldn't tell. The harness over his body didn't let him bend down far enough to see. He examined the lamp on the table made of copper tubing on a cedar platform, with a dial on the front. It branched out at the top like a tree, each piece of copper tube ending with a light hanging down, encased in teardrop-shaped glass bulbs. He memorized its shape with his eyes open and closed. It was the only light in the room, and it flickered occasionally. He appreciated that he was not in the dark this time.

His full bladder protested. He screamed until he was hoarse, and his throat was so dry, it was gritty and painful. Suddenly, grinding gears vibrated his chair, and a series of clicks sounded loud in the small room before his chair unlocked from its upright state. It was the only way he could describe it, as the chair tipped back and rocked inside the stationary cage bars a few times. A gear near his left ear whirred and caught a chain that began to spin him upside down. Wyll was not a fan of the rides at Worlds of Fun that went round and round, but he was flying now. His chair hurtled around the cage as the top and bottom of his chair ran along the rails of the orb in tracks. He thought he'd seen something like this at the space museum. Astronauts used it to prepare for zero-G but only went *one* way around. Wyll was speeding around the various tracks, going upside down in every direction.

He lost his breakfast and hoped it would gum up the tracks enough to derail him. It didn't. When the chair stopped, he was dizzy, sick, and pissed, with a monster headache. If only he had that flask of pain-relieving water. *Damn.* Vomit ran down his chin, but his hands were bound, and all he could do was endure the dripping. His chair rocked at the bottom of the cage. The cycle finished—he hoped. *Thank God.* A pulley grabbed the chains and clicked his chair back into place, and Wyll noticed he now sat in a puddle. Covered in puke, he realized he didn't need to go to the bathroom anymore. He stopped shouting after that.

It felt like an entire day passed before anyone came to see him. His face was tight and itchy. Caked in his own vomit and reeking of pee, he felt disgusting. His clothes were crusty. His stomach knotted from hunger and anxiety, and his tongue felt fat and foreign in his mouth, beyond thirst. By then, he was fairly sure night had passed, and it would remain a dark room. A man he'd never seen entered his room holding a tray in both hands. In the middle of it stood Wyll's oasis. A tall, condensing glass of water, complete with tinkling ice cubes.

Holy shit.

His mouth couldn't even water. He opened it, making a smacking sound as he peeled his tongue off the roof so he could speak. "Is that for me?" he garbled the words as the man stood silently facing him, unmoving.

Apparently not hearing him, the man was a doppelganger for the cartoon version of Ichabod Crane, all knees and elbows with a huge Adam's apple and a nose like a beak. A black velvet ribbon that matched his black coat and pants pulled back his dull gray hair. A gray vest held his pocket watch, and he pulled it out to peek, then snapped it closed and returned it, looking straight ahead.

Wyll watched the drops of water running down the side of the glass, and he wanted to cry. *No*, he was not beaten yet. He would make it through this. All he had to do was hang on. Sira said they were moving ahead in three days. It must be two days away by now. Surely, she was reprimanded and would be searching for him at any time. He thought he still had a grasp on time, though the longer the clock ticked, the less confident he was.

"Do you have a name?" He mumbled the words.

The man ignored him. *Fine. It's too much effort to talk anyway.* Wyll settled for glaring at him through the bars.

A bell chimed from the man's pocket. Wyll was curious about the time and date but knew that silence would meet his query, so he waited. He would have spit at the man if he could—or kicked him.

He attempted to flick his vomit-encrusted boot at the man but only hit the cage bars and lost a warm sock just before the door creaked open and Rozam, the king, stepped in. His smile was dazzling. Nice, warm gloves covered his hands, and he rubbed them together. It magnified the cold tingle of poor circulation in Wyll's fingertips. It was cool and damp in the all-rock room. Wyll guessed he was somewhere in the Reformatory. But where?

"How are you feeling, Wyll?"

"Who's this guy?" Wyll ignored the king completely, nodding toward the living scarecrow. Usually, it riled him, but today, the king just chuckled.

"He's my little gift to you. Call it a good-faith wedding present—if plans fail."

"Excuse me?" Wyll thought he must have missed a page. "Am I getting married?"

"Well, not now, of course. But in time... I don't think Sira bought your death. And if she insists on mating herself with a human ... well, you're it. I understand. And she appears to like you, so, one day, you could be family

The Clockwork Pen

... and here's my gift." He patted the man on the back, grinning at Wyll. "He's your butler. He obeys you. Unless I tell him not to, of course. He's brand new, so you can name him yourself if you'd like. He doesn't speak though—flaw in the design."

More like a flaw in the designer.

"You have lost your marbles. Of course I'm not dead. And Sira isn't going to stay here. Every time you pull her back, it makes her that much more determined to get away. You *should have* let her visit the real world. You should have been honest with her. She deserves it."

"Oh, like you? *Honest Wyll?* Did she deserve what *you* did?" The king lost his smile, and Wyll thought, *stupid, stupid, stupid.* He would have face-palmed himself if he could. Rozam continued, "She *is* going to stay here, and my plan to guarantee it will work perfectly."

"Yeah?" His voice was hesitant. On the one hand, he really, really wanted to know this plan, but on the other hand, it probably involved something he would really hate.

"Do you want to hear it?" Rozam's eyes lit up, and his eyebrows shot to the ceiling. He clapped his hands together and pressed them, palm to palm, waiting for Wyll's answer.

"Sure." He didn't even try to fake excitement, but the king didn't seem to notice or care.

Rozam sat in the wooden chair opposite the cage. "Oh yes." Rozam looked up at Ichabod—he wasn't hard to name—and said, "Give the boy a drink so he can listen."

Wyll would've licked his lips if he could. Ichabod pushed a button on a flat remote and the front half of the bars separated in the middle and telescoped into themselves. The butler stepped into Wyll's prison and held the glass to his mouth. Tilting it gently, the man let Wyll sip the water, draining most of the glass. Satisfied, he tilted his chin up so none would be lost, and the butler wiped his face with a cloth. He felt two thousand percent better. Smiling in relief, he realized the king was watching him like some kind of Truman show, and he frowned.

Rozam cleared his throat. "Here it is. First, I put you in my device, The Reeducator. I told Sira that you died in the Reformatory. Of course, I had to make a clockwork copy of you to show her before your destruction, and I had enough of your,"—he looked at all the chunks of Wyll's last meal on the floor—"DNA to do that already. The problem is, I don't know if she believed it. I mean, getting rid of you is the best option, but she's going to—"

"Wait, she thinks I'm dead?"

"Yes, if it worked. Delightful, isn't it? It'll be a surprise once I fix you. She's going to be so happy later when I show her you're still alive, and she will love that I've made you new and improved. Then she'll love us both and *never* leave." Rozam's maniacal smile was unsettling.

"I'm sorry, dude, but I don't think anyone can convince her to stay here—*especially* me. I mean, no offense, but I don't plan on staying myself." Wyll knew it was useless talking to a madman. There was no logic.

"Aha. Well, you won't convince her *now*. But when the Reeducator is done with you, you will only desire to stay here and restore Sira's relationship with me. It'll be your first priority. You will fix everything, and she'll listen because she cares for you."

Ichabod stepped out of the cage and pushed the button to restore the tracks, standing at attention.

Wyll's mind was going a million miles an hour. The Resistance would move forward with their plans if they believed the king's ruse. They would leave without him in two days. Was it two days? Three? One? When his grandpa died, Wyll's grandma said the hardest part was wanting to talk to him, wanting him to know something desperately, but being unable to know if he heard her. He didn't get it at the time, but he was starting to understand. If he could speak telepathically from sheer effort, Sira would have heard him screaming all through the castle. She'd know he was down here.

"What if it doesn't work?" Wyll knew he was grasping at straws.

"The beauty of this machine is that—similar to the terror machine—it can change your reality. It will make you believe anything I tell you is true."

He snorted. "Like you could tell me I'm a dinosaur, and I'd believe it?"

Rozam picked up one of the boxes on the table and pointed it at him like a TV remote, and he was the comedy … or more like the tragedy. The gears began to turn, and he swung loose again. *Oh no, not this again.*

"You don't have to show me—" The chair seemed like it flew faster this time than before. He lost the water he'd just ingested. The cord tethering the cuffs on his wrists loosened, and his arms flew out in front of him. Then Rozam started talking. "Look at your arms, Wyll. See the bumps all over them? They're greenish. Yellow-green and bulging spots all over your arms. Can't you see them moving? The green worms are burrowing into your skin, one right next to the other. They swim around and eat your flesh. It hurts, doesn't it? You want them out. They itch, don't they?

Wyll's eyes were huge. He was so dizzy that he could hardly concentrate, but he couldn't look away from his arms as he watched the worms moving under his skin. He could feel them wiggling—hundreds of them. He began to scratch wildly. The more he raked across the burrows, tearing the tops off, the more worm heads popped out, and he scraped their fat bodies out, as many as he could at a time, as his stomach lurched repeatedly. Their bodies broke and smeared, and green goo wedged under his fingernails. Once the worms were out and his arms were green and slimy, he saw the small identical holes covering his arms, close to each other. The worms had eaten his flesh and left him cratered. He ran a hand over the torn skin and wanted to throw up again, but he could only heave.

"Stop. Please." Wyll was in tears. He could only take so much.

The chair slowed to a stop, and he returned to the starting position, nearly getting whiplash as it yanked him into place. When he looked down, most of the worm guts were wiped off, but the holes were still in his arms. He panicked. Scratching the skin, his pinky nail fit in each hole. "I thought you said it wasn't real?"

"Oh yes, you are correct. But what I tell you is real *becomes* real for you."

"My arms are stuck like this?" Wyll looked hideous. He only heard the part where the king said whatever he told Wyll became reality. That was enough to mess with his brain. Sira would hate these holes. Sira thought he was dead and would go home without him. He would be stuck here with the insanity. And everyone else believed he sold them out and wouldn't wait for him anyway. Maybe she'd come for him?

"Until you don't believe it anymore." The king stood. "It's all in your control, Wyll. Eventually, you will be released from your bonds and free to leave. But you won't be able to. Your own mind will keep you here until I'm ready for you. I'll have your man clean up." He clapped Ichabod on the shoulder.

Wyll had about a hundred questions. "Where is this place? How is Sira? Is she upset? How—" He stopped talking when he realized Rozam was ignoring him and preparing to leave. Then he had a hundred more. "Wait! When are you coming back? Does anybody know I'm here? Is someone else coming? How long are you going to keep me here?" His voice rose in volume and pitch as he cried out and realized with panic that he was not only alone, but no one would even be looking for him after Rozam's look-alike corpse. He burned with fury and lashed out, screaming and pulling at the restraints. The cord connected to his cuffs retightened and pulled his wrists out to the side. Finally, he stilled, a tear of resolution slipping down his cheek. His nose ran down to his lips.

He wasn't left alone as he thought he would be. The king returned many times. And each time he did, he gave Wyll some new thought to believe. First, it was trivial things like, "You love it here, don't you? It's fascinating. You never want to leave." And things like, "This is your home. You have a place here. You belong in Sepherra. You're so happy to be with Sira. You can't wait to see her." That turned into phrases like, "The Resistance is a plague that must be wiped out to keep Sira safe. You want her to be safe." There were small bits of truth interjected that made it harder for his brain to differentiate between actual reality and whatever the king wanted him to believe. Over time and many visits, it all became mud in his brain—impossible to pick out the nuggets of reality. He lost all sense of what was truly happening.

"Good morning!" The king sat in the wooden chair and perched one ankle on the opposite knee.

"Is it morning?" Wyll asked and smiled at Rozam, not unhappy to have company. He couldn't begin to guess how many days he'd been in that room; it didn't seem like he ever slept, and his thoughts ran together, but having someone to talk to was nice. He got bored all alone and would scratch his arms, absentmindedly sticking his pinky in the holes dotting his skin. It fit perfectly. He wasn't sure he remembered how that happened. Forever ago, he'd lost both boots, and his socks had been pulled off with them, chilling his toes. He had eaten so little that going to the bathroom was not a problem, and he was already soaked in urine.

"You've been doing so well with your treatment this week, Wyll. Very agreeable. Would you like to have some clean, dry clothes today?" he asked jovially.

He'd forgotten where he was or why he was there, but Wyll was ecstatic to be rid of his stench. "Sure." He noticed the bundle of cloth in the king's hands, and a shock ran through his system. His eyes widened as he focused on the material in Rozam's hands. It drew his mind to something. Something about home...

Something...
About...
Home...
What home?

He racked his brain. The king chattered on, but Wyll was on the brink of realizing something important.

How did he know that fabric? Where was it from?

Wait. No, he was forgetting something. This wasn't right. Well, some of it. His head was foggy. He felt a need, a pull inside him. *I must find Sira and make her happy here.* Sira. He wanted to take her home. *Home?* His thoughts stretched as far back as his arrival. All at once, he remembered where he was.

When he first arrived in this cage, he was angry, and then the despair set in. He didn't know how many days or weeks he'd been there, but with Rozam visiting so frequently, he hoped that if Sira left without him, the king would say so or give it away somehow. Maybe kill him. Would that be so bad? He had to believe she was still in Sepherra—maybe searching for him. He needed to believe it. Because if not, he was in a new hell for no reason, at the complete mercy of a madman who'd forgotten he might wish to eat.

Fully realizing how truly helpless he was made him want to go a little crazy. He didn't know if he could handle the emotions of bondage and hopelessness together. Not really sure that he would come out on the other side of this, he'd eventually stopped fighting. All of it. He decided not to resist and drank the Kool-Aid. *The king's right. I'm never leaving this place.* Everything had gone wrong. He gave up. *The king wins.*

But wait.

The fabric of the vest that Rozam buttoned around him now was exactly the same material as the fabric on his mother's sofa. The one she absolutely *had* to buy from Nebraska Furniture Mart when she got the forty percent off coupon in the mailer. It was a dark navy on navy paisley print, and she'd gone on and on about it. How the raised pattern was *sateen*... He smiled at the memory of her euphoric face when they placed it in her living room on Mother's Day and the warm feelings of joy and hope he got from that memory. The king obviously thought the smile was for him. *Ah, let him.*

Wyll had found a trickle of hope.

Chapter Nineteen
Escaping the Deformatorium

Sporadic visits from the king and Ichabod around the clock eliminated Wyll's ability to keep time, plus he'd been out-of-his-mind delirious for a while from lack of food, movement, sleep, and comfort. He invented a game to entertain himself. A rush of endorphins had accompanied his memory of the sofa, and it felt so delicious he began to search his memories and replay all his favorite moments. He sat there, driving to a football game with a pretty girl, his arm around her, the radio loud. Then, he sat in Derec's mom's Corolla at Sonic, drinking blue raspberry slushies.

He focused on his surroundings, picking out the familiar, practicing meditation, anything to lift him from this place of imprisonment. He spent every minute focusing on his sanity by tethering his mind to the past. It made him terribly homesick but grounded him and reminded him of his objective truth. It worked. *Mostly*. He still had holey arms, and Rozam's suggestions so closely mirrored his desires to find Sira and go home that some of the indoctrination took hold.

The Clockwork Pen

Even if Rozam controlled his actions, the king couldn't fully break his mind, not if Wyll didn't allow it. It was a contest of his will against the king's. Each day, his goal of finding Sira grew more essential. He was determined to discover a way out of his cell to find her, pulling against his restraints to stretch the leather. If he had to go back to the little house and break down the damn door to get help, he would get Sira out of this nightmare. He chanted his truth in his head as Rozam spoke. The words echoed in the darkest cavities of his deepest thoughts: *get out, find Sira, stay present, and he can't beat you, get out, find Sira...*

The head shrinker his mom took him to had preached the value of "being in the moment" to keep his mind from slipping into depression. If you could ground your mind in reality, you were actively keeping yourself from going crazy. He'd never been this close to insanity. When he first hit puberty, Mom thought something was wrong with him, like he was broken or crazy. He refused to break now, coaching himself to continue—to focus—to not only exist through the trial but come out ahead. Great strength would be essential to escape and find his girl. So, he stored his energy, biding his time and waiting for an opportunity to strike. *Breathe, Wyll. Focus on the light, feel the fabric on your body, the thumping of your heart, and the rush of blood...*

He didn't get sick from the spinning anymore, and his shirt was dry and warm. Ichabod occasionally helped him with his needs, happily saving him from sitting in another puddle. The silence was so loud—better than the constant screaming of the Reformatory—it couldn't be described as a state of comfort, but it was painless.

He sucked in, filling his lungs, expanding every tiny pocket. It relaxed him. At times, the room seemed unfamiliar, and Wyll succumbed to the utter confusion, his memory inconsistent. The process of ingraining his own messages in his mind had been intense, and he often wondered when he planned to leave. There was no point in sitting here anymore; he knew instinctively that he was ready to go. He calmed himself and released the need to go anywhere or do anything. He had all the time in the world.

The sight of his arms filled him with regret. His mother's reaction wasn't going to be easy when she realized he was deformed and would be considered disgusting by his own society.

He wished he could tell her he'd been kidnapped and taken to Africa, where he got a jigger infestation. And, ah, probably almost got eaten by a lion, too. He was sure he would've flown there in a small white plane with no doors and a red stripe, heat rippling from its wings. Of course, there would be a sweaty pilot in a dirty white button-down shirt with four buttons open, a cigar in his mouth. *Yeah, probably.* Excited to have a new storyline, Wyll let his mind wander down a bunny trail on his own African safari.

He enjoyed creating stories to pass the time and enacting the part of protagonist in each scenario. He was swimming in an oasis pool when the door burst open. He saw a head of red curls duck in the room quickly and turn to leave when she stopped abruptly, jerking her face back to stare at him. Sira's eyes lit up with recognition, and she whisper-shouted out the door, "Indigo! I've got him."

She left the door open and walked over to Wyll's cage. She picked through the remotes on the table and pointed one at him, pushing the button. The bars retracted to the floor and ceiling. Sira smiled with tears in her eyes. He stared at her dumbly until he realized what was happening, and every memory suddenly clicked into place.

Indigo dashed into the room, skidding on the floor. His eyes widened in obvious shock, and he appeared less than thrilled to see Wyll sitting there. It made Wyll instantly embarrassed and angry.

"Let's go," Indigo said, waving them toward the door.

Wyll sat, patiently waiting for Sira to loosen his bonds. She stood staring at him.

Indigo said impatiently, "Sira."

She waved him off with a frown. "What is it, Wyll? Are your legs not functioning?"

It was his turn to frown. "What are you talking about? I'm completely chained up here. Am I invisible or something? I thought you had a key or something to unlock these." Wyll rattled his wrists and ankles.

Indigo looked like he was going to lose his shit. "What is going on?"

"Look, dude. Whatever I did, I'm sorry. But I didn't have anything to do with the raid. I swear. Sira took me there and spent the whole time with me. It was a lie to make you guys mad enough to leave me here and rot. I meant it when I said I'd never do it again."

"See?" Sira turned to Indigo and crossed her arms over the frills on her white shirt, resting them on the most perfect pair he'd ever seen, held up by a satin corset in a wine color with black trim. She looked good enough to eat.

Stop drooling, Wyll.

She spun toward him with a gasp, and he thought maybe he'd said that out loud until she spoke. "I know what this device is. I've seen it before. It's the re—re—"

"Reeducator," Wyll offered.

"Right. It's a brainwasher. He changes your reality. It's all in your control."

A light went off in his brain. "Yeah, that's what Rozam said."

"What?" Indigo cocked his head. He looked a little less pissed but still appeared confused. "He doesn't know?"

"I don't know what?"

"Wyll, tell me what you look like right now," Sira spoke slowly, and he drew his eyebrows together. He wasn't stupid.

What didn't they get? He attempted to squash his sarcasm but was unsure if he was successful. "My ankles are chained to the chair, I think. And this harness,"—he pulled against the straps crossing his chest—"holds me in this chair. My butler put these on me, but I don't know why." He held up his wrists in the leather cuffs. He nodded to his forearms and said, "I know the deformation looks bad." He grimaced.

Indigo closed the door and leaned against it. "What do we do now?"

"I'm thinking," Sira said, scratching her forehead with her pointer finger. She absentmindedly twirled a curl at her temple. She turned to him. "Wyll. What if I told you that you were sitting in a wooden chair, not chained to anything?"

"I'd say maybe you're the one who's nuts."

"That's what I thought." She turned to Indigo. "He's so headstrong. I don't know if I can break him quickly enough. We might have to leave him here and come up with a better plan."

"The hell you will." Wyll strained against his bonds, finding it impossible to imagine the leather straps gone. He felt them. He *knew* they were there. How do you conceive the inconceivable?

"Wyll, listen to me. You must believe the impossible can be possible. Your bonds are gone now. Trust me. You are free."

"How do I do that?" His eyes filled with tears. They couldn't leave him here. He'd believe anything they wanted him to. But he couldn't change reality with his mind, *could he?*

"You've done it before. You believed whatever he told you to be the truth."

"It was the machine. I mean, I fought it, but—I concentrated on getting out and findin—" He shut his mouth before he said something completely humiliating. From the heat of blood rushing to the surface, he knew that his face was flushing a bright pink.

"Well," she said, clearing her throat and turning a pretty pink herself, "you obviously listened to some of it if you think what you do." She tilted her head and squinted. "Indigo, when do you believe in something that's paradoxical?"

"Like weather disasters?" Indigo's hand was tapping his thigh in a nervous twitch of impatience. "I don't know."

"Well, sort of. Those are things that can change your life in ways you don't expect, but I mean a real paradigm shift."

"I don't think I've ever done that." Wyll's mind was blank. Maybe a miracle? His grandma always followed the Miracle News Network on the computer and told him about paranormal events around the world. But he didn't believe any of it, so that didn't count.

"Yes, you have!" Sira spoke excitedly and held up one finger. "When you got here. Clockwork people shouldn't be possible. You shouldn't be able to go through a basement door to another dimension with the same sun and stars. A man shouldn't be able to rule a kingdom of his own creation—with a magic pen, no less. Yet, you believed it all—without question. All the tech you told me you don't understand. You never once imagined it wouldn't work."

"Well, yeah. I could *see* it. I could touch it, hear it, smell it. Like I feel this strap." Wyll ran his fingers along the strap crossing his chest.

"There's nothing there, Wyll." Indigo stepped forward and smiled. "I'm sorry, kid. I should've known better."

Sira smiled with encouragement. "Close your eyes and imagine that all your bonds are gone."

He tried. Closing his eyes, he imagined that he was free to leave, but when he flexed his pec, he could feel the strap lying across the muscle. "But are you saying that they were never here? I've only been told they are? Because I knew the straps were there before the king told me."

"Hush," she said. "I wasn't done. In the beginning, they were there to keep you in the chair. But he probably had someone remove them. Maybe when they gave you a short nap? It looks like you changed your clothes. Maybe then?"

He vaguely remembered Rozam loosening his straps after a spinning or two and telling him he was leaving them on but letting him loose. Maybe that was a hint that he had let him *loose*. Could he believe it? Everything the man had said was half-truth. She was right. He'd accepted even the smallest tech, the magic of the pen, and how much he liked her... *What?* Where'd that come from? *Get your head on straight.* Maybe she liked him back? That was an impossibility that wasn't likely. That a powerhouse livewire like her could like him as an equal romantically... He wasn't afflicted with low self-esteem, but you knew it when someone was out of your league. It was just against the laws of nature.

He concentrated and tried to ignore Sira's intent stare and the impatient bounce of Indigo's knee. Believe the impossible. *Could I believe?* He shouted through the recesses of his mind, trying to deny what he clearly felt, telling himself that he didn't really know what he knew. Squeezing his eyes shut, he bit a flake of dry skin off his lip, worrying the chewy sliver between his front teeth, and forced his thoughts to focus. He'd jumped into the drain of the reformatory even though it felt like he was jumping off a skyscraper. Could he do the same thing here?

"Come on, Wyll," she whispered directly in his ear. "I know you can do this. I believe in you." Her breath bathed his ear in heat, and he shivered. Her minty exhalation teased his senses, waking him up in places he'd long felt grow cold.

Praying he wasn't getting a noticeable erection, his hands slid higher up his lap. Wyll released his preconceived notions and swam in the sensations she caused with her long, slender fingers resting on his shoulder ... her mouth near his ear ... her hair brushing against him ... the warm, cinnamon scent of her skin floating between them. He fought everything within him to keep from turning and kissing her because of Indigo but gave up and quickly pecked her lips before she could move. She feigned indignation while Indigo chuckled. Wyll closed his eyes again and smiled.

I can do this. She believes in me. If Sira believed hard enough, she could make it happen. This was her world, her magic. *I can believe in magic ... and people believing in me.*

They said I can get out of this chair, so I can... I will... At least I can straighten my legs.

"Guys, I heard something." Indigo's ear pressed against the door, and Wyll cracked an eye open to see his panic.

Ignore it. You can stand. Force your legs to straighten.

"Yeah, they're coming this way. Sira, over here. Behind the door."

She ignored Indigo. "Wyll. Listen, I'm counting to three and pulling you out of this chair as hard as I can.

Okay? Try to help me. Ready? One..." Sira crossed her hands and grabbed his, linking his thumbs like an arm-wrestling contest.

Wyll squeezed his closed lids so hard that he saw bright flashes of yellow-orange and purple-red bloom in his vision. Breathing deeply enough to hyperventilate—he'd never concentrated so hard—every ounce of his focus drew him into the mindset of the spinning cage, once again grasping for reality.

"Two..." An angel's voice echoed outside his thoughts.

I will straighten out my legs. I can stand. Ready? Set...

"Here they come," Indigo whispered.

Sweat beading on his forehead, Wyll prepared himself, flexing muscles, delighting in the pain of activity.

"Three!"

Go.

Sira pulled hard, and Wyll poured every ounce of strength into standing. The force of her pull, combined with his push and locked knees, threw him forward. His legs were stiff and weak, and Wyll barreled from the chair across the tiny room, pushing Ichabod backward. They crashed into the back of the door, Ichabod's eyes round as saucers. He swiveled his head, gaping at Sira and Indigo.

"Who are you?" Sira demanded, pulling on the front of his shirt. "Who are you?!"

The Clockwork Pen

"It's okay." Wyll pushed back and steadied his butler, prying her hands from his jacket. "This is Ichabod. He doesn't speak. *Faulty designer*." He would have chuckled, but it wasn't really funny anymore.

Ichabod checked his pocket watch, and his eyes grew rounder with panic. Wyll understood. "The king must be coming soon."

Ichabod nodded.

"Hey," Wyll said with his hands on the old man's shoulders. "I'm leaving with these guys. Do you want to come with me?"

"Wyll, we can't just—"

"He's *my* butler." Wyll felt a responsibility for the man. "Your father made him for *me*, and I'm pretty attached to him."

"Don't you think he's got a tracker on him?" Indigo asked.

"He is probably one giant tracker." Sira nodded in agreement.

He hadn't thought of that. "Well, I can't leave him here for the king to punish when he finds me gone. He doesn't have to stay with us, but we need to smuggle him somewhere."

"We need to go. Now." Indigo opened the door, waving toward the hall.

Sira rolled her eyes and smiled. "Fine, bring him. But we'll have someone in the Resistance scan him and then set him up with a family."

"Perfect." Wyll smiled with relief.

Indigo handed him a hooded cloak, and Wyll swung it on as they walked down the rough stone corridor. "How did you find me?" he whispered.

"We knew you weren't in the Reformatory cells, but he's got rooms down here with different contraptions for private experiments. We've just been ticking them off one at a time." She put her finger to her lips as they changed course and passed a row of open hallways lined with doors identical to the one he'd been staring at for... *How long have I been down here?* They picked up the pace for a few moments. Sira looked both ways, then spoke, "Um, Wyll? Did he ever tell you why he had you down here? What he was trying to accomplish?"

"There are halls and halls of rooms down here," he muttered as they turned another corner, running past closed doors. "How long has it been? How long have you been looking?"

Indigo held up a finger, and they jogged in silence as they entered an open lounge area with a guard sleeping behind a rugged desk. Hallways branched out like the spokes of a wheel from the unguarded hub. Indigo ran timidly for an alcove with a heavy, wooden door. They followed him through it, and while ascending the stairs, she said, "We had to wait until I could get away. We went to the Reformatory the first night we could, but we couldn't find you. We sent people out the next night to search, and Indigo and I began going through the experimental halls. That was five days ago. Everyone else gave up yesterday. I imagine you've been up around the clock. At least you'll sleep well."

"Nah, I slept. But it did seem a lot longer than a week."

"That's because he keeps your body monitored, and when you have fallen asleep, it sets a timer for an hour or so of slow wave sleep, so your body registers that it's had a refreshing night's sleep and time has passed, then they wake you up. Round the clock. Trust me; you haven't rested."

They turned down another dark and empty hall. The stillness was eerie.

"Your father could be a torture specialist for the CIA," Wyll said, and she stopped abruptly. He passed her and walked backward a few steps, facing her. "What's wrong?"

"I'm so sorry, Wyll. I don't want you to think— we're not crazy or anything. He's not a torturer. I mean, *yes*. He is now. But he never used to be. He was a father and an inventor, and we were so happy for so long. I *hate* that pen. I mean, that *ink*. Even *I* keep forgetting it's not the pen that's magic." She started walking again, and he jogged backward in her path. "He knew what he was doing. Oh yeah, Jett said he thinks those pens lying around in Dad's office can all be used with the ink, but he carries the one, so nobody knows the secret."

"What I can't figure out is how the king went missing around the clock for a week, and no one noticed," Wyll said sourly.

"Oh, he was never missing." She nearly crashed into his chest when Wyll stopped.

"How is that possible?"

"I've suspected for years that he had a doppelganger around here somewhere for things he doesn't want to do. This just proves it." At his look of doubt, she assured him. "Oh, his creations will fool you. He's had the look-alike have dinner with us several times that I could tell, but I had no proof. Most of the time, I don't think my father does anything else of importance. He probably sits alone and relaxes while his double does his job. It wouldn't surprise me if your *captor* was as captive as you were, living down there. You're probably the most excitement he's had in a long time."

Indigo came running up to them. "What's the problem? We need to go. You can talk later. Let's move."

Wyll grabbed her hand and pulled Sira out of her funk.

"We're not even out of the castle yet, you two. Don't drop your guard, or else we'll all be in a room."

They crept in silence through the lower basement levels of the castle, above the prisons, where wine and cheese were stored, along with growing plants like mushrooms and other gross-looking edibles. Indigo led them to the servants' stairs—deeper and narrower than normal staircases.

Wyll's thighs burned. He pushed harder, feeling Sira's fingertips gripping his own, hooked together like a yin-yang symbol. Her fingernail gouged his skin, but he didn't care. The pain kept him alert, and he didn't want to let go of her ever again.

They crossed a floor housing a labyrinth of supply shelves and closets, then an immense laundry area, which remained humid and smelled of soap despite the late hour. Finally, they reached the floor of servant residences. They tiptoed single file down the main hall—seeming a hundred miles long—in the dim light of iron sconces, pointing out like triangles from the wall and directing shafts of light on the ceiling. Deep blue, purple, and green glass drops hung from the ends of curling black scrolls.

They stopped at the kitchen, listening for danger, then stepped lightly across the tile. Indigo waited at the half door, the top left open for the cool breeze, refreshing the oven-like kitchen. He held the bottom half open and waved them through like a nervous traffic controller. "Come on. Come on," he whispered. Wyll pushed Ichabod out the door and pulled Sira behind him.

The king-copy had surely discovered the empty room by now. They stood in the shadow of an overhang, looking through the arches surrounding the castle base's lowest floor. *Almost there*, Wyll thought. The bridge staircase gleamed in the moonlight. Time was against them, but if they managed to make it down those stairs, they could be home free—disappear anywhere.

Standing with Indigo by the arch, Wyll looked both ways, making sure the watch guards weren't about to come around the walk. Sweat trickled between his shoulder blades.

"Gotcha!" Wyll panicked when a heavy hand landed with a crushing grip on his shoulder. He turned to see Indigo, the same terrified look on his face, a hand on his shoulder as well. *Crap.* They were caught. This time, the king would—

Chapter Twenty
Agent Double-Oh-Asthma

Derec was dressed in black cargo shorts and a vintage Metallica t-shirt—because it was his only black one. He crouched behind a leafy bush in the dark, leaning against his bike. Across the driveway, on the square concrete pad behind the garage, a dark and shiny Maserati Quattroporte, with a 4.7-liter Ferrari-designed V8 engine and a spacious luxury cabin, was parked and empty. He tried not to drool—much. The lights inside the mansion were all on as the men roamed the house, but each window had darkened one by one over the last twenty minutes, except for the kitchen. He could hear the low rumble of male voices inside the room. He knew who they were now and couldn't afford to let them see him again.

During his spy missions, he'd learned that they were men who knew the guy who lived there before, and they believed he had something of great importance to them. They'd been scouring the house for something. Derec had the feeling it was related to the magic ice land in the basement closet. Why had he let Wyll go through there? Well, both boys knew that if there were two of them, they'd be in trouble, but by himself, he wasn't threatening. It bit a little, but it was the truth. So, he'd locked the door with Wyll on the other side.

By the time he could make it back, Wyll was gone. There had to be someone on the other side with a key, right? Wyll just had to ask around. It was late by the time the men had left that day, and he'd been too afraid to turn on any lights, so he crept down to the basement of the empty mansion in the pitch black to find another, much colder basement shadowed in inky darkness. He knew it was too much to hope that Wyll would be there waiting for him in the dark, but he still deflated when he heaved the door open to an empty vault.

He'd walked Wyll's dog home, made the first excuse he could think of to Wyll's parents, grabbed a bag from Wyll's room—stuffing some clothes in it—and went home. Wyll's bag had been stowed under Derec's bed for weeks now.

Doo! Doo! Yeah! Gimme, gimme, your— Derec panicked as his phone began to blare the newest Muse song, and conversation inside the house stopped abruptly. He fumbled the device, rushing to turn it off, and accidentally hit the answer button. A man's silhouette was outlined inside the kitchen door window as one of them peered through the curtains. Derec ducked back as far as he could into the shadows of the bush and held still. "Derec? Derec, are you there?"

He covered the phone until the guy disappeared and whispered, "Hello, Mrs. Brey."

"I can hardly hear you."

"Sorry. Bad connection. Do you need something?"

"Please tell Wyll we love him, and we understand he needs time. It wasn't fair of us to surprise him the way we did."

"Okay. I will." Derec thought she'd gone and was about to turn the phone off when she spoke.

"His dad's not taking this well."

What am I supposed to say? Derec stammered, "I'm sorry."

"I'm sure you understand." *What?* Her voice was filled with emotion, and he had no idea what she was talking about. Was she asking him something?

"Um, no. I don't know—"

"Tea, stop it. Mommy's on the phone. Darn that dog—oh! Derec! TeaCup says hi. Thanks again for bringing her back. I was starting to worry. My baby—"

"Okay, Mrs. Brey. I need to go."

The lights in the kitchen turned off, plunging the area into darkness, and the door opened.

"Bye Der—" He flipped the phone off and shoved it in his pocket, squeezing himself into a ball as two men in business suits and two men in coveralls emerged into the motion sensor's spotlight. They threw out suggestions of potential pizza toppings as they entered the car. The engine purred like a kitten, and the Maserati backed up, then pivoted to turn up the drive and onto the street.

Derec waited there for a full minute before unfolding his cramped legs and rising to shake out the tension in his muscles. The motion light flicked on, and he felt exposed, so he left his bike hidden and darted across the driveway, swatting away kamikaze June bugs in the light, and slipped inside the kitchen door. He wondered if his key might open the kitchen door—if they ever locked it. But either they had no key, or it wasn't a priority to make one, pretending to own the house before a locksmith. They'd been searching for months, presumably, but nothing in the house seemed displaced. It was as if they expected the man to return at any moment, and they were afraid enough to avoid his discovery, but they were also increasingly certain that his absence meant they were on the right trail.

He squeaked through the kitchen with his new tennis shoes. The dining room's hardwood floor was dustier, though, and his feet slid over the planks to the carpeted hall. He followed it around to the back of the house and the hallway with the game room, half-bath, and stairs to the basement. He knew he was the only one in the building, but the sounds of the house settling still made the hair on his arms stand on end. He pulled his mini flashlight from his pocket when he opened the basement door and shined it down the steps as he

The Clockwork Pen

descended. The basement windows showed the shadowy backyard, but all Derec could see was the glow over the privacy fence from the baseball field's metal halide sports lights over at the high school. He was so glad the season was over for him.

Under the stairs, the ominous door mocked him. Probably the way the wardrobe to Narnia had teased Peter with its frightening delights. Was this a land of talking animals, too? He gripped the old key in his pocket and shined his light at the lock, shoving the key in and turning it to the left. He opened the door, and the squeal of the hinges made him cringe. *I meant to grab that WD-40. Crap.*

He poked his head through the door and shined his flashlight around the adjacent room. It seemed darker than the first basement, but no light came from the frosted basement windows. He stepped lightly across the room to the stairs leading to the other door.

He'd found the little house the second week he'd come, determined to find Wyll. He was glad it was empty and inspected each little item that was strange to him. He'd weighed the possible consequences of leaving the strange house to search for Wyll. He could be lost, or if Wyll was in trouble, he could get one or both of them sentenced to a fate worse than death. The yard outside the house was black and empty. A few porch lights shone down the street, but he was covered in darkness with nowhere to go. What kind of creatures lived in those houses? He'd searched the house for a note from Wyll but found nothing.

This time, he shined his light around, ensuring no new note existed. He needed to be braver. He needed to look beyond the house. Obviously, Wyll hadn't returned to the place. Derec hadn't been able to sneak his coat from the house without alerting his mother, so he strode through the little house to the bedroom and pulled open the drawers in the chest, looking for something warm to wear—nothing but sheets and blankets. The hall closet had towels, soap, and toilet paper. He spun in the living room, trying to think. He could go back to the bedroom and grab the bed covering or check the bathroom for a robe. The front closet caught his eye behind the front door. He pulled it open and saw men's jackets. Well, sort of jackets. They were stylish velvet or had military bell pulls on the shoulders; there was a silky lounge jacket with a satin lapel and a woolen coat that went to his knees. He pulled it on and felt warmer already. His legs would be cold outside, but he'd live. He grabbed the hat from the sideboard and tentatively went to open the front door.

Derec hyperventilated, trying to open the door and step onto the porch. His asthma sent him into a coughing fit, and his hand shook on the knob. If Wyll could have come back and waited for Derec, he would have just stayed in this cute little house, wouldn't he? Wouldn't that make the most sense? *We are talking about Wyll Brey here.* He chuckled, and it relieved some of his tension. He squeezed the crystal knob again and turned it, taking a huge breath. He squared his shoulders, blew his breath out, pulled the door open, and walked out into a light flurry of fresh snow. *I'm a regular Agent Double-oh-Asthma.*

He shouldn't have been surprised. It was an icy, cold place. Was it an arctic land? He closed the door behind him and looked up and down the yards on his side of the street. All was shadowed and quiet. Pacing the length of the tiny walkway to the street, he stopped at the gate. To the left, the road disappeared into the darkness, and he saw shapes that looked like trees in the distance. On the right, though, he saw the glow of lights reflected in the low cloud cover and mountains in the distance. Panic rose in his throat. He shouldn't be anywhere near mountains. *Where the hell am I? Dammit, Wyll. Where the hell are you?*

Derec paced the walkway, gathering the courage to go further. He shook his hands as if they were wet, and he had no towel. Opening the gate, he stepped into the cobblestone street and walked to the middle. He saw a few pointy towers in a massive castle lit in white. *Nope.* Castles and kings could not mean good news. They never did in any fiction he'd read before. Unless you were an evil sorcerer or a brave knight, neither of which described Derec. This was not the night. He still had time. He would have to find a way to come on his day off and look around in the sunlight.

He gave up and went home.

Derec parked his bike in the shed and silently opened the sliding glass door in the dining room. He tiptoed around the table to the hall and turned. He could see his bedroom door down the hall, and he relaxed.

"Stop!" his mother called.

Derec froze in place, mid-motion, and his mom came into the hall from the living room, where he heard the TV talking and saw flashes of blue light erupting with the music of the commercial it played. She saw him and laughed. In Chinese, she said, "You don't have to freeze. I wanted to see you. Daddy is watching TV through his eyelids. Where have you been?"

"With Wyll," he said quickly.

She raised her eyebrows and crossed her arms.

"I went to the store before work, and then Wyll and I hung out after."

"Good," she said. "You and Wyll are good friends. You have been friends for a long time. But he has been distant since he got a car—"

"He doesn't have a car yet. He's got to get it running. Then we can go anywhere we want." He grinned.

"With permission," she said with a frown.

"Of course. You know I always do the right thing."

"True, but does Wyll? I worry sometimes. What are his college plans?"

"Why are you asking?" Derec folded his arms defensively.

"Now, now, *bǎo bèi*, don't take it that way. I think you may be going different directions in life. One Chinese proverb says, *'Each man must ride the road of his own fate.'* I do not wish for you to be hurt by his destiny." She mixed her English and Chinese, but Derec always knew what she was trying to say.

He lifted his elbows and shrugged. "Another says, *'Whether we walk quickly or slowly, the road remains the same.'* Don't worry, Mom. Wyll and I are fine. He's just been going through some stuff. He'll be okay. You'll see."

"Maybe you can have him come to church with you?" Her brows were so high in excited anticipation that he hated shooting her down.

"You know I don't follow all that stuff. It's too strange. Wyll's mom already talked to me about it. He doesn't want to go, either."

"I want you to try it this year. No arguments. You need to go to the right place to find a nice girl. Someone old-fashioned, with family values, who will make me a *Nai Nai*."

"Don't worry, Mom. I have plenty of time for that."

"*Nǐ duì wǒ lái shuō hěn zhòng yào.*"

"You mean a lot to me, too. Good night." He lamely patted her shoulder when she hugged him and wiggled out of the embrace. "Go watch your show. I'm going to my room. Oh yeah. Mom?"

"Hmmm?"

"Wyll and I might go camping next week. Just so you know."

"Okay. Sleep well."

Derec lay back on his bed in a pair of cotton lounge pants. A storm front had cooled the air, and his window was open to let in the breeze. The crickets' shrill song outside his window joined an opera of summer sounds, the rustle of swishing grass, a croaking frog somewhere near the shed, and the sorrowful *ee-er ee-er* of the locust chorus, accompanied by the creaking rattle of cicadas. The flapping percussion of fat green leaves slapping together in the swaying oak and maple trees and the heady scent of the lilac bush lulled him into sleepy thoughts.

He'd been enjoying his days alone these past weeks when he said he was with Wyll. He would have been lectured on productivity if his parents knew he'd been at the mall before work, relaxing at the bookstore, reading deep sci-fi adventures, and sipping iced coffee.

Wyll would call me a pansy. Meanwhile, he rejected the real-life sci-fi nightmare to which he'd sent his best friend. If Wyll wasn't back next week, Derec would *truly* go search for him in the strange world. Of course, that's what he said last week. Derec shook his head. Senior year was starting in three weeks. Wyll was missing football camp and could be cut from the team. Certainly, Derec would do it by the end of next week. *Probably.*

Chapter Twenty-One
Caught Again?

Having just escaped the Reformatory for the third time and not quite clear of the castle, Wyll panicked as he was caught again. He turned to see Jett standing there with the stupidest grin on his face. He cackled, pointing at their livid expressions. Wyll shook his head slowly to keep from punching the douchebag right in the mouth. It wasn't funny.

Judging Wyll's expression of terror, Ichabod pushed Jett back so hard he flew into the railing over the moat. The display of loyalty did manage to cool some of Wyll's anger. If only he'd fallen in… But they were trying to be stealthy, and Wyll wasn't out of trouble yet. He focused on being quiet and didn't yell like he wanted to.

The push didn't faze Jett. "Well, she said you were alive. Guess she was right. You're like a lucky coin that keeps popping up," Jett said in an everyday volume. "Ya had a lovely funeral, *mate*."

"Be quiet, Jett. You're going to get us all caught." Sira pointed back at him.

The Clockwork Pen

Jett obviously believed his position with the king made him invincible—above the law. "Maybe you. I belong here. I have an excuse." He looked at Wyll and said in a jovial tone, "You sure are a lot of trouble. First, you give us all away; then Sira shuts down the mission for you. We could all be free by now if it wasn't for you." The guy poked him in the side with his elbow, like he was just ribbing him, but being a teenage boy, Wyll could recognize barely covered hostility from a mile away.

He chuckled back, glaring at Jett and smiling—but mostly baring his teeth. "Do you have some information for us? Is that why you're here, comrade?"

"He knows you're planning something—but he thinks you're his puppet now. You a puppet, Wyll?"

Ooh hoo hoo. Wyll chuckled, tilting his head to the side before he decked his fellow compatriot. *How does anyone believe this guy is on our side?* Or was it just Wyll that he was threatened by? "It didn't work." He pointed at himself. "Obviously."

"Lucky for you. Just don't choke at the last minute and forget your training. If you don't succeed with your strategy, it's *our* last shot. And he has one of his own." Jett lowered his voice so that Wyll had to lean closer to hear.

"Are you going to share it?" Wyll raised his eyebrow.

"If she tries to make any real attempt to leave, he has finished a complex of apartments in the branches of the Reformatory. She'll be locked in one until she does whatever he says—and he'll blow up the house."

"What house?" Wyll panicked.

"The one with the door to your world." He said it as though Wyll came from the land of cockroaches.

"We'd never make it back," he whispered. Memories of home flashed through his mind. The fire hydrant where he met Derec, the posters on his bedroom wall, the car he'd been rebuilding since he was fifteen, the dining room table with his parents eating pork chops and peas—school, parties, dates—all flipped through his mind, full of emotion.

No, wait—his parents weren't eating dinner at the table together. They were getting a divorce. That was the last thing they'd said to him. And he'd run away. He wasn't particularly proud of that moment now. He'd had no shred of empathy for either of them, entertaining his own selfishness and acting out. But if they hurt nearly as much as he felt at losing Sira, he'd been a real jerk not to notice their pain.

"No crap." Jett smiled like he was the vision of coolness. He must have heard the king say it and thought it was something new. *Douche bag.*

Sira was whispering to Indigo, not paying attention to their interaction at all. Wyll was suddenly ready to go. He needed to get away from Jett before he ended up in prison for clock-slaughter.

The Clockwork Pen

"Let's go. You wanted to go, so let's go." Wyll strode into the moonlight without looking back, stalking toward the stairs. He turned to see Indigo and Sira staring at him—mouths open—but Ichabod stepped lightly behind him like a favorite pet. He chastised himself for the generalization, but the butler *was* loyal—and following him.

Wyll's feet tapped down the steps and to the plaza. He pulled his cloak closer to ward off the chilly mist that fogged the ground, swirling in his wake. He passed the empty stocks left behind, guarding the square like wicked sentinels, his cloak's hem sending the fog into little dervishes dancing among them in whorls of vapor. He turned South for the beach, but a grip on his elbow pulled him around. He spun with karate hands out, but Sira chuckled and pointed North. "There's a lake that way with camping sites. We've moved there. A few people went home, but they disappeared. We're afraid they're in the experimental rooms. We found one and a half." She cringed. "Don't ask. Who knows if he even remembers where he's locked up whom, and for how long?"

"It's like taking a vacation to hell down there. I don't feel quite right. I've been thinking. With so much danger, maybe you'd be safer in the castle. The king is nuts, but everything *else* is awesome; what if we stay for a while? I can keep you happy, and I'm sure you want to make up with your father. Right? Shouldn't we go back and at least try?"

"What!" she whispered furiously, her eyes wide.

Her incredulous expression shocked him, and he hit the side of his head with the heel of his hand. "Where did that come from?"

Her face relaxed. "It's the training. Your subconscious picks it up, even if you fight it. But I get his plan now. He is so predictable. It's despicable. Using you to convince me to stay and make up with him." She was spitting along with her explosive words. "What about me makes him think I'm that simple? I mean, I've never fawned after boys before. Why does he think a human boy's mere presence will supersede my good judgment?"

"You okay?" He grabbed her hand and squeezed.

"Yeah. I just—I still can't believe he tried to convince me you were dead. He even made a copy of you. Did you know that? He might be a madman, taking apart his own creations, but he's never murdered a human that I know of. I couldn't believe he'd do that—especially knowing how much I cared—" She stopped and blushed.

He drew his eyebrows together. "Knowing what?"

She shook her head quickly as they walked.

"How did you know it wasn't … me?" Wyll worked to keep up with Indigo's twenty-foot strides. "The dead me."

"I leaned over your body and hugged you for a while. I wasn't sure at first, and I cried into your shoulder. There's a razor in my ring, and I sliced right behind your jaw joint. Just below your ear. See?" She swiveled the

The Clockwork Pen

base of her ring, and a tiny blade slid out of the center. Not big, but deadly sharp, he could tell.

"What did you find?"

"The teeth of a gear." She smiled.

"Aha. Not very human, huh? What if it was really me? You would have defaced my corpse?"

"I had to know." She shrugged.

"Thanks for rescuing me. *Again*. I'll have to return the favor someday."

"You already did." She squeezed his hand. "I knew my eventual desire was to leave, but there was no set plan. I don't think I was really serious. I was waffling… I didn't know how badly I needed out of here until I met you—coming from the life I've always dreamed of. Obviously, you didn't belong here—and I knew I belonged with you. I mean, where you were. *Oh geez*. Where you're from … in the real world."

He pictured her stalking the halls of his high school in her lace boots and striped stockings, with a ruffled skirt and corset. It didn't seem right to imagine her in jeans and a hoodie. Though literally, everyone wore it as a school uniform. Some layered, some accessorized, and some wore the same ones every day. He didn't care what she wore. She'd never be as sexy as she was in the hayloft in his oversized shirt and white cotton stockings tied above her knee, her deep red hair falling out of its updo, curls resting on her shoulder, and drawing his attention to the top shirt buttons that should have been buttoned. Hey, he wasn't going to say anything. He wasn't stupid.

After passing neighborhoods of citizen residences, they left the pavement and entered an open grassy field of small hills. Exposed, they ran through it, heading for the trees. The area ahead was densely populated with firs and pines. They dodged a few bushy branches, instantly hidden. The trail was invisible in the moonlight; the tall trees covered them in shadow. Wyll noticed a disc on Indigo's top hat; it glowed blue and illuminated the pathway before them. He wanted to grab handfuls of their tech to take home, but he had a feeling he'd be leaving with the clothes on his back. It was a shame. But would their magic even work in the real world? *This world is pretty real, too, I guess.* And why wouldn't it? The king created this world from theirs. The trees still had wooden trunks and green leaves. He ran his hand over the rough trunks and pointy evergreen needles as they passed.

They broke through the trees almost five minutes later, entering a large campsite, and a figure barreled into him. He almost fell over as Keylin wrapped her arms around his neck. "They thought it was you, but Sira and I didn't believe."

He swung her around once and set her on her feet. "Thanks, kid." He pretended to punch her chin, and she beamed.

They sat around the fire, eating and whispering not to wake up the camp, and he stared into the flames. He

The Clockwork Pen

smiled, imagining Keylin in his world, discovering things for the first time in her innocent way. She and Sira would probably be disappointed by the lack of tech in his world. He could see them all together at school in the fall. Derec would save the lunch table in the commons, and Keylin would sit down next to him with her tray while Sira and Wyll spread out the lunch he'd packed for them on the other side. He imagined them going to the drive-in. Kansas City had few left, but they could drive to the one in Raytown. They could take the girls mini-golfing and bowling and to the movie theatre. Ideas flooded his brain.

"—Wyll? Wyll, did you hear me?" Sira nudged his shoulder with her own, reminding his body that she was pressed against his side from ankle to thigh, hip to shoulder. They generated warmth between them, and he nearly sighed when he looked down at how beautiful she was—a few drifting snowflakes catching in her hair. She chuckled. "You didn't hear a word I said, did you?"

"Not a word." He smiled genuinely. "Sorry. I'm a little out of my mind for a moment. Leave a message at the beep."

"What beep?" She tilted her head.

"Oh. Sorry. Old joke. There used to be this machine that answered your phone for you and took messages that you could listen to later."

"What's a phone?"

"Ohhhhh. Hmm. Well, it's kind of like a walkie-talkie…"

"What's a—"

He held up his hand. "Just a second." He patted his pocket, realizing he'd left his phone in his coat at the beach, and by now, it was long gone. *Damn.* "It's about the size of a remote, but everyone has a number. So, if you were in the castle and I wanted to talk to you but was out here, I would type in your number, and *your* phone would ring. Then you push the button on your phone and put it to your ear, and we can talk."

"Nah uh. You're pulling my leg. Any time you want? From that far apart? Not possible."

"Your voice runs on an electric current that is translated at the other end."

She was catching on, "So when you had an answer machine, it would push the button for you and talk for you?"

"Close. When someone calls you, and you don't push the button, the machine records a message from them to you, and you can listen to it whenever you want."

"Oh! We have something like that here. But it's connected to a mouthpiece in each home. We call it the *Messenger*—the king uses it mostly. But if that's old in your world, what do they have now?"

He explained cell phones to her—at least, the best he could. She yawned and leaned his way, laying her head on the seam of their shoulders. They watched the fire, listening to it crackle.

The Clockwork Pen

"I'm going to bed, guys," Indigo stood. "I will explain to the people about what really happened, Wyll. You might as well sleep in. We move tomorrow. Everything's paused but ready to move forward. Hopefully, the schedules are all the same, and none of the planned meetings will fail. We should be ready about noon. Goodnight."

Indigo stood, brushing dirt and snow off his long pant legs, then stepped back over the log and folded himself into a tent. He'd found an older couple when they arrived at camp who needed help, and Ichabod left to sleep in their tent. It was bittersweet. Wyll and Sira turned back to watch the fire silently—the only two still awake. They sat before not a roaring blaze nor embers but a small crackling fire with tongues of flame that licked the black night before breaking into sparks, floating up the vents of heat, rising higher, higher, before winking out of existence.

Wyll wondered, *Is that me?* Was he a temper-fueled inferno on his way to a glowing spark and a final flicker before he was extinguished? His mind went back to the puzzle of conceiving the impossible. He needed to get the idea of arm holes out of his mind. He'd never believed that other dimensions existed on this Earth. He didn't know there was real magic—like this place. He could never have imagined what he'd seen here. So, the question that fully plagued him was: *What else don't I know?* What else was out there in the universe? Wyll felt there was a higher plan than his, but how did he tap into it? How did he learn what he didn't know if he didn't know what he needed to learn?

Sira rolled her head and touched noses with him. They smiled at one another. "I missed you so much," he said, and her lids eased over her pupils, tiny flakes melting on her lashes. He'd been away from her for too long, and by her expression, she wasn't unhappy to be there. He tilted his chin up, and she kissed him, pulling back, intimidated by her own impetuousness. He chuckled and rubbed her nose with his, cupping her face. Her lips, a breath away from his, seemed to swell, and then they were kissing with fire, and this one was raging.

She sighed into his mouth, and the sound melted him. They separated and peered into each other's eyes, hearts, and souls. Matching smiles said *We belong together.*

"How have you been?" he asked softly.

"It was—I've never felt so alone. I'm glad you're back."

"I'm never leaving you again. I'm taking you home." He rested his lips on her forehead. "You ready for tomorrow?"

"My brain tells me I am, but when I think about actually leaving—leaving my home, leaving my father, hurting him—" Her voice shattered.

"Oh, Sira." He wrapped his arms around her, pressing their bodies together. It was like holding your

The Clockwork Pen

favorite thing. The rush of emotions was the same: joy, wonder, admiration, a warm, comfortable feeling that everything was right as it should be. He felt *lucky*. "I can't wait to take you home."

She pulled back, wrapping her hands around his wrists and slipping her fingers under his coat sleeves. He cringed. "How can you touch me? Aren't you—grossed out?"

"What are you talking about?"

He pushed up his sleeves. "The holes, they're everywhere. Don't you see—" He stopped as it hit him. "They're not real, are they?"

She shook her head sadly. "Sorry. It's in your head."

"How am I going to know what he changed in my brain? How do I know what's real? It all ran together; everything. I don't know my own thoughts anymore. It's a helpless feeling, not knowing."

She rested her fingers on his jaw. "It won't last forever. You'll be fine—"

"You don't understand. Before my grandpa died, he had Alzheimer's and forgot who I was every week. He was always so afraid because he didn't know anyone, what was happening, or where he was half the time. My grandma said he was gone long before he died. It's not a life." Wyll's heart skipped to a panicky beat. "I've always wondered, will I get it too, one day? Will they put me in a home with strangers and nurses and no way to tell people I hate it? If I felt like this for the rest of my life?" He shivered. "What a nightmare."

Sira laid a trembling hand on his back, and he realized she was just as afraid as he was, but her fears were present. Her ordeal was still coming. He needed to think of someone other than himself all the time.

Wyll straightened his shoulders—he'd had enough of being captive. He would no longer watch life; he was going to live it. *Starting now.* He pulled Sira's face to his and dove into her. They were sucked under a blanket of fire and smoldered.

"Wyll," she said, breathless. "Whoa."

He smiled. *Practice makes perfect.* He kissed her again, then got up and offered her a hand. "Where's our tent?"

She led him to the metal-framed structure she'd been sleeping in, far away from everyone else, and nestled between two trees bursting with needles that scratched when the wind blew. She shrugged. "I wanted to be by myself. Not many people were happy with me for bringing you in again; no one wanted to volunteer for the rescue mission."

"Geez. I got massively unpopular fast."

"They aren't human and lack a trusting nature. They recoiled from your betrayal, and forgiveness doesn't come easily. It's almost like they're missing their humanity sometimes." She held the tent flap back and followed Wyll as he ducked inside.

"That makes sense." He faced the tent wall and shrugged out of his cloak, throwing his dirty shirt aside. It landed next to a small stack of men's clothing. "Thanks for the clothes."

"Sure," she said, her voice muffled by fabric.

He dug through the pile and found a long cotton shirt. It was going to feel so good to sleep lying down. He smiled at the thought as he kicked off his boots. Done changing first, he turned to see her standing in a pile of skirts. Long white sleeves fell off her shoulders, the shirt ended just under her backside, and he tilted his head for a higher view. Her back was to him, so he could clearly see her fingers fumbling behind herself with a knot in the ribbon lacing her corset. She wore black stockings this time, tied above her knees with pink silk bows in the back, trailing ribbons for several inches.

He ducked under the blanket quickly, pulling it over his lap. The view was much better down here. He cleared his throat. "If you sit down, I can untie that knot."

She crawled over and knelt before him, sitting on her tiny feet. She was a perfect hourglass from behind, and it parched his throat. He scooted as close as he dared and picked up the black silk mess of ribbon. It took him a second, but he picked the knot through. He enjoyed undoing knots. It was kind of like doing a puzzle for him. *Which loop and which strand goes where?* And finishing it was so satisfying.

"There you go," he said.

She rose. He could tell from her tiny "Thanks" that something was bothering her. He waited until she turned off their light and got under the covers. He laid his arm across the pillows, and she snuggled into him, her lips barely brushing his neck. She sighed softly when he wrapped his arm around her, laying his hand on her back.

"What's wrong?" he whispered, looking down at her features glowing in the moonlight that filtered through the tent.

"I'm just tired," she said a little too quickly.

"Not buying it. What's wrong? Are you having second thoughts? I feel like I could stay if you're not ready."

"No. For that reason alone, I need to get you out of here. It's just when I think of how sad he'll be here once I'm gone…" She gave a shaking sob. "He made all this for me, and I'm going to leave him here. I'm giving back the biggest gift he's ever given me—like I don't even care. Aaah." She growled. "He makes me so mad, though. Why did he have to make it this way? Why did he have to keep me from my own place in the world? I mean, is it a real life if you don't live it in reality? He's forced me to do this—there's just no going back. He doesn't believe I'm really part of the Resistance; he thinks I'm playing at being rebellious."

"I know." He stroked her back with his fingertips.

"He will see this as a total betrayal." She sobbed again, letting the tears flow, and he held her as close as he

The Clockwork Pen

could. It was a hug that pulled her heart to his, sealing them together, keeping them safe, as everything fell apart around them.

Her cries warbled and got fuzzy; he could only hear himself breathing then and welcomed a heavy blanket of sleep.

"Wake up, Sleepyhead." Sira leaned over him and kissed his cheek.

"Huh?" Wyll cracked one eye open, took in too much sunlight, and closed it again.

"Hey." She laughed and kissed his nose.

He kept his eyes closed but put a finger to his lips and tapped them twice. Her mouth melded perfectly with his own. He groaned in appreciation, and she chuckled.

"You have to get up." She pushed him back. "It's nearly ten o'clock."

"You're awfully chipper."

"Today's the day I am liberated. I was thinking, maybe I go back for a year and then come back here for a few months and just repeat that? Maybe I can get him to come back eventually and get him some help from a doctor?"

"They can't fix crazy. Not this kind, anyway. What would you tell the doctor? His magic pen made him nuts after living in a world he created in his basement closet? They'd lock you up with him."

She frowned. "Well, at least I can come visit him sometimes. It doesn't have to be forever, right? He'll forgive me in time, won't he?"

Wyll smiled. "Of course he will. He loves you."

Throwing on clothes, he ducked out of the tent flaps to find some coffee. Wyll found the nearest fire and sat with his hands out to shake off the chill of the overcast morning. Energy buzzed through the camp like a live wire, and the electricity soon got to him. With his fingertips barely touching, he felt like he should see sparks between them.

Sira joined him, and they ate, then gathered their backpacks and stuffed in everything they'd need to take with them. The patched bags were army green and full of pockets. Wyll hefted one over his shoulder. "These bags are awesome."

Sira grinned. "They were my parents' backpacking gear. They used to hike the mountains in Colorado when they were young and carried these." She lifted hers with one hand, swinging her arms through the straps. "I had to bring them," she said, apologetic.

"Hey. I get it. I do. I think it's a great idea. Maybe we can go to Denver over spring break or something and take these babies back up there." He raised his eyebrows.

She nodded. "Perfect."

It was almost noon. Sira and Wyll carried their backpacks, following Indigo and Malynda into town. Wyll watched them ahead, strolling arm in arm. Malynda twirled a white lace umbrella over her left shoulder, Indigo on her right. She spoke to him and laughed. He covered her arm with his hand and stared back adoringly.

"They are so cute," Sira said. "I'm not sure if I should applaud or gag."

Wyll's tension broke, and he laughed heartily. "I feel the same way."

It may be an act, but man, they were so convincing. Maybe it was so natural because they were always this way? He took the cue from Indigo and offered his hand to Sira. She laughed.

"Do I look like I need to hold your hand?" She took a few steps in front of him, exaggerating the sway of her hips clad in deep brown leather pants with a bronze-grommeted belt. She turned around to face him and walked backward in his path. She pointed both index fingers at herself. "I'm a woman. I can escort myself." Under a cropped leather jacket, the corset she pointed to was a patchwork of shimmering fabric in purples and bronze trim. It laced up the front, he noticed. Then he tried not to notice. *Better not get distracted.*

"Turn around before you trip and fall on your *woman's* behind." He laughed. Wyll needed to keep his head in the game. She'd gone over the plan with him again, explaining the tweaks and deviations they'd made while the king had him. They'd done a run-through to work out kinks. Wyll felt disconnected from the entire process. He hadn't planned it, made it happen, or donated any supplies or effort, and it made him feel like a kindergartner. Someone insignificant in the grown-ups' plot, doing what he's told for a cookie.

He had one job. Be a pair with Sira. They would protect each other. If something happened to one, the other knew the plan and vowed to carry it out, no matter what. This was it—up to them. This was their chance at freedom. If they failed, the king would know their plans, their intel, and not only would he shut them down, but he'd also blow up the only way to ever achieve it. This could not go wrong—their future depended on it.

"Hey. You okay?" Sira bumped his arm with her shoulder.

He listened to their leather creaking in the chilly air. "Yeah. I'm fine. Just getting my head ready."

"We're going home today." She smiled.

"Together."

She grabbed his hand, and he looked down at their joined grip. "I thought you said—"

"I said I didn't need *you* to hold *my* hand. You're not. I'm holding yours."

He nearly snorted. *Okay.* "However that works in your head, I don't care." He held up her fingers. "As long as the end result is the same."

The Clockwork Pen

They caught up with Indigo and Malynda, who were standing on the sidewalk outside 2224 Olathe, talking to a neighbor. They'd gone this way to pass the house, familiarizing the route and timing the walk. They deposited their backpacks in the yard, dropping them over the fence. Someone would take them inside. Indigo introduced them to the neighbors as they "accidentally" bumped into the couple. The rotund man—jolly pink cheeks matching his cravat—shook Wyll's hand, palming him a piece of paper. It wasn't noticeably big or thick, more like tissue paper. He carefully put it in the short pocket of his vest and tipped his hat toward the man.

They made sure to pass unnoticed through the square, their heads down, meeting no one's eyes. The group paused at the bottom of the main staircase, oddly busy for that time of day. Sira cursed at the stairs—the only way to get to the castle and over the moat. To Wyll's anxious mind, her frustrated word choice was hilarious. Without warning, she took off, weaving between the people on the stairs. Practically running, she pulled Wyll behind her with his hand gripped tightly.

"Ow," he protested at the top, rubbing his shoulder when she released him. "Wrong hand."

"Someone *had* to see us. With all the damn windows and all the damn people who can't mind their own damn business—"

"It's okay, Sira." Indigo caught up to them. He put a reassuring hand on her shoulder, and Wyll's first thought was, *I should have done that.*

"We're going to be out of here so soon." Wyll took her hand with his left, still feeling the pull in his right shoulder. He vaguely wondered how long it was going to hurt. Tucking under the shadowed arches surrounding the castle's base, they followed the hall toward the kitchen in the back. They needed a diversion to clear the help from the kitchen—the fewer people who saw them, the lower the risk. Eleeda would put Wyll to work if she saw him in the kitchen. And she wouldn't be happy that he'd fled in the night without a word. Indigo ducked his head in the door, letting Kipper's son, Juke, know they were ready.

The boy went to his job, and Wyll leaned over the balcony, the first floor jutting out several feet overhead. The castle loomed above him like a weight on his head. *Did the king feel this way?*

"Ready?" Sira tapped his shoulder.

"Hmm? Yeah. I'm right behind you." His nerves were strung so tight they could have played him like a violin.

Juke had recruited the young boy, Pyne, from the kitchens. He'd followed Wyll faithfully when he worked there—it seemed like forever ago. The boys caused some ruckus, and Lyri shrieked like she'd seen a rodent. Eleeda started yelling, and then the voices faded away. Indigo stepped out and waved them over. They darted through the kitchen.

To get to Rozam's office, they could go one of two ways. The first was through the castle's main hall, following corridors adjacent to the family quarters. They didn't even consider that route. The other was through the kitchens to the north hallway, past the stairs for the family suites. Then, down a series of halls to an atrium door, across an open bridge over the moat, to a courtyard. Finally, to a covered walkway winding around a turret—it was all a spectacular tour, but no visiting emissaries to see it—then through the second turret's doors and up a final set of stairs to the curved hallway with the king's office.

Sira mapped it out for them all in case something went wrong and directions were needed. Wyll had it memorized, and he chanted it over in his head. They'd crossed the walkway and were halfway around the turret when Indigo stopped suddenly and lunged backward, his arm stretched out behind him, almost pushing Malynda over the railing into the water.

"What is it?" Sira whispered.

He turned around with his finger up and put it to his lips. Then, he turned his back to them and flattened his body against the wall, inching forward. He stopped. Wyll could feel sweat bead on the muscles of his back. As Indigo crept toward them, Wyll's shirt stuck to his spine under his heavy cloak. Sira had picked out his clothes, and he looked pretty snazzy for someone about to be thrown in the Reformatory.

"The guards that we thought were upstairs are taking a break. They're outside the door smoking their pipes, leaning against the wall, and talking," Indigo whispered. "It's good and bad. No one will hear us in the hall, overtaking the guards, but someone could see us out here." He looked around. "We also lose the element of surprise. They'll see us coming as soon as we go three feet."

"Can we wait for their break to be over?" Malynda asked.

"We can't risk it," Wyll said. "Anybody could come this way at any time. And what if the guards come this way when they leave? They might not be the guards we think they are."

"He's right," Sira said, smiling. She gave him a nod of approval.

Wyll's chest fluttered from earning her respect. He was ready to fight an army—eager to do something reckless. It was the perfect feeling for the perfect time and place. "Why don't you and Malynda waltz over there to ask them a question, like you're strolling and got lost? Then, wham!"

Indigo cringed slightly and nodded with resolve. "Right. We're ready. Aren't we, darling?"

Malynda took his arm. "Yes, my love."

Again, so cute and yet so disgusting. He wanted to make a face, but they might think he was making fun of them, so he refrained. When had he become so thoughtful?

Wyll held his hand out to Sira with his eyebrows raised. He didn't want her to think he was trying to comfort her—she held hands for her own reasons, and he respected it. She grinned and pressed her fingerless leather glove into his palm, gripping with her long, thin fingers.

Wyll leaned out just far enough to see Indigo and Malynda reach the guards, who stood at attention, hands on holsters. He was nervous for them and chewed his thumbnail, ripping the edge off and spitting it out. They were talking. The guards nodded, pointing, and one started to walk toward Wyll and Sira. Wyll ducked back a bit just as he saw Indigo bash the guard on the back of the head with his pistol butt. Malynda spun, throwing her leg high, and kicked the other guard in the face as he reached for his gun. She pulled out her pistol and knocked him out, as well.

Wyll and Sira rushed over, and they split up, undressing the guards and giving the clothes to Indigo and Malynda, who used the guards' keys to open the door and ducked inside with the bundles.

"Cloth." Wyll held his hand out to Sira, and she tossed him a rag. He opened the guard's mouth and put a roll of the white cotton on his tongue. "Tape."

Sira threw him the roll, and they gagged, then hogtied the guards. The waist-high railing of the balcony would keep them hidden if they lay on the walkway. Wyll and Sira debated dragging them inside but thought the guards might be too noisy if they squirmed around to kick the wall or something. Wyll squatted beside a guard, who involuntarily shivered in the cold without his clothes.

"We must take them in. It's too cold."

"When they come back with the keys, we'll move." Sira crouched next to him. "Indi and Malynda can come back for them."

Soon, the door opened, and they pressed themselves against the wall, just in case. Wyll saw a soldier's boot and pant leg and a white glove on the door. A helmet leaned out, looking around, and Wyll thought,. *We're caught.*

Chapter Twenty-Two
Magic Ink Burns

The guard stepped out the door and looked around, but Wyll didn't move. He put his arm straight across Sira's body, holding her to the wall, but she snorted and pushed his arm away. "Come on," she whispered. "If it was a real guard, they would have shot you by now."

He watched her eyes roll, and he laughed. "It was a joke."

She shook her head and walked through the door.

Wyll, you're an idiot. It would be a while before his mind was back to normal. There were more important things to think about, and he followed Sira, pulling the door shut behind him.

The four partners stood at the base of the final staircase, looking up anxiously.

"Ready?" Indigo asked through the mask.

"After you, Captain." Sira motioned for him to pass her.

Wyll inhaled. He knew the plan. She knew the plan. They knew the plan. *Get the pen and magic ink, draw a decoy jar of ink, lock it back in the safe, and leave.*

Indigo and Malynda would set up protection for everyone in the Resistance as soon as possible. They'd make a new key and send him home with Sira. Simple enough plan. Jett's job was to keep the king away for a two-hour meeting that should be just getting started now, giving them plenty of time.

It wasn't a creation event but rather a planning meeting. Jett mentioned he had innovative ideas for expansion—to the king's delight—playing right into their plan. Jett had likewise spent an inordinate amount of time writing up a detailed proposal for constructing a sister country, existing as a ring around Sepherra separated by a freshwater moat. It was a cool-looking design intended to convince the king that Sira would find so much new adventure in the addition that she would be compelled to stay and explore it all. The king could create fantastical wonders of clay and architecture. Jett advised the king to leave his pen in the safe for Sira, who was coming by to "practice writing" after the meeting.

Indigo and Malynda escorted them up the hall and slowed in their surprise, noticing a second pair of guards stationed outside the king's office, just down the hall from the family suites. Good thing the other guards left their helmets where they could find them. Thinking fast, Indigo said to the guards, "We are escorting the princess and her friend to the family suites, and we are here to relieve you."

The Clockwork Pen

"We weren't told of this," the guard on the right said, laying his fingers on the grip of a wicked-looking pistol with a saber blade attached to the handle.

"Whew!" The other guard slumped, shaking out each leg, and said, "Thank my gears, my feet are killing me. Damn new boots." He punched his partner in the chest and said with enthusiasm, "We've got a break, dummy. Let's take it before they give us some other job, like watch this plant or guard that chair, or maybe we'll get another door!"

The first guard sputtered his laughter at the absurdity, and they clapped each other on the back. "Let's go see what Eleeda's got to eat." The first guard gave them the side-eye but left in a jovial mood.

Wyll exhaled and blew it out with a silent whistle. "That was close. Come on."

They clustered around the door, and Sira pulled out her tool set—a flat leather case the size of his Geometry calculator. She unfolded it to show an array of slim silver tools. Nodding at Malynda, they put their keys in both locks and turned them together. The door clicked open, and a series of beeps let them know the alarm was counting down. Wyll and Sira ducked inside while Indigo and Malynda left to drag the guards inside at the bottom of the stairs.

Sira directed Wyll to the alarm box on the wall. He would never have figured it out on his own. It was one of many gears and intricately designed pieces of steampunk art covering the walls. The office seemed like it revolved around a theme of sea life. By the window, a cluster of multi-colored, blown-glass starfish caught his eye, hanging from the ceiling by thin wires, confirming his theory.

The alarm box itself looked like the front half of an old diving helmet embedded in the wall. It had a dial on the front and mesh circles on the sides and top of the helmet. The shoulders sported brass piping, and copper coil ran from the top to the breastplate. Sira opened the flip-top head of a tiny octopus clinging to the side of the helmet, flicking a switch that popped the panel open. It was like the inner workings of a clock—gears, wires, and spinning parts everywhere—but tucked in the center was a brass-plated panel with a number pad.

Wyll pulled the tissue paper from his navy-striped vest and unfolded it. There was a sequence of numbers and instructions to cut the third blue wire to the right of the fuse. He typed in the numbers, whispering to himself, "One, two, one, two, two, zero, zero, three." The little red light turned yellow and emitted four high-pitched beeps.

"That means you have ten seconds before the alarm goes off." Sira tapped his shoulder.

"Yes. I know." He tried not to sound angry, speaking through gritted teeth.

"Sorry." She didn't sound sorry.

Nervous sweat trickled from his temple, absorbed by the brim of his black hat. He'd been warned that any misstep in this process would cause the alarm to belt out an insanely high-pitched scream, so high and loud that your eyes and ears would spew blood before you could leave the room. He opened the brass panel with trembling fingers and saw a nest of tangled wires. There were black, white, red, yellow, and blue-coated wires. How was he supposed to find the third one on the right? Where the hell was the fuse? He'd thought it might be self-explanatory at this point, but Rozam didn't make anything easy. If you were going to hack into his alarm system, he wasn't about to hand it to you. You'd have to have the balls to do it. *Well, I've got the balls.*

Wyll stuck his hand in the tangle and felt for the back of the panel. A few wires were long and folded up, so he gently pulled them out and let them hang. It opened the space a bit. He felt several bumps and screws on the back, then a glass cylinder. He parted the wires and folded them back so he could see it.

"Wyll. You need to hurry. I'm not pressuring you—"

"I know. I'm hurrying." He saw the tube full of red liquid and thought, *that must be the fuse.* The alarm started a new series of beeps. He didn't know how much time he had. One beep. He touched the fuse and felt for the wires. Two beeps. He pushed the wires away from the panel so he could see. Three beeps.

"I need a light. Quick!" he shouted.

Sira shined her penlight on the panel, and Indigo peeked his head in the door. "Everything all right?"

"Not now!" they both shouted.

He could see the first wire; it was blue. The next two were red. Then a yellow. A blue, a black, two whites…

Four beeps and a pause. *Beep beep beep beep beep*—they came faster, one after the other, increasing in volume and getting shriller. The sour taste in his mouth compounded the dryness of his throat. Sweat ran from his forehead, dripping off the tip of his nose. He could *not* mess this up. The next wire was blue. The third blue! *Beep, beep, beep, beep.* Now so quick that the beeps were running together, the screaming alarm had to be attracting attention. He reached in with Sira's scissors and snipped the wire.

The light turned green, and there was a loud click. The following silence was so loud that Wyll's ears almost hurt as the blood pulsed around his eardrum, thumping with his rapid heartbeat.

They stared at each other, and Sira laughed lightly. "One down…"

"One to go," he said, following her across the room. A living room sofa and two chairs surrounded an oval coffee table on an oval rug in the front half of the turret room. The woodwork was rich and dark, the colors matching his mother's bathroom. He'd heard the names of those colors over and over when they were decorating.

The Clockwork Pen

"We need the cranberry rug, the navy toothbrush and soap holders, the hunter green trash can...Oh, and they'll match the cranberry, navy, and hunter-striped towels. We'll get those next. What kind of switch plate are you getting? Do we need a new one? Do you hear me, Frank?"

She'd talked to them all the way through Target and Home Depot. Wyll could have sworn his dad had in ear plugs, just nodding the whole time, whether she was speaking or not.

Guess that should have been a red flag.

The king's desk was a massive piece of furniture—shiny, dark walnut inlaid with strips of oak and cherry, a masterful work of art that curved around his chair. The chair itself was a brown leather monstrosity with smooth, wooden arms sporting carved scrolls along the top of the back. Seashells and coral emerged from the carved frame, and under the seat, an octopus with eight wheeled legs curled around. He pushed it back toward a giant, round, convex window. The frame touched the floor and ceiling.

"Over here." Sira leaned down to the right of the desk, facing a black safe door covered with all sorts of gadgets. She zeroed in on the keypad. "It's six digits. I was right. Hopefully, I know the number."

"Hopefully? You don't know? Are you telling me we got this far, and now you're *guessing?*"

She glared at him as she unfolded a note. "Well, I couldn't come in here and practice, you know. I wrote down all the dates I could get my hands on."

"Sorry. I know. Just edgy. Go ahead—hurry."

She typed in her birthday, then her dad's, and finally her mom's birthday. *Nothing.*

"What about their anniversary?" Wyll asked.

"Good call." She typed the numbers in. *Nothing.* She continued to try each number on her list, and he tried to think.

"What about social security? No, that's too many. Or the zip code? No, that's five." He was counting on his fingers.

"How many are in a cell phone?" she looked up.

"What?"

"You know, when you talk on your cell phone. That thing you told me about where people talk from far away?" She made a rectangle with her fingers, the size of his cell phone.

"Yeah, I know what a cell phone is. You mean a phone number?"

"Beats me." She shrugged.

"No, that's too many numbers. And I wouldn't know your dad's cell number anyway."

She tapped the panel with her fingernail. "Think. Think. Think. What date would be important to him?"

She tried a few more numbers from her paper. Nothing. There was a rapping at the door, and one of the

The Clockwork Pen

helmeted guards stepped inside quickly and shut the door behind them. Indigo spoke, "There's another guard here who says we've been re-stationed. He says we have to go with him. I told him we were instructed to stay here with you while you wait for your father, but he insists we have new orders. I don't like it. But I don't want to blow our cover. We'll go with him, but we'll get away as soon as we can and double back here. If we miss each other, meet us at the house with the ink. If we can, we'll draw a key and go from there. With any luck, you'll be in the human world by supper."

"Go ahead," Wyll said, but he didn't like this. There wasn't supposed to be a guard change. Was the king on to them? Or was it instructions from the guards who'd been here before?

"We'll catch up," Sira said over the desk.

The door clicked as Indigo left. Sira was mumbling ideas to herself—addresses, special days, combinations of the above. She continued to type in her calculations.

"Damn!" She hit the safe. "We can't have gotten this far only to lose because we can't figure out the mind of a madman."

The mind of a madman, huh? What was Rozam's only goal here? To make the perfect world for his daughter... "Do you know the day your father got the pen?"

"No. I didn't even know he had it until I got older."

"What about the date when he started making Sepherra?"

"I don't know. I don't know any of it."

"What about the day you moved here? Do you remember when that was?" Wyll knew they had lost and were grasping at straws. At this point, they needed to make a few more guesses and then get the hell out of there before they were caught in the king's office by the wrong people. Plan B would have to be concocted. He sighed. They could go back to the lake tonight and camp out—maybe have everyone make a list of dates. Of course, they'd need to switch the rest of the plan around now—

"I know that one! It was four days after my fourth birthday." She started punching numbers in. "April twenty-ninth, two thousand."

Beep, beep, beep.

The tiny light beside the panel switched to green, and a heavy click pushed the thick door open an inch. She looked up at him with such unbridled hope and joy; his heart leaped in his chest. She looked like an angel in a top hat, peering up at him through wisps of dark red hair curling around her forehead. He wanted to grab her by the straps of her top, haul her up, and kiss her senseless. But this wasn't the time.

"Open it. Let's make the decoy and get out of here. I can taste a double cheeseburger and fries. I can smell freedom."

She laughed lightly and swung the door open, reaching in. He watched her feel around with her hand and then bend down to peer inside the dark space.

"What is it?"

She pulled out a short bottle of black liquid with a cobalt glass stopper full of little bubbles frozen in time. It was the same full jar her father had started with. She placed it on the desk next to a pile of papers and stood up.

"Where's the pen?" he asked.

"It's not in there." She looked around on the king's desk, picking up papers and moving books.

He turned and saw one that looked just like it in the holder. It was ornate and heavy in his hand, with a silver nib and an empty glass chamber streaked with dried black ink. It could be the one. He turned to her, holding out the pen.

"I found it," they said in unison as she held an identical pen toward him.

"Which one is it?" She was desperate. "There must be five right here. There's one on the coffee table, and I see at least two on the bookcase. What do we do? What do we do?"

She was losing it and looked near to tears. He needed to step up and make a decision. This is what he was here for—to be Sira's rock. "We know that the ink is the magic part, and the pen is just a conduit. So maybe every pen he made is a conduit. Magic doesn't make magic, but the pen just has to hold it, right?"

"I don't know. I don't know if it would work, but if the ink is magic, it *should*..." Her breathing was shallow and quick. "Right?"

Afraid she would hyperventilate and pass out, he gripped her shoulder. He couldn't carry her *and* escape. Wyll needed to pull his head out of his ass and take charge. "I'll fill the pen; you find me some blank paper." He knew there was a clear price to using the magic, but he was only going to do it this one time, so he should be okay, *right?*

"This is my fault; I should do it." She dug in a side drawer, pulled out a sheet of paper, and placed it before him as he uncapped the bottle. He twisted the pen open, stuck the opening of the glass chamber into the valve, and drew the lever upward to suck up the black liquid, then screwed the pen together.

"This is not your fault. It's his." He smiled at her to calm her worry. "Let me be the one to set you free. Plus, I can draw fairly well."

"Okay," she said with an exhale of relief and stepped back.

Wyll closed one eye for perspective like his art teacher told him and memorized the curved lines of the bottle. He held the pen over the paper and pressed down,

The Clockwork Pen

but nothing happened. "Damn fountain pen." He shook it downward, tapping the nib on the page surface.

He held it over the paper, ready to begin, when the door opened wide, slamming on the inside wall. The king barged through the frame with Jett at his back.

"See, Your Highness? I told you she was a traitor. They've come to steal your pen." Jett smiled viciously, pointing at them over the king's shoulder. Wyll should have known he wouldn't give up on Sira that easily. *He* wouldn't have.

"You dick." Wyll glared at Jett.

"Hurry, Wyll, draw it now," Sira urged him in a whisper, grasping his elbow.

The king was saying to Jett, "But she knows it's not in here. She knows I always carry it with—" At that point, the king saw Wyll shaking the pen and lowering it to the page. He reached out his hand toward them, a look of terror in his eyes. "No! Don't!"

Thinking the king was worried about him taking Sira away, Wyll quickly pushed the primer button, touching the nib to the absorbent surface.

In Wyll's mind, one of two things was going to happen: either he'd draw the inkwell, and they'd manage to trick the king into leaving, or Indigo would show up and clobber Jett, subduing the king to let them leave. Maybe he should just draw a key so they could run. What Wyll *didn't* expect was the ink being drawn out by the paper's thirst and rising, like a sentient glob over the nib, then—nearly gushing forth—traveling up the pen, rapidly covering his hand and flowing around it, swiftly crawling like hungry vines, up his right arm, burning the fabric away as it leeched into his skin.

"What's happening?" Wyll's eyes were as round as the window behind him. Then, the fire of intense pain began. He shouted in agony.

The king hung back in despair, holding up his magic pen. "This one is the only conduit that can control the magic of the ink. It has a life of its own." He stepped around the room, hugging the curved wall. "Sira. Sira, come to me. Get away from him."

Sira stepped behind Wyll like a shield.

The ink burned, and Wyll cried out as it dove into his skin. His arm spasmed and knocked over the bottle, splashing ink onto the paper in a jagged blob. Immediately, the sharply pointed globule came to life, standing next to the desk as a seven-foot mindless monster shrieking. Its pointed sprays of ink had become long spikes rising from its body, and it growled angrily, turning toward Wyll and Sira. Giant hackles raised, and a gaping maw, full of sharp and pointy black teeth, opened, sneering and baring black gums. Drool, like dirty oil, strung to the floor. It moved with clunky steps, its Clockwork body straining and clicking but fast for its size. It stretched its appendages, trying to reach them over the desk, spikes like thin arms flailing in every direction. It appeared to be blind.

The Clockwork Pen

The ink had coated Wyll's hand and slithered to his elbow. He could barely keep track of what was going on, the heat increasing as if his arm was held in a furnace, with red-hot needles doing surgery on his veins—and he could feel every bit of it. In a state of delirium, all he could do was scream repeatedly. The ink created a brilliant light as it seeped into his skin, the poison growing. It climbed up the inside of his bicep where the skin was bulging, and a coil emerged. A set of gears erupted where his knuckles should have been. It felt like hot lava, destroying his arm from within, melting his bones, and stripping his muscles. He screamed, trying to claw it off, but Sira held his left arm back, barring him from touching the mess that resembled his melted right arm.

Drawn to Wyll's screams, the monster inched around the side of the desk. Sira was using all her strength to keep Wyll from losing two arms as he thrashed and cried out, but when she saw the monstrous smear coming for him, she pulled his arm and ran between the two, pressing Wyll behind her. He could see her through his tears as a wobbly saving angel.

Seeing his little girl in danger, the king awakened from his trance. He shoved Jett out the door, yelling, "Go get my men, idiot."

He ran across the room, diving in between the monster and his girl. The creature advanced, and the king tried to push it away, but it was clear they had a problem.

The monster's oily flesh stuck to his skin like hot tar. The king began to cry out.

"Daddy!" Sira yelled, with her hand on his shoulder.

"Get back!" he yelled. "Don't touch me, Sira. Get behind Wyll."

With one arm stuck in goo and a string of black slime trailing from his armpit to the beast, the king pulled his sword from its sheath with his other hand, swinging at the creature's mouth. The black mass glopped around the weapon and oozed down his other arm. Strings of black sludge flung everywhere, burning the walls like acid. The streams smoked a bit and sizzled as they ran down the wall and pooled on the desk and floor.

Wyll was panting—getting lightheaded—the king screaming in agony. Sira, in tears, turned from one man to the other, unable to help either of them. The monstrosity blared a primal scream and grabbed the king by both arms, pulling him into the goo toward its mouth. Rozam released his sword, letting it swing into the mass, and it slid harmlessly to the floor. Sira freed one of the king's arms, even as he cried for her to get back.

"Pull your other arm out. Get free. You can do it." She sobbed, and Wyll watched in a daze as the tears gathered on her lashes and spilled down her flushed cheeks.

Wyll forced a measure of control over his senses, enough to see straight when the king pushed Sira away.

The Clockwork Pen

"Keep her back there!" he shouted to Wyll over her head.

Wrapping his left arm around her middle, he pulled Sira back, thrashing, and almost dropped her as she went limp in his arms.

"Help him, Wyll. Help him, *please*. I'm begging you." Her voice broke apart and caught on her last few words.

The king turned his head, looking back at them with eyes shining, and used his free hand to rip the key and its cord from his neck. He held it out to Wyll. "Take it."

"Daddy, no. We can't. I can't leave you now."

The oily mess crawled over the king's body like ivy on a trellis. She reached toward her father, pushing Wyll closer to the king and the monster.

"Sira! Sira, no. You can't help him."

"It's burning him! I can see it." The acrid stench of burning hair and flesh surrounded them.

Smoke rose from the king as black ink covered the back of his head, his eyes rolling. He was beyond pain—he was giving up.

"Aaagh!" Wyll released a deep yell as he picked up Sira with one arm and held her back against him. He reached down and grabbed the key from Rozam's palm.

As he straightened, the king reached back and pressed a cylinder in his hand, nodding gravely. "Take her back to our world. Make her happy. And keep this safe—they'll be coming for it."

He looked at the pen in his hand. *The magic pen.* "Who's coming?" Wyll asked desperately.

Sira screamed then as the black blob swung its largest appendage toward Rozam. Wyll saw him duck the heavy hit, but the strings of hot tar caught in his red hair and covered his face. He flailed about, blowing a bubble from his lips while the blob drew him closer into its embrace. He twisted toward them, his face black and eyes closed, the sticky tar running into his mouth, and he spat it out, shouting, "Take her! Now! I can't … hold it long enough…"

Ignoring his own searing pain, Wyll reached for the king but realized he could do nothing. It was an agonizing way to go. Sira began to scream, realizing the hot tar covered her father's face and seeing his body in the death throes of suffocation. Over and over, she screamed. All the air her lungs could hold came back out in a forced, desperate, broken cry.

Wyll knew they needed to move. Jett would be back with the troops at any second. This would not look good—and Jett wouldn't help matters. He tucked the pen and key in his pocket, then plugged the stopper into the inkwell and placed it in the side pocket of his bag. He gathered Sira up, and she turned into his chest, sobbing. The monster—devouring the king—growled its anger and came toward them, dragging the king's body across the floor. Thankfully, it slowed the monster down to a crawl.

Wyll's shoulder was a deep core of lava, and he could feel the trails of heat, like surgical knives, licking up his neck to connect with his leather band, then to his hearing device, burning, fusing it to his ear. His yell warbled in pain. Needle-thin black lines crept slowly over his right cheekbone before dripping down along his jaw and stopping.

He set Sira on her feet and looked deep into her glacial gaze. "We need to go." She looked around wildly, all sense gone. *She just lost her father*. He couldn't even begin to relate. The thought of watching his parents die usually filled him with nausea and a cold sweat. He turned her face to him with his good hand. "Sira. Look at me."

Her eyes welled up when she focused on him, and she cried harder. "Oh, Wyll. I'm so sorry. This is all my fault. I've done this to you. Your beautiful face—"

"Come on. Snap out of this. We need to get back to the house and meet the others. All hell's gonna break loose when they find the king here. Sira! Sira!"

She inhaled and shook her head before blowing the air out. "Okay. I'm okay. I'm—Oh God, my father—"

"Don't think about it. Not now. Not yet." He took her hand. "Can you run?"

She looked around the office wildly, and he thought he'd lost her. She wasn't going to be able to do this. But she ran to a set of hooks on the wall and pulled down her father's cloak and a smaller one that must have been his wife's. She rushed back, threw it over his shoulders, carefully covering his gooped-up arm, and delicately pulled the hood over his head.

"Okay." She swung on her cloak as well and put up the hood.

Wyll could hear stomping feet and men's agitated voices getting louder. He held out his hand to her, and she grabbed it, running out the door and down the hall. They stopped at the top of the stairs when they saw the guards taped up at the bottom. A squad of soldiers was cutting their bonds, untaping them, and they pointed up the stairs.

Wyll pulled Sira back just in time, and they went the other way. Heads down and pretending to be in conversation, they slipped into a closet as a fleet of guards ran past them, heading for the king's office.

They waited only a few seconds for the guards to pass, then hurried through the conference rooms to the courtyard. When they got there—to their first checkpoint—they found Keylin frustrated by a soldier with his back to them.

"I'm not interested, you jerk. I said I'm busy." She tried to pull away from him, but he stood before her in a lazy, relaxed stance, holding the ribbon of her corset.

"You don't look busy to me," he drawled as if he had all the time in the world. "Sitting out here by your

The Clockwork Pen

lovely self. What are you doing out here alone?" He slowly curled and uncurled the finger that tethered her.

"Isn't there some emergency you're supposed to take care of?" She stomped on his foot with her heeled boot.

He shot upright as he shouted out in pain and slapped her. She gasped.

Wyll reached back and plucked the tranquilizer pistol from the other side pocket in his coat. The guard started to turn as Wyll clicked off the safety and fell once the dart landed between his shoulder blades.

"Thanks," Keylin said, looking up. "Hey, what happened to you?"

Wyll's right side screamed in pain, but he didn't have a chance to ask what she meant before Sira dragged them all across the bridge toward the atrium doors. "Come on." They ran through the halls, Keylin's dainty boots clicking on the tile while Wyll and Sira's boots clomped loudly. He ignored the lightheaded feeling as if he was about to black out and pumped his arms, running full steam, passing Sira and pulling her behind him. They slid through the elegantly gilded foyer, then the atrium, surrounded by climbing stairs and hallways, and were turning for the kitchen when the alarm rang out like a tornado siren.

"Screw the kitchen. We're going this way." Wyll gripped Sira's hand and snatched Keylin by the back of her coat. He spun both girls toward the castle's main entrance and the huge set of ornate doors he'd seen the first day, rising two stories high, the back covered with golden scrolls and animals on the hunt. Wyll covered his ear and watched as Sira pulled the hunter's gun up, pointing it toward the birds, and gears in the door spun, causing the animals to look like they were running across the door. Their little legs went back and forth, and the bodies jolted up and down while the door inched open.

Wyll was nearly shaking with his need to get out of the castle. They absolutely could not be caught in there. Especially with the king killed by a hot tar monster and Wyll covered in the same burning slime. It wouldn't look good. And though he knew there was a large resistance group, a larger number of people loved their creator and didn't desire a change of government. They would be furious when they discovered he had the pen. He bounced his knee, pulling open the massive door with his left hand, his right arm throbbing and hanging uselessly.

When it was wide enough to squeeze through, they ran. Guards amassed in clusters. Wyll had no idea what the order could be, but he wasn't slowing down to find out. Were they looking for him? For Sira? Keylin tapped down the stairs, and Wyll pounded every other one, his heavy feet thumping the stone. They entered the square at the bottom of the stairs, and a guard behind them yelled, "Stop! Hey, you three! Stop!"

Wyll heard feet behind him, and Keylin said, "Wyll! Gun!"

The Clockwork Pen

Her cry was a shrill siren in his right ear, and it vibrated down his neck and arm to his fingers. He threw her the tranq pistol and kept going, glancing back when he heard her shoot and saw a man's body hit the cement, skidding along the pebbly gravel. His body was in agony, but he increased his speed and gritted his teeth.

The deafening sirens of the castle held no comparison to the Sepherran Alarm, which had only gone off three times in its history before now. People turned toward the castle curiously, and many walked at various speeds in that direction, so they looked highly suspicious, speeding the opposite way as if their tails were on fire. When they arrived at 2224 Olathe, Wyll stopped by the picket gate in front of the house, sucking in air. He looked up and down the sidewalk. Faintly, he heard the commotion of the castle grounds with the alarm that continued to blare.

He leaned on the gate nonchalantly, smiling at neighbors walking by but mostly showing his gritted teeth as hot pain radiated through his shoulder and neck. One man stared at his face, looking confused, but when he stared back with narrowed eyes, the man cleared his throat and faced forward again. Keylin speed-walked down the sidewalk toward them, and he waited a minute, slowing his breath while she caught up. Sira stood numbly, holding his hand, clearly in shock.

He followed the girls through the gate and clicked it shut. His head spun. They hurried up the walk, ducking into the small house. The glass case stood inside the door, where he'd found it upon arrival, but now he knew what most of the multi-use items were for—reading magnifier, pipe and glasses, glass and cigar holder, lighter and bottle opener, that kind of thing—must be the king's favorites. He shut the front door and turned around. "Indigo? Malynda?"

"They're not here yet," Keylin said, coming back from the kitchen and biting the nail on her ring finger. "And my mom is late."

Wyll checked the clock. *Two-thirty*. They were right on time. Everyone should be here. His mind was fuzzy from the intense pain, and he tried to stop the hammering of his heart as he watched Sira's face—drained of all color—standing motionless just inside the door. She was shutting down. *Come on, Indigo. Hurry.*

There were glasses in the kitchen, and he filled one with water for Sira. She sipped it and handed it back absently. He reached out and took it but realized his other hand was completely black, shining metal. The mechanisms were intricate and pristine, no longer goopy and covered in sticky tar. Pistons pumped where his finger bones had been, pushing the gears in place of his knuckles. He moved them to hear the tiny hiss of each piston. His fingertips were silver lima bean-shaped caps with a rough copper pad. He clicked the tip of each one to his thumb and watched the clockwork mechanics glide and fit together smoothly.

The Clockwork Pen

He carried the glass to a side hutch with a mirror and set it on the marble top next to a pipe and a pair of glasses. A feathered cap hung from a golden hook on the mirror frame. He looked up at himself and gasped in shock.

Chapter Twenty-Three
The Human Monstrosity and the Door Home

Sira appeared behind him in the mirror, watching him absorb his new form. She folded the cloak away from his right shoulder and eased the hood back. The material of his shirt was burnt along the edges, forming something like a tank top on that side. His forearm was a sheath of black metal with shiny rivets and a mesh oval. A set of intertwined hoses ran from his wrist to his elbow, and three small, round knobs sat in a row on the inside of his arm, near his palm. The coil he saw erupting from his bicep in the castle was now copper and shiny. It began next to a raised dial on his elbow and ran the length of a cylindrical brass cage that made up his new bicep.

Inside the cage, oily brown and blood-red tubes ran the length, and working gears whirred when he moved, connecting to a pulley that used to be his shoulder and armpit. It was covered with a shoulder pad of leather, edged in black metal trim, interspersed with gold half-circles, like tiny marbles cut in half. Chunky black metal scrolling embedded in the flesh near his collar and climbed up the side of his neck to his ear.

The Clockwork Pen

The hearing device Sira had given him was now permanently fused into his ear. The tiniest gears he'd seen so far—other than on a bug—crawled from his lobe up the shell of his ear. A small brass tube circled behind his ear, over the top, and connected to the dial nestled in his ear canal. An amber dome made the body of a tiny octopus nestled into his jaw, which spread eight tentacles, with moving parts that came to life as he worked his jaw around. Two tentacles squiggled as they reached out toward his cheek. How was he going to take a shower? Would he rust? Could he even have surgery to remove this? What would be left of him once it was gone? He felt like shutting down, too, but he knew Sira needed him to be strong now. He struggled with the strong pull to use it as an excuse to hide from reality, but what better reason?

Indigo burst through the door, calling their names, and stopped abruptly when he saw Wyll. Malynda ran into the back of him and pushed him forward. She stepped to the side, and her face fell when she looked at Wyll.

"It's that bad, huh?" He chuckled wryly.

"No. No, of course not," she said. "It was just a shock. We've never seen … um. We've never—"

"Never seen a human monstrosity before?" He pointed to himself. "Clockwork on the outside, idiot on the inside?"

"Stop that," Sira said, laying a hand on his other shoulder with a shrug. "It's different—but cool."

He sputtered his laugh. "Yeah, you could say that. What're my parents gonna do?"

"It won't matter in the important ways. They'll love you anyway," Sira whispered. "I know they will." Her face fell. "At least you still have a mother ... and a father."

"Oh, oh, oh, Sira-honey." Keylin opened her arms as she crossed the room and embraced Sira, who hung her head. "You know we share a mom; always have. You aren't alone. Not as long as I'm here. You remember?"

"Yeah." The soul drained from her voice. It was still hitting her.

He was completely inept in this department. Girl emotions, he understood. How they worked and what to do about them, not so much. So, he let Keylin do the consoling.

They were still standing around the living room like an awkward chess set when the back door swung open, and a small herd of people rushed into the kitchen. The first one he saw that he knew was Alva. The moment she spotted her girls holding each other up, she rushed over and joined the group hug, consoling them both with motherly gentleness that made him miss home with a deep ache.

The men—in an assortment of hats, goggles, and masks—gathered around Indigo and Malynda in the kitchen, chattering with news. These must be the council members. He was part of it now, so he went to meet them and stood next to Indigo, crossing his arms. The mechanics in his shoulder pulled, and the gears in his arm fit together like they'd been freshly oiled. A man with an eye patch raised his eyebrow, and Wyll was self-conscious enough to drop his hands—shrugging his arms and shoulders under the cloak.

"—army amassing. You need to send her now," a lady in a long coat was saying to Indigo. "The castle is in chaos. They're trying to keep things quiet, but it's spreading like fire."

The man next to her, with a long mustache, nodded as she spoke, and as soon as she finished, he piped up. "People are running to the castle for confirmation, and some of the servants have gone home in fear, telling everyone the king's dead." He pointed toward Sira in the other room. "The word on Sira is mixed. Jett didn't help us any, and not everyone knew whose side she was on. The question is whether she's dead, too, or if she killed him herself."

Things didn't look good.

One woman said, "She was noticed coming in this direction."

Another woman whispered, "She wasn't exactly secretive about how badly she wanted the king out of her way."

Wyll frowned at her. This wasn't a good day for him, and the last thing he wanted to do was listen to someone blame Sira for wanting out of her cage. If they were correct, every minute they remained put Sira in danger of some radical follower thinking she'd committed king slaughter and taking the initiative to mete out justice on behalf of all clockwork.

"They're right." Wyll turned to Indigo, interrupting whoever was already speaking. "I need to get her out of here now. Are any of you coming? Taking turns? I never listened to the plan past this point." He shrugged apologetically.

Indigo looked tired. His eyes seemed to cast purple shadows that Wyll hadn't noticed behind his small glasses. The toll of stress was on all their faces. Everyone looked at Malynda, who smiled at him. "Alva and Keylin are going with Sira to live in the house owned by the king. Indigo and I will pull the community together, and the Resistance will rebuild the government into a self-run society. We'll manage Jett. Most people don't know of any other world than ours, so we'll keep it to ourselves as much as we can. As long as you don't mind a visit from a few of us now and then?"

"That's a good idea—" Suddenly, Wyll cried out and grimaced as a sharp pain burned through the front of his shoulder. He wanted to touch it but refrained and watched the pointed tip of a black spike emerge from his skin with a drop of blood and loop through a spiral, then curve lazily into a grommet joining his shoulder to the cage of his arm. He wanted to cry, like, *really* cry, *baby* cry, until he was spent. He'd never imagined leaving this place with anything other than his normal body. And apparently, he was still transforming. *How far will this go? Will I become completely Clockwork?* Could he survive a change like that? Would he still be human?

"Here." One of the men had gone behind the group and tapped Wyll on the back. He held out a small bottle with a rubber stopper full of blood-red fluid. Really cool, but he didn't know what it was for.

He scrunched his brows together and moved his arm to put the bottle in his pocket. "Thanks."

The man's bushy beard wiggled when he laughed. "It's for the pain. Put two drops under your tongue or four drops in a glass of water."

Oh. He squeezed two drops into his mouth and groaned in relief as it immediately hit his bloodstream. He was blissed-out for a second and felt like they'd won a battle for the planet. *It's all going to be okay,* he thought, picturing his house, his street, and his car. He would even be glad to see TeaCup. It was time to go.

He thanked the man again and returned to the living room, where the women sat on couches and chairs, chatting excitedly around a statue of Sira. He caught the end of Sira's conversation with Alva.

"—can't believe he's gone." Sira's face was blank.

"The man who was your father has been gone for quite some time now, love." Alva curled a red tendril over Sira's ear.

Wyll cleared his throat on the other side of the coffee table, and she looked up. "Are you about ready? I don't want to keep you somewhere you're in danger, and I'm kinda ready to go home." He smiled gently at her.

Alva hopped up. "I packed your bags, but Wyll said they wear different clothing there. At least you can take your personal things." She headed to the bedroom, still talking as if they could hear her. "I left your—mumble, mumble, mumble—bedroom, so we could see later. If you want?"

"Sure," Sira said woodenly.

She wasn't Sira-the-leader like she had been since the moment he met her. She was Sira-the-broken right now, and he was terrified of her. He didn't know what to do or how to fix it. He just wanted her ... *better*. Gently, trying not to spook her, he edged around the table and picked up her limp hand. Alva was dragging carpet bags from the bedroom and called a protesting Keylin to help her.

He leaned down to place his mouth near Sira's ear. "Come on, sweet girl. Let's go home."

She looked up with eyes shining. "I'm not sweet. I'm poison. I've killed both my parents."

Uh oh. He was treading deep water. "Not poison. Maybe not sweet, probably spicy. Maybe you're a spice girl?" He started to chuckle before he realized she wouldn't get it, but she rewarded him with a small smile anyway.

"Let's go," he said as if he were begging her for water in the desert. "Please."

"Yes." She nodded and seemed to wake up a little. "We've got to get you home. What will you tell your parents?"

"I figured I'd say I got hit by a car, and some strange hospital did this." He shrugged.

"Unfortunately, I don't have anything better." She matched his shrug with a sweet smile.

He picked up as many bags as he could carry, and they descended to the basement. Wyll looked at the small door and took a deep breath. He didn't know what he'd find on the other side, any more than the people there would expect him with his automata arm. He reached into his pocket and took out the key. It turned in the lock with a click. He put his head to the door, and it creaked open a few inches. Pushing it with his cheek, he tried to peer into the concrete basement of Rozam's mansion. Not that he was looking for blood or anything, but he was relieved when the door opened, and Derec's body wasn't lying on the floor, decaying or anything.

He stepped in, smelled the musty heat, and then turned back to see everyone hugging through the door. A shaft of loneliness pierced his heart, and he was ready to go. "Sira," he called. "I think I'm going to go ahead."

"Wait!" She bounded through the door. "I'm going with you."

Keylin hefted her bags with both hands and squeezed through the door frame. "I'm coming, too."

Wyll opened his mouth to tell them they didn't have to accompany him, but Sira saw it and spoke first. "Don't even try it. I want to come. I want to meet your mom and Derec. And I want to support you when they see you."

He'd almost forgotten for a second; he was a freak now. How could he forget that?

Keylin followed Sira further into the basement and dropped her bags, saying, "And I'm coming just because I want to. You can't tell me no, or I'm going to follow you anyway, so get used to it."

Wyll gave one last wave to Malynda and Indigo. "Come on, then." He hauled the carpet bags upstairs, and it got hotter and hotter as he ascended. Squeezing down the narrow hall, he deposited the bags in the dining room. The house was humid and stifling. He began to sweat profusely, hoping he wouldn't rust.

"Why is it so hot up here?" Keylin asked while Sira walked around, peeking under sheets.

"It's summer here. It gets wicked hot. You guys have summer, right?"

"Yeah," Sira said. "But our dimension must be somewhere else to have such different seasons at the same time." She popped open the fastener at her throat and shrugged off her cropped jacket, leaving her in bronze pants, gun belt, and corset. She tossed the jacket on the table, and he noticed matching bronze bands circling the tops of her arms like some Aztec warrior—or maybe that was gold? Scooping up most of her curls in the back with one hand, she fanned her face, neck, and the swell of her breasts with the other. Her skin glistened with perspiration.

Wyll was suddenly heating up for all the wrong reasons. *Get a hold of yourself.* He removed his cloak and vest and unbuttoned what was left of his shirt. The pen and inkwell bulged in his pocket as he folded the cloak over his arm. He was going to miss looking so cool. Maybe he'd save his clothes for Halloween, or they could look up a Steampunk Con to visit. The girls would like that. They could show Derec what Sepherrans looked like. Wyll couldn't imagine he'd ever be going back.

"Are we leaving?" Keylin asked, dropping her coat in the chair next to her.

"You might want to leave your hat and gloves, too." He knew this was going to be odd for them. They'd start small. He wasn't ready to explain to his parents yet. Better to find Derec and feel out the situation first.

"But we're going out." Keylin looked confused.

He walked over as she unpinned her flowered hat and peeled off fingerless lace gloves. Wyll pointed to her extra leather belts and the shoulder harness, then her stockings, along with a few smaller accessories, saying, "You can leave this, and this, and this—"

"But I'll be practically naked!"

He laughed. Wait till they saw what girls at his school were wearing… He imagined Sira in some of those shorts that stopped just high enough to make the teachers look horrified but not enough to be sent home for. His mouth went dry. He couldn't wait to show her off to Derec.

"You'll be fine." He chuckled as he strode to the front door, opening it to the sun. "Come on, girls, let's see your new world."

Chapter Twenty-Four
METATRON? WANTS WHAT, NOW?

Wyll, Sira, Derec, and Keylin sat spaced around Derec's bedroom, drinking raspberry lemonade—it was Derec's mom's summer crack. She didn't always understand his English—she spoke only Chinese with Derec—and thought Wyll and the girls were going to a costume party. She was just ecstatic that Wyll had brought a girl "for Derec."

Wyll sat in Derec's computer chair, Sira on an oversized beanbag, and Derec and Keylin perched on the edge of his bed, glancing nervously at each other. Derec's mom stood in the doorway holding a loaded serving tray, the biggest grin plastered on her face.

"Moooom." Derec's nasal rendition was almost a song. "Go awaaaay."

"You need more drink? Cookie?" She held out a package of Oreos with the metallic film curling up from the top. Wyll reached out toward the Double Stuft treat.

Derec got up and headed for the door, and she moved into the hall for him to pass, but he shut the door and shouted, "Thanks, Mom. We'll tell you if we need anything."

"Okay!" She rapped on the door. "You want more, you yell. Okay?"

"Okay, Mom! Geez!" Derec shook his head, peeking at Keylin from the corner of his eye.

"So, what happened after I went through?" Wyll leaned forward precariously in Derec's ancient rolling desk chair, pressing his elbows to his knees and feeling the bite of a gear on his right kneecap. He winced.

"I put the key in my pocket and curled up under the burlap so he wouldn't see me."

"So, the guy didn't find you at all?" Wyll didn't know how he felt about that.

"Oh no. He didn't see me." Derec's fine black hair stood up from static electricity. "But it was so dusty down there, and with my allergies…"

"You sneezed."

"I sneezed." He nodded.

"So?"

"He grabbed me and pulled me up by the front of my shirt. But I didn't tell him anything—said a few things in Chinese. I almost peed my pants, but after the guys yelled at me, they decided I was a squatter or something. One of them said I was just a punk kid. Yeah, I'm definitely punk."

They all laughed lightly.

The Clockwork Pen

"I took TeaCup to your house later and told your mom we were going camping. I grabbed some of your stuff." Derec pointed to a gray duffle next to the bed. "Told my mom we were hanging out every day, but I said we might be going camping—in case I had to go hunt for you. I was planning to come back and search for you, but there were so many variables—"

"It's okay. We had about all we could handle with my appearance." Wyll smiled at Sira and looked at the bag. "Great. I can change here, then."

"Yeah. Your mom said to tell you she's sorry and to please come back. Your dad even got upset. What's going on?"

It hit Wyll in the solar plexus like a gut punch. He'd missed them so much. "They're getting a divorce."

"Oh..." Derec nodded somberly. "Sorry, man."

"What's a divorce?" Keylin asked Sira, who shrugged.

Derec explained it to them, but Wyll only half-heard the discussion. He was already trying to think of a better explanation for what had happened to him. *What was* still *happening*, he reminded himself. Fine wire crept inside him, arcing, piercing the flesh slowly with sharp points.

They heard tapping, and Derec yelled, "Go away, Mom," but the tapping continued.

"It isn't the door," Sira said. "It has a *ping*, like glass."

Heads swiveled to Derec's window, but open curtains framed a typical view of his backyard in blue and green plaid. The tap thumped again, three times, and someone cleared their throat.

Keylin shrieked, pointing to the mirror. The image of an older man was luminous, his white hair and beard flowing around his head like he was underwater or somewhere without gravity. It was eerie.

Wyll stood and faced him with a frown. "Who are you? What do you want?"

"You don't seem shocked to see me?" The man smiled with affectionate ease.

"I haven't had the best day. So, who are you? And what do you want?"

"Straight to the point." The man nodded. "I like that. I really think you might do."

"Might do what?" Sira stood next to Wyll, placing herself in front of his shoulder protectively.

The man chuckled. "I mean you no harm. I'm incredibly happy to meet you. I'm known as Metatron, Heaven's Scribe."

"Heaven?" Derec was enthralled with the idea of the supernatural in stories and movies, but there was no room for stories in reality. Order ran the universe, right? Wyll's mother tried to convert him once, but that hadn't gone well. Derec was picky about what he believed.

"Yes, and you've found my pen and ink."

"Yours?" Wyll squinted one eye. "How do you know about that, and what makes you think it's yours?"

Looking as patient as a preschool teacher, Metatron explained, "I felt their presence when they entered this dimension."

"I get it." Keylin popped up off the bed and spoke to the mirror. "If you're a scribe, then you used the pen—"

"To create life on this planet, yes. The tools were designed specifically for me about thirteen trillion Sagaropama ago."

Metatron's blue eyes were mesmerizing, but Wyll shook his head. "You said we might do. Might do for what?"

"Someone stole my entire desk set, the tools sent to worlds I cannot enter. I have no corporeal form in the dimensions of man." He pointed to the mirror's frame. "I can only appear to you in reflections of life."

"What do you want us to do? We're a bunch of teenagers—stuck in *this* dimension." By his pale face, Derec was having an issue with this. His eyebrows raised, and he jumped up to discover the mirror's trick. He felt the exterior of the mirror's frame, pulling it away from the wall and peeking behind it, searching for a camera or an answer.

Metatron looked on—waiting for Derec to finish hyperventilating and return to the bed—with a patient smile.

Jennifer Haskin

"So," Wyll said in a deep rumble, "what makes you think we want anything to do with this?"

"You found my pen and ink and returned it from another dimension. It can't have been easy." He looked at Wyll and then Sira. "It must have been painful ... to leave."

Wyll grabbed her hand and squeezed.

"I'm okay," she said. "But can you help Wyll?" She stepped aside and pointed to his shoulder.

Hope flooded him at the idea, and Wyll perked up, but only for a second.

"I cannot. Without my tools, I don't have the right power. But once you find the items and my desk set is again complete, I can reverse the ink's destruction. You must follow the instructions carefully—"

"Who said we were going?" Wyll interrupted. "I get your point—we're capable—but it's complicated. I'm the one who needs to be fixed here, so if any of us was stupid enough to join you, it should be me. But I didn't rescue your pen and ink. Sira's the one who brought them, and I *know* she's smarter than falling for whatever you're selling. Besides, we both have people here to protect."

Derec said indignantly, "Yeah."

At the same time, Keylin gave him a confused side glare, saying, "Hey! I can be part of a mission. You don't need to protect me! If you guys are going, so am I." Propping her little fists on her hips, still covered in ruffled

The Clockwork Pen

satin fabric, she was an angry China doll in impressive cosplay.

Wyll chuckled at her forceful loyalty. How would they do in another dimension? It dawned on him, there must be many more. Was this an answer to his silent questions—the answers he didn't know he needed? Maybe it wouldn't hurt to hear more. "Tell us about these other worlds."

Metatron nodded. "A decree made here—where I am—affects the creation of a new human planet in a binary galaxy of the Milky Way. We've never put two human galaxies so near each other, and there was much controversy over it. The host divided and took sides on the issue."

"I meant the worlds on *this* planet, mister. We don't have a spaceship." Wyll folded his arms, bending and straightening his knee.

"Does he want us to go to another planet to look for his stuff?" Derec leaned toward Wyll.

"No, no." Metatron held his palms toward them. "The new star's system hasn't been manufactured—it would involve the use of my full set to write it into creation. A snap of my shears divides space, creating the system's timeline with the explosion of a new star. My slide ruler gauges the perfect distance to place the planet, relating to its star, for human life to thrive—an exact tool for the size of every object in creation. I usually move to the planet during the Creation phase to take notes on the

Jennifer Haskin

Creator's instructions—I need my pen and ink for that—composing new flora and fauna. I will need a new paperweight as my map home, from the new planet, but this galaxy's map must be found. Everything you need to find my tools is on this planet."

"You want us to agree to jump into parallel dimensions to find a desk set for creation? I don't—why don't you have it anymore?" Wyll wondered if there was a good reason somebody disseminated this man's items.

Metatron opened his mouth, but Sira cocked her head and cut him off. "And you said you go to new planets, so why can't you just come here and get your own stuff? I'm missing something."

The old man nodded. "The disagreement progressed to rampant protesting, and my office was upended, the desk set stolen. We believe one of the protesting leaders must have—never mind. It's not important. To stall the project, my set was divided and hidden in man-made dimensions where I could not detect them. But you know firsthand how destructive these things can be in the hands of mortals—the tools' power distorts, the item's true purpose is skewed, and the user suffers the consequences."

"I get it," Wyll said. "But why us?"

"There is no one else. You are the first to have found anything in two hundred years, which is lucky for us. We could be back on schedule within your lifetime…"

The Clockwork Pen

Wyll didn't know if the scribe was finished or not. He'd heard enough mind-bending information to think himself into next year. He held up his hand. "Can we talk about this?"

"Of course," Metatron said, gesturing to them with his palm up.

Wyll turned Sira's shoulder, and they faced away from the mirror. He pulled Derec up by the sleeve to complete their little huddle with Keylin. "What do you think, you guys? We don't have to do this, but—"

"Sure sounds like an adventure." Sira crossed her arms and tapped her elbow. Then, her lips curled into a smile. "I don't have anything to lose. I always wanted out, you know? But maybe I really wanted something different—something unusual and exciting—and maybe a little dangerous ... to be able to do what I want, and not just what my—father—told me."

Wyll grinned at her, dimples deepening his smile.

"Well, I'm in. I don't even have to say it." Keylin rolled her eyes.

They all looked at Derec, who appeared as though he'd just run a marathon. His skin was flushed and sweaty, and he peered back in terror. "Wha—What? I can't do anything. You don't need me." He shook his head maniacally, making his wispy hair swirl around him. "What if you leave me again? I could get stuck somewhere else, lost in time—"

Jennifer Haskin

Wyll tempered the force of his mechanical hand, laying it on Derec's shoulder. "First of all, you left me. But you were brave enough to stand up against the thugs by yourself. Come on, buddy. It's no fun without you."

"I'm not as brave as you, dammit. You're the one who always wants to explore and have an adventure. I'm side-kick material, and you know it."

"Oh yeah? Who walked to Quik Mart when my tire popped that night past curfew? Who splinted my arm when I fell out of the tree by the lake? And who covered for me when we went to the game last year—that day we skipped school? You're like my lucky charm."

Derec turned eight shades of tomato. "Well, technically, *you* skipped school. I was already home sick."

"Whatever." Wyll's dimples deepened. "What if I need you?"

Derec shrugged his shoulders around his ears, and his lips curled as he looked out the window.

"Is that a yes?"

"Okay." Derec nodded, relaxing his shoulders.

Wyll turned back to the mirror. "All right, Mr. Metatron, we acc—" On the floor directly behind him sat a small, coffee brown, leather, hard-shell briefcase with a black handle. "What's this?"

"That is the case you will need, to keep the set together until it's complete. Guard it well. In it, you will find a leather bookmark with a half-round gemstone you will use to enter each dimension we believe hold the remaining items. When we are sure, I will let you know where to go. Step forward, young man."

Wyll stepped over the case. "My name is Wyll."

Metatron smiled again. "Yes, Wyll. I see you have an implement in your ear. Was that made with the pen to understand language?"

"Yes." Wyll subconsciously covered his ear with his hand, letting his bumpy fingertips trace the metal scroll implanted along his cheekbone.

"And your voice has been enhanced. Yes? Also by the pen?"

Wyll squinted an eye. "How would you know that?"

"You are speaking in the Language of Ancients. It is understood in every language. The pen creates *universally*. You will be able to hear and speak whatever language you come across. There are attachments for your group—though not as invasive as yours—to be able to communicate in new dimensions. Many of the human creators avoid their native tongue to control infiltration."

"Oh, I'm familiar with that one." Wyll's adrenaline was starting to crash. He'd been through so much already today; his head was spinning. "Just tell me what to do. Plain and simple."

Metatron spoke slowly. "When you are ready to leave, you will hold the bookmark with your thumb on the stone and say the name of the man-made dimension you wish to arrive in. For example, 'Ludisha.' Speak aloud the words, '*Aperto caelo*,' then name the dimension you wish to enter, in this case, 'Ludisha.' You will find yourselves there in the blink of an eye. My sources say this is where the paperweight is."

"Your map, right?" Derec asked.

"Clever boy. Yes. It is shaped like a jewel, and each facet displays a different symbol that matches a set of constellations and, when held to the sky, it points to the exact location of Heaven's gateway. It's why I cannot travel to Earth now. I have many matters to attend to, and if I were to appear there, I would be stranded on the planet until the paperweight was retrieved."

"Can *we* see this Heaven place when we find the paperweight?" Keylin had her head cocked. Surely, this was all very confusing to someone who'd never known religion. *Probably about as strange as she felt crossing into another world.*

Metatron's chuckle ceased. "No, no. In the hands of mortals, it shows the future of an object or person—it can give the odds of a situation. But the more a *human* uses the prophetic crystal, the more they lose their past increasingly until they must live every moment as their first."

Wyll tried to wrap his head around it. Your first moment must be very confusing, not knowing where you are, where you came from, where you're going… It would be *terrifying*. "I'd rather be in a coma."

The Clockwork Pen

"It might feel about the same as waking from one." Metatron nodded. "I will know when the tool returns to this Heaven-made dimension, and I will find you."

He disappeared about three seconds before Derec's mother burst through the door with her tray. Her face was expectant and hopeful at first, but her smile dropped, ineffectively masking her confusion as they each faced Derec's mirror. "Snacks?" A trembling hand balanced the tray, her other one gripping the lemonade handle. She looked like she'd walked in on a cult meeting, and they were all naked. "Lemonade?"

"I told you we were fine, Mom. Wyll was showing us his costume. Right, guys?"

"Oh yes. Very, um, clean, and tidy..." Keylin said, oblivious to the differences in their clothing.

Sira tried as well with a serious face. "I think it's very handsome."

Derec's mom smiled and nodded. "Yes. *Handsome* boys. My Derec, too, yes?"

"Of course." They both nodded.

Wyll failed to catch his burst of laughter as Derec groaned, and the girls laughed lightly with Derec's mom. He was ready to see his own family now. The summer was nearly over, and his mom would want to go supply shopping soon. *How am I supposed to go to school like this?* Lots of long-sleeved shirts were in his future—turtlenecks, in fact.

When would they find time to embark on this new mission? The last one had changed him more than he could have anticipated. What would they find in Ludisha? Would it be clockwork as well?

He touched the silky fabric of his vest, tracing the grooves of stitching with his fingertips absently, and felt the key in his pocket. They'd check with everyone in Sepherra when things died down. They'd forgotten to leave the Sepherrans a key of their own. He was interested in how they would set up their new government and how they punished Jett—that backstabber. If he hadn't brought the king in, Wyll wouldn't have knocked over the inkwell—maybe… At least the king saved them in the end. Sira's dad wasn't really a bad guy, just insane from the pen. Crazy from making what any man in his position would've made.

Wouldn't I have done the same? Wyll wondered. *Will any of the people we find with these items be truly evil or just misguided humans? And what does that mean about me? Which side am I on?*

He stood at the mirror a new man, arms crossed, and looked at Keylin, laughing into her hands, his best friend rolling his eyes, and beautiful Sira—smiling at him—and he knew. For the first time, he knew which side he was on.

Hers.

Epilogue

Wyll's parents never bought his phony explanation that an unknown hospital had turned their son into a half-machine, but they had no idea what could have happened to him. Wyll wasn't giving any other ideas, so they warily accepted his claim and stared at him over the dinner table.

Given Wyll's extreme reaction to their news, his parents decided that the last thing Wyll needed in his last year of school was to deal with a divorce, so they remained together in their home. It brightened his heart to see his parents forget about the divorce and laugh with each other at the table. Maybe it took enough pressure off to change things permanently? He grinned, happy his family was intact.

He had to promise to see a head-shrinker, but he was okay with it. He'd done a lot of introspection in Sepherra and liked the idea of changing into the man he always imagined he'd be. He realized that before, he hadn't been on the road to becoming a great man, but he could choose to be one now.

Wyll had gone with his mom to buy a few extra supplies for school, paper, pens, a new calculator, and a backpack since his had a hole from the cheap strap ripping off at the end of last year. She took him to the men's section and tried to choose the style he was accustomed to, but Wyll wanted clothes that covered his arms, with collars that might cover his scrolling and attached leather neck strap. There weren't many choices as the fall clothing was just coming in. He also decided to let his hair grow longer to cover his ears, and it had started to curl a bit on top from growing all summer.

As Derec feared, Wyll was cut from the football team with an offer to sit on the bench his senior year. It was too insulting. So, he quit. All over email, of course. He dreaded the day he had to appear in person and show people his new form.

"You know we will be with you," Sira said as he sat at the mahogany table in the mansion, having dinner with her, Keylin, and Alva. They'd had a shock of their own when they went shopping for school clothes and now wore shorts and T-shirts. Sira's hair hung down her back in a ponytail of loose curls, and Keylin had opted to cut hers in a wavy bob.

Derec had changed, too. His normally fearful personality was disappearing as he acclimated to the idea that there were other man-made dimensions that they would visit. He was excited, researching all he could find regarding them on the dark web. He read facts, stories, and even the wildest of beliefs in personal articles stating the most unbelievable experiences with dimensions, angels, and Heaven. He wanted to know everything and was happy to report his findings to the group.

When school started, there would be a lot of talking, staring, whispers, and snide comments about Wyll's metallic half and the girls—now inhabiting the haunted mansion. They worried about the strange men returning, so they called an alarm company to secure the property and install cameras around the house.

In Rozam's home office, Sira found his checkbook, and Wyll showed her how to find his banking information using his little book of website passwords. Luckily, Sira was named on his accounts along with her mother. He'd kept his accounts open to pay for things he may need, like the annual insurance on the house. The money, kept in an interest-bearing account, had been multiplying over the years. They didn't know if Rozam had tried to make money with the pen and deposited it or if he just had that much when they moved to Sepherra, but there was plenty to cushion them once they had jobs. Though Alva insisted the girls wait until second semester at least and concentrate on school and graduating. They debated telling Alva about Metatron and the mission but decided they'd keep it to themselves as long as possible.

Their anticipation was palpable. In the meantime, Metatron's case was safely nestled in Wyll's closet, looking unremarkable under some shoe boxes, waiting for the day Metatron called them to go to Ludisha. Until then, they prepared to enter high school together on the first day, circling Wyll and supporting each other as a team.

Senior year, Wyll thought with a chuckle. Who could have imagined life would change this much? *But now I'm ready. Let's go.*

End Book One

Dear Reader

Thank you for joining us on our adventure to Sepherra! I anticipate your return to see where Wyll and his friends go next and who will tell the story. And I'm glad you stuck it out till the end to discover the broader plot.

I hope you loved the dark steampunk world and enjoyed *The Clockwork Pen*! If you did, I would be so grateful to everyone who could leave me a short review on Amazon. Don't worry about being eloquent.
A sentence or two works, too.

Authors rely on reviews for feedback, and other readers need them to know if this is a book they want to read. So, every review is essential.

I'm so excited to meet you again in book two, coming soon!

Acknowledgments

Thank you, first and always, to my God. And thank you to my mom, who believes in me enough to read these manuscripts while they're still garbage—to give me her honest opinion. Thank you to my long-time writing partners, Alisha Davis and Zachary Drummond, and the new members of our writing group: Mark McGuiness and Berkay Karakurt. Thanks to my best friends and first readers: Kristin Freeman, Cindy Ziegelman, Angela Renczarski, Christie Leigh Babirad, Alice Wakefield, Wendy Walsh, and Kat Hardesty. I have other readers who come and go, and I thank them all for their advice and support. An author really needs fresh eyes on their work to tell them if they're hitting the mark or missing it. So, thanks, everyone!

I also dedicate this book, as I do each of them, to my kids: Ben, Noah, Jayna, Zach, and Emmy. One day, when I'm gone, these words will be all they have left of me. Maybe then they will be interested in reading them, maybe not. But they'll be here—all the weirdest plots my mind conceives. May they find peace in them. This is my legacy, and may it grow in skill and imagination and prosper as God's will directs.

About the Author

As her kids are growing up, Jennifer Haskin remains a teen at heart. Jenn remembers reading her first fantasy book in the second grade when she read *Island of the Blue Dolphins*. It opened her mind to the world of escapism. She could open a book at any time and not be where she was. It was bliss and made her an avid reader. Then, she read all the ones under Mom's side of the bed. Ahem. She went back to YA, and first kisses, hand-holding, and the beginnings of romance, when you feel that first tingle like an icy vine growing up your spine because your eyes meet theirs during just the right song.

Determined to create that feeling but with a bad-A heroine, she wrote a YA fantasy romance trilogy with magic, wizards, and a subculture of biomechanical people. The next trilogy is inside a mined-out dwarf planet colony where a death match winner gets to be the Ambassador's Bride. And this series is about a teen who opens a closet door to find another world. Her books are full of sword-fighting and surprises, books that people can escape into—books people say they can't put down.

Jennifer Haskin

I binged this series over the weekend, and once I started on the first book, I found myself unable to put them down! I didn't get much sleep, that's how you know you're reading a good book. ~Amazon Reviewer McLovin

I found that I could not put down the book once I started reading it. It is so packed with action that there was no place where I could say, "Ok time for bed now. I'll finish it tomorrow." A must-read. ~Amazon Reviewer Eloise

Other Titles by Jennifer Haskin

THE FREEDOM FIGHT TRILOGY:

BOOK ONE — *PRINCESS OF THE BLOOD MAGES*
www.amazon.com/dp/B07XWVSH2B

BOOK TWO — *THE QUEEN'S HEART*
www.amazon.com/dp/B07XWTH6ZB

BOOK THREE — *THE FINAL RESCUE*
www.amazon.com/dp/B07Z5PFYVW

THE FIVE COLONIES:

BOOK ONE — *HIERARCHY OF BLOOD*
www.amazon.com/dp/B0B66H85VS

BOOK TWO — *HIERARCHY OF CROWS*
www.amazon.com/dp/B0CTJQ6919

Printed in Great Britain
by Amazon

54081229R00267